Elegy for a Lost Star

The Symphony of Ages Books by Elizabeth Haydon

Rhapsody: Child of Blood

Prophecy: Child of Earth

Destiny: Child of the Sky

Requiem for the Sun

Elegy for a Lost Star

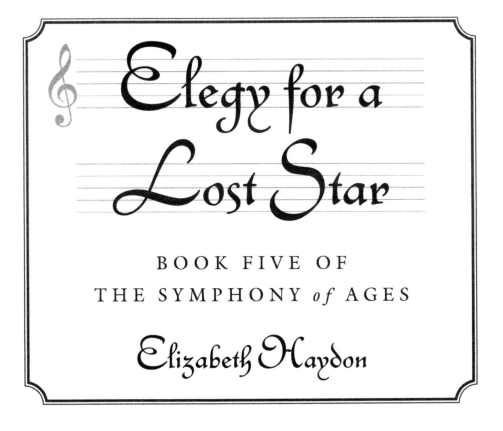

Elegy for a Lost Star

BOOK FIVE OF
THE SYMPHONY *of* AGES

Elizabeth Haydon

GOLLANCZ
LONDON

The right of Elizabeth Haydon to be identified as the
author of this work has been asserted by her in accordance
with the Copyright, Designs and Patents Act 1988.

First published in the United States of America in 2004
by Tom Doherty Associates, LLC.

First published in Great Britain in 2004 by
Gollancz
An imprint of the Orion Publishing Group
Orion House, 5 Upper St Martin's Lane, London WC2H 9EA

A CIP catalogue record for this book
is available from the British Library

ISBN 0 575 07309 8 (cased)
ISBN 0 575 07414 0 (export trade paperback)

www.orionbooks.co.uk

Printed in Great Britain by
Clays Ltd, St Ives plc

For my adopted siblings
Daughter of the Earthly Garden
Son of the Sea
for all they've done
to keep it going
with love

ACKNOWLEDGMENTS

Many thanks to three sets of innkeepers whose hospitality was inspirational in the places I visited while researching this book:

The Taste of Alaska Lodge, Fairbanks, Alaska

Quagmire Manor, Homer, New York

King's Inn, Huntsville, Alabama

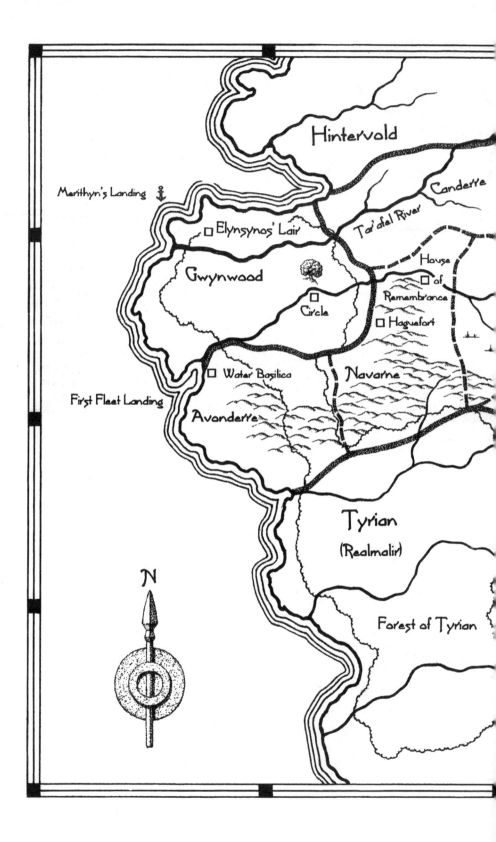

Hintervold

Merithyn's Landing ⚓

Elynsynos' Lair

Canderre

Ta'afel River

Gwynwood

House
of
Remembrance

Circle

Haguefort

Water Basilica

Navarne

First Fleet Landing

Avonderre

Tyrian
(Realmalir)

N

Forest of Tyrian

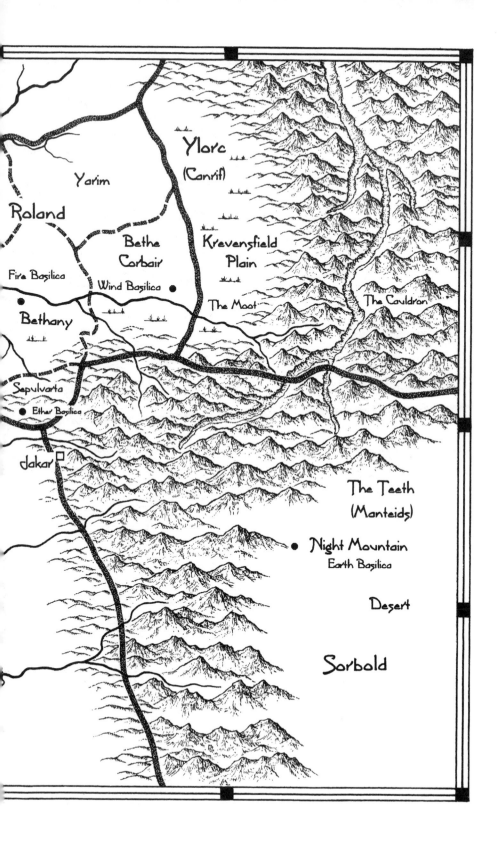

ODE

WE are the music-makers,
And we are the dreamers of dreams,
Wandering by lone sea-breakers,
And sitting by desolate streams;
World-losers and world-forsakers,
On whom the pale moon gleams:
Yet we are the movers and shakers
Of the world for ever, it seems.

With wonderful deathless ditties
We build up the world's great cities,
And out of a fabulous story
We fashion an empire's glory:
One man with a dream, at pleasure,
Shall go forth and conquer a crown;
And three with a new song's measure
Can trample an empire down.

We, in the ages lying
In the buried past of the earth,
Built Nineveh with our sighing,
And Babel itself with our mirth;
And o'erthrew them with prophesying
To the old of the new world's worth;
For each age is a dream that is dying,
Or one that is coming to birth.

—Arthur O'Shaughnessy

Seven Gifts of the Creator,
Seven colors of light
Seven seas in the wide world,
Seven days in a sennight,
Seven months of fallow
Seven continents trod, weave
Seven eras of history
In the eye of God.

SONG OF THE SKY LOOM

Oh, our Mother the Earth;
Oh, our Father the Sky,
Your children are we,
With tired backs.
We bring you the gifts you love.

Then weave for us a garment of brightness. . . .
May the warp be the white light of morning,
May the weft be the red light of evening,
May the fringes be the fallen rain,
May the border be the standing rainbow.

Thus weave for us a garment of brightness
That we may walk fittingly where birds sing;
That we may walk fittingly where the grass is green.

Oh, Our Mother Earth;

Oh, Our Father Sky.

—Traditional, Tewa

THE WEAVER'S LAMENT

Time, it is a tapestry

Threads that weave it number three

These be known, from first to last,

Future, Present, and the Past

Present, Future, weft-thread be

Fleeting in inconstancy

Yet the colors they do add

Serve to make the heart be glad

Past, the warp-thread that it be

Sets the path of history

Every moment 'neath the sun

Every battle, lost or won

Finds its place within the lee

Of Time's enduring memory

Fate, the weaver of the bands

Holds these threads within Her hands

Plaits a rope that in its use

Can be a lifeline, net—or noose.

The Awakening

1

*W*hen the mountain peak of Gurgus exploded, the vibrations coursed through the foundations of the earth.

Above ground, the debris field from the blast stretched for miles, ranging from boulder-sized rubble at the base of the peak to fragments of sand that littered the steppes more than a league away. In between, shards of colored glass from windows that had once been inlaid in the mountain's hollow summit lay like a broken rainbow, glittering in the sun beneath an intermittent layer of sparkling dust.

Below ground, a small band of Firbolg soldiers felt the concussion rumble beneath their feet, though they were some miles east of Gurgus. A few moments of stillness passed as dust settled to the floor of the tunnel. When Krarn finally released the breath he was holding, the rest of his patrol shook off their torpor and resumed their duties. The Sergeant-Major would flay them alive if they let something as small as a tremor keep them from their appointed rounds.

A few days later, the soldiers reluctantly emerged under a cloudless sky, having reached the farthest extent of this section of their tunnel system, and the end of their patrol route.

Krarn stood on the rim of the craterlike ruins of the Moot, a meeting place from ancient times, now dark with coal ash and considered haunted. Nothing but the howl of the wind greeted him; no one lived in the rocky foothills that stretched into steppes, then out to the vast Krevensfield Plain beyond.

Having finished their sweep of the area, his men had quietly assembled behind him. Krarn was about to order them back into the tunnels when the hairs on his back—from his neck to his belt—stood on end.

It began as the faintest of rumblings in the ground. The tremors were not enough to be noticed on their own, but Krarn noted the trembling of vegetation, the slightest of changes in the incessantly dry landscape, little more than the disturbance that a strong breeze might make. He knew that it was no wind that caused this disturbance; it had come from the earth.

Silently ordering his men into a skirmish line, Krarn scanned the area, looking for any more signs. After a few minutes, the feeling passed, and the earth settled into stillness again. Nothing but wind sighed through the tall grass.

"Aftershocks," he muttered to himself.

With a shake of his head, Krarn led his men back into the tunnels.

And in so doing, missed the chance to sound a warning of what was to come.

$\mathcal{A}$s the days passed, the tremors grew stronger.

The surface of the Moot, baked to a waterless shell by the summer sun, began to split slightly, thin cracks spreading over the landscape like the spidery pattern on a mirror that had broken but not shattered.

Then came steam, the slightest of puffs of rancid smoke rising up ominously from the ground beneath the tiny cracks.

By day it was almost impossible to see, had eyes been in the locality to see it. By night it mixed with the hot haze coming off the ground and, caught by the wind, wafted aloft, blending with the low-hanging clouds.

Finally came the eruption.

Waves of shock rolled through the earth as if it were the sea, waves that intensified, growing stronger. The earth began to move, to rise in some places, shifting in its underground strata.

Then, with a terrifying lunge, it ripped apart.

The rumbling beneath the surface suddenly took on movement. It started outside of Ylorc but traveled quickly. It was heading north.

Unerringly, determinedly north, toward the icy land of the Hintervold.

All along the eastern rim of the mountains, then westward across the plains, a movement within the ground could be felt, a shifting so violent that it sent aftershocks through the countryside, uprooting trees and splitting crevasses into the sides of rolling hills, causing children miles away to wake in the night, shaking with fear.

Their mothers held them close, soothing them. "It's nothing, little one," they said, or uttered some similar words in whatever language they were accustomed to speaking. "The ground trembles from time to time, but it will settle and go quiet again. See? It is gone already. There is nothing to fear."

And then it *was* gone.

The children nestled their heads against their mother's shoulders, their eyes bright in the darkness, knowing on some level that the shivering they had felt was more than the ripples of movement in the crust of the world. Someone listening closely enough might sense, beyond the trembling passage, a deeper answer from below the ground.

Much deeper below.

As if the earth itself was listening.

$\mathcal{D}$eep within her tomb of charred earth, the dragon had felt the aftershocks of the explosion of the mountain peak.

Her awareness, dormant for years, hummed with slight static, just enough to tickle the edges of her unconscious mind, which had hibernated since her internment in the grave of melted stone and fire ash in the ancient Moot.

At first the sensation nauseated her and she fought it off numbly, struggling to sink back into the peaceful oblivion of deathlike sleep. Then, when oblivion refused to return, she began to grow fearful, disoriented in a body she didn't remember.

After a few moments the fear turned to dread, then deepened into terror.

As the whispers of alarm rippled over her skin it unsettled the ground around her grave, causing slight waves of shock to reverberate through the earth around and above her. She distantly sensed the presence of the coterie of Firbolg guards from Ylorc, the mountainous realm that bordered the grave, who had come to investigate the tremors, but was too disoriented to know what they were.

And then they were gone, leaving her mind even more confused.

The dragon roiled in her sepulcher of scorched earth, shifting from side to side, infinitesimally. She did not have enough control of her conscious thought to move more than she could inhale, and her breath, long stilled into the tiniest of waves, was too shallow to mark.

The earth, the element from which her kind had sprung, pressed down on her, squeezing the air from her, sending horrific scenes of suffocation through her foggy mind.

And then, after what seemed to her endless time in the clutches of horror, into this chaos of thought and confused sensation a beacon shone, the clear, pure light of her innate dragon sense. Hidden deep in the rivers of her ancient blood, old as she was old, the inner awareness that had been her weapon and her bane all of her forgotten life began to rise, clearing away the conundrum, settling the panic, cell by cell, nerve by nerve, bringing clarity in tiny moments, like pieces of an enormous puzzle coming together, or a picture that was slowly gaining focus.

And with the approaching clarity came a guarded calm.

The dragon willed herself to breathe easier, and in willing it, caused it to happen.

She still did not comprehend her form. In her sleep-tangled mind she was a woman still, of human flesh and shape, not wyrm, not beast, not serpentine, and so she was baffled by her girth, her heft, the inability of her arms and legs to function, to push against the ground as they once had. Her confusion was compounded by this disconnection between mind, body, and memory, a dark stage on which no players had yet come to appear. All she could recall in her limited consciousness was the sense of falling endlessly in fire that had struck her from above, and blazed below her as she fell.

Hot, she thought hazily. *Burning. I'm burning.*

But of course she was not. The blast of flame that had taken her from the sky had been quenched more than three years before, had sizzled into smoky ash covering the thick coalbed that lined her tomb, baking it hard and dry in its dying.

Fighting her disorientation, the dragon waited, letting her inner sense sort through the jumble, inhaling a bit more deeply with each breath, remaining motionless, letting the days pass, marking time only by the heat she could feel through the earth when the sun was high above her tomb, and the cooling of night, which lasted only a short while before the warmth returned.

Must be summer's end, she mused, the only cognizant thought to take hold.

Until another image made its way onto the dark stage.

It was a place of stark white, a frozen land of jagged peaks and all but endless winter. In the tight containment of the tomb the memory of expansiveness returned; she recalled staring up at a night sky blanketed with cold stars, the human form she had once inhabited, and still inhabited in her mind, tiny and insignificant in the vastness of the snowy mountains all around her.

A single word formed in her mind.

Home.

With the word came the will.

As the puzzle solidified, as the picture became clearer, her dragon sense was able to ascertain direction, even beneath the ground. With each new breath the dragon turned herself by inches until, after time uncounted, she sensed she was pointed north-northwest. Across the miles she could feel it calling, her lair, her stronghold, though the details of what it was were still scattered.

It mattered not.

Once oriented in the correct direction, she set off, crawling through the earth, still believing herself to be human, dragging a body that did not respond the way she expected it to relentlessly forward, resolute in her intent, slowly gaining speed and strength, until the ground around her began to cool, signaling to her that home was near. Then, with a burst of renewed resolve, she bore through the crust of the earth, up through the blanket of permafrost, hurtling out of the ground in a shower of cracking ice and flying snow, to fall heavily onto the white layer that covered the earth like a frozen scab, breathing shallowly, rapidly, ignoring the sting of the cold.

She lay motionless for a long while beneath that endless night sky blanketed with stars, thought and reason returning with her connection to this land, this place to which she had been exiled, in which she had made her lair.

The dragon inhaled the frosty wind, allowing it to slowly cleanse her blackened lungs as the dragon sense in her blood was cleansing her mind.

And along with thought and reason, something else returned as well, burning hot at the edges of her memory, unclear, but unmistakable, growing in clarity and intensity with each moment.

The fury of revenge.

2

The king of the mountainous realm was away when the peak exploded.

A man born as an accidental by-product of depravity and despair, of mixed bloodlines that came from the earth and the wind, his skin was almost magically sensitive, a network of traceries of exposed nerves and surface veins. He was, as a result, innately aware of the vibrations in the wind that others defined as Life, could oftentimes tell when things were not as they should be, when something was disturbing the natural order of the earth, especially the earth that was his domain. Had he been in his kingdom when the wyrm awoke from her sleep, he would have known it.

But Achmed the Snake, king of the Firbolg and lord of the realm of Ylorc, was half a continent away, traveling overland on his way home when it came to pass.

So, like his subjects, the guards who walked the edge of the grave itself, he missed the chance to intervene, to stop what was to come.

And, by chance, because of a weapon of his own design, the cwellan, which he had adapted just for the purpose of penetrating the hide of a dragon, he alone might have been able to do so while the wyrm lay in her sepulcher, prone and disoriented. His weapon had drawn her blood before.

By the time he returned home, the beast was long gone.

His mission in the west accomplished, he had chosen to return to his kingdom in the eastern mountains alone, riding the same route as the guarded mail caravans, but refusing to wait to travel with them in the safety of numbers. In addition to his natural tendency of isolation, his complete disdain for the majority of the human race, and his desire not to be slowed down in his return by traveling with others, Achmed needed time alone to think.

The heat of summer's end was waning as he traveled the trans-Orlandan thoroughfare, the roadway built during the most prosperous days of the previous empire. The thoroughfare bisected the land of Roland from the seacoast to the edge of the Manteids, the mountains known as the Teeth, where he now reigned. The cooling of the season and the fresh wind that came with it gave him a clear head, allowing him to sort through all he had experienced.

The western seacoast he had left behind him was burning still, though the fires had begun to be extinguished by the time he left. The ash from the blackened forests had traveled east on the wind as well, and so for the first few days of his journey his nostrils and sensitive sinuses were sore from their exposure to the soot. But by the time he reached the province of Bethany, the midpoint of the realm of Roland, the wind had turned clearer, and so had his head.

His mind, distracted by the disappearance of one of his two friends in the world, was able to refocus on what had been his priority for the last few months. Now that she was safe, his thoughts were locked obsessively on the completion of his tower.

Many of the reasons for his obsession with rebuilding the instrumentality that had once been housed in the mountain peak of Gurgus were lodged in the past. But the most important one was the future.

The pounding of the horse's hooves was a tattoo that drove extraneous thoughts away. *The Panjeri glass artisan I hired in Sorbold has had a good deal of time to make progress on the Lightcatcher; the ceiling of the tower must be complete by now,* the king thought, ruminating on what Gurgus would look like when restored. A full circle of colored glass panes, seven in all, each precisely fired to the purest hues of the spectrum, the mountain peak would soon hold a power that would aid him in his life's mission.

Keeping the Sleeping Child safe from the F'dor, fire demons that endlessly sought to find her.

From the time he had begun the undertaking of building the tower, the Firbolg king's mind had known even less peace than usual. His obsession was coupled with uncertainty; he was by training and former trade an assassin, a murderer, an efficient killer who had for centuries plied his trade alone, choosing only the contracts that interested him, or that he felt warranted his attention. Life and circumstance had taken him from an old land, his birthplace, now dead and gone beneath the waves of the sea, and deposited him here, in this new and uncertain place, where he had put his skills to good use, seizing control of the loose, warlike tribes of mountain-dwelling mongrels, forging a ragged kingdom of demi-humans. Under his hand, with the help of his two friends, he had built them into a functioning nation, a realm of silent strength and resolute independence. Now he was a king. And he was still a skilled killer.

What he was not was an engineer.

When he had discovered the plans for the Lightcatcher buried deep in the vault of the kingdom he now ruled, once a great civilization fallen into ruin by its own folly, he had broken into a gray sweat. He could not read the writing on the ancient parchment; it was drafted in a tongue that had been old when his long-dead homeland was still young. As a result, he could not be certain of the specifications of the drawings, of the directions to build the instrumentality, and, more important, of what its powers were. He only knew he recognized in the detailed renderings something he had known in the old world as an apparatus of unsurpassed power, a device that had held an entire mountain range invulnerable from the same evanescent demons that were now seeking the Earthchild he guarded.

That device had apparently been duplicated here long ago.

From that moment on it had become a challenge to rebuild it. For the first time in his life he'd had to rely on outside help, on expertise other than his own, to fashion something that was part weapon, part scrying device, part healing instrumentality. And it was being done in secret, in the hope that he was not being betrayed or misled. Achmed did not really believe in hope, and therefore had suffered mightily, plagued with doubt and worry mixed with the burning belief that this apparatus, and this apparatus alone, would be able both to make his kingdom invulnerable to the invaders he knew would someday come, bent on its destruction, and, far more important, to help him protect the Sleeping Child from those invisible monsters that endlessly sought to find her.

One of his two friends in the world was a Lirin Namer, schooled in the music of words, ancient lore, and the dead language of the drawings. She had been disquieted by the depth of the magic she saw in the renderings, had implored him not to meddle in matters he didn't fully understand, but in the end her loyalty to and love for him had won out over her reservations, and she had given him a brief translation of one of the documents, at his insistence. It had contained a poem, a riddle really, and the schematic of the color spectrum, along with the power each color held.

He chanted them to himself now as he rode, trying to commit them more naturally to his memory, and finding that the words refused to remain there. He had never been able to recall the words in the ancient tongue; he could retain only the color translations, only for a short while, and only by concentrating resolutely. Even then, he was still uncertain of them, as if some innate magic within them was refusing him right of entry.

Red—Blood Saver, Blood Letter, he thought, trying to employ the techniques of visualizing the words that Rhapsody, the Namer, had taught him. That one, at least, was easy for him to recall. *Orange—Fire Starter, Fire Quencher.* He was fairly certain of that one as well. *Yellow—Light Bringer, Light . . . Queller?* His mind faltered. *Damnation. I can't remember.*

But soon it would not matter. He had finally found a glass artisan in the neighboring kingdom of Sorbold, a Panjeri master from a tribe known the world over for their expertise in molding the sand of the desert and the ashes of wood into the most exquisite of glass, capturing rainbows in a solid yet translucent form to adorn the windows of temples and of crypts. He had given her free rein, under the eye of Omet, his head craftsman, to move ahead with the firing and inlay of the glass ceiling of Gurgus, which, once finished and outfitted with the other pieces of the apparatus, would become the Lightcatcher. He had even dared to look forward to that being completed by the time of his return.

So it was with more than a little shock moving to unbridled fury that he dragged his hapless mount to a halt upon discovering the rainbow grit that was scattered across the Krevensfield Plain at the foothills of his kingdom.

Achmed dismounted slowly, his considered movements mirroring the motion of the reptile he had received a nickname from. He walked in measured steps to a place where the layer of colorful glass powder was somewhat thicker, crouched down, and scooped some of the tiny shards up in his perennially gloved fingers. The glass was little more than dust, but it still contained the unmistakable colors that he had seen being fired when he left home some weeks back.

Achmed sighed deeply.

"*Hrekin,*" he swore aloud.

He glanced up from his crouch to the multicolored peaks of the Teeth, where he reigned over the Firbolg hordes in what was known in their tongue as the kingdom of Ylorc. Gurgus, the peak in which the colored windows had been inlaid, was deeper in, past the guardian ring of mountains at the edge, so it was impossible to see what had befallen his tower from this distance. He could, however, see that the guard tower of Grivven, one of the westernmost and highest peaks, was still standing.

At least the entire bloody kingdom didn't blow to bits while I was gone, he thought ruefully. *I suppose I should be grateful.*

He tossed the glass powder angrily behind him, mounted, and urged his horse into a steady canter, growing more irate with each breath of the wind that poured over his face as he rode.

Sergeant-Major Grunthor, commander of the united Firbolg forces and Achmed's only other friend in the world, was directing a massive reconstruction that had clearly been under way for quite some time when the king returned to the mountain. As Achmed strode down the interior mountain corridor leading to the former entrance to Gurgus, he could hear the Sergeant bellowing commands to the workers, his voice occasionally straining with exertion as he moved massive broken pieces of earth himself.

The Firbolg king rounded the corner and stopped for a moment, beholding him. Grunthor was paused as well, though he hadn't caught sight of Achmed yet; with a dray sled at his feet piled high with broken basalt, a hand cart gripped in his massive hands, the giant commander was catching his breath, his skin, the color of old bruises, glistening with sweat from the exertion. Even at rest he was a terrifying sight, seven and a half feet of musculature at rest for the moment, preparing to resume the strenuous task, directing a squad of Firbolg soldiers in their tasks while he rested.

The sheer scope of the destruction took its toll on Achmed's limited patience. The king stormed to the end of the hallway, stopping just short of the Sergeant's presence.

"What in the name of every ridiculous evil god that never existed happened here?"

An ugly light came into the giant Sergeant's amber eyes.

"Birthday party got a little out o' hand, sir," he said, his voice sharp with sarcasm. "So sorry. Won't 'appen again." As the cords in the king's neck tightened, Grunthor tossed the cart aside. "You might want ta pose that question to that 'arpy glassmaker you brought in 'ere to build the tower windows. Oh, no, wait! Can't do that."

The king's eyes narrowed in rage that was tempered with panic. "Why not?"

The Sergeant crouched down and grasped another massive rock, lifted, and heaved it angrily into the dray sled.

"Because Oi cut the bitch's head off 'er shoulders," he snarled as the small boulder bounced against the earthen floor with a resounding thud. "Then Oi tossed it in a crate and shipped it back to the *assassin's guild* in Yarim, from whence she had come in the first place." He watched without sympathy as the fury in his sovereign's eyes muted into realization. " 'At's right, sir, the artisan you 'ired in Sorbold to build yer bloody glass tower turned out to be the mother of all assassins, the mistress of the Raven's Guild." He wiped his forehead with the back of his wrist and indicated the destruction around him. "This was the lit'le present she left just for you. We're findin' all sorts of other traps, lots o' nice surprises—"

"The Child?" Achmed demanded, sounding as if he were strangling.

Grunthor exhaled deeply. "Safe, for now," he said more calmly, the latent anger in his voice gone. "Oi combed every inch of the tunnel down to 'er chamber; appears that it was broached, but only a few feet of it. The assassin didn't 'ave time to get down there, by sheer bleedin' luck. But if Oi was you, sir, Oi'd be careful not to insult any ridic'lous gods that never existed, as they apparently been watchin' yer back in a major way."

"Now there's a terrifying thought." Achmed crossed the broken hallway and stopped before the thinning pile of rubble. "How?"

"Picric acid. Apparently she 'ad it shipped in from the guild while you were gone. In a liquid state it's stable, but explodes when it dries. She 'ad it annealed into the glass of the dome; kept a wooden cover over it ta keep the sun off. But Shaene and Rhur—both dead, by the by—pulled the cover; the sun 'it it square on, the 'eat dried the enamel, and—well, you can see the rest." The Sergeant ran the toe of his enormous boot through the grit of the floor.

"Except the Sickness—lots o' dysentery and a lot of Bolg bleedin' out their eyes. That seemed to come with it."

Without a word the Firbolg king turned and left the scene of the destruction.

"Oh, by the way sir," called Grunthor as Achmed disappeared around the corner, "welcome 'ome."

℧he tunnel down to the chamber of the Sleeping Child began in Achmed's bedchamber, its entrance secreted in a trapped chest at the foot of his bed. It took him only a moment to ascertain that each of the guardian traps, deadly locks he had set himself, had been serially disarmed, their triggers sprung with an expertise he had not witnessed since his own assassin training at the hands of an undisputed master a lifetime before.

"Hrekin," he swore again.

Grunthor exhaled. "Aye, well, at least she was a master. Oi remember back in the old land when the thieves' guild kept sending their trainees after ya for a while. Remember that, sir? That was just plain senseless carnage, it was. Not even really useful as target practice for you."

Achmed said nothing, but rose from the chest and traced the path around his chambers, looking for all-but-invisible signs of disturbance.

They were everywhere.

Dust disturbed in only the slightest patterns, the occasional repositioning of an object in such close proximity to where it had originally been left that only one trained at the level he was trained would have seen it. Subtle traps as well; a thin rim of poison on his mealtime cutlery, his comb, on the brace of the doorframe, so discreetly laid out that he might not have noticed, which meant that only a master assassin could have laid them. Achmed's already sensitive skin prickled with gray sweat at the thought, because it was clear that the woman had only had a few moments in the room before being discovered.

"If you ever find that I have misplaced my head this badly again, Grunthor, please be sure to have me bend over and check my arse for it," he said gloomily, removing a tiny spring-loaded pin from the toe of one of his spare boots. "It must be wedged up there tightly enough to qualify me as a Cymrian."

"Very well, sir," Grunthor said with exaggerated respect. "Oi 'ave a button 'ook ya might be able to use ta get it out o' there, but it may not be long enough."

Achmed opened the door to his chambers carefully, avoiding the mercury-coated wire that had been filed hair-thin and positioned invisibly along the doorjamb.

"Get me a set of glass calipers," he ordered one of the guards standing watch in the hallway. "Drop them outside the door loud enough for me to hear, then withdraw. Do not touch the handle." The Bolg soldier nodded and jogged up the corridor.

"Is Omet still alive?" Achmed asked Grunthor, closing the door again.

The Bolg Sergeant nodded. "She poisoned 'im and left him for dead, but Rhur and Shaene found 'im and took 'im to the tower."

The Bolg king's eyes, mismatched in color and position in his pocked face, darkened at the significance of the Sergeant's words.

"Is that why they pulled the tower dome cover off? They were trying to use the Lightcatcher? To heal Omet?"

Grunthor nodded, his expression guarded.

Achmed's movements slowed and he ran a gloved hand over his mouth, pondering.

"And you say Omet is alive?"

"Yeah."

The Bolg king's head snapped up sharply. "How alive? Is he debilitated, or hovering near death?"

Grunthor exhaled, his jaw set so rigidly in disapproval that the tusks showed over his bulbous lips.

"Good as new," he said finally. "As if it 'ad never happened."

Achmed stood motionless, pondering, even the tides of his breath invisible in the intensity of his concentration. Grunthor could see the realization spreading, first over his face, then through his body, like a stain. "It worked," the king said finally. "The Lightcatcher worked—or at least the healing aspect of it, the red section."

"One might believe that the orange section worked as well," muttered the giant Bolg. "Started the fire that blew the damned thing up."

A clank of metal sounded in the hallway, followed by the noise of footsteps hurrying away.

"It worked," Achmed repeated. "You fail to see the significance now, Grunthor, but I can assure you, if we can rebuild it, make it function completely, we are setting in place a defense for both Ylorc and the Child that is unparalleled." He strode to the door, disregarding the Sergeant's rolling eyes, and carefully opened it. He retrieved the metal calipers lying on the stone floor, then closed the door again.

"Before anything else, I want to see the Earthchild," he said.

As they traveled the rough-hewn tunnel that led from the chest at the foot of Achmed's bed to the chamber in which the Earthchild slept, Achmed could still smell a hint of the smoke of the battle fought to save her four years ago. To any other nose it would have been indiscernible, but along with his skin-web of nerve endings and surface veins, Achmed's sinus cavities and throat were exceptionally sensitive. This strange anatomical system, bequeathed to him by his Dhracian mother and his unknown Bolg father, was both blessing and bane; it gave him early warning of hazards others might miss, and a memory of things others had long forgotten.

Even Grunthor. He cast a glance at the Sergeant-Major as they descended, noting the blank expression on his friend's face in the cold light of their lantern formed from glowing crystals that had been found in the depths of the mountains. Grunthor was in a state of watchful autonomy, listening to the song of the Earth that only he could hear. Whatever the Earth was singing had him guarded, concentrating, but he was not feeling the same dread that Achmed felt every time he came down to this place.

Each time he descended into the fractured remains of the Loritorium, the sepulcher deep within the mountains where the Earthchild slept, the Bolg king was assailed with frightening memories of the battle they had fought near there. The F'dor had corrupted a root of one of the World Trees, using it to slither through the Earth's crust, past the guard towers and bulwarks he and Grunthor had painstakingly assembled, into the very heart of the mountain range to the hidden chamber in which she had slumbered for centuries.

They had had no warning at all, except for the nightmares of the Child. And the Child could not speak, could not tell them what was coming.

Achmed quickened his pace as they neared the opening to the chamber. He ran to the rough-hewn entranceway and climbed quickly over the barricade of rock and loose stone that was the last bulwark before the broken Loritorium. He held his breath as he crested the gravelly hill.

In the distance he could see her there, still slumbering. Achmed exhaled slowly, then nodded to Grunthor, who followed him down the slippery rockpile and over to the altar of Living Stone on which she slept. They peered down at the Earthchild, their eyes searching for any change, any discrepancy since the last time they had seen her.

An icy chill descended on them both at the same time.

"She's withering," Grunthor whispered.

Achmed nodded. He pulled out the glass calipers and carefully measured the body that at one time had been taller than his own. She had lost some of her smoothly polished flesh, once alive with the colors of the earth, green and brown, vermilion and purple, twisting bands of color that now seemed to have faded somewhat beneath her silver-gray translucent skin. How much was lost he was uncertain, but at least now he had a point of reference.

Hesitantly he stretched out his hand and brought it lightly to rest in the Earthchild's hair, brittle as strawgrass at summer's end. The roots of her hair were golden as ripening wheat, a sign that the earth from which she had come was preparing to celebrate harvest before slipping into slumber with the coming of winter. But below the grasslike locks were strands of wasted black weeds, burned as if in fire or slicked with poison.

"No," Achmed whispered. "Gods, no."

"Do ya think she's sick, sir?" Grunthor asked in concern, his eyes scanning the empty vault. Achmed didn't answer. " 'Ere, let me 'ave a look."

The Bolg king moved numbly aside as the giant Sergeant stepped up to the catafalque on which the Sleeping Child lay. He watched as Grunthor stared down at her pensively for a moment; the giant was tied to the earth as the king was, but more so, had a connection with it that had been established long ago. Earth spoke to him in his blood. Sometimes all Grunthor gleaned from this connection was an impression, an image in his mind, and could never communicate it fully to the Bolg king in words. But that wasn't necessary anyway. Achmed could gauge the severity of the message by the expression on Grunthor's face.

He continued to watch, nervous, as the giant reached out a hand and laid it gently on the Child's midsection, resting it on top of the blanket of eiderdown Rhapsody had covered her with years ago. The Child's face was the same cold and polished gray it had always been, as if she were sculpted from stone, but Achmed felt a nauseating dizziness as he noticed tiny rivulets of muddy water trickling down her forehead.

It looked like she was sweating in the throes of a fever.

The tides of her breath, once almost indiscernible in sleep, were now ragged. There was a wheeze in the depths of her inhalations, a sound that did not bode well for her health, if an ancient being formed from Living Stone could have such a thing as health.

Let that which sleeps within the Earth rest undisturbed; its awakening heralds eternal night, the words over her chamber had once read, words that had been inscribed in letters the height of a man, as if to emphasize their importance. Whether the prophecy referred to the Child herself, or other, more terrifying things that slept within the Earth, Achmed did not know. But having seen some of those things with his own eyes, he knew that keeping this being at peaceful rest was of consummate importance, not just to his safety, or that of his subjects, but to the whole of the world.

And now she was flinching, moving from side to side, as if preparing to awaken.

Achmed thought back to the first day he had seen her, almost four years before. He had been shown her by the Grandmother, a Dhracian woman of ancient years who had lived alone with the Child for centuries, guarding her, the last survivor of a colony of his mother's race who had given their lives in the Child's rescue and protection. He had stared down at the remarkable creature under her guardian's careful eye, observing that her features were at once both coarse and smooth, as if her face had been carved with blunt tools, then polished carefully over a lifetime. He had marveled at her eyebrows and lashes, which appeared to be formed of blades of dry grass, matching her grainy hair, delicate sheaves of what looked like wheat.

She is a Child of Earth, formed of its own Living Stone, the Grandmother had said in her delicate buzz of a language. *In day and night, through all the passing seasons, she sleeps. She has been here since before my birth. I am sworn to guard her until after Death comes for me. So must you be.*

He had taken the edict seriously.

"Well?" he finally demanded softly, unable to restrain his anxiety. "What is happening to her?"

Grunthor exhaled, then walked away from the catafalque, out of the Child's possible hearing.

"She's bleeding to death," he said.

$\mathcal{F}$or time uncounted they waited together in the darkness in which smoke from years past still lingered, standing watch over the Sleeping Child, searching for any clue as to what was causing her to wither.

Grunthor, in whose veins ran the same tie to the Earth, whose heart beat in the same rhythm as her own, attempted futilely to find the source of her dissipation by communing silently with her, but discovered nothing more than an agonizing sense of deep loss. He finally stepped away, shaking his massive head sadly.

"P'raps you can give it a try, sir," he suggested to Achmed, who crouched beside the Earthchild's catafalque, his elbows resting on his knees, his hands entwined before his veiled lips. "Can ya use yer blood-gift?"

The Bolg king shook his head as well. "That was broken long ago," he murmured in a passive undertone so as not to disturb the Earthchild. "The *gift* is but a sporadic one now. And it only was truly in place with those born on Serendair. So while I am useless in helping her, the heartbeat of every living Cymrian still rings clearly in my head, and you know how much I *love* those idiots. The irony is sickening; the gods must be choking with laughter."

The Sergeant-Major exhaled sharply. "Yeah? Well, let 'em choke. What do you want to do, sir?"

Achmed rose from his crouch and rested his hand on the Earthchild's own. He leaned over her, brushed the grassy wisps of hair back from the muddy sweat of her forehead, and pressed a kiss on it.

"Do not worry," he whispered. "We stand guard. We will find what is doing this to you and make it stop."

He turned away and walked off into the darkness, back toward the rubble barrier and the tunnel entrance. As soon as they were out of earshot he spoke the only three words he would utter the rest of the night.

"Summon the Archons."

$\mathcal{C}$he dragon lay still as day came and brought light, if not warmth, to the frozen world around her.

As night followed day, the cycle repeating itself again and again, her broken mind was slowly knitting, coming back to itself, though she still had not comprehended her form, could not yet remember how she had come to be entombed in a cavern of smoke and ash so far away from this place of cold clarity.

The world here had already been in the grip of autumn when she arrived; now winter, early and bitterly windy, was signaling its imminence. Though she was still not whole, her instinct told her that warmth and shelter must soon be found, or she would die.

With great effort the beast lifted her head, then hoisted herself onto her forearms, crawling over the earth as once she had crawled through it; across the frost-slick ground and the endless plains pocked by dry vegetation, to the shores of an almost-frozen lake. In the distance she could see what looked like steam rising from it, though in all likelihood it was merely the crystals of ice taking to the wind as it gusted sharply over the tundra.

As she made her painful way through the thick brush at the lake's edge she tentatively extended her hand to touch the surface, endeavoring to ascertain whether the water had frozen deeply enough to bear her weight.

The mirrorlike surface, not yet fully ice, reflected a sight that caused her breath to choke in her throat.

No hand hovered over the meniscus; instead she could see a gnarled claw, red-gold and scored with scales, ending in cruel talons, some razor-sharp, some broken, one missing, jointed with phalanges that no longer resembled anything even vaguely human.

The beast recoiled in horror.

The great claw disappeared, leaving only ripples in the frigid water.

The dragon's still-foggy mind fought off the implications of what she had seen, but realization was taking hold in her belly.

Slowly she crawled forward, steeled her resolve, and looked down into the water.

Partially obscured by fireweed and bracken was a face that rang a chime in her memory, but it was not one she recalled as her own.

She tore the vegetation aside and looked again.

Then loosed a cry of rage, a long, sustained howl that trailed off in despair, dragging the snow from mountain faces in great white avalanches.

When she could force herself to look once more, her eyes were cloudy with unspent tears.

Gone was her proud beauty; she had been a handsome woman, with the tall, statuesque frame of her Seren father, and the gold cast of his skin in hers as well. The dramatic bone structure of her face, which long ago had adorned myriad court paintings, statues, and coins, was gone as well, replaced with the hideous aspect of a beast, a wyrm, as her despised mother had been.

The dragon continued to stare at her face, locked in disbelief mixed with dread, her nose and mouth jutting forth in a serpentine snout, her skin now mottled red scales that glinted in the light with traces of black and copper, horned at the edges, metallic, with webbed wings, one of them brutally scarred, hanging limply from her back. Only her eyes remained as they once had been, blistering blue eyes that could level a man with a glance, eyes so compelling that she had been able to enslave, enchant, or entreat almost any soul she had ever caught in her gaze.

Staring now at her reflection in the almost frozen lake, those commanding blue eyes spilled over with grief. The rocks on which her tears fell glistened gold in the sunlight, as they would forever after.

The dragon shook herself violently, as if the force could shake the body in which she was now housed from her. She willed her form to change back to what it had once been, resorting finally to scraping at her hide with her cruel talons, leaving brutal gashes in her own thick flesh. It was all for naught—the fire that had struck her, that had haunted her awareness from the moment she had awakened—had come from the stars, the element of ether, purified in living flame. The form she had chosen to wreak havoc in was now her own permanently, the human aspect of it having been purged forever by power that was older than her own earth lore.

Her stomach rushed into her mouth and she vomited caustic flame, kindled in the firegems that now were part of her viscera. The patchy vegetation ignited beneath its hoary coat and crackled, blackening immediately and filling the air with dull smoke.

As bright blood blazed in stripes and flecks on the permafrost, the dragon's grief mutated into anger. The easy and inadvertent destruction of the grass pleased her on some level, lessened the pain somewhat.

She took a deep breath and exhaled, allowing her fury to vent itself in her breath.

A billowing wave of orange heat rolled over the frosty plain, melting the snowcap and singeing the small trees, leaving the landscape smoldering all around her.

Destruction, she thought in the mind that was still not entirely clear. *Destruction eases the pain a bit.*

It was easy medicine to take.

In the distance she could feel the place that had been her lair calling to her from the west.

Too weary to yet be able to contemplate the ramifications of her new form, the wyrm dragged herself forward, aiming for the place she hoped to find answers.

And rest that would cause her strength to return.

3

FISHING VILLAGE AT
JEREMY'S LANDING, AVONDERRE

*W*hen Quayle the fisherman first found Faron on the beach, he thought he had stumbled across nothing more than a thick strand of pale seaweed clogging the inlet.

Upon further investigation, he discovered what resembled a large jellyfish or squid, a grotesque mass of colorless skin hanging on a frame that did not resemble anything human.

Except that it had a head vaguely shaped like that of a child, its eyes closed, thick lips fused together in front, with black water draining out the sides of its mouth.

The fisherman's first impulse was to pummel it with a board and toss it to the cats to shred. This is what he would have done, in fact, had he not observed the shallow chest quivering with breath.

His dockmate, Brookins, who was trimming the nets, saw him recoil in disgust and called to him from the pier.

"What is it?"

Quayle shrugged. "Somethin' from a nightmare," he called back.

Brookins wiped the slime from his hands onto his trousers and made his way over to where Quayle stood, staring down at the mass entangled in the weeds at the edge of the inlet.

"Sweet All-God," he said, shielding his eyes.

The creature lay in the fetid water, still as death, with only the faint movement of the nostrils in its flat, bridgeless nose and the shallow rise and fall of its chest to indicate otherwise. Its sallow skin, faintly golden but bleached gray by the sun, hung loosely over a skeletal frame that the men could tell was monstrously misshapen, even beneath its blanket of seaweed.

"Do you think it's alive?" Brookins asked nervously after a moment.

Quayle nodded silently.

Gingerly Brookins picked up an oar and lifted some of the seaweed off the creature.

Both men cringed as more of its body was revealed—twisted limbs that appeared almost boneless, as if fashioned from cartilage instead, were bent at all-but-impossible angles beneath its torso. The creature was lying on its side, mostly naked; the ratty remains of fabric that covered its body bulged slightly in spots to suggest both nascent male and female traits.

Brookins swore again, then tossed the weeds into the sea.

"A freak of nature, that's what it is," he said, having no idea how little nature had had to do with what he saw in the inlet before him. "Part jellyfish, part man, or somethin' akin to it."

"Perhaps part woman," Quayle noted, pointing at the buds of what appeared to be breasts.

"Pour pitch on it and light it," Brookins muttered. "I've got some in the boat."

Quayle shook his head, thinking. "Naw," he said after a moment, "we may be able to turn a crown or two on it. The catch was miserable today."

"Turn a crown? Are you daft, man? Who would be willing to eat something so vile?"

"Not to eat, you fool," said Quayle contemptuously. "We can sell it to a traveling carnival, a sideshow—that's what buys freaks like that. There was one up the coast in Windswere just a sennight or so back."

Brookins cast a glance up the coast, where smoke from the forest fires that had only recently been quenched still hung in the air. Until a few nights ago, the entire western seacoast had burned with rancid heat, acrid black flames that carried with them the unmistakable taint of evil. Now that the conflagration had been extinguished, a few of the evacuated villagers had begun to return, to pick through the rubble of the scorched homes on the water and in the charred forest. There was a stillness to the air that was unnerving, as if the coast was waiting for the next wave of destruction.

"If they was in Windswere, they probably fled east to Bethany with the other refugees," he said, poking the creature gently with the oar. "This thing'd never make it that far."

"Ayeh, looks to be a fish of some sort," Quayle agreed. "The fish-boy."

"Or girl."

"Ugh. Well, the types that deal in curiosities and freaks and the like might have use for it, whatever it be, alive or dead. I'll get the net; we can drag the thing out of the inlet and put it in the wagon. Might as well smoke the pitiful catch we have and cart it into Bethany. We'll sell the wares and buy the ropestock and whatever provisions we were gonna get later in the month, and while we're there we can look for that sideshow. The thing won't take up much room in the cart."

Brookins exhaled. "If you think so," he said doubtfully. "But I'm thinking we're going to need to keep it wet. After all, The Amazing Monstrous Fish-boy won't survive out of water all the way to Bethany. Alive or dead, it will start to stink. Maybe will stink less if we can keep it alive."

Quayle, already on his way to the boat, chuckled at the thought.

Saron was jarred to semiconsciousness by a violent jolt when the cartwheel made contact with a deep rut in the road. The creature opened one wide, fishlike eye, covered with a milky cataract, and winced, too weak to even recoil from the pain. The midday sun was baking its fragile skin with both light and heat, two elements that caused its body to blister. It closed its eye and wheezed with the exhalation of its breath. Faron was already so frail and ill from exposure that, in its foggy perception, death could not come quickly enough.

Despite being imprisoned all its life in a monstrous and malfunctioning body, Faron's mind, while primitive, was keen, and even as close to death as the creature was, it was aware enough to recognize the vibrations that reverberated on its sensitive eardrums through the water in which it lay as voices, and unfamiliar ones. Involuntarily it shuddered, trying to piece together what had come to pass.

Having been kept from birth in darkness in a comfortable pool of gleaming green water, the creature had very little understanding of the outside world, although its father had told it tales during the evenings when he came to visit, bringing marinus eels for its supper. Faron's father had been a tender caretaker, even if he had been given to sudden outbursts of rage and cruelty. Faron loved him, as much as an unevolved mind could love, and was bereft in his absence, so bereaved at his loss that death now was welcome.

Faron curled up a little more tightly, wishing it would come.

The sun beat down on the creature's back.

And in the midst of its agony, it sensed another source of pain.

Hazily Faron tried to concentrate on the sharp edges that bit into the flesh between its arthritic fingers, in the sagging folds of its underbelly.

With the last ounce of available strength Faron unbent an elbow, bringing the soft bones that, formed normally, would have been a forearm up close to the fishlike eyes in its face.

And opened its eyes in tiny slits to spare them from the sunlight.

The creature's hideously deformed mouth, with its lips fused in the center and gapping open over the sides, curled slightly at the corners in a shadow of a grimacing smile.

The scales were still there, one wedged into the flesh between its fingers, the others digging into the folds of its belly where they had been hidden.

Faron opened the first two fingers on the hand before its eyes, just slightly enough to see what they held.

The sun glimmered onto the irregular green oval, pooling there, making the center shine like the light in a glade, leaving the tattered edges of the scale cool and dark as the forest's core.

The creature's failing heart leapt. It peered into the scale, fighting off the assault of sunlight in its stinging eyes.

Faron twisted the scale slightly, allowing the light to run in shining ripples off the lightly scored surface; in the creature's hand the scale took on an infinitesimal film, an iridescent surface, like a veil of mist, behind which a cool and verdant wood seemed to beckon. When it ascertained which card it held, its smile grew brighter.

It was the Death scale.

Since the creature had taught itself to read the scales, it only knew how to summon into its primitive mind the future they could foretell. Ofttimes in the past, when scrying with the scales for its father in the cool and delicious darkness of its safe haven, Faron would become confused, bewildered by the images that it saw reflected in them.

Thankfully, the Death scale was clearly interpretable.

Faron tilted the scale and peered into it.

All around the scale, the world melted away, replaced by darkness.

Life as Faron knew it was now depicted in, and limited to, the small oval surface defined by the tattered borders of the scale.

Against the frame of flat blackness, the scrying card hummed with power, like the deep green iris of an enormous eye.

Within its center Faron could make out a forest, the same sunless glade that was always visible in the Death scale. No birds sang in this place; stillness reigned unchallenged by even a breath of wind.

Faron waited, oblivious of the bumps in the road and the excoriating sun on its skin.

After a few moments a translucent figure formed in the glade, as if from the mist itself. It was the figure of a pale man, garbed in robes of green that blended seamlessly into the forest behind him. His eyes, black and devouring as the Void, were crowned by thick thundercloud brows, the only part of him that seemed solid, which gave way to snowy white hair. It was Yl Angaulor, the Lord Rowan, whom men called the Hand of Mortality.

The peaceful manifestation of Death.

Despite his stern appearance, Faron had never feared Yl Angaulor. The creature watched, entranced, as the Lord Rowan slowly shook his filmy head, then disappeared into the mist from whence he had come.

The Death scale went dark.

Faron's eyes closed as the heat of the day returned.

Not for me, the creature thought in its semiconscious mind. *I not die now.*

A single caustic tear welled beneath a heavily veined eyelid and burned as it fell.

The snow muted the sun's light as it hung over the edge of the world, pausing as if reconsidering its descent.

With the last measure of her strength, the beast pulled herself up from the chasm, over the ice-covered battlements that scored the mountaintop in wide, frozen rings, to rest on the flat, cold ground outside the walls.

The word that had been driving her on, inspiring her to fight off the sleep that hovered on the edge of her consciousness and the numbness of her limbs, echoed in her brain, growing louder as she climbed.

Home.

She stopped and wearily inclined her head, her three-chambered heart thudding loudly.

Above her in the snowy air a castle reached to the clouds, formed of marble that had long ago been coated with so much ice as to appear chiseled from it. The three towers loomed above her in haughty splendor, unchallenged in the winter sky.

Home. Home. Home.

The dragon's eyes opened slowly, widely, the vertical pupils that scored the searing blue iris contracting in the last of the afternoon light, drinking in the sight of the vast fortress and with the sight, the memory of it.

In her foggy mind the pieces of those memories were scattered in the dark corners, confused. Slowly, however, they seemed to crawl together and form a clearer picture.

The first memory that returned was an old one, the sight of the castle as she had first beheld it in her exile. She had come to believe she might have been a queen at one time, or a woman of some kind of import, because even as she had been walked to the edge of the icy slopes by someone whose face had not yet come into the picture, even as he had turned and left her in the blinding snow, alone for all time, her back had remained straight, her head unbowed.

As the wyrm stared up at the frost-covered crenulations, the icy windows glazed over so thickly that sunlight would never again pass through them clearly, the towers piercing the clouds above, the images continued to return. She could now recall years of being alone in the cavernous halls that lay beyond the gates, the silence of her marble prison broken only by the echoes of her own footsteps and the crackling of the fires that burned in the mammoth hearths. Each century, each year, each day, even down to the hour came slowly back to her, her dragon blood surging with each beat of her heart, recalling the infinitesimal details as none other than a wyrm could recall, obsessing over them as none but a wyrm could obsess.

They exiled me to this place, she thought bitterly, an anger whose source she could still not remember burning in her blood now. *Left me alone in the cold mountains, alone with nothing but memories. And now someone has taken even those from me.*

At that thought, another image began to form in her mind. It was of a face, a woman's face, though she could not make it out completely. A woman with golden hair and emerald green eyes, though little else was clear.

At the edges of the dragon's mind, the fire of hate began to burn again. She still did not know who the woman was, or why her own caustic blood boiled with fire at the thought of her, but she knew that the memory would return eventually.

And when it did, she vowed that all the unspent fire, all the contained hate, would be unleashed in a thunderous fury that would rock the very foundations of the world, cracking the endless ice into hoary dust and shattering even the marble walls of the prison that was her home, her lair.

The beast crawled on toward the castle, seeking shelter from the coming night.

4

HAGUEFORT, NAVARNE

Gwydion Navarne waited anxiously in the opulent hallway outside the doorway of the Great Hall of Haguefort, the rosy-stoned castle that was his ancestral home. His sixteen years had been marked by loss, first of his mother, then his father, and scarred by near-loss as well, so whenever the doors closed on the place where critical discussions were undertaken and decisions of great import were made, leaving him out in the corridor, it made him anxious.

He was particularly nervous now, given that his guardians, the Lord and Lady Cymrian, had gone to great lengths to include him in virtually every decision of state that had been made since his father's death three years prior. That they had politely requested he remain outside during their discussions was upsetting, though he told himself there was no reason for it to be. He trusted both his godfather and his godfather's wife, the woman who had adopted him as an honorary grandchild, implicitly. Somehow, despite that trust, his nerves were on edge this morning.

His anxiety deepened into genuine dismay as one by one his guardians' most trusted advisors began to arrive in the corridor outside the Great Hall. Each was announced, and quickly admitted, while Gwydion continued to cool his heels on the thick carpet of woven silk.

Finally, when a familiar advisor entered the corridor, Gwydion intervened. That he chose to approach Anborn, the great Lord Marshal and General during the Cymrian War, was less because the man had been a mentor of sorts to him than because the Cymrian hero was lame. Anborn had to be carried in on a litter, there had been a delay in his announcement, and so Gwydion seized the opportunity to speak to him before he entered the Hall.

"Lord Marshal! What is going on in there?" he asked, coming alongside the litter and interposing his body between it and the doorway.

Anborn signaled to the soldiers who bore the litter to set him down and step away. His azure eyes, blue in the color of the Cymrian dynastic line, blazed beneath his wrinkled brow in a mixture of annoyance, amusement, and fondness.

"How would I know, you young fool? I haven't even made it past the door, thanks to you. Move aside, and then perhaps I will have an idea."

"Will you come back out once you do know and tell me, then?" Gwydion pressed. "If Rhapsody and Ashe have invited you to confer, the subject must be of great importance."

The general shook his mane of dark hair streaked with the silver of age and snorted.

"Certainly, though I doubt I am going to stay for much of the discussion. Where you attend a trade apprenticeship is of little interest to me."

Gwydion's face contorted in shock as the icy horror took hold of his viscera.

"A trade apprenticeship? They are sending me away to be apprenticed? Please say it isn't so."

The general signaled to his litter bearers. "All right, then. It isn't so. Now move out of the way, cur, and let me get this cursed conference over with so that I might get back to more useful pursuits—training my men, cleaning my boots, picking my nostrils, moving my bowels—anything other than this folderol."

"*Apprenticed?*"

"Oh, for goodness' sake, buck up, boy," the General said as the soldiers lifted his litter. "Going away to continue your education is a necessary part of your training to be duke one day. Your own father was apprenticed to any number of different masters in his youth. You will survive and be better for it. " The doors opened; the General's litter was carried into the Hall, and the doors shut decisively behind him.

Gwydion sank onto a bench of carved mahogany and groaned.

"What's the matter?"

He looked up to see Melisande, his nine-year-old sister, watching him, concern in her dark eyes. Gwydion smiled quickly.

"Perhaps nothing, Melly," he said reassuringly. Melisande had suffered many of the same tragedies he had suffered, but she was much younger. It had been an unspoken agreement between Gwydion and his guardians that her life be made as stable and free from worry as possible.

"You're lying," Melisande said evenly, tucking away a bag of jackstraws and sitting down beside him on the bench.

"No, I am not," Gwydion said. He turned in time to see a man he recognized as Jal'asee, the ambassador from the distant Isle of the Sea Mages, enter the far end of the corridor. Both siblings watched in respectful silence as the elderly man walked past with his retinue of three. Jal'asee was an ancient Seren, born of one of the five original races of men that originated in the time before history. His race was unmistakable in his tall, thin frame, his golden skin and dark, bright eyes; the Seren were said to have been descended of the stars. Gaematria, the mystical island on which they made their home, along with other ancient races and ordinary humans who had come as refugees there centuries before, lay three thousand miles to the west, in the midst of the wide Central Sea. It was said to be one of the last places on the earth where magic was still understood and practiced as a science.

"If the Sea Mages are sending a representative, there must be something else going on here," Gwydion mused aloud. "It would be vain beyond measure to imagine that my schooling was of any interest to them—or to anyone else in that room except Rhapsody and Ashe, and perhaps Anborn."

"Maybe they are going to execute you instead," Melisande said jokingly, rising from the bench and drawing out her jackstraws again. "Your report from the tutors must have been worse than we imagined."

At that moment the doors opened, and their guardian emerged. Both children stood immediately. The Lord Cymrian, whose given name was also Gwydion but whom they both referred to in private as Ashe, was attired in court dress, a happening so rare that it made both Melisande and Gwydion begin to fidget.

The Lord Cymrian's eyes, cerulean blue with vertical pupils that told of the dragon's blood in his veins, sparkled warmly as he beheld the children.

"Melly! You're here as well. Excellent. Please remain here in the hallway for a moment, and then they will bring you in." He held out his hand, banded at the wrist in leather at the end of a sleeve of white silk slashed with dark red, to Gwydion. "Will you come with me, please, Gwydion?"

The youth and his sister exchanged a terrified glance; then Gwydion followed Ashe through the vast double doors, which closed almost imperceptibly behind him.

As they passed through the entrance to the Great Hall Gwydion's eyes went to the vaulted ceiling on which historical frescoes representing the history of the Cymrian people had been meticulously rendered in a circle around a dark blue center. When his father was alive, they had entered the Great Hall only on rare occasions, spending most of their time in the family quarters and the library, so the grandeur of the Hall never became commonplace to Gwydion. He found himself unconsciously following the story of his ancestors who had refugeed from the doomed Island of Serendair fourteen centuries before.

Each vault on the ceiling covered a period of the history. Gwydion stared up at the first panel, a fresco depicting the revelation made to Lord Gwylliam ap Rendlar ap Evander tuatha Gwylliam, sometimes called Gwylliam the Visionary, that the Island would be consumed in volcanic fire by the rising of the Sleeping Child, a fallen star that burned in the depths of the sea. It made him even more nervous when he realized that the court clothing that Gwylliam was wearing in the painting was very similar to what Ashe, who was walking before him, was wearing now.

Each of the additional ceiling frescoes told more of the story—the meeting of the explorer Merithyn and the dragon Elynsynos, who had once ruled undisputed over much of the middle continent, including Navarne; her invitation to the people of Serendair to take refuge in her lands; the construction and launch of the three fleets of ships that carried the Cymrian refugees away from the Island; the fates of each of those fleets; the unification of the Cymrian royal house with the marriage of Lord Gwylliam to Anwyn, one of the three daughters of the dragon Elynsynos; the building of the mighty empire over which the first Lord and Lady Cymrian had ruled, and its eventual destruction in the Cymrian War.

Gwydion had once suggested to Ashe that the blank blue panel in the center be painted to commemorate the new era into which they had recently passed, known as the Second Cymrian Age, with his godfather's ascension to the Lordship along with Rhapsody, who had been named Lady by the Cymrian Council three years before. Ashe had merely smiled; the panel remained blank.

In the Great Hall itself numerous chairs had been set up. Occupying those chairs were the dukes of the five other provinces of Roland and representatives from each of the other member nations of the Cymrian Alliance, the loose confederation of realms loyal to the Lord and Lady. Rial, the viceroy of the forested kingdom of Tyrian, where Rhapsody was also the titular queen, nodded to him pleasantly, but with a look of sympathy that was unmistakable. The back of Gwydion's neck began to tingle.

Before they passed under the arch that demarked the second vault, Ashe turned and took him by the arm.

"Come in here for a moment," he said, diverting him into a side room.

Gwydion followed blindly, his stomach clenching with worry. Ashe closed the door behind him. The echo of the vast hall was swallowed immediately by the smaller room's carpets, drapes, and tapestries.

In the room near the windows the Lady Cymrian was standing, watching the leaves on the trees beginning to lose their verdant hue and turn the color of fire. She, too, was dressed in heavy velvet court clothing, a deep blue gown that hung stiffly away from her slender frame, hiding the swell of her belly. Her golden hair was swept back from her face and plaited in the intricate patterns favored by the Lirin, her mother's people. She turned upon hearing them enter the room and eyed Gwydion intently for a moment, then broke into a warm smile that faded after a second into a look of concern.

"What's wrong?" Rhapsody asked, coming away from the window. "You look like you're about to be executed."

"You're the second family member to suggest that this morning," Gwydion replied nervously, taking the hand she held out to him and bowing over it formally. "Should I be worried?"

"Don't be ridiculous," she said, pulling him close and tousling his hair fondly. The skin of her face, normally a healthy rose-gold tone, paled visibly; her clear green eyes brightened with tears of pain. She released him and walked over to a chair where she sat quickly. Her pregnancy was a difficult one, Gwydion knew, and she became fatigued and nauseated easily.

"We have a few announcements to make shortly, but since all of them concern you directly, I thought you should hear of them before the general council does," Ashe said, pouring a glass of water for his wife and handing it to her. "And, of course, if you object to any of them, we will reconsider."

Gwydion inhaled deeply. "All right," he said, steeling himself. "What are they?"

Ashe hid a smile and put his hands on Rhapsody's shoulders. "First, Highmeadow, the new palace I've been having built for your—grandmother"—his dragonesque eyes twinkled in amusement at the word—"will be ready on the first day of autumn. I plan to move our lodgings there; it is time we leave Haguefort and set up our own residence."

Gwydion's stomach turned over. Rhapsody and Ashe had been living in his family's home since the death three years prior of his father, Stephen Navarne, who had been Ashe's childhood friend. Their presence was the only thing that had made living in Haguefort tolerable; otherwise the memories would have been too strong to bear. Even though he had been a young boy, and Melisande an infant, when their mother was murdered on the road to town, he still remembered her, and missed her when the night winds shrieked and howled around the castle parapets, or on warm, windy days, like the ones on which he and his mother had flown kites together. And the loss of his father in battle, before his eyes, had dealt a death blow to his optimism. Though he knew he would always carry the weight of these tragedies, the load seemed lighter when shared with people who loved him, and who had loved his father.

"We also think it would be a good idea for Melisande to come with us for the time being, and live at the new palace," Ashe continued.

"Melly? But not me?"

"Right. We will get to that in a moment."

Gwydion nodded numbly, his every nerve screaming inside. *They* are *sending me away,* he thought, his mind reeling at the thought.

"Second," Ashe continued, oblivious of his consternation, "Rhapsody and I would like to reinstitute the winter carnival this year."

Gwydion's nausea grew exponentially. The winter carnival had long been a family tradition at Haguefort, something his father had relished hosting, on the days that spanned the winter solstice. Each year a great festival was undertaken, coinciding with holy days in both the Patriarchal religion of Sepulvarta and the order of the Filids, the nature priests of the Circle in Gwynwood, the two faiths of the continent. The festival lasted for three days, marked with games of winter sport, feasting, singing contests, minstrelsy, and dozens of other forms of merrymaking.

The last of the carnivals had taken place four years before and had turned into a bloodbath. The horror of it was still raw in Gwydion's mind.

"Why?" he asked, unable to contain his revulsion.

"Because it is time to get back to the business of living," Rhapsody said gently. "Your father loved that celebration, and understood how important it was to the folk of his province, and in fact all of Roland. It is the one time of year that the adherents of the religion of Sepulvarta and that of Gwynwood convene for a happy purpose; that is critical to advancing understanding between both sects. And besides, we have an announcement to make; that seems like the best place to make it."

"What announcement?"

"Third," Ashe said, "we have decided, after deep discussion and consultation with a few of our most trusted advisors, that you are ready to take on the full mantle of your inheritance, as duke of Navarne."

Gwydion stared at his guardians in silence.

"That is why we are offering to take Melisande with us," Rhapsody said quickly. "Once you take on the responsibility of the duchy, there will be much for you to accustom yourself to, and caring for your sister, as much as we know you are willing to do it, should not be a distraction to you. Our new home is less than a day's journey on horseback anyway; she can come and see you whenever either of you wish."

Ashe came over to the young man and stood in front of him, looking down gravely into his eyes.

"Your seventeenth birthday is the last day of autumn," he said seriously. "You have more than proven yourself worthy of being fully invested as duke; you are both brave and wise beyond your years. This is not a gift, Gwydion; it is both your birthright and a title you have earned. I need you as a full member of my council, and Navarne needs a duke who looks out for its interests as his main concern. Anborn believes you to be ready, and that is high praise indeed. My uncle is not the quickest to offer support or praise; if he feels you merit the title, there are few that will gainsay it."

"But there may be some who do," Gwydion said, his heart still racing.

"None," Rhapsody said, smiling. "We have met already, and all agree. We're sorry for keeping you waiting in the hall, but the council needed to be able to speak freely. You would have been flattered to hear what they said. No one objected." She glanced at Ashe; Tristan Steward, Gwydion Navarne's cousin, had expressed concern, but in the end had acceded and given the idea his support.

"And even if there are, that is something you may as well become accustomed to," Ashe said. "It is the lot of a leader to be questioned; it is the sign of a good one when that leader takes the praise and blame with equanimity, without being swayed too far from what he believes by either of them. So, what say you? Shall we call in Melisande so that she can witness the first moment of her brother's investiture?"

Gwydion walked over to the window where Rhapsody had stood and pulled the drape back, causing a bevy of winterbirds that had been perching in the nearby trees to scatter noisily. He gazed out over the rolling green fields of his ancestral estate, scored by a twelve-foot-high wall his father had built to fortify the lands around the castle. The townspeople had begun to move their dwellings within the wall, turning it from the once-pristine meadow into a village, as Stephen had predicted would happen. It was an ugly reality: the trading of innocence and beauty for safety and security.

"I suppose this is childhood's end," he said, his voice tinged with melancholy.

Ashe came to the window and stood behind him. "In some ways, yes. But one could make the case that your childhood ended long ago, Gwydion. You've seen more loss in your young life than any man should have to see. This is just a formal recognition that you've been a man for some time."

"Your father never truly lost the innocence of childhood, Gwydion," Rhapsody said. "He had seen the same kinds of early loss that you have—his mother, your mother. Even your godfather—for many years Stephen believed Ashe to be dead. But he had you, and Melly, and a duchy to be strong for. He could have embraced the darkness of melancholy, and he would have had every right to do so. He chose instead to laugh, to celebrate, to live in the light instead of the darkness." She rose slowly. "That choice is yours as well, as it is for each of us."

Gwydion turned back and regarded his guardians. They were watching him closely, thoughtfully, but in their eyes was the silent, common understanding of people who had taken on leadership reluctantly, at great personal sacrifice. He knew that they had both lost much, too—most everyone in the world they had ever loved. In their loss, they clung to each other.

Something his godfather had said to him on their wedding day three years before came to mind.

If your grandmother were to have her way, she would abandon all of the trappings and the power and live in a goat hut in a remote forest somewhere. Grow herbs, compose music, raise children. And with but one word from her, I would move the mountains with my hands to make it happen.

Then why don't you? Gwydion had asked.

Because there are some things that you cannot escape, for they are inside you, Ashe had said, putting on his wedding neckpiece. *One of them is duty. She is needed in the positions she has been given, as I am.* His eyes had twinkled. *But on the day when we are no longer specifically needed, I will ask for your help in building that goat hut.*

Gwydion met the eyes of the Lord and Lady Cymrian.

"I'm honored to accept," he said simply.

Rhapsody and Ashe smiled in response.

"Know that we are here for you, always," Rhapsody said.

"Let us go share the good news, shall we?" Ashe added, crossing to the door of the small room and opening it. "We have a festival and an investiture to plan."

On his way down the aisle of the Great Hall behind the Lord and Lady Cymrian, Gwydion Navarne paused long enough at Anborn's seat to lean in and utter one word.

"Apprenticeship?"

The Lord Marshal broke into an evil grin.

"I *told* you it wasn't so," he whispered back as the duke-to-be walked past.

Through Ashe's announcement, Gwydion kept his eyes fixed on the Lord Marshal's face. It remained frozen in the same formal aspect, a court face, Ashe would have called it, immutable and showing no emotion, giving no indication of his thoughts one way or the other. But in the Cymrian hero's azure eyes Gwydion thought he saw more—sympathy, perhaps; he and Anborn had forged a strong bond, and he knew that Anborn disdained titles and court responsibilities, valuing instead his freedom from duty. Given the sacrifices he had made as a young man in the court of his father and mother, Gwylliam and Anwyn, and the war his father forced him to lead against his mother, Gwydion well understood Anborn's distaste for titles and the responsibilities they carried. The Lord Marshal had long counseled Gwydion to stay away from them until he could avoid them no more; now that day had come.

When finally the announcement was over, and the congratulations had all been passed around, Ashe announced that a state dinner in Gwydion's honor would commence immediately following. The invited guests swirled politely around him, proffering their congratulations again, and talking among themselves.

Just as the group prepared to depart the Great Hall for the dining room, the ambassador from Gaematria, the Island of the Sea Mages, Jal'asee, bent his head slightly and spoke in a tone inaudible to all but Ashe. The Lord Cymrian nodded.

"Uncle," he called to Anborn, who was preparing to be carried out of the Hall, "indulge us for a moment?"

The Lord Marshal's brow furrowed, but he signaled to his bearers to wait.

"Go along to the dinner, Melly," Gwydion Navarne said to his sister. "I will be right there."

"I'll see if I can save a seat for you," Melisande said, amusement in her black eyes. "It would be unfortunate if you had to stand in the back at your own celebration." She turned and followed the heads of state out of the Great Hall, her golden curls bouncing merrily.

The dukes of the provinces of Roland and Tristan Steward, the Overlord Regent, remained as well, watching with interest as Jal'asee walked slowly down the carpeted aisle and came to a stop in front of the Lord Marshal. He nodded to two members of his retinue, who opened the doors of one of the side rooms and disappeared inside, returning a moment later with an enormous pallet on which a huge wooden crate was carried. With great effort they set it down in front of Anborn, then respectfully and quickly withdrew.

"What's all this?" the Lord Marshal demanded, eyeing the wooden crate suspiciously.

The elderly Seren cleared his throat, his golden eyes gleaming.

"A gift from your brother, Edwyn Griffyth, High Sea Mage of Gaematria," he said. His voice, soft, deep, and crackling with an alien energy, sent shivers down Gwydion's spine. The duke-to-be glanced over at Rhapsody, and saw that she was similarly affected; she was listening intently, as if to music she had never heard before.

Anborn snorted. "I want nothing from him," he said disdainfully, "least of all something that has to be carried in on a litter. It's an insult. Take it away."

Jal'asee's placid expression did not change in the face of the harsh reply. He merely reached into the folds of his robe and pulled forth a small sheaf of cards, and held them up silently, indicating they were instructions from Edwyn. Ashe nodded.

"With respect," the tall man said in his pleasantly gravelly voice. He consulted the first card, cleared his throat again, and read it aloud.

"'Don't be a childish ass. Open your gift.'"

A low chuckle rippled through the hall among the dukes. Anborn glared at them, then at the Seren ambassador. Jal'asee smiled benignly. The Lord Marshal inhaled deeply, then exhaled loudly and signaled to the attendants to open the crate.

The members of Jal'asee's retinue hurried to unlatch the crate, then stepped back as the wooden walls fell neatly away.

Inside was a gleaming machine, fashioned in metal. It stood upright, with steel foot pads supported by articulated joints, which seemed to be controlled by two geared wheels with handholds. The assemblage took in its breath collectively; otherwise, silence reigned in the Great Hall.

"What in the name of my brother's shrunken, undersized balls is *that*?" Anborn asked scornfully.

Jal'asee coughed politely, flipped the top card to the back of the sheaf, and peered at the next one.

"'It's a walking machine, you dolt. It has been designed precisely to your height, weight, and girth, and should serve to allow you to walk upright, assisted, once again. And you would do well not to comment on the size of my genitalia—it may give rise to embarrassing questions about your own manhood.'"

Anborn raised himself up angrily on his fists. "I don't want it!" he roared. "Take that infernal contraption back to my brother and tell him to bugger himself with it."

Patiently Jal'asee flipped the top card back again, and read the next one.

"'There is no need to be foul. And I am not paying to transport it back. It's staying. You may as well make the best of it.'"

Anborn eyed the metal walker with a blackening brow, then suddenly turned in the direction of the Gaematrian ambassador once again.

"Tell my brother I said 'thank you,'" he said with exaggerated politeness.

Jal'asee blinked, then quickly riffled through the remaining cards, finally looking up with a pained expression on his ancient face.

"I—er—do not appear to have a response to that," he said in amused embarrassment. "I don't believe your brother anticipated that as a possible reply."

"HA! Got him!" Anborn crowed. He signaled to his bearers. "Get me out of here; I'm missing dinner." His attendants picked him up and carried him from the Hall, leaving the dukes, the ambassadors, and the lord and lady staring after him in a mixture of humor and bewilderment. The dukes, talking among themselves, followed behind him.

Ashe went over to the walking machine and examined it carefully. "Edwyn's abilities as an inventor and a smith never cease to amaze me," he said, a tone of wonder in his voice. "It is marvelous to see the genius he inherited from his father put to good and helpful uses, rather than the destructive ones that Gwylliam employed."

"Gwylliam wasn't always destructive," Rhapsody said, watching as Ashe turned the hand crank slowly, making the right foot pad rise and step forward, then reversing it. "He is responsible for many useful and pleasant inventions—the halls of Ylorc are lighted with sconces he designed; the mountain is warmed and cooled through ventilation systems of his making; there are even privies within the depths of the mountain. When Ylorc was still Canrif, his masterwork, it boasted some of the most sophisticated and clever inventions in the world. You should take pride in your grandfather's accomplishments as well as ruing his follies."

She felt a light touch on her elbow, and turned to see Jal'asee standing behind her. She looked up into his face and returned his smile.

"M'lady, if I might, I would like to speak with you alone for a moment," Jal'asee said pleasantly.

Rhapsody looked over at Ashe, who was watching her questioningly, and nodded.

"Go ahead with the dukes, Sam," she said quietly, addressing him by the name she called him privately. "I will be along in a moment." She waited until her husband and Gwydion had left the room; once alone, she looked back up at Jal'asee.

"Yes?"

The Ancient Seren ambassador's pleasant expression faded into one that was more serious.

"M'lady, is the Bolg king to be invited to young Gwydion's investiture at the winter carnival?"

"Of course," Rhapsody said. "Why?"

"Is he likely to attend?"

She exhaled, then shrugged. "I really couldn't say. He has been away from his kingdom for an extended period." Her face flushed; it was her rescue that had required him to be away thus. "Why do you ask, Your Excellency?"

The tall man looked down at her seriously. "I am hoping that you will do me the honor of introducing me to him, and arranging a brief moment of consultation." The gravelly voice was light, but Rhapsody could hear in it the unmistakable seriousness of the words.

"I can certainly introduce you if he is there, but I cannot promise he will be willing to speak at length with you," she said. "Achmed is—well, he can be—unpredictable."

"I understand," Jal'asee said. "And I am grateful for whatever intervention you can provide. I plan to stay until the solstice and attend the investiture; it would be impossible to travel home and back in the two months' time from now until then." His eyes sparkled brightly. "Without extraordinary measures, that is."

Rhapsody smiled. "Someday I would like to learn about such measures," she said, rising and gathering her skirts in preparation of leaving the Hall. "Though I understand that the Sea Mages are very guarded when it comes to their magic."

The ambassador nodded noncommittally. "I would be honored to tell you a little about it, given your status as a Namer, m'lady," he said, offering her his arm. "Your vow of speaking the truth and guarding the ancient lores makes you one of the few people outside of Gaematria with whom it would be appropriate to discuss such things. When you are feeling up to it, perhaps we can take a walk in the gardens and do so."

"Thank you; that sounds very appealing," Rhapsody said, taking his arm.

"And perhaps in return you can tell me a bit more about the Bolg king," Jal'asee continued, starting across the floor of the Great Hall. "He is one of the two men with whom you traveled along Sagia's roots to this land from Serendair, is he not?"

The Lady Cymrian jerked to a halt in shock. She pulled her arm away, shaking. Other than Ashe, no living soul knew of how she and her two friends from the old land had escaped the death of the Island of Serendair, to arrive here, on the other side of time.

"How—how did you know that?" she asked, her voice trembling. She had been caught by surprise so deeply as to be unable to cover gracefully; the nausea of her pregnancy and the exhaustion she was routinely fighting prevented her from it.

Jal'asee smiled at her.

"Because I saw you leave," he said.

5

ON THE TRANS-SORBOLD ROADWAY, REMALDFAER, SORBOLD

Dusk was coming, taking the remaining light of the afternoon sun with it.

Talquist, regent of the vast, arid empire of Sorbold, had been scribbling notes and poring over balance sheets throughout the latter part of the day in the back of his opulent coach, the shade of the window up to allow him both fresh air and illumination in the course of his task. Now, with the approach of night, he paused in his work for a moment, taking care to blot the last of his writing before allowing himself to stare out the window at the sunset.

For all that he had modestly chosen to remain regent for a year, even when the Scales of Jierna Tal had weighed in his favor and selected him as emperor, Talquist did not deny himself any of the luxuries of the position that would soon be his. He had been nibbling all day upon the bounty of the shipping trade from which he had arisen as the hierarch of the western guilds: sweetmeats from Golgarn, flaky pastries layered in honey and cardamom, roasted nuts and delicate wine from the Hintervold, where the frozen grapes were pressed through ice to make an incomparable nectar. He had worked in the trade of the shipping lanes of the continent all of his life, and as a result he had developed a taste for and access to the finer things, even when he was a mere longshoreman. Once he became First Emperor of the Sun in a few months, he would have even better gastronomical delicacies to look forward to. The kitchens of the palace of Jierna Tal were considered among the finest in the world.

The splendor of nightfall over the Sorbold desert was impossible to ignore, even for so focused a man as Talquist. The air, normally static and dry to the point of bringing blood from the nose, took on a sweeter, moister aspect for a moment, as if tempting the sun to return in the morning. The winds had quieted, leaving that air clear as well; the firmament of the heavens was darkening to a cerulean blue in the east, with tiny stars glimmering through the cloudless veil of night. In the west was a swirling dance of color, fiery hues that tapered away to a soft pink at the outer edges, wrapped around a blazing ball of red orange flame descending below the distant mountains.

Talquist sighed. *There is such beauty in this land,* he thought, the fierce pride of his nation welling in his heart. *She is a harsh land, this dry, forbidding realm of endless sun, but her riches are undeniable.*

The clattering of the hooves of the horses in his escort, fifty strong, roused him from his musings. Talquist reached for the platinum tinderbox, removed the flint and steel, and struck a spark to the wick of the lamp of scented oil on his table. A dim glow caught, then expanded, bringing warm light into the deepening darkness of the coach's velvet interior.

Three more days until we reach Jierna Tal, Talquist thought, his eyes returning to the detailed ledger before him. The thought made him itch; he was eager to return to the grand palace with the parapets nestled deep in the mountains of central Sorbold after so much time on the western coast, attending to business there. An unfortunate accident at the time of his selection by the Scales had taken the life of Ihvarr, the hierarch of the eastern guilds, Talquist's friend, cohort in trade, and only real competition. Talquist had quickly absorbed Ihvarr's network of miners, carters, tradesmen, and store owners, which required extensive oversight, and he himself had always had the shipping concerns, which needed even more. But the heavy workload didn't bother him, because Talquist was an ambitious man.

The sound of a horse approaching broadside of his coach drew his attention away from his books. Talquist looked out the window to see one of his scouts riding up, signaling for the coach to slow. He tapped the interior window at the base of the coachman's seat.

"Roll to a stop," he ordered, then leaned out the window.

"What is it?" he called.

The soldier, attired in the emperor's own livery, reined his horse to a halt as well.

"M'lord, there is a caravan ahead approaching the mountain pass, four wagons."

"Yes?"

"They appear to be traveling under cover of darkness to avoid detection. The wagons are full of what appear to be captives."

Talquist leaned farther out the window, his brows drawing together in displeasure.

"Captives?"

"Yes, m'lord. They are bound and blindfolded; probably were brought ashore to the south along the Skeleton Coast."

Talquist nodded angrily. Slave trade was increasing by leaps and bounds in Sorbold; the sale of human prisoners into the mines and fields had been on the rise since the death of the previous ruler, the Empress of the Dark Earth, whose demise had led to his ascension. Renegade slavers who attacked villages or caravans and impressed their captives into fieldwork or sold them were one of Talquist's greatest irritations.

"Where do they appear to be going?" he asked.

The soldier removed his helmet and shook the sweat from it. "Based on their route, I would hazard they are headed for the olive groves of Baltar," he said.

"Intercept them," Talquist ordered. "Divert my procession; I want to see who is smuggling slaves in my realm and put a stop to it personally. I'll batten down in here; tell the coachman to go full out."

"Yes, m'lord."

Talquist lowered the shade and put out the light, seething with anger.

Evrit rubbed his tongue futilely inside his mouth, hoping to generate spit, but there was none to be had.

Five days with his eyes blindfolded and his hands bound before him had made him somewhat more aware of things around him: the cooling of the air with the coming of night, the stench of the waste in the wagon, the moans of pain and whimpers of fear among his fellow captives, especially those of his young sons, whose voices he could recognize even when no words were spoken. He tried to listen for any sign of his wife, who had been thrown, struggling, into another wagon, but the endless clatter of the horses and the clanking and groaning of the wagons made it impossible.

Selac, the younger of his two boys, had ceased making sounds some hours before. Every time the wagon noise lessened, Evrit had called to him, his ragged voice all but unrecognizable, but had received no reply. He prayed that the boy had merely fallen asleep or unconscious rather than trying to remain upright in the stench and the thirst, but could not rid his mind of the thumping sound that occurred every time the wagons slowed for the daily feeding and watering of the captives. He had counted five such sounds. The whipping sands of the desert wind stung against his skin, serving as a fine substitute for the tears of fear that could not come from his eyes for lack of water and the blindfold.

Over and over again he cursed himself for being enough of a fool to undertake the sea voyage to Golgarn. He was the titular leader of the expedition; he and his fellow passengers on the *Freedom* had timed their departure to take advantage of the last of the southerly summer trade winds, before autumn turned the current near the Skeleton Coast deadly. They had taken to the sea ultimately seeking tolerance of their gentle religious sect in Golgarn, which was a state that espoused no particular faith. They had survived the sinking of their vessel only to find themselves prisoners of the people who had helped them ashore—the people they had thought were rescuers.

Their captors had not been completely unkind to them; there had been no rape of the women from the sundered ship, as far has he could tell, no beatings or abuse. They had been bound and blindfolded after being given water and food, and allowed to relieve themselves, though the harshness of the summer in the desert, the roughness of their transport, and the general conditions could not help but add to their collective misery. The leader of the slave traders had even asserted that two seasons of olive picking, were it done dutifully and well, would buy their freedom. Evrit was not addled enough to believe the word of a slaver, but at least it had given the women and children hope. Ever since their vessel had lost course on its way to Golgarn and had struck the savage reef at the outskirts of the Skeleton Coast, Evrit had believed it was just a matter of time before death took his family. Their survival had thus far not proved to be a better lot than death would have been.

In the distance he heard a horn blast, once, long and sustained, then again, three times short. Evrit could feel the men in the wagon around him sit up or go rigid; they had heard it as well.

Around them their captors began to shout to one another, calling out in a tongue he did not understand. There was panic in their voices.

"What's—happening?" the man next to him murmured.

The ground beneath the wagon began to rumble. Evrit recognized the sound.

"Horses," he whispered. "Many of them."

The wagons slowed, the creaking giving way to the sound of thundering hooves muted by the sandy roadway.

One of the captives began praying aloud; the others joined in quietly as the vibrations of the oncoming horses whipped up the grit of the desert against their skin.

Evrit tried to sort out the maelstrom of sounds that followed. It seemed to him that some of their captors had tried to run, abandoning the wagons and fleeing on horseback, but were quickly pursued by other horsemen greatly outnumbering them. The din around them made it clear that the wagons themselves had been surrounded, and from the shouting of commands, he could tell they had been taken into the custody of a military entity, though what it was he could not be certain.

Finally, after a long time of noise and confusion, he heard a carriage roll to a stop beside the wagons, and a door open amid the sounds of protocol. He listened intently, trying to catch the words, but they, too, were in a tongue he did not recognize.

At last a command was uttered, and someone leapt into the wagon, causing it to shudder violently. A moment later, he felt hands gently removing his blindfold.

At first he thought he might have lost his sight entirely; the world around his eyes, freed from their bandage, was dark, but after a moment they adjusted and he could see a soldier, dressed in dark red cloth studded with leather strips, releasing the eyes of the rest of the captives in the wagon.

Evrit looked around quickly, desperately, and caught sight of his eldest son, who sat across from him, staring wildly back at him. He nodded encouragingly, then looked behind him.

Standing in the midst of the four wagons was a swarthy man with heavy features, dressed in loose white robes with a heavy neckpiece inlaid in gold. The robes were embroidered with the symbol of a sword and the sun. He was giving orders to what appeared to be an entire cohort of mounted soldiers, similar in skin texture and features to their leader, some of whom rode between the wagons while others released the eyes of the captives or passed out water.

A wineskin was offered to him and he drank gratefully, his hands still bound, then looked around for Selac, finding him in a nearby wagon. Evrit bowed his head in relief, whispering a prayer of thanks for their rescue.

Finally the man in the robes waved the soldier he was conferring with away, then turned and addressed the captives in the common tongue of the maritime trade.

"I am Talquist, regent of Sorbold and emperor presumptive. I welcome you to my lands, and apologize for any mistreatment you may have suffered at the hands of my subjects. The ringleader has been executed, and the rest of these renegade slavers are now in the custody of my army."

Evrit exhaled in relief and flashed a slight smile at both of his sons to reassure them.

"You will be continuing on with the my caravan now, so that my soldiers can protect you," the regent continued. "In a moment, you should all be freed from your blindfolds if you are not already. If anyone is in need of water, tell the soldier attending to your wagon. Who among you is the leader?"

For a moment there was silence. Then Evrit found his voice.

"Our—our expedition had no real leader, m'lord," he said, his voice cracking. "But I signed the bill of lading when we set sail on the *Freedom*."

The regent turned in his direction and walked over to the wagon, smiling agreeably.

"The *Freedom,* did you say? A fine ship. I have sent cargo aboard her many times. Did she founder?"

"Yes, m'lord, I'm sorry to say, against a reef. We came ashore at the Skeleton Coast, but were taken prisoner by the men whom you have captured."

"Well, on behalf of my nation, I apologize. They had no right to do that." The regent gave another command to the soldiers, who in turn broke off into four groups of two and mounted the wagons, preparing to drive them on. Then he started back toward the carriage from which he had descended.

"Er—m'lord?" Evrit called nervously, compelled by the looks of shock on the faces of his fellow captives.

The regent stopped and turned around. "Yes?"

"Might—might we have our hands unbound?"

The regent considered for a moment, then walked back to the wagon and stood next to Evrit, regarding him thoughtfully.

"The woman in the green skirt—she is your wife, is she not?" he asked finally.

"Ye—yes," stammered Evrit.

The regent nodded. "Would you like her brought to sit beside you?"

"Yes, yes, m'lord," Evrit said gratefully.

The regent placed his hand on the wagon slat, and leaned closer in toward Evrit. "I fear I may have unintentionally misled you. You see, the slavers who took you captive had no right to do so, because all slave captures are specifically sanctioned and controlled by the Crown—in other words, me," he said pleasantly. "And while these miscreants probably would have sold you to an olive farmer or the owner of an apple orchard, I have much better use for you men—in the salt mines of Nicosi. You look like a strong lot. You should survive awhile. The women we will put to work in the linen factories, the children will labor in the palace as chimney sweeps and cleaning the sewers while they are small enough to fit."

The regent turned and headed back to his carriage, pausing long enough to call to the captain of his guard.

"Mikowacz, bring me that woman in the green skirt. I'll start with her. By morning I want you to have found the youngest and prettiest among them. We have three days until we reach the mines."

He cast a glance back at Evrit, whose face was white as the crescent moon that hung over the Sorbold desert.

"When I'm finished with the leader's wife, you may allow her to sit beside her husband in the wagon until we reach the salt mines."

He climbed into his carriage, leaving the door open.

6

RAVEN'S GUILD,
THIEVES' MARKET, YARIM PAAR

*Y*abrith, petty thief, assassin, and thug that he was, had a gift for knowing when a man was about to crack. He had used this talent many times over the course of his criminal career, amassing an impressive reputation for prying information and secrets from the most unwilling of victims.

His sensitivity to situational precariousness was in a heightened state of alarm now, deep within the dark confines and crumbling walls of the Raven's Guild hall in the Inner Market of Yarim Paar. The air was thick with the static of danger, of black rage only slightly held in check.

Yabrith had no desire to be the weight that tipped the scales. He set the heavy crystal glass down in front of the guild scion and stepped quickly to the side of the table, trying not to draw the man's notice while hoping silently that the spirits he was providing would quell the nervousness that had taken hold of the scion, and all his fellows in the Guild over the last few weeks.

Dranth, the guild scion, extended a hand that shook only slightly and seized the glass, downing the amber liquid in one bolt. He clenched his teeth and inhaled over the burn, drawing the vapors into his sinuses, hoping they would soothe his mind, and realizing dully that they could never be strong enough.

For a full cycle of the moon he had been plagued, for the first time since childhood, with nightmares from which he woke drenched in sweat and the sour smell of fear. Dranth had taken to pacing the floor after these dreams, hoping to drive the images from his mind, but he could only succeed in making the pictures fade into the dark recesses for a short while, lingering in the shadows until sleep took him.

Whereupon they would emerge to clutch at him again.

He dropped the glass onto the thick board of the new table, wincing as it thudded. It was a sound similar to the one that haunted him, the dull thump of a box that had been placed on this table's predecessor two fortnights before.

Dranth had opened the small, leather-bound crate, sealed and wrapped in parchment paper carefully, believing it to be yet another package sent home by the guildmistress, who was working surreptitiously in the mountains of Ylorc, deep within the Bolg king's lair. Upon removing the internal wrapping, however, he had discovered instead the guildmistress's own head, her eyes open and festering with maggots that crawled through the sockets, her mouth frozen open in an expression of surprise.

He had lurched back and vomited all over the floor of the guildhall.

It was not horror at the ghastly fate that had befallen the guild's erstwhile leader which caused Dranth's stomach to rush into his mouth. Nor was it any loss he might have felt for the woman herself. In the twenty years he had known Esten, there was no one to whom he had been more devoted, more enslaved, more loyal, but now, beholding her disembodied head rotting before him on the table, it was not grief or revulsion that racked Dranth.

It was abject fear.

Because, until he beheld the evidence of it himself, he would never have believed it possible that anyone could visit death of any kind, let alone such a gruesome and violent one, upon the guildmistress.

From the moment he had first seen her in a dark alleyway, ripping her blade mercilessly into the belly of a startled soldier at the tender age of eight summers, eviscerating the man as coolly as she might play jackstraws, Dranth had been painfully aware of Esten's extraordinary powers of murder and self-preservation, as well as her utter lack of a soul. She had held the guild, the city, and much of the province of Yarim in her merciless grasp for her entire adult life, propagating the Raven's Guild's undisputed reign in black-market trafficking, murder, thievery, assassination, and a host of even more brutal crimes, raising their skullduggery to the level of pure artistry.

Dranth, the man who loved and respected her more than anyone in the world, believed her to be Evil Incarnate, and more—he believed she was invulnerable.

Yet someone had managed to kill her, to rip her head from her shoulders, beheading her while alive.

And whoever it was had caught her completely by surprise, something else Dranth had believed impossible.

So if invulnerable Evil could be so stripped of life, so torn, snuffed without so much as a skirmish, it was clear to Dranth that he had lived his entire life underestimating just how powerful his enemies, and those of the guild, could be.

He was still shaking now, a month later. He had slipped into the desert when the moon was new, and in the devouring darkness of the wilderness buried Esten's remains beneath the sandy red clay, blinded by the blackness of the night and his tears. Dranth did not wish to remember where her grave had been, because there were so many who would seek to steal its contents, to mock her in death as they never had dreamed of doing in life, putting her skull on display in some ignominious place like a tavern, a brothel, or a privy.

As she herself had done to innumerable opponents.

He had burned the leather crate, the table, and everything it had touched.

Dranth glanced up from staring at the new table board. In the dim light of the guildhall three score or more of thieves stood, clinging to the shadows, waiting for instructions.

When his voice was able to be forced into his mouth, it was soft, harsh, deadly.

"It was to the court of the Bolg king that the guildmistress went, seeking revenge for an old wrong," he said, his eyes glinting black in the fire-shadows that roared on the hearth behind him. "It was from the court of the Bolg king that the package containing—that the package was delivered.

"Esten built this guild with the labor of her hands, with her very blood. Any that would dare to spill that blood must answer to the guild."

A quiet chorus of voices rose, murmuring assent, then fell into silence once more.

"The Bolg king has earned our undying enmity, and he shall have it visited upon him. But anyone with the strength to fell Esten will not be vulnerable to traditional attack, not even the kind of murder we practice in the shadows." He lapsed into silence as well.

"What, then, Dranth?" one of the journeymen asked.

Dranth stared into the fire. He watched the flames flicker against the soot that stained the bricks of the back of the hearth, letting his mind wander with them. Finally he turned back to the guild.

"We will stand ready to aid his enemies," he said simply. "Before her death, the guildmistress sent back meticulous plans, maps of his inner realm, details of his stockpiles, armaments, treasury, manpower. This information will be invaluable to anyone who seeks to bring him down, and has the army to do it."

He tossed the crystal glass into the fireplace.

"There are any number of such men out there," the guild scion said. "But I think I will make inquiries first in Sorbold. It lies on his southwestern border, and has a new regent. I hear he was once a guild hierarch himself." Dranth's eyes glittered. "And as the mistress always said, a guildsman knows the value of the goods; it is merely a matter of making him feel an overwhelming need to have them, whether he needs them or not.

"So we will make them available at a price he cannot resist."

The gargantuan doors of the ice castle were frozen over almost beyond recognition.

The dragon stared at the entranceway, her body beginning to slow from the loss of heat. Snow now caked her mammoth claws, packed between the phalanges of what had once been her fingers, hardening with each painful step. Her eyelids stung from the crust that had formed on them, her skin peeling under the weight of the ice on her scales.

The life that she had felt returning to her after so long in the grave was ebbing now.

Open, she whispered, *please open.*

Her dragon sense, fading along with her life force, felt a stirring in the doors, as if the very steel of them had recognized something in her, but was too weak, or too unwilling, to respond.

Deep within her, in the part where her will remained, steely and haughty, the refusal rankled.

The dragon's ire at the rebuff sparked, then roared like a hedgefire through her.

"Open," she said, louder now, her voice stronger. It issued forth from her mind and her sinuses, rather than her throat—wyrms are absent vocal cords, and thereby must manipulate the element of air to be able to speak as men do—in a tone that could be heard above the howling of the autumn wind.

Before her the gigantic slabs of ice seemed to soften slightly. The crack between them shuddered; the doors trembled, but remained closed.

The beast trembled, too, but with rage. Fury, full-blown and all-encompassing, heated her blood, and her anger radiated out from her, causing loose snow on the distant crags to crumble and fall into the crevasses below.

"Open!" she howled, the winds shrieking with the sound of her words. "I command it!"

The ice that had glazed the doors for three years undisturbed cracked and began to slide down in great rolling sheets, avalanches of snowy shards falling onto the frozen stones of the courtyard. The dragon, her searing blue eyes burning hot in frenzy, inhaled, then loosed her wrath in her breath.

The blast of acidic fire from the brimstone in her belly almost blinded her with the intensity of its light.

The wave of boiling breath blasted the frozen doors, melting the ice completely, along with the snow that caked the walls around them. Rivers of liquid steam rushed like waterfalls down them, even as the ice underneath sublimated into the air in the beat of a three-chambered heart, revealing sheets of towering steel.

Slowly the palace doors swung open.

The beast watched, panting, triumphant, as the vast, cold inner chamber of the palace was revealed. *I may not have reclaimed my memories yet,* she thought, watching the melted ice refreeze in rivers of gleaming glaze, *but I recall that this is* mine. *And all that is mine will bow before me.*

Ignoring the pain in her limbs, she crawled forward, dragging her stinging body through the vast doorway and onto the cold stone floor beyond.

The great doors swung shut silently.

The cavernous halls echoed with the sound of metal on stone as the beast pulled herself across the floor of the towering center hall, scraping her claws on the granite as she moved.

Before her in the central hall was a massive fireplace, black with long-cold soot. The vault of the ceiling towered above, not far from where her head would reach should she rise to her fullest height. Behind her, tall windows thickly glazed with ice allowed muted light to enter.

Her dragon sense, as innate a sensory tool as her sight, hearing, or touch, rose from within her, dormant from the cold, as if it were thawing gradually. She was distantly, then more acutely, aware of the contents of the castle—its three towers, the winding stairs, the deep basements filled with stores, frozen now that the fires of the enormous hearths had been extinguished for years. She turned slowly, absorbing the information, as if through her skin, from the air around her.

There were very few memories here; she had lived alone, from what she could glean, within these frigid walls, these empty rooms. She could tell that there were chambers above and below that she would never be able to see again because of her massive size; the doorways to all but the largest common rooms of the ground floor would deny her access. Still, at least there was shelter here from the endless cold of the pale mountains.

A powerful hum drew her attention; she turned her massive head away from the empty hearth in the direction of the tall window. Before it stood an altar, simple, of heavy, carved wood; atop of it lay a tarnished spyglass.

The dragon closed her sore eyes.

Even blind, she could still see the instrument, power radiating from it in the darkness behind her eyelids. All of her focus was drawn inexorably toward it; the vibrations rippled over her skin, thrumming with the rhythm of her blood.

Remember, she thought desperately. *What is it?*

She opened her eyes again and made her way across the cold stone floor to the altar, then stared intently down at the spyglass.

In her mind images swirled willy-nilly, scenes of ferocious battle, desperate suffering, struggles, triumphs, events of world-shaking import and the tiniest significance, all vying for her attention. The dragon's mind burned with the intensity of it; bewildered, she slithered back away from the altar, closing her mind as if in defense.

Pain, hollow and clutching, twisted inside her, even more than the constant ache of her broken body. It gripped strongly enough to make her weak; her head sagged rapidly toward the ground, leaving her dizzy, until she righted it.

Then, amid all the confusion, she heard a voice ring clear in her scrambled memory, like a bell tolling through a storm at sea; it was that of a woman speaking clearly, as if pronouncing a sentence.

I rename you the Past. Your actions are out of balance. Henceforth your tongue will only serve to speak of the realm into which your eyes alone were given entry. That which is the domain of your sisters, the Present and the Future, you will be unable to utter. No one shall seek you out for any other reason, so may you choose to convey your knowledge better this time, lest you be forgotten altogether.

The great beast shuddered.

She thought for a moment about slapping the spyglass from the altar, shattering it, crushing it beneath her weight, or hurling it from the castle battlements into the crevasse below, but the thought brought her pain, physical pain, as if her mind were being stabbed with the icepick thought. In the limited scope of what she knew, she was certain that the instrument was older than she, ancient, from a realm that was no more, a place the winds could no longer find, that Time had all but forgotten. She also felt sure that it was tied to her in some way, some deeply significant, almost holy way.

I rename you the Past.

The spyglass glimmered in the fading light.

It sees the Past, the dragon thought, and with the thought came new certainty, as if it had unlocked doors in her mind to small, hidden places previously inaccessible. *It sees the Past.*

It can see me.

With the realization came a surge of power, of revitalization. The beast, still lost in her own life, was no longer invisible to the eyes of Time, no longer alone in the vast white of the endless mountains. Somewhere in the Past her memories were hiding, waiting for her to find them.

And the glass could see them.

The pain in her belly grew stronger, followed again by the weakness. *Hunger,* the dragon thought. *This is what hunger feels like.*

She moved to the icy window but could see nothing beyond the frozen panes. Innate survival mechanisms began to burn within her, her dragon sense making note of everything that might possibly be considered sustenance within the range of her senses, about five miles.

Minutiae became mammoth; the tiniest crumb of grain was suddenly as clear to her as the sun. She knew instantly that there was food to ease human hunger in the subterranean vaults of the castle, but that to get to it would require the breaking down of walls and strength she did not, in her weakened state, possess. Her mind turned outward, scanning the hillsides and the crevasses.

An eagle was passing a mile and a third away, flying southeast at thirty-two—no, thirty-one—knots. Farther out a flock of ptarmigans was scattering to the wind. The dragon discarded the thought. She did not know if she was capable of flight yet; one of her wings ached with an infuriating stiffness and hung off-kilter, likely a result of whatever wound had scarred it so deeply. She would have to seek food on the ground for the time being. She concentrated harder.

A glacial stream ran through her lands, she realized, the water silver-gray and cold, having been ancient blue ice a moment before it turned to runoff and slipped, laughing, down the frozen hillsides. She might find food there, she thought, but discarded the notion a moment later. Winter was coming; the great red and silver fish had come and spawned, laid their eggs and died, having completed what life expected of them. There would be nothing to ease her hunger in the gray water now.

Then, tickling the very edges of her consciousness, she felt something else. Near the river's edge, tucked away beneath a wide, sheltering ridge, was a small hunting camp.

Men. Humans, from the smell that the dragon sense inspired in her nostrils.

At first the thought repulsed her. She was, or at least had been, a being like them once herself, a woman, though not human—her blood was much older than that, she suspected. Dimly she recalled words spoken to her by another dragon, a beast she believed might have been related to her; her mother, perhaps. Hate, bitter and foul-tasting, came to her mouth at the memory.

If they are encroaching on your lands, why do you not just eat them? she heard herself saying in the voice of a child.

Eat them? Do not be ridiculous, the wyrm had said. *They are men. One does not eat men, no matter how much they may deserve it.*

Why not?

Because that would be barbaric. Men are alleged to be sentient, though I admit I have not seen evidence of that. One does not eat sentient beings. No, my child, I limit myself to stags, sheep, and tirabouri. They digest well, and carry none of the guilt that men would in the stomach.

I know no guilt, thought the dragon bitterly. *Only hunger.*

She allowed her dragon sense to explore further, to wander closer to the hunting camp, where the snow had walled the huts inside the ridge, forming a frosty barrier between the humans and the river. They had dug a pathway—four feet, three and three-quarters inches wide, seven feet, four and five-eighths inches high, her dragon sense noted—between the camp and the river. In her mind's eye she could see the footsteps that had tramped to the water's edge, and the skids where the buckets had been hauled back.

With the rising hunger and the expansion of her dragon sense, the wyrm's eyes narrowed in thought.

I have no such qualms about men, she ruminated. *They are a large source of meat, warm of blood and thin of skin. I imagine they roast nicely, and will keep well.*

And I am famished.

The decision was an easy one.

Open, she commanded the doors of the castle in a voice that rang with bloody intent. They slammed open in response; the icy wind blew in, swirling angrily through the cavernous hall.

Spurred by hunger, and the desire to vent her pain in destruction, the beast slithered out through the doors into the dusk, over the battlements, and down into the crevasse, where she disappeared into the earth beneath the snow.

7

The Rampage of the Wyrm was an epic poem penned in the Cymrian era, inscribed on an illuminated scroll and found, after centuries uncounted, hidden deep in the vaults of the library of Canrif by Achmed, who presented it, with wry amusement, to Rhapsody just before she undertook a long journey with Ashe to find the dragon Elynsynos. The Bolg king had sat smugly, scarcely able to contain his glee, watching her expressive face as she read the tale, which told of the murderous exploits of the dragon she was about to seek.

Elynsynos, the wyrm for whom the continent was named, was older than Time, the manuscript said. It related in breathless detail the story of the primordial dragon, said to be between one and five hundred feet long, with a mouthful of teeth the size and sharpness of finely honed bastard swords. As dragons possess some of each of the five elemental lores, she was able to assume the form of any force of nature, such as a tornado, a flood, or a blazing forest fire, the manuscript said. She was wicked and cruel, and when her lover and the father of her three daughters, the sailor Merithyn the Explorer, did not return to her as he promised, she went into a wild fury and rampaged through the western continent, burning it with her caustic breath and decimating the lands up to the central province of Bethany, where her fire sparked the eternal flame which burned to that day, in Vrackna, the basilica consecrated to the element of fire.

Rhapsody was quick to point out to the gloating Bolg king that the account was mostly nonsense, which was evident to her without even meeting the dragon. As a Namer she was familiar with folklore as well as lore, the first told by untrained storytellers and woven over time into tales that tended to be filled with falsehoods and exaggerations, as opposed to the latter, which was as pure as possible, related by those trained to keep the history accurate.

Even so, the descriptions in the tale carried enough possible truth to make her nervous.

Sometime later, when she finally did meet the wyrm in her lair, Elynsynos quickly debunked the manuscript and its false account of history.

You've been reading that tripe, The Rampage of the Wyrm, *haven't you?*
Yes.

It's nonsense. I should have eaten the scribe who penned it alive. When Merithyn died I thought about torching the continent, but surely you must be able to tell that I didn't. Believe me, if I were to rampage, the continent would be nothing but one very large, very black bed of coal, and it would be smoldering to this day.

The continent and its people, for all their fear of the dragon legends, for all the tremulous whining in the manuscripts that recounted their history, had never in fact seen the immolation the tales told of, had never lost more than a stray sheep to the beasts, and certainly had never experienced a true rampage.

And therefore were totally unprepared.

The men of the Anwaer village in the midlands of the Hintervold were a quiet lot.

Unlike the seasonal nomads who spent the summer culling fish from the area's fertile streams and trapping fur-bearing animals, then relocating to the southern part of the realm when autumn came, the families of Anwaer braved the bone-chilling cold and the towering snowfall to stay together in their ancestral lands. They were all related in some manner, and found the beauty of the isolated tundra, the verdant forests of spiraling spruce, and the silence that reigned unchallenged by any but the mountain winds to be reason enough to endure the harsh winter in the place their families had called home for generations.

So when the autumn came, and the nearby villages thinned out, Anwaer ended its season of transport of skins and fishing and prepared to hunt.

Usually the hunting time lasted only a few weeks, less than one turn of the moon. With the heat of the summer fading and the merciless swarms of blood-sucking insects dispersed by the approaching cold, the game animals of the Hintervold would come out from their summer hiding places, down from the summits of the white crags and into more sheltered areas, seeking vegetation or prey, and a more hospitable clime for the coming winter.

The endless expanse of the land at the top of the world caused game animals to grow to substantial size, and a single one, carefully dressed, was generally enough to feed an Anwaer family for the winter. So the hunters moved away from the villages into the thicker woods, and waited for the game to come.

But this year, it never did.

After two weeks without a single kill, the men determined that something was terribly wrong. Whatever had spooked the game animals had frightened them not individually, or in clusters, but as a herd; the caribou and the northern tirabouri had last been seen ranging north, contrary to nature. The solitary animals, the moose and the predators that the Anwaer men hunted for pelts, were gone as well. The hunters sat in their blinds in silence, hearing little and seeing less. Even the customary birdsong of the migrating raptors had been stilled.

Finally, with winter approaching, the men of Anwaer decided it would be necessary to follow the herds north. If the hunting party could come upon a cluster or even the outer edge of a ranging herd, it might be possible to bring down enough meat to salvage the winter. If they could do it within another turn of the moon, the shallow glacial river would not yet be fully frozen, and could be floated in makeshift barges back to Anwaer in time before the heaviest snow came. If the new moon came before they had gathered their stores, however, it would be too late, and for the first time in memory, the village would have to join the migration, hurrying to keep ahead of the weather.

Should the men not be back by the time the moon had faded to a slim crescent, the women were told to start ahead alone.

The youngest member of the hunting party was tying down the boats on the rushing silver river when nightfall came.

The wind was chill; the water, shallow in most places to the depth of a man's knee, with deeper spots up to his shoulder, was rippling beneath the breeze, causing the makeshift rafts to bump against each other on the shoreline, tugging at their rope and stone moorings.

Sonius, as the hunter was known, struggled to keep the barges from breaking apart in the chilly water. Racing against the falling sun, he muttered obscenities under his breath, finally pulling the doeskin gloves from his hands in an effort to handle the ropes more efficiently.

He glanced back at the smoke seeping from the vent in the snowpack that sealed the huts into the shelter beneath the wide ridge. The landfall from an avalanche soon after they had made camp had fortuitously sealed in the area they inhabited, keeping them sheltered from the worst of the winds and any predators that might come, lured by the scent of their kills. They had brought down five moose and two tirabouri, and were in the process of smoking the latter to assure it keeping until their return to Anwaer. Sealed behind a solid wall of snow, with nothing but the tunnel they had carved out to the river and a crescent-shaped opening at the top of the snow wall where the smoke escaped, the rest of his hunting party was settling down to sleep before heading for home on the morrow.

Sonius had drawn the short straw, and so, despite his exhaustion, he kept at his task until he was certain the boats were secure. When at last he had tied the final knot, he rose tiredly and looked out over the silver-gray river before him.

The wind had died down to almost still; white chunks of ice from farther up the glacier were floating downstream now, spinning slowly in the rushing current. The dim light of the crescent moon reflected off the river, pooling in swirls, then vanishing into darkness again.

Sonius wondered absently why the silence had deepened, then exhaled, casting the thought from his mind, and turned around to head back through the tunnel in the snow into camp.

At first he didn't see the movement, but as he came within a few steps of the snow wall a flicker in the mountains above him caught his eye. He stepped back and looked up, trying to get a better glimpse, thinking that it was the mountain ice calving again, praying that it was not another avalanche that would bury his fellow hunters inside the sheltering ridge.

Sonius stared up into the endless crags of snow, and thought he saw a shadow slithering down the mountain face. He shaded his brow from the dim light of the moon. *There is some movement of snow,* he thought, *perhaps just from the wind.*

But there is no wind.

He rubbed his eyes, then looked back up to the peaks.

The movement was gone.

Sonius shook his head, then started for the tunnel.

The dragon's massive head crested the ridge, rising above the snow wall, then thrust down directly in front of him. The stench of brimstone filled the air, which cracked in the heat.

The serpentine eyes narrowed, the vertical pupils expanding in the light of the moon.

A ragged gasp tore from the young hunter's throat. He stared, glassy-eyed, at the beast looming before him, then made a scrambling dash for the tunnel below her.

Suddenly the shoreline of the river was drenched in light as bright as day. A rippling blast of flame rolled in a caustic wave down from atop the ridge, illuminating the human shadow, lighting his young face to brilliance for a split second before it turned black and withered to skeletal ash, along with the rest of his body.

Then, in an instant, the light was snuffed; darkness returned again.

The dragon lay crouched on the top of the rock ridge, staring ruefully down at the baked skeleton in the pile of ashes at the edge of the snow wall. *Damnation,* she thought. *The skin is even thinner than I had imagined. This will not serve if I want the meat.*

She turned around on the ridge. With a thundering slap, she brought her spiked tail down on the snow wall, crushing the top of it and causing the ice to collapse into the tunnel. Then she climbed down onto the wall and slithered to the crescent-shaped opening, behind which her dragon sense told her the humans were sleeping before a dwindling fire.

There were eleven, she knew; her mind, flooded with the sensory information from the primordial element in her blood, was aware of each of them, how much each one weighed, where he was sleeping, and the relative depth of slumber each of them was enjoying. There were also four dogs, all in various stages of repose. She stared at the camp behind the snow wall for a moment, thinking what a good place to store this cache of meat it would be.

Then she slid through the opening.

The first man was in her grasp before any of them had a chance to waken; the dogs saw her, smelled her probably, and began to bark agitatedly as she barreled over the wall and slid through the fire into the first makeshift hut, crushing it like a nutshell beneath the weight of her body. He was wrapped in wool blankets; the beast squeezed him with a crushing force in her talons and slashed his throat, then tossed his dripping body to the ground to turn her attention to the man who had been lying beside him.

That man, who watched in stark terror as she disposed of his bunkmate, began to scream, a gargling, high-pitched sound that rippled painfully over the dragon's sensitive eardrums. He continued to caterwaul as she seized him and lifted him from the ground; she severed his head in one clean bite and spat it into the fire to make it stop squealing.

From that point on it became an elegant, joyous dance of death. The men, trapped behind the immense wall of snow, scattered to the corners of their small shelter, hiding behind rocks, scrambling in vain to the wall itself and trying piteously to scale it. They fired their crude hunting weapons— spears and longbows—at her, but the missiles bounced off her armored hide, impotent.

The firecoals, scattered about in the fray, cast weak shadows on the massacre, sparked with bright blood.

And in the heat of the skirmish, as one by one she cornered the hunters and slaughtered them, the beast laughed aloud with delight, a harsh, ugly sound that rang with soulless malice. *Destruction eases the pain,* she thought as she seized the last of them, crushing him slowly, taking pleasure watching the life being squeezed from him inch by inch, while the dogs, who had ceased to bark, whined in terror. *And I have so much pain to ease.*

Then the feast began.

8

It was deep in the night of the Bolg king's return when Trug was summoned.

He felt as if he had been called to rise even before he had finished exhaling his first breath of sleep, yet he did not complain. Complaints were useless, and something about the quiet nervousness of the guard who had come for him told him he was being observed. Trug rose silently and dressed quickly in the manner of all of Achmed's Archons. He had experienced many such midnight summonses in the seven years of his schooling.

He followed the guard past his training ring, noticing by smell that the two horses he had quartered there for the night had been taken, and replaced with two others of similar size and markings. His brows knit together in puzzlement; such a test of his notice had been undertaken less than a year into his training, when it might still have been possible that he did not yet know every one of the three hundred fifty head that he was responsible for stabling. But that trick had not even worked at the time; why anyone was attempting it now was perplexing to him.

Trug, like most of his race, did not give voice to his inner thoughts but rarely, and so he kept his silence as he walked behind the guard. He listened for signs of conversation or movement, but heard nothing except his own breath and the footsteps of the man leading him out of the mountain tunnels.

Unlike most of his fellow subjects, it was part of Trug's training to be able to speak; what he was speaking, however, were the thoughts of the Bolg king, both within the mountain and outside it. It was his path to be trained as the Voice, the Archon that King Achmed expected to handle all of the communications, both official and secret, on behalf of the Bolglands, including the management of the miles of speaking tubes that ran throughout the mountains, left over from the Cymrian Age. In that capacity he had been trained from childhood for the last seven years, selected at an early age by Rhapsody as having the potential for the task at hand, and systematically familiarized with language, cryptography, anatomy, and a thousand other studies of communications, verbal and otherwise. A year ago he had been deemed worthy to supervise the aviary, with its extensive fleet of messenger birds, as well as the mounted messengers who rode with the mail caravans. Eventually it was planned for him to assume responsibility for King Achmed's network of ambassadors as well as his spies.

But even though he would one day be the master of all the communications within Ylorc and from the Teeth to the outside world, Trug had not been told why he was being summoned. Nor did he expect to be.

An hour's walk, up out of the mountain to a small softened peak, like a cavity in the Teeth, brought him to a listening post, a way station in the system where the Eyes, Achmed's elite spies, made daily reports on what they had observed in the mountain passes. The guard stopped inside the hollow peak, lit and hung a lamp, and motioned for him to take a seat at the table that became visible in the light.

On the table was a tube made of bone, sealed with the king's imprimatur. Trug said nothing, but beads of sweat broke out on his dusky forehead. The guard motioned to the tube, then stepped away from the wind cave.

Trug stared at the tube for a moment, knowing that what it contained would mark a turning point in his destiny. He, as well as all his fellow students, had long been told about the eventual arrival of this sealed message, and he knew what it foretold. It would hold either the order of his banishment, as it had for at least one other Archon-in-training, or his elevation to full status, along with all the others. Either way, at least one part of his life would end that night.

With clammy hands he broke the seal and opened the tube.

He stared at the page, trying to absorb its import. It contained nothing more than the imprint of a hand.

Trug stood up, held the edge of the parchment in the flame of the lamp until it ignited, waited for it to burn completely, then cast the ashes into the wind atop the hollow mountain peak.

When the very last black cinder had caught the updraft and was carried away, Trug doused the lantern and hurried down the mountainside, making his way in the darkness for a passageway into the depths he knew all too well.

Deep within the mountain, at the convocation of five tunnels known as the Hand, they gathered, each summoned in the same manner.

Upon arriving, the Archons nodded to one another but did not speak. It was not only customary to remain silent until the king or his representative spoke, it was mandatory. Achmed wanted to be certain that when his Archons were called to assemble, the words that their ears heard were as pure and unpolluted by secondary noise as possible.

The future Archons were, in a way, Achmed's children, though none of them had ever seen his face. Taken from their clans when he first became king, as hostages some thought, they had been kept apart as a new clan, with the Bolg king and Grunthor, and Rhapsody for a time, as masters and parents, along with such tutors and models as he could hire and trick and persuade from the outside. Grunthor was known as the Chief Archon, lending a credit to the title that instantly made it coveted.

They were raised as Achmed had been raised, in study and to an unrevealed purpose, given knowledge as a religion, fed, threatened, and cajoled into the belief that they must grow into their potential or their people would be doomed.

None of them had seen more than eighteen summers.

They came from an assortment of tribes that before Achmed's arrival had roamed the Teeth, preying on each other and whatever unfortunate creatures, human or otherwise, they could catch. Some were the spawn of the Claw clans, the warlike marauders that had lived in the borderlands, the lower foothills and rocky steppes that abutted the human realm of Roland. Others had been culled from the Guts clans, those living deeper in the realm of what they called Ylorc, past the guardian ridge of the Teeth into the deep forest glades and decimated cities that had once been the inner lands of the Cymrian stronghold. Possibly the most valuable of them had come from the Eyes, those demi-humans most adapted to thinner air, who crawled the ledges and peaks of the Teeth, watching the world from above, wrapped in clouds.

And some had come from the Finders. The Finders were not a clan in and of themselves, but rather were the descendants of those unfortunate Cymrians who had remained or been left behind a thousand years before when the Bolg overran Canrif. Their blood still contained some of the odd, magical elements of longevity and elemental power that their unknown and hapless ancestors had bequeathed them, but until Achmed came, they had no idea how to put that power to use.

Achmed saw them regularly but rarely, coming in to test them and redirect them. They were uncertain about his motives, as if it were not clear to this small grove whether the forester measured them in anticipation of cutting, or to be confident they could bear his weight on a climb to the clouds. There were ten of them that remained in this, the fifth year of training; some of the original children sent to him had been redirected to other lessons, one had perished, one had been banished. Those who had been released no longer studied the history of the Cymrians and of Roland, world geography and currency, and were no longer subject to the rigors of the king's direct attention.

It was a sweet relief to them, and a horrific dishonor to their clans.

Those Archons that had survived the training came now, one by one, to the black tunnels of the Hand, where no light entered or escaped.

The first to arrive was Harran, the Loremistress, a Finder who had been selected by Rhapsody and trained by her personally until she had left Ylorc to rule the Lirin realm of Tyrian. Harran was thin, even by wiry Bolg standards, and her shadowy form barely disturbed the darkness at the bottom of the tunnel in which she hovered, waiting.

A few moments later came Kubila. His long shanks made him a superior runner, and generally guaranteed that he would arrive before most who had to travel to the Hand, even though his abode was the farthest away. He nodded to Harran in the dark, then came over to the finger in which she lingered and sat down before her to wait.

One by one they came, Yen the broadsmith, training to hold the position of Armorer, whose responsibility for building the unique weapons that armed Ylorc and were sold for trade already had made him one of the most powerful men in the kingdom; Krinsel the midwife, who came from a long line of respected clan mothers that managed all the medical needs of the realm; and Dreekak, Master of Tunnels, the brilliant young engineer who was in the process of inspecting and renovating the hundreds of miles of passageways and underground complexes that the Cymrians had built a thousand years before. Additionally, he had restored a number of the systems that Gwylliam had designed to make life within the cavernous mountains more civilized; the Cauldron, the great inner city of the guardian mountains, now had working ventilation, sanitation, and irrigation systems that circulated heat and air, provided rainwater for drinking and cooking, and channeled waste into vast central cisterns at the base of an unoccupied mountain crag, where once it had been ubiquitous and uncontrolled. In these matters, the demi-human Bolg were considerably more advanced, more civilized, than their neighbors in the human nation of Roland, who had long considered them monsters beneath contempt.

Until the arrival of King Achmed, the Earth Swallower, the Glowering Eye, the Night Man, Warlord of the entire deep realm, that had in fact been true. But he had changed all that, had forged the Bolg as he had Trug, into something greater, for a greater, if unknown, purpose.

A whisper of sound was heard at the arrival of Vrith, the Quartermaster, whose duties included the inventory and supplying of the entire kingdom, in particular the Bolg army. Vrith had been born with a clubfoot, a deformity that had resulted in him being left out on top of Kurmen crag to die on his tenth birthday. Rhapsody had rescued him and, seeing in him a fastidiousness for detail and an impressive head for numbers in his early lessons, had trained him to keep track of all the kingdom's stores as Ylorc was evolving from a wasteland of loose marauders into a realm whose army was feared, its leadership respected, and its goods coveted.

Greel, the mining Archon known as the Face of the Mountain, arrived in the company of Ralbux, who had been trained as a scholar to oversee the education of the Bolg populace. They took their places on the ground at the index-finger tunnel.

Finally, the only Archon who was not Bolg arrived. Omet had been rescued from slavery in Yarim by Achmed and Rhapsody three years earlier. A human child whose mother had given him over to the mistress of the Raven's Guild to broil in indentured servitude in the tile factories of that desert city, he had adopted Ylorc happily as his home. *Somewhere in those mountains greatness is taking hold,* Rhapsody had said upon setting him free. *You can be a part of it. Go carve your name into the ageless rock for history to see.* They were words that had echoed in his heart, and in his own words now, and led him to his post, the most secret of all the Archonic responsibilities.

Omet was the builder of the Lightcatcher.

After a few moments' silence, the ten Archons became simultaneously aware of the presence of the king among them. Each knew that had Achmed not wished to be observed he would not have been, but the static hum of the tunnels indicated silently to them that their attention was being commanded. If any of them had been deaf to that hum, they might have also been made aware by the seven-and-a-half-foot-tall shadow that lurked behind the shade of the king in the darkness.

They crowded into the Hand, and the king motioned for them to sit. Grunthor stood in the Thumb, with Krinsel the midwife seated on the stone floor in front of him. Kubila and Harran sat at the opening of the next passage, the index finger, he with his lanky legs stretched out and his hands spread behind him, she crouched, knees drawn up as if she felt cold this deep in the mountain. Omet and the broadsmith Yen chose the next passage, while the others grouped into the last of the fingers. When they were in, silent and motionless, Achmed took his place in the large central passage, the palm of the Hand, on a stool that had apparently been waiting for this ceremony. He looked at them for a dozen breaths. "My children," he said, his sandy voice as flat as any of them had ever heard it, "your trials are nearly over."

Half a score of exhalations echoed through the chamber, and the Archons sought each other's eyes in the blackness.

For Harran, the Loremistress, who was barely fifteen, this was especially welcome news. She had been commanded to recite a hundred genealogies, Cymrian, Nain, Lirin, and Bolg; read and memorize pages she was never allowed to see more than once in seven languages, a few of them long dead; commit to memory the names and leaders of every Bolg clan, as well as each soldier of the army; and manage a score of resources scattered or buried in the Great Library of Canrif, where the librarians and lore students under her direction researched meticulously in shifts that never ceased.

Seeing the relief in her eyes, Achmed smiled slightly. "That does not mean the tests are over, Harran," he said dryly. "That is not the way of things. The tests of your knowledge are to come soon, and for the rest of your lives. The sword is tested when it leaves the forge, before it is finished and cooled in water—but that is not the real test of the sword. That comes later, in clashing and blood. But for now I am satisfied."

He stared at the broadsmith.

"Yen. I know the metal from which you were made, drew the hammer across your edges myself, but have not yet cast you to the stones to see if you sing or shatter." The smith swallowed visibly, but said nothing.

The king then turned to the Archon he was training in diplomacy and the ways of trade. "Kubila. I know your stock, taught you speed for the great mountain race, yet you will still need to show whether you or the coming storm shall prevail. But enough of tests for now.

"You are my Archons, keepers of our thousand and one secrets. Remember to count and hold them carefully."

The young trainees turned to each other in puzzlement. None had ever heard him refer to anything by that name before. Achmed took notice of their confusion, and turned to Trug, who would one day be the Voice, and nodded his permission to speak. Trug cleared his throat.

"We hold many secrets, sire," he said in a voice that had been trained to lose the harsh tones of the Bolgish tongue. "Which, my lord, are the thousand and one secrets?"

The king's mismatched eyes, one light, one dark, gleamed with intent. "Who can answer?"

The Archons looked at each other again, then returned their gaze to their leader.

"The secrets of the fortifications, the breastworks and trapped tunnels," the Master of Tunnels, Dreekak, whispered nervously.

"The secrets of the spies," said Trug.

"The secrets of the Lightcatcher," added Omet. His voice always scratched on the Bolg ears when he spoke in his attempt at their tongue, but none of the Archons winced.

"Those are all worthy answers," the king replied. "There are greater secrets, secrets I will impart to you in a moment, to keep locked in your hearts, guarding them with your very souls. But we are guardians of many smaller, sometimes more urgent secrets as well." He turned to Vrith, the Quartermaster. "How long can we stand a siege of the mountains if we are totally beset and surrounded?"

"Two months and sixteen days during this season," Vrith answered rotely, as he had done many times before in several different languages. The Archons were accustomed to being questioned in this manner, and had been since early childhood. "Two days less in winter."

"How many of our traders and agents are now outside Ylorc?"

"One hundred twelve," Kubila replied.

"How many of the invisible routes used by the doves of Roland has the master of hawks discovered?"

"Nine," said Trug.

"What lies at the bottom of the passage opened by the recent explosion of the Lightcatcher?"

"We don't know yet, sire," Dreekak said reluctantly. It was an answer that an Archon hated to give, but was best given quickly, lest the king believe that one was covering a weakness in his or her training.

The king nodded. "All these small secrets, and countless others, make up the thousand. But what is the one?" He watched them for a moment, then turned to Harran and called upon her wordlessly.

The young Loremistress thought for a moment, then answered. "The secret of why you have chosen us, what you are training us for."

"That is it," Achmed replied, pleased. "Your training is finished, at least that which was needed to bring you to the status of Archons. This is my last word to you as students: What is the secret of wisdom?"

Greel, responsible for mining, spoke. "Before acting, envision your act carried out a million times."

"Before speaking also," added Yen.

Achmed assented silently, then gestured for them to move closer.

"For all this time that I have taught you such secrets, I have kept one to myself, unshared, unrevealed to any but Grunthor." *And Rhapsody,* he thought bitterly, *but she did not retain it.* "But if you are to fulfill my wishes for you as Archons, there can be no secrets between us. I share with you now the thousand-and-first secret. But you will need light in this lightless place in order to grasp it."

Achmed took from his cloak an egg-sized stone that glowed clearly with light as bright as that of midday. The Archons shrank away from the radiance, but discovered a moment later that it was cold, and did not sting their night eyes, the eyes of cave dwellers who had lived in the belly of the mountains for centuries.

"The Nain discovered these stones a thousand kings before Faedryth, their present ruler. Their use was lost and found a hundred times between then and now. Let none of the lore you learn be ever lost in the same way." He handed the glowing stone to Harran. "You will need this to see what must be seen before you can understand."

As he spoke, he slowly lowered his hood and began to unwrap the cloths from his face. Between the mesmerizing effect of his words, and the vision in the bright light before them, only Grunthor, who had seen and heard it before, was breathing.

"To comprehend my purpose, my reasons for training you thus, you must understand something that you do not know about me as of yet. I was born from an unholy union to a terrible purpose: to find, hunt, and kill a spirit that no one could see. That purpose came to me as a racial imperative; I never knew my mother, but feel her blood in my veins still."

The pale, purplish skin of his forehead, etched all over with veins, was no preparation for the sight of the whole of his eyes, mismatched in color, shape, and position, resting in skin so translucent and light that they might have been floating unsupported in his skull. The Archons swallowed in unison.

"While through my veils you may have recognized the traits of my Bolg father, one of a dozen soldiers that raped my Dhracian mother, who they chose to kidnap by a toss of the bones, what you now see is the bastardization of the race of which I was the first of a generation. The Dhracians are an old people, born of the wind, descended from the race of Kith, as you have studied, Harran. But the purpose of the Dhracians was singular—we were jailers, guardians. Eventually, when we failed in that task, we became hunters. But instead of being brought up with the training, the knowledge, and the understanding of the lot that was bequeathed to me by my Dhracian blood, I was instead raised by Bolg on the other side of the world, tortured and tormented and eventually imprisoned." The voice held no trace of regret, no plea for sympathy, just a flat, toneless sound that indicated the import of the words.

"One day the urge in my blood became too great to deny; I knew I needed to find out what was driving me to murder. In order to escape from the Bolg, I was forced to kill he who had been made to guard me, my brother of sorts, really not much older than myself."

The Archons stared at the newly revealed nose, its flaring nostrils almost like that of a horse, but made of delicate flower-petal filigree, underlaid all through with the vein lattice.

"In order to survive my flight, I was forced to consume him."

The Archons nodded nonchalantly. Cannibalism had been common among their tribes before Achmed took the mountain. At Rhapsody's insistence, it had been outlawed; the king had acquiesced not because of any of her arguments against savagery or because of how the practice was viewed by the outside world, but because he needed as many of his subjects whole and intact, and therefore uneaten, as possible.

The king's virtually lipless mouth, made for tasting air for traces of fear, whispered in the darkness.

"Now that you have finally seen my face, you can understand. This is how I know what I know. How I feel you enter a room. How I hear you breathe any curse, smell your fatigue. It is in my skin. It is my blessing, and my bane. I can feel the rhythm of the world around me; I cannot hide from it. It is not flawless, but it is rarely wrong. And now I will tell you what you need to know in order to understand why we guard the thousand and one secrets."

He turned to Harran and leveled his uneven gaze at her, as if he were sighting down a weapon. The Loremistress maintained a stoic aspect, but her thin body was quavering like a leaf in the wind.

"I have allowed you to study the lore of Roland, and of other lands on the continent, but have often indicated to you that what you were learning was really folklore, tales that have been polluted because they were told by generations of idiots, rather than preserved by Lirin Namers and others skilled in the art and sworn to the truth. What do you remember about the lore of the F'dor?"

The young scholar swallowed, her dark face growing pale.

"F'dor were the children of Fire, the ancient culture that sprang from it," she intoned, reciting from the texts she had studied. "It was the F'dor who tamed fire, and gave it to mankind for its use in protection, in the warming of homes in winter, in the forging of weapons. The F'dor, now long deceased, were the forefathers of steel, of hearths, and the givers of the gift of flame to man."

Achmed nodded thoughtfully. "That is what texts say, indeed. That is what the imbeciles who tend the Fire Basilica in Bethany preach to the hapless numbskulls who attend services there. That is what the world believes. I tell you now, it is the greatest lie that has ever been told." His eyes glistened and he motioned them closer, to keep his words so soft as to barely be audible.

"In the Before-Time, when the world was being formed, there were five races that sprang from the primordial elements. Four of these races— the Seren from ether, the material that makes up the stars, the Kith from air, the Mythlin from water, and dragons from earth—lived in a fairly harmonious state, it is said, in that era of prehistory. The F'dor, the second-born of those Firstborn races, however, were not an ancient culture that gave the world the hearth and smithing—they were demons of unimaginable destructiveness, bent on consuming all the life on the Earth, and finally the Earth itself. They were formless, evanescent, without corporeal bodies, and were able to take possession of a human host—or one any other race, as long as its victim was lesser in power than it was. They did an impressive job of almost bringing the world to an end until the other races joined forces and thrust the lot of them into an impenetrable Vault of Living Stone, deep in the Underworld, the belly of the Earth near its fiery core. Each race played a part in the capture and imprisonment, but it was the responsibility of the Kith to act as jailers. And so a tribe of them, the Elder subrace of Dhracians, was given the onerous task of guarding the Vault, living deep within the earth, separated from the wind that is their mother, day into day into eternity.

"All went as it was prescribed for millennia, until one day a star fell from the sky into the sea, and its impact ruptured the Vault, allowing many of the

F'dor that had been imprisoned there, biding their time in futile dreams of destruction, to escape to the upworld, and take their place among the unsuspecting human population that had evolved from those Firstborn and Elder races. And so the destructive element was free."

Achmed paused in his diatribe. The Archons were barely breathing, probably from the combined shock of seeing his face for the first time and hearing more words spoken together than he had uttered since coming to Ylorc four years before. He willed himself to be calmer, to make his voice less harsh.

"Those beings still live, some of them imprisoned in the remade Vault, others free, hiding in broad daylight, their poisonous, parasitic spirits clinging invisibly to a human host. They are almost impossible to discern from the rest of the mass of human flesh that walks the world. And those that are upworld want but one thing: to free their kin in the Vault from their imprisonment, so that together they can satisfy the primal longing that consumes their race—the hunger for destruction, for annihilation, for the obliteration of all life, not just in this world, but beyond it. They seek a return to utter Void, even at the cost of their own existence. And their presence is felt in the tides of the universe, in war, in conquest, in murder, in betrayal. In short, in the ways of men.

"And what they ultimately seek—that is the last secret. I tell it to you now. A prophecy long ago told of a Sleeping Child—three such children, actually. Do you know this prophecy, Harran?"

The Loremistress nodded, closed her eyes, and intoned the words in a soft, toneless voice.

> The Sleeping Child, the youngest born
> Lives on in dreams, though Death has come
> To write her name within his tome
> And no one yet has thought to mourn.
>
> The middle child, who sleeping lies,
> 'Twixt watersky and shifting sands
> Sits silent, holding patient hands
> Until the day she can arise.
>
> The eldest child rests deep within
> The ever-silent vault of earth,
> Unborn as yet, but with its birth
> The end of Time Itself begins.

Achmed nodded as Harran fell silent. "The first child in the prophecy is sheltered within these very mountains," he said gravely, watching the faces of the Archons, their eyes glittering in the darkness. "She is an Earthchild, a being made of Living Stone, left over from when the world was born. For all I know she may even be the last of this race, which the dragons fashioned out of elemental earth. The ribs of her body are made of the same Living Stone that comprises the Vault—and would thereby act as a key to it were she to fall into the hands of the F'dor. And they know she is here."

An audible shudder arose from the assemblage. Achmed glanced at Grunthor, whose face remained impassive. The Bolg king exhaled, then continued.

"The second Child mentioned in the prophecy is the star that fell millennia ago into the sea on the other side of the world, the same star that shattered the Vault. That burning star, which slept beneath the sea for thousands of years, rose and consumed the Island of Serendair in fiery cataclysm centuries ago. And for all the destruction that ensued, for all the lives that were taken, she brought about far less damage than the other two could." The Bolg king fell silent, the noise in the tunnel disappearing with the sound of his voice.

Finally Omet spoke. "And the third, sire? The eldest?"

The Bolg king remained quiet for a long time. Finally he spoke, and when he did, his voice was soft.

"Long ago, at the beginning of Time, when there were none on the Earth but the five Firstborn races, the F'dor stole something from the dragons—from the Progenitor of the race, the eldest of all wyrms. It was an egg. They took this nascent dragon, this unborn wyrm, which had in its blood all the elements, and tainted it, made it impure, though it was kept in a state of stasis, allowed to grow until it was part of the very fabric of the world. Deeper even than the Vault, lies the last Sleeping Child; a beast of unimaginable size, slumbering in cold downworld caverns, waiting for its name to be called, to be summoned to life, as all dragons must be in order to hatch. It has grown thus, and remained asleep, because when the F'dor were imprisoned in the Vault, all the heat of their evil fire was taken with them. But should they be freed, they will immediately call it to life—and it will awaken.

"And it will consume the world."

The king stood a little straighter, trying to avoid noticing the glances that were being exchanged in the Hand.

"I fled from the grip of an upworld F'dor more than a thousand years ago, because in the course of my servitude I looked across the threshold of the Vault itself. And seeing what was inside caused me to understand that there are things worse than death, worse than exile, worse than endless torture. And seeing that, knowing that, I came to understand why the Dhracian blood in my veins screams for the death of all F'dor, why I must hunt down whatever hint of their foul stench I catch on the wind, to rid the Earth of each and every one that I can find. It is a calling that surpasses all other duties. And while I am a hunter, I am also now a guardian—the guardian of the Earthchild. The guardian of the Bolg. And, in a hideously ironic sense, I am the very guardian of the Earth. Trained and experienced as a killer, an assassin, a dealer in a catalogue of death that once held an entire continent in fear, I am now the one who has the ultimate responsibility for guarding Life, and possibly the Afterlife, for the F'dor hate them both, and seek to snuff both of them out if they can.

"So, my involuntary children, while there are some who believe that age will never take me, that I can die, but not by the hand of Time, there is a legacy that I must not only leave to you, but must enlist you in, beginning now, as you come into adulthood. I can no longer carry this mantel alone. Grunthor has always been my aide in this, but he cannot do it alone, either. I do not know what direct power the F'dor have outside the Vault, how many demonic spirits are abiding in human hosts, but I can see their influence growing in the hearts of men, that longing for destruction rising beyond the mountains where we reign. You will stand with me—like me, your destiny is not a choice that you made, but was made for you. It is as much beyond your control as the beating of your own heart. There is no option, no way of shirking or avoiding it.

"This is the thousand-and-first secret: Your lives will be spent in endless vigil, guarding the Earth, and all that lives on it, and after it, from that which seeks to extinguish it. Your training, your dedication, your wisdom—your very lives—are pledged to hold these mountains, to guard the Earthchild, as I guard her, to be the first, and possibly last, barrier, between the F'dor and the wyrm that sleeps in the heart of the world."

The Archons nodded one by one in understanding.

The Bolg king lifted his veils back into place.

"But lest you think the task is too onerous to be borne, remember that at least you were born Bolg. If you begin to feel sorry for yourselves, keep in mind that you could have been born human or, far worse, a human *Cymrian*. Self-pity usually disappears when you consider that could have been your lot."

Grunthor chuckled for the first time that night.

"Yeah, and if ya want ta see what it's like being one o' those, Oi can rip 'alf yer brain out and send ya to Roland to live. Any takers?"

The vigorous shaking of heads raised a faint cloud of dust in the stolid corridors of the Hand.

$\mathcal{U}$pon returning from the Hand, Achmed discovered a nervous messenger waiting for him in the Great Hall.

Impatiently he put his hand out to him, a boy even younger than Trug, and was quickly given the ivory tube which had been delivered by the mail caravan. He broke the wax seal, and, seeing that it was from Haguefort, drew the parchment it contained across his veiled face between his nose and lips. Rhapsody's scent still clung to the paper, the fresh aroma of vanilla and spiced soap. The odor pleased him, though he was not consciously aware of why. Where it could have carried the perfumes of myrrh and amber sought by other queens, other monarchs, the scent was instead that same sweet spice she learned to cleanse herself with as a farm girl on the other side of Time. It was innately comforting to know that at least some things about her had not changed in the time since she had taken on the title of Lady Cymrian, and the role of being Ashe's wife.

"Somethin' from the Duchess?" Grunthor inquired.

Achmed nodded. "Just a note requesting in code that I be on the lookout for a messenger bird to arrive sometime in the next few days."

The Sergeant-Major let out a low whistle, and reached into the bandolier that adorned his back. The hilts of his prized collection of weapons, spread out in a fan like the spines of some ferocious reptilian creature, squeaked as he felt around for one to play with. Upon settling on The Old Bitch, a serrated short sword named in honor of a hairy-legged harlot he had known in the old world, Grunthor drew the weapon forth and ran it along the palm of his hand.

"Sounds like we may be seein' 'er again soon. Good; Oi've missed 'er."

The Bolg king exhaled. "Let's just hope that she's not going to need rescuing again. She hates that even more than I do, if that's possible. But for now, I can't be concerned about her and whatever she wants. I have a shattered kingdom to rebuild."

9

OUTSKIRTS OF THE CAPITAL CITY,
PROVINCE OF BETHANY

$\mathcal{J}$or most of the wagon trip to Bethany, Faron was mercifully unconscious.

The creature's insensible mind, primitive at its best, sank into an almost comatose state, a hazy realm where half-formed dreams and images appeared in fragments, dashed away by the splash of tepid water the fishermen routinely tossed on its body, causing it to sizzle in the hot sun. Faron lay beneath the seaweed that the fishermen had blanketed its pale body with, wishing for death when conscious, flitting through nightmares when not, burning in the sun in either case.

Finally, after a time that seemed endless, the wagon rolled to a slow stop and did not show signs of starting up again.

Quayle climbed down from the wagon and stretched painfully. He shaded his eyes and looked at the round-walled capital city of Bethany, surrounded by its exterior ring of villages and settlements, then pointed into the depths of the shops and huts and foot traffic swirling within it.

"The tinker said the fellow in charge of the sideshow is in the alley out back of the Eagle's Eye Tavern," he said to Brookins, who stretched as well and nodded. "You go into the city proper and sell the catch to the fishmonger, and I'll go into the outer circle, see if we can make a bargain for our Amazing Fish-boy." Brookins nodded and clicked to the horse.

Quayle watched as the cart wended its way up to the western gate, one of two of the entrances that were allowed by law to give access to animals of trade and other mercantile traffic. Entry through Bethany's eight gates was strictly enforced, and therefore much of the trade that did not fit within the law was conducted outside the ringed ramparts, in the external villages and settlements.

It was to this place he went now, seeking the Eagle's Eye, and the alleyway behind it.

Quayle was no stranger to this place, or places like it all over Roland. He chose to sell his wares and spend his profits in just such fringe settlements— the margin was higher, and the goods were cheaper. In addition, there was a variety and availability of merchandise that no self-respecting merchant in the city proper would handle.

Along the route to Bethany they had passed many other tradesmen of their ilk, asking if anyone had seen the traveling circus that had been performing along the coast a few weeks prior. Finally a tinker had told them, amid the rattle of the pots and pans hanging from his cart, that the carnival had traveled to Bethany and was doing a fair business in the grim streets outside the walls.

He had also provided directions to the tavern.

Quayle made his way through the cobbled streets, past the rows of small shops, inns, and houses, absorbing the sights and sounds of the place— the squawking of chickens at the poulterer, the merry, screeching laughter of street children, the haggling of the old women in the air market, the appetizing smell of food wafting from within the taverns. Quayle was hungry, and he wanted to remain that way until he had made his bargain; it assured that he would be more virulent in his negotiations.

Finally he came to the place where the tinker had directed him. The Eagle's Eye was a seedy building in need of repair, fronted on a dark thoroughfare known as Beggars' Alley. Quayle slipped into the lane that led behind the building, following the sound of commerce in the back streets.

A small group of men, with a plain-dressed woman and a few boys, were gathered in a circle around a brawny, bald man, shirtless, wearing hobnail boots and a length of wire whip looped around his shoulder that hung to his waist. He was leading something on a chain, a bear perhaps, that was jumping around on the filthy street, growling and squealing. Quayle moved closer to get a better look.

Once he broached the circle he could see that the creature on the end of the leash was a man, or at least manlike; it was covered completely with hair, even to its eyelids, walking around like an ape on its knuckles. Every now and then the freak would lunge at the crowd, causing them to reel back in amused consternation; the huge man dragged the hairy being back by the leash, growling at him in a menacing voice. Quayle's lip curled in disgust.

His obvious disdain caught the keeper's eye, and the muscular man glowered back, then loosed the chain a little and nodded in Quayle's direction. The hairy creature lunged wildly at the fisherman, scratching at his leg and crawling in frenzied dementia up as far as his waist, slobbering on his clothes, before the keeper tugged on the chain, dragging him back to the ground again. The other bystanders stepped hastily away from Quayle. The fisherman's gaze did not waver; he glared at the keeper but otherwise did not move.

"All right, then, who wants a ticket?"

The voice came from behind Quayle. He continued to stare down the keeper as the others moved away; he could hear the sound of coins being exchanged and directions to a place at the outskirts of the town being given. Finally when the people who had been watching moved away, the man behind him came around to the keeper's side.

He was tall and thin, with a similarly thin black beard that brushed the edges of his cheeks. The man was dressed in gaudy silk pants, striped in red and gold, with a green waistcoat and a tall black hat.

"Well, my friend, can I interest you in a ticket?" the man said; his voice was deep and pleasant, with a sinister ring to it.

"If that's what you call a freak, I think not," said Quayle, pointing to the panting creature.

The tall man stepped closer. "I assure you, my good man," he said, his voice inviting and threatening at the same time, "the Monstrosity is a sideshow of incomparable interest. There is something for every taste. You can't help but be entertained. As for freaks"—he leaned closer, speaking as if he were delivering a secret—"the darkest recesses of your mind cannot possibly imagine all the horrors the carnival holds."

Quayle rubbed his chin, as if considering. "And who is in charge of this carnival?"

The tall man's dark eyes roved over Quayle's face.

"Who's asking?"

"Someone with somethin' to sell," the fisherman replied stoutly. He had seen too much dark action in his days on the wharf to be intimidated by a clown in striped pants, a muscle-bound deadglow, and a hairy man behaving like a monkey.

The tall man's eyes narrowed.

"I am the Ringmaster of the Monstrosity," he said darkly. "And I doubt that you have anything that is of interest to me. I have collected the finest specimens of freakdom from every corner of the world—"

"What about a being that is both man and woman, and part fish?" Quayle interrupted.

The Ringmaster snorted. "Got one," he said.

Quayle crossed his arms. "This one's *real*."

Rage began to brew in the tall man's black eyes. He cast a glance around the alleyway to ascertain whether anyone had heard Quayle's derisive comment. "All of the Monstrosity's freaks are real," he said, unmistakable menace now in his voice. "And now, if you don't wish to buy a ticket, you should leave."

Quayle considered without blinking. "Tell you what," he said, ignoring the blackening anger on the face of the keeper, "I'll buy me a ticket, but you will come meet me outside the sideshow half an hour before it opens at dusk. I'll show you my Amazing Fish-boy, and if you want him, you'll buy him from me—and buy back the bloody ticket. Bargain?"

"Half a crown," the Ringmaster said, extending his palm.

Finally Quayle blinked. "Truly, I am in the wrong business," he muttered, pulling forth his coin purse and depositing the coin grudgingly in the tall man's hand. "But at least I know that when you want to buy my freak, you will be well flush to pay me handsomely."

Quayle met up with Brookins outside the western gate.

"How'd the catch sell?"

Brookins offered him his hand and pulled him into the wagon.

"Surprisingly good," he said, taking the reins again. "The fires on the western coast shut down the flow of fish. The mongers were pretty hungry for it. An' I found ropestock for dirt cheap."

Quayle rubbed his hands with delight. "This is shapin' up to be a very prosperous trip, Brookins," he said importantly. "How's our fish-boy?"

"'Twas alive the last time I checked him, but he's startin' to shrivel. They'll need to get him into a tank or something fairly soon. And he stinks to beat all."

"By sunset he will be out of the wagon; we can scald it good before headin' back," Quayle said. "Well, I'd best check on him and see if we can pretty him up before he meets the Ringmaster tonight."

He crawled into the back of the wagon, stepping gingerly around the seaweed blanket, and pulled it back carefully from the creature's face.

Unconscious, exposed to the sun, Faron merely blinked and exhaled, the air escaping through the fused sides of its mouth in a hiss.

Quayle reached over and shook the creature, recoiling at the slimy feel of its skin.

"Hey! You! Wake up, beast. You're going to the grand ball! At least for your kind."

The creature did not move.

Quayle's brows drew together. "Wake up," he urged the creature again. When it still did not respond, he looked over his shoulder at Brookins. "Not good—they won't want to pay as much if all he does is lie there."

"Mayhap he's sick," Brookins suggested.

"Mayhap. Fish out of water—can't be feelin' too well." Quayle steeled himself, then gingerly took hold of the creature's thin wrist and raised its soft arm, folds of skin hanging loosely, only to have it fall limply at its side again. The fisherman exhaled in annoyance, then blinked, moving closer for a better look.

In between the long, arthritic fingers something was wedged.

Quayle reached out and took hold of one end of it. It was thin and hard, with a ragged edge, green. At first it had blended into the seaweed so that he had not seen it. He gave a tug.

The creature's eyes flickered open.

Quayle tugged again.

The fishlike creature hissed, louder this time, its head lolling back and forth, struggling to awaken.

"What the—?" murmured Quayle. He tugged once more, with as much torque as he could muster. The object broke free of the creature's grip, leaving a thin trail of black blood dripping between its spindly fingers.

The creature's eyes snapped open, and its fused lips shook with agitation. It hissed wildly, and flailed its weak arms, reaching for its treasure.

Ignoring its protestations, Quayle held the object up to the light of the afternoon sun. It was hard, like an insect's carapace, with tattered edges, at the same time flexible, with tiny etchings that scored its surface. At first he would have said that it was green in color, but when the light hit its surface, it refracted into a million tiny rainbows, dancing over the object.

"Bugger me," Quayle whispered, entranced.

The creature hissed louder and spat, its eyes focused on Quayle, brimming with anger. It made another weak grab for its object, but Quayle moved easily out of reach.

He stared at the thin disk for a moment more, then looked back at the creature, who was glaring at him with all of its remaining strength.

"You want it back?" he asked softly. The creature nodded angrily. "Good—you do understand me. Well then, my friend, if you want it back, you'd best look lively in front of the Ringmaster; if he likes you enough to buy you, then you can have your treasure back. And only then." He slid the ragged disk into his shirt and climbed back onto the wagon board, turning a deaf ear to the piteous wails and whimpers coming from the back.

The Monstrosity was set up to the north of the city, just beyond the edge of the outer villages, in a ring of torches and lanternlight that cast twisting shadows on the Krevensfield Plain beyond.

In the light of the fading sun and the flickering brands, Quayle and Brookins could see ten circus wagons, each painted gaily in dark, rich colors with images that defied the imagination. In addition, there were several carts and a number of dray horses, with a multitude of tents set up all around.

A steady stream of people were en route to the sideshow, a host of wide-eyed spectators mixed with unsavory characters undoubtedly seeking other pleasures than the mere spectacle of viewing the monstrous. Quayle knew that sideshows were often fronts for peddling flesh, particularly flesh of the more perverse nature.

A ring of burly guards, dressed in the same fashion as the keeper he had seen in Beggars' Alley, stood at intervals around the perimeter of the sideshow. The ticket taker, a hunchback with a harelip, waited at the entrance, carefully collecting the pieces of fishskin parchment that the Ringmaster had sold to the curious in the alley; sideshows often operated only with presold tickets, to avoid keeping their lucre on the premises in case of bandits or authorities who wished to harass them or shut them down. The hunchback waved two young boys away, followed a moment later by one of the guards, who growled at them.

"Ya can come back tamarra!" the hunchback shouted as they ran. "We here fer two more days!"

Brookins shielded his eyes from the torchlight and looked around. "I don't see anyone waitin'," he said nervously. He clucked to the horse, who was dancing anxiously in the torchlight.

Quayle glowered in agreement. There was no one outside the ring of tents and wagons waiting to meet them.

"I can go in and find him," Brookins offered.

The other fisherman laughed. "I'd forgot you had a taste for this sort of thing, Brookins," he said, scanning the scene again and still seeing no sign of the Ringmaster. "But we don't want to meet him on his own twisted ground. Such places are havens of monsters, after all."

"So how are we gonna talk to him?"

"We'll get him to come out to us."

Brookins scratched his head, perplexed and agitated. "But what if he don't come out?" he said, watching the crowd begin to enter the gate.

"Oh, mark my words, he'll come out," Quayle said confidently.

He jumped down from the wagon, then pulled the oilcloth covering back. The creature in the seaweed hissed at him, its eyes full of hate.

"There ya go, bucko, hold that thought," he said to it, ignoring its withering glare as it struggled to reach him with its bent limbs.

He pulled the oilcloth covering over the creature once more, then stood up in the wagon, cleared his throat, and began calling in the barker's voice he had used in his days as a monger on the wharf.

"Step rightly, lads and lasses, come one, come all—see the Amazing Fish-boy! A better freak you'll not find within the show you've already paid for—and what's more, it won't cost you a thing!"

The crowd of onlookers heading into the Monstrosity continued streaming past him, though a few turned and looked in his direction.

Quayle tried again. "Come now, if you dare, look into the face of *true* monstrosity! Come and take a gander at a being who is half man, half woman, and half fish!"

A few men slowed their gait, but otherwise the crowd ignored him, hurrying to the tents.

Not to be deterred, Quayle addressed a heavyset woman strolling with her husband, a redheaded man with a barrel chest.

"You, madam! You appear to be a right brave soul. You want to be the first to see the *real* freak? Somethin' so frightening that the Ringmaster of the Monstrosity himself is afraid to come out and see it?"

The woman paused, intrigued, and plucked at her husband's arm. The man shook his head disapprovingly, but she dug in her heels.

"Come along, Percy, he picked me! I want to be the first!" she bleated. "Come on, now, love. Let's have a look."

"Yes, manny, listen to the little lady," said Quayle in a manner he believed to be smooth. "You can look, too. And it won't cost you nothing. Be the first! Or move on."

The barrel-chested man cast a longing glance in the direction of the Monstrosity, then looked back at his wife's expectant face and sighed.

"All right, Grita, but then we are late for the gate," he said grudgingly.

Quayle clapped his hands together in delight. As he had expected, a small crowd had started to form, willing to delay for a moment their entry into the carnival of freaks in anticipation of what might be hiding in the wagon. The light from the torches cast long fireshadows that scurried across the oilcloth, making it seem like a menacing bog or a cave from which something hideous was about to appear.

"Come 'round this side, missus," he said to the woman, who eagerly made her way around the wagon to the place where the fisherman had indicated; her husband followed her, exhaling loudly. Quayle glanced over his shoulder in the direction of the sideshow; as he expected, enough of the crowd had been diverted to have caught the attention of the hunchback at the gate. The ticket taker muttered something to one of the bare-chested guards, and the muscle-bound man slipped through the gate and disappeared into the Monstrosity.

Quayle returned his attention to the woman, who was dancing impatiently next to the wagon. He adopted as polite a tone as he could muster.

"Are you ready, missus?"

The woman nodded eagerly.

"Now, make sure you stay within grasp of your fine husband here. This is a savage beast."

"Get on with it," her husband growled.

Quayle glanced up at the small crowd once more, and, determining the size to be right, he nodded.

"Very well, then. Behold the Amazing Fish-boy."

He grasped the oilcloth and tugged it up so that the woman and her husband could see inside, while the rest of the crowd around the wagon watched their faces.

The man and the woman peered into the depths of the wagon.

At first all they could see was darkness. The woman stood on her tiptoes and leaned in for a better look, while her husband crossed his arms, looking annoyed.

"I don't see nothin'," he said in a surly voice.

"Neither do—"

Just as the words left the woman's lips, the creature in the wagon lunged at her with all its might, hissing and screeching ferociously. Black water poured from its gaping mouth, its lips fused in the center over its soft yellow teeth, its eyes, cloudy with cataracts, filled with unmistakable murderous rage.

Both of them reeled back in shock, then screamed in unison. The woman's face went completely gray, and she darted behind her husband, sobbing; he could do little to help, as he seemed rooted to the spot, gibbering like a monkey.

The unveiling had its desired effect. The response was so genuine, the husband and wife so aghast, that it caused ripples of residual horror to wash over the small crowd, which gasped in fear, even without seeing the freak in the wagon.

Quayle chuckled at the shock on Brookins's face; the ripple of terror had caught his dockmate unaware. He pulled the oilcloth back over the wagon.

"All right," he called to the crowd around his wagon, which had tripled in the wake of the scream, "who's next?"

Brookins, recovering, had been watching the gate. "Quayle," he murmured, "he's comin'."

Without looking, Quayle nodded. "You, sir?" he asked quickly, pulling a tall, brawny man in from the wagon's edge. A group of other people around him stepped quickly back.

The man was coaxed into place just as the Ringmaster and two of his keepers came into the circle around the wagon. Quayle timed his revelation to coincide with the Ringmaster's arrival; when he was just a few steps away, the fisherman pulled the oilcloth off again, once again eliciting a strangled gasp and a cry of genuine horror rising from the brawny man's viscera.

The crowd of peasants began to talk among themselves in an enthusiastic blend of excitement and fear. The Ringmaster shoved his way through the convocation, followed by his keepers, trying to talk above the din of chatter, endeavoring to convince the group to move on to the gates of the sideshow, but the promise of free viewing of what must be a heinous monster served to make them insistent upon seeing it for themselves.

"What do you think you are doing?" the Ringmaster demanded angrily of Quayle, who was watching the proceedings with a look of smug satisfaction on his face.

"Why, just giving your sideshow customers a little — a little — "

"Side show?" Brookins piped up.

Quayle chuckled. "That's it! A side show to the sideshow." He glanced from the boisterous crowd, which was now jockeying to see who would peer into the wagon next, to the livid Ringmaster and his bristling henchmen, and leveled an insolent stare at the man. "Now, don't get uppity, Ringmaster," he said patronizingly. "Remember, it's *you* what stood *me* up. I offered you first crack at this freak, and you didn't bother to come to our arranged appointment."

The Ringmaster pushed his way through the crowd and came around to the side of the wagon where Quayle stood.

"Let me see it," he demanded. He seized the edge of the oilcloth.

"Ah, ah," Quayle chided, slapping his hand away. "It's not free for *you*, Ringmaster. You charged me to come into *your* show. Seems only fittin' that you should pony up a crown to see mine."

The crowd, caught up in the excitement, began to babble in agreement.

Inhuman sounds began to issue forth from under the oilcloth.

The Ringmaster's face slackened. "I don't carry money," he said sullenly.

Quayle nodded. "Mayhap that's true. So I will show you what a gentleman I can be. Despite how rude you've treated me, I will spot you the crown. But if you want to buy my fish-boy, you will have to pay me my price, plus the crown, plus the first half-crown you charged me." He looked to the growing throng for support. "Does that seem fair?" he asked the assembly.

A chorus of assent replied.

"All right," the Ringmaster snarled. "Show me your damned freak."

Quayle broke into a wide smile and stepped aside, bowing and gesturing politely at the wagon. "Be my guest, sir."

The Ringmaster lifted the tarp high.

A pale arm shot forth from the bowels of the wagon, its sickly skin almost green in the flickering light of the brands, followed a moment later by the misshapen head, its huge, cloudy eyes blazing, its grotesque mouth hissing and screeching sounds that were clearly inhuman, and possibly demonic. It clawed at the Ringmaster, clutching his waistcoat and dragging itself toward him. The man pulled free and stepped away. The creature swiped helplessly at Quayle before sinking weakly back into the depths of the wagon.

The crowd gasped collectively, the spectators in the front pushing and shoving to get clear of the wagon.

Only the Ringmaster stood still. He turned to Quayle, who was still unable to disguise his gloating.

"How much do you want for it?" he asked tersely.

Quayle pretended to consider. "Well, this afternoon I had planned to ask for fifty crowns," he said, continuing on through the Ringmaster's shocked intake of breath, "but since you've been so downright rude, the price is one hundred gold crowns. Plus two."

The Ringmaster started to protest, but then caught sight of the crowd surging enthusiastically toward the gate of the Monstrosity, and reconsidered.

"Done," he said. He motioned to one of the keepers, and the man disappeared in the direction of the outer villages of Bethany.

"We'll give you an hour," Quayle said, climbing back into the wagon. "My friend Brookins here would like to use his ticket, if you don't object. Then we're gone, with our money and without our fish-boy, or without it and with him. So if your lackey ain't back with the money—"

"He'll be back in time," the Ringmaster said through his teeth.

"Good," said Quayle, stretching out on the wagon board. "And just to show you what a generous chap I am, you can take its fish; that's what it eats, though it likes eels better. And maybe next time you'll show up when you're expected."

The creature was handed over in the dark, when the sideshow had closed for the night. It had spat and hissed, but its soft bones and weakened state made its transfer a fairly easy one.

"Don't forget to keep it wet," Quayle had cautioned the Ringmaster as the creature was placed in a canvas sling and carried away beyond the gate and into the strange world of the Monstrosity. "It dries out easy."

"Take your money and get out of here," said the Ringmaster, watching the keepers carry the creature into one of the tents within the carnival. He turned and followed them without another word.

Later that night, as they rejoined the trans-Orlandan thoroughfare, heading back west to the coast, Brookins finally spoke. He had been staring directly ahead of him for hours, trying to process what he had seen beyond the gates.

"There was a—woman in there with two—two—purses," he whispered, gesturing between his legs. He shook his head, trying to expunge the sight from his memory.

Quayle laughed aloud. "Good thing I was holding the gold, Brookins," he said with a crude tone. "You wouldn't want to deposit any of your 'coin' in either of those 'purses.'"

"And one that ate manflesh," Brookins continued, still attempting to exorcise the experience. "Severed arms all around her, tearing at the muscle and fingers with her teeth—"

"Stop now," Quayle directed, annoyed. "I just want to enjoy our good fortune." He patted his chest where the wallet of tender was kept, and felt something sharp scratch across the skin over his ribs. He reached inside his shirt and pulled forth the ragged, multicolored disk he had taken from the creature. It shone, prismatic and radiant, in the light of the sliver of the setting moon.

"Well, lookee here," he said, pleased; he had forgotten about the strange object altogether. "I guess we have another memento of our fish-boy."

"Didn't you promise to give that back?" Brookins asked.

Quayle shrugged. "A promise to a fish don't count," he said nonchalantly. "I make 'em promises every day to lure them into the nets. I don't keep those, neither. Besides, by the time we would get back there, that sideshow will have packed up and moved on." He turned the scale over, admiring his own face in the reflection.

"Did they say where they are goin' next?"

Quayle thought for a moment, trying to recall, then nodded.

"Sorbold," he said.

They drove most of the rest of the way in their accustomed silence, Quayle planning how he was going to spend his share of their good fortune, Brookins trying to forget how they got it.

10

Faron awoke in water.

The creature blinked; it was dark inside the tent. It could make out dim shapes through the blurry glass of its container; with a little effort it floated to the surface and took a breath, bumping its soft skull on the ceiling of reinforced canvas that had been chained around the outside of the glass.

It tried to remember what had occurred to bring it to this place, but the picture in its limited mind was hazy and painful to contemplate. Faron vaguely recalled being wrestled from the wagon onto a sling of some kind, and fearing drowning when plunged into the tank, but other than that, everything was a blur.

It banged helplessly on the glass, futilely pressing its bent hands against the canvas ceiling, but gave up after a few moments, spent. At least it was out of the blistering sun, back in the comfort of water without salt.

The thought of salt water made Faron melancholy. The last time the creature had seen its father was aboard a ship; he had left and gone ashore in an angry state and never came back. Faron had seen him pass through the Death scale into a deep abyss; the Lord Rowan, Yl Angaulor, had refused him entrance to eternal peace. Its father's death had broken Faron's heart; deep despair had set in, but only for a moment.

Grief had fled in the wake of the tidal wave that followed its father into the Underworld.

Faron had been belowdecks, down in a pool of glowing green water in the darkness of the ship's hold, when the wave struck the ship broadside. The creature could hear the screams a second before, but had no idea what was going on above until the ship lurched violently, upending the pool and slamming the creature into the hull. Faron had lost consciousness and awoke in the sea, surrounded by flotsam and jetsam, and no sign of another living being.

And remained thus, suffering the sting of the salt and the thunder of the waves, until it washed ashore, unconscious, in the fishermen's net.

The flap of the tent was pulled aside, spilling light within. Faron winced.

A stout woman in many tattered layers of ragged dresses, soiled aprons, and torn petticoats came into the tent, a tray in her sharp-nailed hand. She wore no shoes; her enormous feet, easily twice as large as would seem proper, were splayed at an odd angle, flat and covered with calluses. The toes appeared to have a webbing of skin between them.

She came straight up to the tank and peered inside. Faron wrenched away to the back wall, treading water furiously. The woman's wrinkled lips skinned back, revealing an almost toothless smile; what teeth she did possess were black or broken.

"Yer awake! Aw, dearie, Sally's so glad to see yer feelin' better."

The woman set the tray down on the dirt floor, clucking sympathetically.

"Now, now, little 'un, nothin' to fear. Old Sally would neva hurt ye." She undid the knot in the chain that held the canvas cover on the tank and, reaching over her head, slid it off and onto the floor.

Faron's arm went up defensively, and the creature hissed at the odd woman. She didn't blink, just crossed her arms and regarded the new arrival fondly.

"Now, you just stop that, little 'un, my sweet. Ye got nothin' to fear. Ye hungry?"

Faron's cloudy eyes narrowed. The creature looked askance at her, then nodded guardedly.

"Poor dearie. Well, I've brung ye some nice fish, live 'uns. Will that do ye?"

A mix of hunger and excitement came into Faron's eyes. The woman chuckled at the response, then pulled the cloth from the tray to reveal a small bowl full of goldfish. She held it up before Faron's face, and chortled with delight as the creature began salivating and whimpering with anticipation. She extended a long taloned finger and, with a motion so quick Faron could not follow it, speared one of the fish on her nail, then held it, wriggling, over the tank.

"Here ye go, my beauty, my sweet little 'un," she whispered. "Come an' eat."

Faron floated in the back of the tank for a moment, considering; finally, hunger won out over suspicion and the creature swam forward, bracing itself against the front wall of the tank. With quivering lips Faron reached up and plucked the writhing fish from the woman's nail, shivering with delight as it slithered down its gullet into a stomach that had known nothing but hunger since the shipwreck.

Outside the tent, voices could be heard as two men walked past.

"Ye seen Duckfoot Sally? Ringmaster's looking fer her."

"Ayeh, she went into the tent ta feed the new 'un."

The canvas tent flap pulled aside again. Faron shrank away from the light. Duckfoot Sally scowled at the man who opened it.

"Sally—"

"I 'eard him. Tell him ta keep his stripes on; I'm busy feedin' the new 'un," she said harshly. She turned back to Faron, and the snaggletoothed smile spread over her face again.

"So sorry, my luvly; come back now. Here's another." She speared a second fish and held it up.

After a moment's hesitation Faron returned to her and allowed her to continue to spear fish and hold them up to be eaten. She didn't seem to mind the touch of the creature's lips; in fact, took delight watching the wriggling fish disappear, sating its hunger. She spoke softly to Faron, crooning occasionally as a mother would to a child.

Her ministrations were so tender, so kind after so long being tossed about in the sea, abused on the land, that it brought a memory back to Faron's mind, the recollection of the father that had tended the creature so gently, even though given to fits of rage and cruelty. Then there welled up a sense of loss as profound as Faron had ever felt, and a tear rolled out of one cloudy eye and down the loosely wrinkled cheek beneath it.

Duckfoot Sally's grisly smile dissolved to a look of sympathetic consternation.

"There, there," she said quickly, setting down the empty fishbowl and turning back to the weeping creature, "what's wrong, luv? Ol' Sally's here, and she won't let no one harm ye." She extended her hand and carefully closed the talonlike nails into a fist to keep from scratching the creature, then ever-so-gently brushed the tear from its cheek with her knuckles. "Don't cry my sweet little 'un, my fair 'un."

Faron's eyes snapped open, recognition clear for a moment in them.

Duckfoot Sally's eyebrows shot to the top of her forehead at the reaction.

"What, luv?"

The creature's gapped lips quivered, and its gnarled hands banged against its chest.

Sally's brows now drew together in puzzlement. "'Fair 'un'? That be yer name?"

Faron nodded enthusiastically.

The hag clapped her hands together in delight.

"Well, well," she said brightly, reaching out to caress the creature's cheek again with her knuckles, "pleased ta meet ye, Fair 'un. Be ye man or woman?"

The creature blinked, no understanding in its eyes.

Duckfoot Sally shook her head. "Never mind; doesn't matter. There are many here that dun' know, either. No worries, luv. Sally's lookin' out fer ye, and that's all ye'll need." She drew closer, her tatters rustling as she pressed herself against the glass. "Jus' 'member this, my Fair 'un: yer as good as any livin' soul born in this wide world. They may pay to see folks like us, ta laugh and throw things, but mayhap where you come from, why, yer king of yer kind! Mayhap somewhere, in a distant sea, yer the lord above all the fish that swim, an' all the clams; the oysters, too! And what are they that laugh at ye? Peasants, all of 'em. Mindless peasants who save up their miserable coppers to go hoot at others, all in the 'tempt to ferget that their lives are of no consequence." Her smile brightened, and her voice grew warmer.

"But ye and me, my Fair 'un, we perform fer kings and queens! Kings and queens, ladies an' lords, Fair 'un! We go to grand cities, and palaces the likes of which those wretches will *never* see. So never ye mind when they laugh at ye, my Fair 'un. It's us, ye and me and our like, that will have the last laugh."

The Monstrosity remained three more nights in Bethany, one night longer than they had planned. Each night the crowds swelled to capacity and overflowed in long lines, waiting to catch sight of the horrific fish-boy. Word had spread from the outer towns into the city proper, and there was so much interest that even the Ringmaster, who kept to a rigid schedule, could not resist the business.

But after keeping the sideshow open from dusk to the end of the dark hours just before dawn three nights in a row, the Ringmaster decided there was such a thing as too much good fortune. He called for his exhausted menagerie to pack up and put rein to horse.

An entire empire awaited, a harsh realm where trade and commerce of all sorts, honest and otherwise, flourished.

Sorbold.

11

HAGUEFORT, NAVARNE

Rhapsody was pale throughout the dinner in Gwydion's honor. After the meal had been cleared away Ashe hoped that she would regain some of her stamina and that her stomach would settle, but she remained nervous and quiet, even when the toasting began.

Ashe had been worried ever since he had walked back into the Great Hall and found his wife conversing with Jal'asee. Rhapsody's choice of professions, attuned to the music of life as it was, usually assured that the vibrations in the air around her matched her mood. For the most part, ever since she had been returned to her home and family, she had been at peace. But the dragon sense within Ashe's blood told him now that behind the calm court face she was terribly distressed. Whatever the Sea Mage ambassador had said to her had unnerved her immeasurably, but she had declined to tell him what it was.

Now, as the various dukes of Roland rose, each in turn, and offered words of wisdom and congratulations to his young ward, Ashe reached over and silently took Rhapsody's hand. It was blazingly warm, either from the pregnancy or the element of pure fire she had absorbed, long ago, on her trek through the belly of the Earth with Achmed and Grunthor. In addition, it was perspiring, the nervous sweat of panic. He leaned over casually and whispered in her ear.

"Do you want me to make a polite excuse?" Rhapsody shook her head imperceptibly. "Are you all right, beloved? You are frightening me."

"I have to find the time and strength to speak with the Sea Mage ambassador," Rhapsody murmured. There was very little air in her statement; Ashe heard it in his ear, a Namer's trick.

"Tomorrow," he said quietly in return. "I think you should offer your toast and then rest. I can ask Jal'asee to come to the garden after your morning devotions. Will that suffice?"

Rhapsody exhaled, then nodded reluctantly. Finally, when the dukes of Roland had finished saluting Gwydion, and toasts had been offered by Rial of Tyrian and the other ambassadors from members of the Alliance, she rose a little unsteadily and turned to her adopted grandson.

"Gwydion Navarne, you are the son of a great man and the namesake of another. You have carried both their names, and the honor that accompanies them, all your life. On the last day of autumn you will finally come into your own name. I have no doubt that when the Singers and the Namers of history record it, the tales they will tell will be songs of greatness; of nobility, honor, bravery, loyalty, leadership, and kindness toward your fellow men. You have shown all these traits, even before gaining your birthright. Carry that forward into your life, as a man, as duke of Navarne." She paled, then reached for her husband's hand. "I'm sorry—I—must go lie down now." Ashe started to rise, but she waved him back to his seat. "No, no—please stay, all of you, and keep the merriment going. I want my grandson to be properly celebrated, even if I am not in appropriate voice as a Singer of lore tonight. My apologies, Gwydion, and congratulations." She wanly lifted her glass to Gwydion Navarne, finishing her toast, then smiled and blew him a kiss. She gathered her heavy velvet skirts.

Ashe rose and took her arm. "I will return forthwith," he said to the guests, "as soon as the Lady Cymrian is safely settled. Pray continue, ladies and gentlemen." The dukes and ambassadors stood as the couple left, then returned to their dinner conversations.

"Are you in pain?" Ashe asked as the two made their way through the resplendent hallways of Haguefort toward the Grand Stair, past the lovingly displayed suits of armor, heraldry, tapestries, and other antique objects that Stephen Navarne, once the Cymrian historian, had collected. "More than usual? Is the baby in distress?"

Rhapsody slowed her steps as they came to the foot of the Stair, and shook her head.

"No," she said, her face paling. "I think I am just unsettled by what happened earlier."

"You can tell me about it once I have you safely ensconced in bed," Ashe said, slipping an arm behind her as she prepared to ascend, then reconsidered, lifted her into his arms, and carried her up the stairs. Her lack of resistance worried him; Rhapsody hated to be carried.

A palace guard opened the door to their tower chamber as Ashe approached, then closed it behind the couple and withdrew, leaving the hallway quiet.

Ashe carried Rhapsody to their bed and laid her down, drawing the bedcurtains around them in the candlelight. Then he sat beside her and looked deeply into her eyes, trying to assess her condition. He allowed his dragon sense, that innate part of his blood bequeathed to him by his lineage from Elynsynos, his great-grandmother, to wander over his wife, examining her on a level that was invisible to the eye.

Her breathing was shallow, a sign of the discomfort she routinely bore in the course of her pregnancy. The Seer of the Future, Manwyn, the Oracle of Yarim, had predicted her pain, but had offered a comforting reassurance.

The pregnancy will not be easy, but it will not kill or harm her.

Watching his wife now, struggling to breathe, clenching her jaw to maintain control over the pain, Ashe wondered angrily how broadly the Oracle defined harm.

Rhapsody's green eyes, which darkened to emerald when angry, amused, or deeply touched, were blazing the color of spring grass. Ashe had noted that her blood was changing as the child grew within her; the dragon essence of their offspring was strong, palpable already, asserting itself, however innocently, by controlling the environment in which it was growing.

His stomach sank as he remembered the words of warning that Llauron, his father, had imparted about their marriage, and the death of his mother in childbirth.

I assume you are aware of what happened to your own mother upon giving birth to the child of a partial dragon. I have spared you the details up until now — shall I give them to you? Do you crave to know what it is like to watch a woman, not to mention one that you happen to love, die in agony trying to bring forth your child, hmmm? Let me describe it for you. Since the dragonling instinctually needs to break the eggshell, clawing through, to emerge, the infant —

STOP. His own voice had rung out in draconic tones.

His father's eyes had held a stern light, but there was something more — a sympathy, perhaps. *Your child will be even more of a dragon than you were, so the chances of the mother's survival are not good. If your own mother could not give birth to you and live, what will happen, do you think, to your mate? I watched with horror the greatest sadness of my life in the face of what should have been my greatest joy. And I don't wish for you to repeat my mistake, nor do I want to lose Rhapsody to our world.*

Rhapsody had been unwilling to allow his father's warnings to dictate their lives, however. She had insisted they visit his great-aunt, the Oracle, and ask about what her fate would be should they undertake to have a child. Manwyn, the Seer of the Future, was unable to lie, and her answers seemed quite clear. Rhapsody had indeed suffered in the throes of the pregnancy, but seemed to be getting better day by day. At least now she could see most of the time, where at the beginning her eyesight had been adversely affected. Ashe knew she was suffering, and hated it, but endured it, knowing that she had made her choice, was happy in it, and that the end result would be worth the discomfort she was routinely in.

For now, however, she appeared more distressed by whatever the Sea Mage had said to her than by anything that was happening within her. He squeezed her hand gently.

"Tell me."

Rhapsody's grip on him tightened. "He knows. Jal'asee knows about Achmed and Grunthor and me traveling through the Earth from Serendair."

Ashe blinked, then considered for a moment. "All right," he said finally. "What is the harm in that, Aria?" He addressed her by the name he called her in the most tender of moments, the Lirin word that meant *my guiding star*, in the hope that it would ease some of her distress.

Rhapsody released his hand and drew the pillows behind her. "It has always been a secret that we have held closely," she said uncomfortably, as if the words pained her. "You are the only living person, outside of the three of us, who knows the details of how we got to this place—or at least we believed that until now."

Ashe caressed her face, then began to unlace the bodice of her court dress, loosening the stays to allow her to breathe more easily.

"I can understand why learning what you believed is not so in this manner would upset you," he said, pulling the cord from the holes, "but when you examine the impact of it, I think you will see that it was only a shock because you had believed it to be unknown. The knowing of it—where is the harm?"

Rhapsody exhaled as the garment loosened, pondering his words. "Achmed was always very specific about the need to guard this information closely," she said, raising herself up to allow her husband to remove the heavy velvet outer dress, leaving her clad in the lighter white chemise beneath. "I think knowing that there is someone—someone from as distant and mysterious a place as Gaematria—that knows our past, our history, would make him angry, or at least suspicious."

"When is Achmed ever *not* angry and suspicious?" Ashe said humorously, tossing her dress into a nearby chair; his dragon sense noted the inner flinch that resulted in Rhapsody, whose upbringing on a farm had engendered a sense of neat orderliness in her that he, the child of a royal line and the head of a religious order, had never learned.

Rhapsody smiled slightly. "True," she admitted. "But it unsettles me as well."

Ashe pulled back the crisp sheets and the duvet for her, then tucked them around her body, his hand pausing on the swell of her belly. "When the dinner is over I will ask Jal'asee to meet you tomorrow in the garden after your sunrise devotions," he said, feeling the movement of the child within her and smiling. "Then you can ascertain what he knows, and whether it is a threat or not. The Sea Mages guard many secrets lost to time and the rest of the world. My guess is that yours is safe with him. But you can be the judge of that in the morning. In the meantime, there is nothing more to be done about it tonight." He leaned forward and kissed her gently, then lowered his lips to her belly and pressed a kiss on their child as well, and rose. "Sleep now, beloved. I will return in a very short while."

Rhapsody caught his neck and drew him into another kiss, then patted his face. "Very well," she said. "Please make my apologies again to Gwydion for my poor attempt at a toast. When we name him duke in two months' time, I will be in better form."

"Rest now," Ashe said, then extinguished the candles and left the room.

Rhapsody turned on her side in the dark and allowed sleep to take her. Her dreams were filled with unsettling images, recalled from the recesses of her mind. For what seemed like forever she was back in the darkness and cold, wet fear of traveling through the belly of the Earth along the Axis Mundi, the centerline of the world, crawling along the root of Sagia, the great tree her people worshiped as sacred. In her dreams she stepped forth from the ground, emerging into the world they had come to on the other side of Time, only to find it in the grip of war and terror; before her, people were running in every direction, screaming in fear, their voices swallowed in the cacophony of destruction that was burning all around them. *What war is this?* she wondered, walking through the devastation that encircled her, charred bodies littering the landscape. *Is this the Seren War that tore my home-land asunder after we left, or the Cymrian War that shattered this new land while we were still traveling within the Earth?*

In the distance the sky lit up with fire; Rhapsody strained in her dream to see what was illuminating the clouds. She thought she could make out the image of a winged beast circling, a billowing cloud of black-orange flame that smoldered of acid raining down from its maw. *It's Anwyn,* she thought hazily, tossing in her sleep. *This is neither war; it is a memory of the battle that took place three years ago at the Cymrian Council, when the wyrm called forth the Fallen of history from the dead to wage war on us.* She willed herself to breathe easier, reminding herself that the battle was over, that the wyrm was long dead. Ashe's draconic grandmother lay buried in a grave outside of Ylorc, having been struck by starfire from the sky.

By Rhapsody's hand, and the power of Daystar Clarion, the elemental sword of starfire she carried as Iliachenva'ar.

But the memory of Anwyn's destruction did little to assuage her uncon-scious fears, did not drive from her mind the dreams of annihilation and death. It only permuted into the present, making her heart pound even more furiously, as images assaulted her unawake mind, pictures of herself running from a wave of caustic fire, her hands on her belly, shielding her child. In some scenes she was pushing the child before her, sometimes carrying it in her arms as a baby; sometimes it was within her still as she hid in darkness, calling to its great-grandmother, giving their location away. Each time she found a new place for them to hide, the dragon would find her; Rhapsody fled with the child, until at last she looked down to find herself alone, her arms empty.

Her dreams changed to visions of the sea roiling, of ships on fire and the coastline burning beyond the edge of the shore, of a continent, a world, at war. Great winged shapes circled above the land, strafing down suddenly on the dark human shadows that ran through the smoke, plucking them from the ground and taking them, writhing, back into the sky.

She was in a gray sweat by the time Ashe returned, muttering to herself in a low, panicked voice. He hurried to the bed and took her into his arms, gentling her down, quieting her as his dragon nature chased away the nightmares, banishing them from the ether that surrounded her. He whispered words of comfort to her in her sleep until her breathing deepened, her fever broke, and she slept dreamlessly on his shoulder.

He lay awake for a long time, stroking her damp forehead, caressing the silk of her golden tresses, wondering what could have caused the nightmares she had once suffered from, and from which she had been free for so long, to return so virulently. Perhaps it was the kidnapping she had lived through recently at the hands of a depraved man from the old world, who had long ago made a pact with a demon to ensure immortality, then had come to find her. Even her captor's destruction, and her return to safety, could certainly not be expected to expunge all of the horror from her mind. Perhaps that was what was plaguing her.

Eventually he drifted off into dreams of his own, dreams in which he was walking through water, traveling through the ocean, formless and without bodily limitations, communing with the element to which he was bonded, as Rhapsody was bonded to fire. It was something he had done many times in the past, wading into the sea, turning his body porous while he was within the waves, letting it cleanse his soul and his mind from care.

What neither of them knew, as they slept in the darkness of their bedchamber, their hearts beating in time, if not in unison, their breathing measured breath for breath, was that while Ashe dreamt of the past, Rhapsody was dreaming of what was to come.

*H*er hunger sated, the wyrm ascended the cold peaks again.

The night sky stretched out, endless with promise; stars winked at the dark horizon, but above, all across the firmament of the heavens, the aurora blazed, pulsating bands of multicolored light, dancing to the silent music of the universe.

The dragon inhaled the frosty wind. *I remember this,* she thought, watching the twisting light strands gleam in the darkness above her. *The northern lights; how intensely they shine; how cold.* She could recall standing beneath them in a woman's body, beneath the black sky and the glistening stars, watching her breath form icy clouds in the darkness as she pondered the power of the aurora, its beauty, its distant majesty. It was a sign of the power of ether, the element that was born before the world was born, that lighted the stars, that burned beyond the Earth, out in the vast void of space. As a being with dragon's blood in her veins, she had been able to feel a whisper of the element within herself then; now, in dragon form, it pulsed within her, in tune with the vibration of the aurora.

Ether. Its cold beauty was hypnotic to her. But it was also the power of ether, mixed with that of pure fire, that had trapped her forever in this form, this wretched, serpentine body.

At the remotest edge of her awareness, a fragment of a memory jangled.

A young memory, recent; not from the old time, when she was a still a woman, but in her dragon form.

She was flying, hovering on the hot wind, something grasped in her taloned claw. It struggled, like the man whose head she had bitten off had struggled in her grasp.

A pretty sight, isn't it, m'lady? How do you like the view from up here?

An image flashed through her mind, duplicated in her skin a moment later; it was the flash of a burning weapon, the sting of a wound in her wing, as the searing heat ripped through her, tearing her flesh. The agony of it echoed in the webbing between the hollow bones in the crippled appendage; involuntarily she winced at the recollection of the pain.

Damn your soul, Anwyn!

Too late, the wyrm whispered, her voice echoing her own in her memory.

She followed the path of the memory back, looking down in her mind's eye into her blood-drenched claw. It seemed to her that the creature struggling within her grasp was a woman, a small woman with golden hair, brandishing a weapon of flame. She tried to form the woman's name in her mouth, but the word escaped her still.

Hatred, black as the night sky above her, burned like the cold fire of the aurora within her three-chambered heart.

Anwyn, she thought; the name resonated, ringing a chime in her memory. *Anwyn.*

Her name.

Her own name.

She remembered.

12

Morning crept through the eastern windows, unbidden and unwelcome.

In the gray light of foredawn Rhapsody sat up, hazily aware and partially refreshed. She pressed a warm kiss on her sleeping husband's cheek, then leaned back and watched him for a while, lovingly admiring his face, its chin and jaw shadowed with a night's growth of beard. With his eyes closed, his human and Lirin heritage was more evident than when he was awake; the vertical slits in his eyes were the only real sign of the draconic blood that ran in his veins. Asleep, he was human, undeniably human. Rhapsody's heart swelled at the sight.

Finally, when Ashe sighed in his sleep and rolled over she rose, running a hand gently across his shoulder, then made her way into the privy closet to dress for her morning devotions.

The air in the garden was chilly; autumn was coming, and the earth was beginning to cool in preparation for its long sleep that would soon begin. If this year was to be as most were, the snow would fall a sennight or so before the winter solstice, blanketing the middle continent with an unbroken layer of frost that sank deeply below the ground until Thaw, that time in midwinter, after the yule, when the harsh weather abated for one turn of the moon before going back to its frozen dominion until spring came. That warmth in the depth of winter held a special place in Rhapsody's heart; it had been Thaw when she, Achmed, and Grunthor had first come to this place, stepping out of the dark belly of the world into the relative warmth of winter's abatement.

But before winter came again, there would be autumn, harvest time, which was her favorite season. She had seen the first signs of it upon returning to Navarne from the seacoast, where her abduction had left the shoreline burning from Gwynwood to Avonderre. After Ashe and Achmed brought her back she had been confined to her bed for almost a sennight before she rebelled, and had hurried to the window in time to see the beginnings of the autumnal change, the tips of the leaves turning bright hues of red and orange, yellow and brown, in the trees beyond the balcony of her tower chamber.

Now, as she wandered the neatly manicured pathways of Haguefort's gardens, waiting for the first ray of sun to crest the horizon, Rhapsody took the time to inhale the morning wind, scented with hickory and pine, and the sharp odor of leaves burning. It was a smell that put her in mind of her childhood home on Serendair, the farm country where she was born, where harvest had been a time alive with excitement, with urgency, with the year growing shorter, the days growing darker as each one passed.

She watched the sky now; Liringlas, the skysingers of the Lirin race, were accustomed to greeting the dawn with songs called aubades, and therefore could sense when the cobalt hue of the horizon lightened to the richest of cerulean blues, signaling the sun's approach.

The first ray of morning cracked the horizon, sending a thin shaft of radiance into the clouds, bathing them with golden light. Rhapsody cleared her throat, and slowly began the ancient devotion, the song of welcome that her Liringlas mother had taught her while her human father stood and listened, entranced.

She sang the first aubade welcoming the sun, then turned westward and moved into the second one, the song which sang the daystar farewell. Rhapsody watched as the bright celestial light dimmed in the brightening sky, then began to sing her last customary aubade, the song to Seren, the star she was born beneath, on the other side of the world.

Aria, she chanted softly; *my guiding star.* Tradition held that each Liringlas soul was tied to the star which ruled the day of his or her birth; Rhapsody's birth star had been Seren, the bright celestial body for which the island of Serendair had been named. The aubade to Seren had always been particularly poignant when sung in this new land, as she could never see it; it sparkled in darkness half a world away when the sun was high above her, and slept in the light of day when she was out beneath the stars of this new land. Rhapsody had taken to chanting the traditional evening blessing in the morning out of a sense of futility, choosing to honor her birth star at the time it was shining, even if she could not see it.

As she sang the namesong of the star, she heard a rich, crackling voice join with her, chanting in the same tongue she sang in.

Seren, si vol nira caeleus, toterdaa guiline meda vor til.

Blood flushed her face; she broke the song off in midnote and whirled around to see Jal'asee behind her, smiling pleasantly. His expression faded at her reaction.

"Pray forgive me, m'lady," he said, bowing respectfully, "I did not mean to intrude."

Rhapsody crossed the garden, her hand going instinctively to her belly in an unconscious gesture of protection.

"How—how do you know the Lirin aubades?" she asked nervously, struggling to keep her own voice in an appropriate tone.

Jal'asee smiled. "You forget, m'lady, that when the Liringlas of your homeland—*our* homeland—refugeed from Serendair, most of them sailed with the Second Fleet. And most of those that did chose to land in Gaematria after the fleet was blown off course by a storm, rather than continue on to this continent, or to follow the rest of the fleet to Manosse. So I live among a good number of your people. No doubt more than you have ever seen, if you were raised among humans." He tucked his long-fingered hands into the sleeves of his robe and stepped cautiously toward her as the sun crested the horizon and the sky lightened to robin's-egg blue.

"I have only met a few of my mother's race in my life," Rhapsody admitted. A wave of nausea rose and she struggled internally to force it down. She mimicked Jal'asee's gesture, her hands suddenly cold, either from the morning chill or from the shock of surprise at his joining in her aubade.

The elderly, golden-skinned man stepped closer, then stopped when he was within gentle earshot. "In addition, it might be noted that I am of a race even older than your own, ancient as the Lirin may be," he said congenially. "The Seren are said to be descended of the stars, a race born at the place where the element had its birthplace on Earth, where starlight first touched this world. We are, of course, named after that star, as was the Island. Your aubade is the musical vibration that rings the star's true name. So I suppose it is not beyond reasonability that I might know the song as well." He winked at her. "Failing that, I have a good ear for catchy tunes, I'm told."

Rhapsody chuckled, half embarrassed. "How arrogant of me. I beg your pardon, Your Excellency."

"Please, m'lady, address me by my given name. Among my people that is a sign of friendship as well as respect." Rhapsody nodded. "Your husband asked me to meet you here; I apologize if I am early."

"Not at all."

"Excellent. Now, what I can do for you? I am at your service."

Rhapsody struggled to keep her voice calm, while her stomach churned in distress. "You can elucidate your comments of last night, as I am confused by them."

"About seeing you leave the Island?"

"Yes."

Jal'asee studied her face; Rhapsody noted that he seemed aware of the rise and fall of her nausea, the movement of the child within her. When the sickness abated for a moment, the Sea Mage ambassador extended his arm and led her to a marble bench at the foot of a splashing fountain.

"Do you know why people become seasick?" he asked in his gravelly voice as they sat down on the bench. "Humans especially—for all that they are descended of a race born of water, and are themselves composed largely of it, one might think they would be naturally attuned to the rhythm of the ocean. But it is in their unconscious resistance to it, the desire to be a separate entity, that the vibration is unbalanced, thereby making them ill. If only they could learn to embrace the element within them." He reached out one hand to the water cascading in pulsing rivulets in the fountain, the other to Rhapsody's forehead. Unconsciously she closed her eyes.

She heard the sound of the fountain grow louder, and realized after a moment that it was Jal'asee's voice, perfectly matching the vibrational tone of the splashing water. Within her she felt the nausea abate; her stomach settled, and her balance returned, along with the clarity of her sight that had been blurry since the child's conception. She felt a sudden sense of wellness, as if she were floating in a bubble, protecting her from the jounces and jolts of the air that had been assaulting her for the last few months of her pregnancy. She opened her eyes to see the tall, golden-skinned man with the bright eyes smiling down at her.

"Better?"

"Yes, thank you," Rhapsody said. "Now, please tell me what you meant last night."

Jal'asee looked at her thoughtfully for a moment. Rhapsody was certain that she heard the splashing of the water in the fountain growing louder.

"When you lived on the Island of Serendair, had you ever seen one of my race?" he asked finally. His voice was soft, less scratchy than before, blending into the sound of the falling water.

Rhapsody considered his question. "No," she said, "though I had studied a bit about the Ancient Seren. My mentor, Heiles, the man who instructed me in the science of Singing, had introduced me to the ancient lores, and told me of each of the Firstborn races, but before we could go into more depth he disappeared. I never saw him again, so I had to finish my studies alone."

Jal'asee nodded. "Had you lived always in the fields, or did you ever go to a major city?"

"I—ran away from home as a young girl, and lived for several years in Easton." Rhapsody's face flushed with the memory of her life there and what she had done to survive.

"Easton was the largest city on the Island, a port city, with commerce from all parts of Serendair, as well as from other lands. And yet you never saw an Ancient Seren in all the years you lived there?"

"No. In fact, I thought they—you—were extinct; that except for Graal, the king's vizier, who was known in the tales of the traveling storytellers, your race had died out in an earlier age."

The Sea Mage settled himself more comfortably. "M'lady, long ago, before the grandfather of the king that ruled the Island you knew as a child was crowned, I was an instructor, a lecturer, at Quieth Keep, the royal college of Serendair. I also am a professor in the study of natural magic and tidal vibration in the academy of Gaematria. I tell you this for two reasons— the first is that I wish to present my information to you and have you see it, as a Namer, as close to lore in its accuracy." Rhapsody nodded. Jal'asee chuckled. "Additionally, while telling you my tale, should I adopt an imperious, condescending, or arrogant tone, it is because once an academician, always an academician. I mean in no way to condescend to *you,* but some things are bred into professors, and sanctimony is one of them. I apologize heartily in advance." Rhapsody laughed.

Jal'asee cleared his throat. "Forgive me for reiterating anything you already know," he said. "In the history of this world, the earliest age, before recorded history, was known as the Before-Time. It was in this age that the Firstborn races, those sprung directly from the five elements themselves, came into being. The Seren were the first to evolve, as the element of ether was the first element. Ether came into the world from another place; it is the fire of the stars, and has a natural music to it, the music of light—I assume you know this, yes?" Rhapsody nodded. "Good. And had you ever seen a member of another firstborn race? Had you ever met someone who was Kith, or Mythlin, or a F'dor? Nor wyrm—you had never met a dragon in the old world, had you?"

"No," Rhapsody said. "Mostly humans. A few of later races descended of the Firstborn—I saw a few Gwadd, and my mother was Lirin. I think I may even have seen a few Nain, though I did not know what they were at the time. But I never saw someone of a Firstborn race. I thought they had all died out, as we had been taught they had."

"Well, as you can see, we did not." Jal'asee covered his eyes as the sun rose higher in the sky, brightening the garden with intense light.

"So where were you, then?" the Lady Cymrian asked.

"In hiding," the Sea Mage ambassador said seriously. "For many ages."

"Why?"

"Self-preservation," Jal'asee said. "The Seren were the first race to appear on the Island, but we were not alone for long. In the early days, after the F'dor were imprisoned deep within the world, peace reigned for a time; a long time by your measure. But eventually came the younger races, the Lirin, and the Nain, who did not care for each other's ways. In their day, the Island still saw peace for the most part, because the place each race chose to live was distant from and unlike that of the other race, so there was little conflict.

"But then, after millennia had passed, came man—humans, or half-men, in our language. They were long generations removed from the primordial magic which had brought the Firstborn races into being, and mortal, bent on living short, violent lives. At first it seemed they would come and go more quickly than the wind, snuffing themselves out in their impatience, but we underestimated their strength, their endurance—and their pure bloodthirstiness. They were avaricious, jealous of land and power, and they set about taking it in any and every way they could, through war and murder and genocide.

"And there were many of them. They filled our once-open and spacious land with their settlements and cities, their fortifications and their prisons, continuing to multiply, until they had all but choked out what had gone before. We had welcomed them as refugees—and now they were poised to eradicate all the civilizations that had come before. Much the way Gwylliam did, ironically, to this land."

Jal'asee paused for a moment, as if the tale had winded him. Rhapsody looked into his eyes; within the golden irises a dark swirl was dancing, as if he were looking directly back into a painful history. She waited quietly for him to continue, watching the bronze color return to his lanky, hairless forearms after a moment. Finally he shook his head and looked down at her, an awkward smile crooking his wide, thin mouth.

"I beg your forgiveness, m'lady," he said hastily, mopping beads of sweat from his forehead with a quick motion. "When one is designed to live forever, history sometimes takes on an immediacy that Time strips from it in the eyes of those over whom Time has sway. It is as if a thousand years ago was yesterday."

Rhapsody nodded, continuing to wait. Finally the Sea Mage shook himself, as if shaking off sleep.

"And that is the way of the world, I have learned over Time. In each era of history a civilization is formed, holds sway for a time, and then is displaced by another, either over centuries, or quickly, brutally, in conquest, until history is but a swirling sea of change, supplanting what had been before, keeping pieces of it, moving on. It is foolishness to hope that what you have built will survive—though we all do."

The golden-skinned man blinked in the light of the sun, then turned his gaze on her once more.

"When, in the Second Age of history, known to scholars on Gaematria as Zemertzah, literally 'The Broken World,' it became clear to the Ancient Seren that our culture and in fact our people were facing destruction from the advancement of the human habitation of Serendair, and the conflicts that habitation brought with it, we decided there were but two choices for our people if we were to survive. We could leave the Island, emigrate to a distant and unoccupied land, as Gwylliam later did at the end of the Third Age, or we could go into hiding in the earth, deeper than the mountainous realms where the Nain lived, in catacombs left over from the birth of the world.

"The first choice was unimaginable—our race, few in numbers as it was, had been spawned from the very light of the stars, sprung from the clay of the Island where the starlight touched. Even in the face of war, of death, we could not abandon our birthplace, our home. So instead we disappeared from the sight of the world, the bulk of our population slipping away to those undercrofts, those vaults deep in the earth, leaving a few of our number in the air of the upworld to watch out for us, to wait for a time when it might be safe to return.

"The races of men, the Nain, the Lirin, the humans, and their like, barely noticed we were gone. They were busy in their own racial wars, and when the dust settled, the humans emerged victorious, as your history must have taught you. Each racial kingdom maintained its sovereignty under the human High King, the line which eventually ended with Gwylliam. That confederation of kingdoms shaped the Island to their will. So it was when you were born, and until the time that the fleets left it was still so. All that remained, in the eyes of the world, of my race was a handful of upworld Seren, Graal, the king's vizier, as you mentioned, myself, and a few others numbering less than would need two hands to count. Eventually only Graal remained; when one of our remaining number of upworld brethren was brutally killed, the rest of us save for Graal quit the air and sought refuge in the catacombs with our people.

"And there we remained, until the Sleeping Child began to signal it would arise. Then we came up into the world again, those of us who chose to leave Serendair for life elsewhere beyond the Cataclysm."

"I had no idea," Rhapsody murmured.

Jal'asee smiled. "Had you remained, rather than leaving the Island with your friends, you might have known it. But it happened while you were traveling through the Earth, along the root of Sagia. And yes, m'lady, I know that you entered the World Tree with a key of Living Stone, in the company of he who is now the Bolg king, and his Sergeant-Major, because when you were climbing down into the darkness, along the Tree's taproot, I looked out from the catacomb entrance that the Tree guarded and saw you myself."

The memory of the journey within the Earth roared back in Rhapsody's mind, the suffocating feeling of being underground, disconnected from the sheltering sky, and beads of sweat broke out on her forehead. She closed her eyes and swallowed, trying to fight back the fear that she could still taste, even four years later, though the journey within the world had been timeless. When they had emerged, they discovered that fourteen centuries had passed without them; all they had known in the world was gone. It was a loss she no longer thought about consciously, but still felt keenly when it was recalled.

"What did you see?" she asked haltingly.

The smile left Jal'asee's eyes, and he regarded her seriously.

"I saw a girl, fearful and yet brave, an unwilling captive who struggled futilely but did not give in. I saw a creature, half Bolg, half Bengard, I would wager by the height of him, who seemed intent both on holding her captive and helping her along at the same time. And I saw someone else, someone I thought I recognized." His forehead wrinkled deeply, but otherwise his face did not change. "I may know your friend, the Bolg king, but I will not be certain until I see him again.

"Those of us who lived beneath the surface of the world were in a state of half-sleep, m'lady. Had I been able to aid you, and had I been certain you were in need of such aid, I would have tried. But all that I saw, all that I relate to you now, was like a very intense dream; for a long time thereafter I was not even certain if it had been real or only a prescient vision, which the Ancient Seren were prone to. I apologize for not being able to help you, but it seems as if you have come out the better for surviving whatever hand Fate has dealt you."

The Lady Cymrian smiled slightly. *"Ryle hira,"* she said softly, intoning the old Liringlas adage. "Life is what it is."

"Indeed," Jal'asee agreed. "I know that your path has not been one that followed a predictable pattern, but it has led you to places you might never have lived to see, and inspired in you powers that you might never have known had you followed a more traditional route. You say that your mentor disappeared before you had finished your study of Naming, and that you had to complete your training alone. Forgive me when I say this, but it shows. I have had the privilege of knowing many Lirin Namers, both on Serendair and Gaematria, and it is evident that you missed out on the final step of the process of becoming one—the baptism in the light of *Aria,* the Namer's guiding star."

Rhapsody flushed red with embarrassment. "I—I don't even know what you are referring to," she said nervously.

"It's nothing to be ashamed of, and not surprising that you do not know of it," said Jal'asee soothingly. "It is a ceremony that marks the end of a Namer's studies, and is not revealed to him until it is upon him. If your mentor was not with you at the end of your training, it is not surprising that you did not benefit from the baptism. As you are undoubtedly aware, each Lirin soul is tied to the star he or she was born beneath—and each day and each night of the year is dedicated to a different one. That is what you think of as *Aria,* is it not?"

"Yes," said Rhapsody. "I was born beneath Seren itself. My aubades have always been to Her."

Jal'asee nodded. "And they have no doubt drawn power from that star, even half a world away. So while you are self-taught, while you have not had the advantage of the final baptism in the light of your guiding star, you have undoubtedly gained other strengths, other insights, because you have had to make your own road, rather than following the prescribed path, much as you and your companions found your way within the Earth. If anything, your link to the star may be even stronger than it would have otherwise been, because you have kept vigil for it, lost as it is to you. It is a special celestial body, you know, an old star by the way the universe reckons. Your husband carries a piece of it within his chest—how it came to be there, I do not know, but I sense its song within him."

A chill ran through Rhapsody's blood again. It was as if Jal'asee knew not only all of her secrets, but those of the people she loved as well. The Sea Mage ambassador noted the change in her eyes and took her hand in his long, articulated one.

"Your child will be blessed, and cursed, with the power of all the elements, Rhapsody," he said in a voice as warm as Midsummer's Day. "You walked through the fire at the heart of the earth—do not fear; of course I know this, because you clearly absorbed it. In what the rest of the world mistakes for mere beauty, one such as myself, who has seen the primordial elements in their raw form, can recognize them. You and your child were cradled in the arms of the sea during your recent captivity—I know this too, not by seeing it, but because the waves told me of it during my journey here from Gaematria. Your husband is the Kirsdarkenva'ar, the master of the element, so there is a tie to water in both parents. The earth is in you both as well—you because you have traveled through Her heart, your husband because he is descended of the wyrm Elynsynos, and thus linked to it, as you are both linked to the star Seren. And finally, as the Lirin Queen you are a Child of the Sky, a daughter of the air. So your child will have all of the elements nascent within his blood. Do you know what all of those elements add up to?"

"Tell me," Rhapsody said. Her voice came out in a choked whisper.

Jal'asee smiled broadly. "Time," he answered. "He will have the power of Time. I hope you will do me the honor of allowing me, when the child is old enough and the occasion permits, to help teach your child how to use it."

The child within her belly lurched. Rhapsody flinched; the song of the fountain's splashing had come to an end, and with it her nausea returned. She stood slowly, trying to maintain her balance, and put a hand over her brow to shield her eyes from the ascending sun.

"Thank you," she said noncommittally. "I will discuss that with Ashe when the time is right. I thank you for all the lessons you have imparted to me today, and hope that you will convey my thanks to Edwyn Griffyth for the walking machine he sent to Anborn." She sighed regretfully. "I hope he will deign to make use of it. I confess that it strangles my heart to see him so impaired."

The Ancient Seren ambassador rose as well and looked down at her, his shadow blocking the sun.

"Why?" he asked, taking her arm and leading her back up the garden path to the keep.

"Because he was injured in battle saving me, as I assume you know," Rhapsody said, struggling to walk steadily. "I tried to employ my skills as a Singer and Namer to heal him at the time, but as you can see, the hapless state of my training and the limits of my abilities kept him from healing completely. Perhaps that is because, lacking a baptism in my guiding star's light, I am only fooling myself into believing I can draw on its power."

Jal'asee continued walking, but his voice moved closer to her ear, as if he could cause it to sink on the air.

"A tie to a guiding star, like love, is often stronger when it has to be found at great cost," he said softly. "And Anborn is not crippled because you were unskilled to heal him, but because he was unwilling to allow you to do so. Perhaps someday he will forgive himself, and then you might try again. But having watched him over the last seven centuries, I am not going to wager anything valuable on it. Your child may benefit from the blessings of all five primordial elements, but he will undoubtedly be cursed with pigheaded stubbornness of epic proportions. It runs in deep rivers on his father's side of the family. You have my deepest sympathy in advance."

Rhapsody laughed in spite of herself all the way back to the garden gate.

13

THE MONSTROSITY

True to her word, Duckfoot Sally set herself up as Faron's protector.

The long ride south from Bethany to Sorbold was a difficult journey under normal circumstances; housed in a fragile tank of fetid water, in the back of a circus wagon lurching over pitted and unkempt roads was just short of agony. Sally moved her cot into Faron's wagon after the first night, when the creature's tank was nearly shattered by the lion-faced man and the sword-toothed geek, two of Faron's wagonmates, who saw the new arrival as a source of jealousy or food, or both. Duckfoot Sally had interposed herself between the ravenous freaks and the cowering creature's tank with a broom handle and a snarl of such intensity that the men, both more than twice her size, had shrunk back into the dark recesses of the wagon, muttering threats and grousing quietly until sleep took them into a realm of relative silence.

For several days the Monstrosity traveled without stopping except for the night; no shows were given, because there was no place along the route with a population worthy of the effort. The Ringmaster had chosen to avoid the holy city-state of Sepulvarta, which was the citadel of the Patriarch of the largest religion in Roland, knowing the Patriarch would have them arrested and tried for peddling human misery. So there was little to do but travel by day, and camp by night. Duckfoot Sally tended lovingly to Faron, and the creature seemed to settle into relative calm, though it still shrank away whenever anyone else came into the wagon. Sally happily took on all of the responsibility of Faron's maintenance herself.

The keepers, the Ringmaster's henchmen who served as control for the freaks and guards for the audiences, began grumbling among themselves about Sally's new obsession. Malik, an older keeper with a scar running from the base of his skull down the centerline of his back to his waist, took to lying in wait outside the new freak's wagon, watching her comings and goings and reporting them back to an increasingly displeased Ringmaster. On the night before they came to a small farming settlement on the Krevensfield Plain to the south of Sepulvarta, he caught her as she came off the ladder, empty fishbowl in hand. Malik leaned around the wagon's side and grabbed her around the waist.

"Ahoy, now, Sally, where ya been? Seems like yer slightin' the rest of us to wait upon the fish-boy hand an' foot—if he had a foot, that is."

Duckfoot Sally gave him an impatient shove, extricating herself from his grasp. "He has feet, ye rock-headed lout. They just be soft."

"Aye, an' I'll betcha all the rest of his parts are soft as well," Malik grinned, catching her waist and turning her around again. "But you know that ain't the case with me, Sally, doncha, girl?" He buried his bearded face in her neck, nibbling playfully.

"Yeah, ye have a right hard *head*, Malik," Sally said crossly, but the keeper's lips were having an effect.

"'Sss been a long time, Sally," Malik crooned, his hands moving higher. "You fed him jus' now, right?" The carnival woman nodded, her eyes starting to glaze over. "And is he asleep?" Another nod. "Then he should be all right for the moment, eh? Let's go off behind the privies, and I can have my way with you."

Sally snorted contemptuously. "'Twill be the other way round," she said, setting the fishbowl down on a barrel and glancing furtively around the camp for any sign of the Ringmaster; he was not to be seen. "Always is."

"Either way," said Malik agreeably. He took her clawed hand and led her into the darkness.

As soon as Duckfoot Sally had disappeared into the night, three of the other keepers came out of nearer shadows and made their way quietly into the wagon.

The creature was asleep in its cloudy tank, floating limply in the water, as the shirtless men crawled through the dark wagon, stepping carefully over the bedding of the other freaks who were out taking the air or eating their nightly meal. When they were finally in the back of the circus cart they conferred quietly through hand signals, then leapt out of the darkness, banging noisily on the tank, pressing their faces up against the glass walls and screeching hideously.

The new creature bolted awake, squealing piteously, its fused mouth flapping at the sides, gasping and cowering in the back of the tank.

The keepers were still making faces at the creature, banging on the canvas lid of the tank with sticks, when Duckfoot Sally charged into the wagon, fastening the stays of her many bodices, fire blazing from her eyes. Behind her Malik, his pants still unlaced, glowered angrily.

She raked her nails savagely across the backs of two of the keepers, drawing blood, and bellowed in a voice that threatened to shatter the glass tank.

"Ye bloody *bastards!* Get away from my Fair 'un!"

The only keeper not in range of her swinging talons gave her a mighty push that sent her sprawling backward, where she landed at the feet of the Ringmaster, who stood in the doorway of the wagon, a lantern in his hand.

"What is going on in here?" the tall, thin man demanded.

"They're bedeviling my poor Fair 'un!" Duckfoot Sally spat, rising furiously from the floor and starting into the fray again, only to be pulled back as the Ringmaster seized her arm.

"If you idiots have harmed the fish-boy in any way, I will draw and quarter you," he said in a deadly hiss. "That freak has tripled our take." He turned to Malik and gestured at the floor. "Move this bedding to the carnivore wagon, and bring the dead displays in here." He turned toward the trembling creature in the tank. "I don't want to take any more chances with the fish-boy's bunkmates."

"The contortionists and oddities won't get no sleep in with the meat-eaters," one of the keepers protested. "All that howling and pacing don't bother the dead 'uns."

"Get out of here, and do as I ordered!" the Ringmaster snarled, shoving the man toward the curtained door.

He stepped aside and let the sullen henchmen pass, then turned back to Duckfoot Sally.

"You can stay in here. Make certain nothing else happens to him."

"Aye, that I'll do," Sally said, still panting from the fight.

The Ringmaster glared at the creature in the glass tank once more, then turned and disappeared through the curtains.

Duckfoot Sally wiped her nose with the back of her arm, then made her way across the wagon to the tank that gleamed dully in the dark. She untied the canvas cover, then pulled a small wooden chest over to the tank and stood atop it, plunging her arms into the unclean water.

"There, there, Fair 'un," she said softly, gesturing, making smooth ripples in the creature's prison. "Yer safe. I won't leave ye; and the Ringmaster's word is law here. No one will bother ye again. Come, my pet. Let Sally rock ye back to sleep."

The creature hovered in the water at the back of the tank for a long time, staring wildly at her in the dark. She could see the cloudy eyes, open and round like moons, above the wrinkled skin of its face, the rest fading away into the watery green. Finally it swam cautiously over to her, and laid its head in her open hand.

Duckfoot Sally smiled her broken smile, curled the fingers of her other hand into a fist, and wordlessly caressed the creature's cheek with her knuckles, crooning a melody she had heard, though where she had long ago forgotten.

The night before the sideshow caravan entered the mountain pass leading into northern Sorbold, the Ringmaster opened the gate to a contingent of Sorbold's mountain guard, soldiers in the elite unit that patrolled the border between that nation, Roland, and the Firbolg realm of Ylorc.

The soldiers, long away from home and without anything much to do except train and watch for invasions that never came, welcomed the Monstrosity enthusiastically. While the whoring tents saw the longest lines, the tents that housed the most deformed and grotesque exhibits were patronized eagerly as well.

Faron had been displayed between the dead specimens of preserved freakdom with which it shared a traveling wagon, the two-headed baby, the winged man, and a score or so of other malformations that floated, pickled, in salt solution. The creature by that time had grown so despondent that the crowds of soldiers didn't even notice that it alone in the tent was a living specimen; they walked through, talking among each other, much as they would at a museum, then hurried on to the more exciting tents where danger, however staged, lurked.

Afterward, when the keepers were loading the wagons up for the night, the Ringmaster stormed angrily through the curtains at the door of Faron's wagon and strode over to the tank, slamming his hand against the glass.

"Wake up, you damned fish!" he snarled, shoving a horrified Duckfoot Sally, who had been sewing on a stool next to the tank, out of the way. "I paid dearly for you, lad, one hundred gold crowns, plus two! Rescued you from those imbecile fishermen. And *why?*" He slammed his hand against the tank again, causing it to rock crazily, water leaking from the seam at the side. "Because you were a hissing, spitting *nightmare,* that's why! And how do you repay me? By floating lifelessly in your tank, no different from the dead ones, who the audiences think are *fake!*"

"Leave my Fair 'un alone!" Duckfoot Sally shouted indignantly.

The Ringmaster wheeled and belted the odd woman to the floor with the back of his hand.

Faron, who had shrunk to the far side of the tank, cowering, while the Ringmaster ranted, screeched in rage and slammed against the front glass pane, scratched futilely with its soft, curled hands.

"Ah!" the Ringmaster exclaimed, his dark eyes glinting with understanding, "that's it. You need to be angry, do you?" He turned and kicked Sally squarely in the forehead as she tried to rise, knocking her unconscious, then smiled as the creature screeched again, yellow teeth clenched, its eyes bloodshot with hate. It pressed itself against the glass, clamoring to get out, scratching at the canvas covering above its head.

The Ringmaster's eyes widened in amazement.

Jutting from the folds of the creature's belly was something he had never noticed before. A series of multicolored fins, or something like them, were hidden in the freak's sagging skin, one of which dangled at the edge of the skinfold, ready to fall. A moment later it did, as the fish-boy continued to pound on the canvas covering, its arms elevated. An irregular oval, the size of the Ringmaster's hand or so, with tattered edges, blue in color, drifted down into the offal at the bottom of the tank, sparkling as it fell.

Faron stopped rampaging at the look of amazement on the Ringmaster's face and followed his eyes down to the tank floor. Fury fled in the face of panic; the creature darted quickly to the bottom and snatched the blue scale, returning it rapidly to its belly folds, glaring at the Ringmaster.

Shouting for his henchmen, the Ringmaster began to roll up his sleeves.

"Give it to me," he said in a low, menacing voice.

The creature shook its head, retreating to the far side of the tank.

The Ringmaster grasped the edge of the glass and rocked the container violently.

"I said *give it to me,* freak. Before I pull you from the water and toss you into the sand of the Sorbold desert to wither."

Faron hissed and spat in return.

Amid loud tromping the keepers came into the wagon. With an efficiency born of years of experience dealing with unwilling monstrosities and beasts of violent capabilities, they wrestled Faron to the back of the tank and pinned the creature, amid sloshing water and shrieks of inhuman noise. Then, once the freak was secured, the Ringmaster, his clothes drenched in fetid water, plucked the blue scale from Faron's belly, ignoring the creature's howls of distress, and stared at it in the lanternlight.

It was a concave oval, tattered slightly at the edges, gray when held flat, its blue coloration only noticeable when it was turned in the light, which then refracted into a shimmering spectrum that danced across the scored surface. On one side of the scale the image of an eye was engraved, surrounded by what appeared to be clouds. The Ringmaster turned it over carefully in his hand, noting that the other side, the convex one, bore a similar etching, but the eye on this surface had clouds obscuring it.

He looked back at the trembling creature, bound in the arms of the keepers, still squealing in fury, black blood trickling from the skin folds of its abdomen, clouding the water.

"Well, isn't this a pretty thing?" he mused, holding up the scale, taunting Faron with it. "At least now I know how to make you perform the way you should, Fish-boy." He nodded to the keepers. "Let him go."

The henchmen released the creature, allowing it to slide back into the now half-full tank, and trooped out of the wagon, followed a moment later by the sodden Ringmaster.

Faron continued to howl, sometimes angrily, sometimes piteously, until Duckfoot Sally finally came around. She pressed her hand to her bruised forehead and made her way amid her wet, rustling tatters to Faron's side, whispering words of comfort and solace, until the creature finally gave in to racking sobs.

"There, there, my Fair 'un, don't fret, luv. It's all part of the life, I'm 'fraid." She stroked the soft head gently with her knuckles. "All part of the circus life."

14

THE CAULDRON, YLORC

𝒜chmed had been poring over his dusty volume for more than an hour when the messenger bird arrived.

Grunthor had become accustomed to standing or sitting in silence of late, contemplating the field maps and reports that came from the Eyes in the farther outposts, the more distant guard towers in Ylorc, past the Blasted Heath and the blue forests of the central kingdom, deep into the crags of the Teeth. The Sickness had spread throughout the Claw and Guts clans, but the Eyes had seemed to remain unscathed, so most of the information now being delivered to him was from their leaders, as they maneuvered to consolidate his favor in the absence of competition. The news they were sending his way was increasingly disturbing.

The stone walls hewn from the mountain that formed the Cauldron's main meeting room were flecked with shadows from the large hearth fire that burned steadily in the corner, the occasional crack and pop of the wet wood the only sound in the room. When the messenger from the aviary opened the door, therefore, the hum of the hinges and the whine of the wood reverberated through the silence. Grunthor looked up to see the hairs on the Bolg king's sinewy arms standing at irritated attention.

The soldier coughed politely, a sound that a human would have thought to be a grunt. Achmed waved him in impatiently.

He stared at the scrap of oilcloth that the messenger handed him for a long time, then sat back in his heavy wooden chair, his hand resting on his thin lips in the position he frequently assumed when contemplating. Finally he looked up and leveled a sharp glance at the Sergeant-Major.

"I'm going to need to leave again in a few weeks," he said to Grunthor.

"Ya just got back," the Sergeant said grumpily. "What is it now?"

"I have to go to a carnival," Achmed said.

"Oh. Well, if that's it, certainly, by all means, 'ave a wonderful time, sir," Grunthor said sarcastically. "Bring me back some of those pretty lit'le sugared almonds if they 'ave any."

Achmed tossed the oilcloth scrap into the fire and watched it burn before he spoke, appreciating the hiss of cured paper in smoke.

"Rhapsody and her ne'er-do-well husband have decided to confer the title of duke of Navarne on Stephen's son Gwydion," he said finally. "Hard as it is for me to imagine the words coming from my lips when pertaining to someone or something Cymrian, I have to admit I have taken a liking to young Gwydion, as I took one to his father."

"Yeah, ol' Lord Steve was a dandy fellow," Grunthor said, the earlier gruffness in his voice dissipating a little. "But, if Oi might be so bold to suggest it, sir, you 'ave a few other things to attend to, if ya know what Oi mean. The Sickness is spreading—or at least those who survived coming in contact wi' the glass of the Lightcatcher all seem to be in fairly great agony. Strange rumblin's in the breastworks, word from the Eyes that Sorbold seems unusually quiet—Oi don't like the feel o' the wind these days. Might be a good time to stay close ta home."

"Undoubtedly it is," Achmed agreed. "But I have my reasons for going other than court ceremony and the appeal of spending a frivolous day in the company of a bunch of self-important Cymrian nobles."

"Oi never would o' guessed that, sir," said the Sergeant dryly. "We all know 'ow much ya love those sorts o' parties. Oi assume that givin' the Duchess what she wants is at least a part of it?"

The Bolg king rose and crouched near the fireplace, allowing the pulsing heat to ripple over the sensitive exposed nerves of his skin. "Not at all, actually. I have something I need her to do for *me*. And she owes me." He rose and returned to his dusty reading. "In addition, I have something I want to give to Gwydion Navarne—a spoil of fortune in the rescue of Rhapsody. I claimed it, though Ashe had already determined Gwydion was the one to have it. I want to be the one to confer it to him, so that it is used properly. I need to make that clear to all involved. Finally, I want to test the Archons in my absence. They've been commissioned at last, brought into the light. They understand what I expect of them, what their purpose is now. I will only be gone for less than a fortnight. Surely you can hold things together without incident that long, Grunthor."

The giant Sergeant did not answer, but stared into the twisting flames, wondering what new horror would come to pass this time.

High at the topmost frozen peak, the wyrm clung to the snowy rocks, trembling in the wind. She had slithered out through the gate of the frozen palace and up into the mountaintops, battling the screaming wind all the way to the dark peak.

Wrapped around the summit, the spines of her serpentine tail anchored into the frost, she set her teeth against the wind and struggled to open her eyes. The gale that whipped around the mountaintop slapped her again, digging icy fingers into her eyelids.

Damnation, the beast thought.

She did not feel the cold as much as she had, for within her a fire of a sort had been lighted. With the remembrance of her name had come a burning power, smoldering deep in her viscera, a source of strength and energy that had been sapped from her by her near-death and entombment. Not knowing her name, her past, how she had come to be in the state she now was in had left her weak, disoriented, impotent. But now that she had remembered at least part of her past, she was hell-bent to seek the rest of it.

And return whatever power resided there to herself.

She steeled her will against the icy blast and shouted with all the power of her mind into the screaming wind.

Anwyn! Anwyn!

From the beast's draconic throat, absent a traditional larynx, no sound emerged. But the will to speak was enough; from all around her the air thickened, then vibrated, bent to her will as all the elements bend to the command of a dragon.

Anwyn!

The updrafts caught the elemental sound, stretching it on the gusts of air until it hovered, dancing around the mountaintop, in long, moaning circles.

Annnnnnnwyyyyyyyyynnnnnnnnnn!

The sound molded, swelled, and filled the thin air of the summit. It grew in volume and intensity, the vibrations of it shaking the snow from the peaks, causing avalanches to slide, shimmering, down the mountains and into the foothills below.

The noise of it grew and ebbed, catching currents of wind and stretching across them, whispering off into the wide world on the breeze, multiplying the noise of her shout over and over again, until it had expanded to the edge of the sea.

The beast clutched the icy stones of the peak, the fog in her mind lifting as much as it had since the time of her Awakening. She braced herself in the wind, her reptilian blood coursing in a sort of ecstasy, feeling the echoes of her name's reverberations in the world, sensing its vibrations as it danced on the wind, thundering off the hillsides, wailing down through the chasms.

And then, in the distance, a thousand leagues or more away, a noise rose up to greet it, to echo its sound. It was a vibration from a history long past, centuries old, rumbled in a voice that was unlike that of the wyrm, though it had silt in its timbre, as if it, too, had in some way been tied to earth. Though the word was the same, the elongated melody of its syllables almost identical, the power of it was vastly different. Where the dragon's shout had been victorious, the call that answered it was from a voice in torment. Even centuries later, thousands of miles away in time and space, the fury in the word, the hatred that swelled to an agonized lament was unmistakable.

Annnnnnnwyyyyyyyynnnnnnnnn!

The beast's head rose above the wind, her senses immediately heightened to crystalline clarity.

Her inner dragon sense, honed and eager, caught the answering vibration like a beacon from the Past. She turned slowly, ignoring the icy buffeting of the insistent gale, and concentrated, shutting out all other thought, all other interference, and locked her mind onto the sound of her name, fragile and windblown now as the breeze on which it was carried began to dissipate.

Her name, spoken in hate, rang like the deepest note sounded from a iron bell, like the roar of the sea, the music of the stars in the cold lifelessness of the night sky.

And her mind had caught it. Now it rang, over and over again, ceaselessly behind her eyes, calling to her from the darkest depths of history.

She did not know who had invoked her thus, or why it had been with such animus, but that didn't matter. Somewhere south of the frozen peaks, somewhere beyond the viewable horizon, somewhere in the past someone had known her. Someone possessed of a power similar to her own. Someone whom she had enraged; there was a grim joy in her heart at that aspect of it.

She had a tie now to whatever place that scream had occurred.

She could find it now, and in so doing, perhaps find more of herself, her power.

And the woman she hated.

The wyrm slithered down from the peak, following the sound of her own true name, mindlessly through the jagged wind, heedlessly over the barren wasteland, southward until the never-ending winter gave way to late summer again. Once the ground was warm enough, she burrowed into it, following the harsh song of her name below the surface of the earth.

Hunting for echoes.

Her joyful excitement in the anticipation of bloodletting building with each mile she traveled.

15

TERREANFOR, THE BASILICA OF
LIVING STONE, SORBOLD

Talquist waited impatiently in the gray light of foredawn.

Whenever he came to Night Mountain now, rather than approaching through the ravine that twisted and wound its way through the dry rocks that served as a natural fortification, as all the other visitors to the temple did, he instead scaled a small hidden trail that he had found many years ago, when he was an acolyte in the basilica. In his younger days it was a climb that left him winded; now, though an older man, he had learned enough, had strengthened himself enough, to make the journey without breathing hard.

While he waited for the secret door to open, he glanced around at the dry, stony rock formations that ringed Night Mountain. Their colors were glorious—streaks of pale pink and burnt rust, hints of green and darker purple that had all baked in the hot and merciless sun of Sorbold, drying them to a pale wash of their former splendor in the sandy brown stone of the desert. Deeper within the holy mountain, in the cool realm of Living Stone where the light never touched, those colors were true, deep and rich with life.

A hint of deeper glory hiding within the mountain, he thought. *How appropriate.*

The stone slab before him rustled; Talquist turned back to see a dark doorway appear in the shadows. He hurried inside.

Lasarys, the sexton of Terreanfor, stood just past the doorway, holding a dim lantern. Talquist noted, as the stone doorway swung shut again, blotting out the light, that the Earth priest's pale face was more sallow than usual.

"Good morrow, Lasarys," Talquist said solicitously. "How does this new day find you?"

"Very well, m'lord," the chief priest whispered. "And yourself?"

"Well, that depends, Lasarys. How has your project been coming?"

Lasarys swallowed visibly. "I—I have found a few more places to harvest, my lord."

"Excellent!" Talquist said, trying to contain his glee. He knew that shearing the flesh of the living earth was a task beyond onerous to Lasarys; as a cleric consecrated to the element, it was much like being asked to cut off one's own mother's breast. "Show me."

Lasarys bowed slightly and held up the cold light, illuminating the pathway down into the cathedral.

Terreanfor was the most ancient of the five basilicas dedicated to the elements, and the only one housed in Sorbold. It was old as the earth, one of the last repositories of Living Stone on the continent, and the most well known. The magic of the place was extant in the air; from the moment he came from the hot, dry wind of the outside world into the cool, moist depths of the hallways leading into Night Mountain, Talquist could feel its power.

He followed the shadow of the sexton through the winding tunnels he remembered from his days of servitude here, the dark walls gleaming in shades of green and rose, purple and blue as the light flickered over them. Living earth, unlike its dark counterpart, was alive with color.

The ceiling of the tunnel disappeared into a huge vault above them as they entered the temple proper. Lasarys extinguished his lantern; the only fire that was allowed within the outer hallways of Terreanfor had been kindled in a golden plate by the sun. Inside the basilica itself, no light was allowed save for the glowing phosphorescent stones that gleamed with a cold radiance of their own in the otherwise complete darkness.

They passed the first of the immense pillars shaped like trees that reached to the towering ceiling into the main apse, where a great menagerie of animal statues stood, life-sized sculptures of lions and gazelles, elephants and tirabouri that, carved as they were from living earth, seemed almost to breathe. Above, in the pillar trees, Living Stone birds were perched, their feathers the deep, rich colors of the earth in the cold light. Talquist thought he could almost hear them twitter.

Lasarys led him through the earthen garden to a pathway flanked by immense statues of soldiers, a score and ten of them, each standing ten feet in height atop a three-foot base. The stone warriors formed an arch with their primitive swords, their faces reflecting the features of the indigenous people who had lived in this place long before the Cymrians came, the people who had found and preserved Terreanfor, had carved the beautiful stone tributes within Terreanfor by planting within the living earth the seeds of the trees, the feathers of the birds, and an unknown essence of the animals that had grown, as if by magic, from it.

Finally, when they were standing in a dark alcove in which a bevy of earthen flowers grew, their petals shaped like tiny stars, Lasarys stopped, then slowly pointed at the ground.

"There," he said sadly. "I have been through the entire cathedral, and though it pains me greatly, I suppose if you must have more of the Living Stone, we can harvest one or two of these flowers. There are more of this kind than any other."

Talquist coughed, choking on a laugh, then cleared his throat and put his arm around the shoulder of the sexton.

"Lasarys, surely you jest." He gave the man a friendly squeeze, then released him, his face growing more solemn in the almost-dark. "I'm afraid you misunderstand, my friend."

He turned around and surveyed the stone garden, its trees and plants, flowers and lily pads all formed from Living Stone, pulsing in the light of the phosphorescent crystals. "When I asked you to harvest the stone that I used to tip the Scales in my favor, and end the Dynasty of the Dark Earth in favor of my ascension as Emperor, I needed only a small amount, because I had this." He reached into his robe and drew forth a tattered oval, slightly concave, violet in color had it been visible in the light. "The New Beginning; that's what this scale portends. Its power is older even than the Living Stone, or so the ancient books say. And between the stone you gave me, and the scale, that new beginning has come to pass.

"But it was only a beginning, Lasarys. What I plan requires much more than the tip of some ancient Scales, the rigging of a weighing. No, Lasarys, I have much bigger plans. When I am crowned emperor, I want my domain to be worthy of my vision. And I can see for miles, Lasarys." His eyes glowed brightly in the dark. "Thousands of miles."

The elderly priest began to tremble. "I don't understand, m'lord."

"That's all right, Lasarys, you don't need to. You served me well as a teacher many years ago, when I was your acolyte. I came to you long ago in the hopes that I would discover how to use this scale that I had found, buried in the sand of the Skeleton Coast. You were unable to shed any light on that for me, but it wasn't waste, any more than my apprenticeships with scholars and foresters, ships' captains and Filidic priests were, because in each place I looked for answers, I found other things that would one day complete the picture, like—well, like pieces of a puzzle." He smiled, pleased with his analogy. He held up the violet scale. "And this, Lasarys: this is the centerpiece."

"Yes, m'lord." Lasarys settled into quiet compliance, as he always did when the emperor began to pontificate in this manner.

"Where is the benison?" Talquist inquired. Nielash Mousa, the Blesser of Sorbold, was the chief cleric of the patrician faith in the nation, and one of the five benisons of the Patriarch, his highest religious councilors. Lasarys maintained Terreanfor under his supervision.

"He's—he's in Sepulvarta, at the Patriarch's meeting, with the other benisons. He won't be back for another six weeks."

"And he isn't scheduled to be in Terreanfor until the high holy days, on the first day of summer next year, correct?"

"Yes, m'lord," Lasarys whispered, a sickening feeling crawling through him.

"Excellent." Talquist's black eyes gleamed in the dark. He turned away from the garden and walked back to the arch of soldiers, their expressionless faces staring stalwartly above them. He pointed to the last in the line on his right.

"I think this will do nicely, Lasarys."

The sexton's eyes grew wide in the darkness. "The soldier, m'lord?" he asked in horror.

"Yes. I want you to harvest it."

"Which—which part of the soldier?"

"The whole soldier, Lasarys. I need a great deal of Living Stone, and he will provide just what I need."

The cleric choked audibly. "M'lord—" he whispered.

"Save your pleas, Lasarys—you are too deeply entrenched, and too deeply compromised, to protest now. I will return on the morrow, and when I do, I want you to have felled this statue and left it for me on the altar of Terreanfor. Use all of your acolytes to help you carry it so that it will not be damaged. Do be careful—I'm sure it is over two tons, possibly three. Slice it through the base to avoid damaging the feet; I will make use of whatever stone is left from the base as well." Talquist patted Lasarys, who was weeping silently, on the shoulder. "Cheer up, Lasarys. There is always pain in birth. And when you behold what is about to be born, and the nation that will come from it, you will finally understand its worth is a thousand times the suffering."

He turned and strode past the sexton and made his way through the dark cathedral back to the light and hot wind of the upworld.

JIERNA'SID, PALACE OF JIERNA TAL,
SORBOLD

*L*ater that afternoon, as he pored over the reports of the shipping transactions from the western coast, Talquist's eyes were drawn once more to the scale.

He paused in his work, putting down his quill long enough to reach out his hand and absently caress the brittle surface of it, to run his finger over the lines etched in it, the tiny tatters along its perimeter that looked like the edge of baleen from a whale.

How beautiful it is, he mused, recalling his first sight of it, as nothing more than a purple glimmer in the misty sand of the Skeleton Coast. He had known from the moment he first held it in the bleeding fingers of his hand, the flesh torn by digging it out of the volcanic sand, that it was an ancient thing, an artifact of great power. It had tasted his blood then, and had done so again recently.

He thought back to the night, in the height of the last summer, when he had placed it, his hands trembling slightly, on the Scales of Jierna Tal, the enormous instrumentality from the old world whose gigantic column and beam, balanced with large weighing plates of burnished gold, towered in the square outside the royal palace where the empress of Sorbold had reigned undisputed for three quarters of a century. Until that night, the dynasty of the Dark Earth had held the nation in a death grip of control.

He had changed that, had broken the death grip with a death blow of his own. And the violet scale had allowed him to do it.

The scale on one great golden plate; a totem of Living Earth, carved in the shape of the Sun Throne of Sorbold, had balanced the scale in the other plate.

Talquist glanced down at the back of his wrist, marred by a fading scar, a reminder of the last element of the equation—seven drops of his blood, freely given, counted meticulously as they fell, one by one, onto the scale in the plate.

A blood offering to join the one of Living Stone; his life essence on one side, the Earth's on the other.

The Scales had shifted; the bloody scale was lifted aloft, then the Scales balanced. The totem of Living Stone had burned to ash in a puff of crackling smoke.

And the power of the Dynasty of the Dark Earth had ripped in one metaphysical heartbeat from the hand of the empress to his own.

Later, amid great ceremony after the empress's death, each of the contenders to the throne from the various factions of Sorbold made their way to the Scales of Jierna Tal to be weighed against the Ring of State, the symbol of power. Each that stepped into the plate before him had been found wanting, until finally he took his turn and was lifted high, for all the assembly to see, by the holy artifact that had been used to make the most important of state decisions for centuries. The Scales, and the benison, had proclaimed him emperor, but Talquist, aware of the political instability caused by the sudden turn of events, had modestly offered to only be confirmed as regent for one year's time, after which, if the Scales confirmed him again, he would ascend as emperor.

And he was using that time well. The strictures the empress had put upon his trade were now gone; his domain over aspects of sea mercantile and indentured human labor was growing like wildfire. The arenas of bloodsport, once only tolerated by the Crown in a few places and strictly regulated, now were flourishing throughout the land; slave captures at sea and to the south, in the Lower Continent, were filling the mines and rocky hillside vineyards with much-needed workers. The coffers of the royal treasury were being filled handsomely.

In short, life was good.

And he owed all of it to his beautiful discovery, the ratty-edged scale of the New Beginning.

A knock at the study door shattered his musings.

"Come," Talquist said, closing his books and tucking the scale back inside the folds of his garment.

The chamberlain entered, a man of the same swarthy skin and dark chestnut hair as the rest of Sorbold bore, as Talquist himself had.

"M'lord, a representative from the Raven's Guild in Yarim has begged an audience with you under the auspices of the golden measure."

Talquist sat back in his chair. The golden measure was a guarded code, known only to hierarchs of guilds, a tradesman's countersign.

"Show him in."

The chamberlain stepped aside to allow the visitor to enter. The man moved through the doorway like a shadow, stepping instinctively around the patches of hazy afternoon light that shone dustily through the windows, clinging instead to the dark spots, blending in with them as he moved. He was dressed in the simple garb of a traveler, plain brown broadcloth cloak and trousers, his dark eyes glinting from within his hood. As he approached the emperor presumptive's desk, he took down his mantle to reveal a cadaverous face topped with thinning hair, with long tapers of sideburn joining the razor-sharp beard that darkened his cheeks like the shadows he traveled through.

"I bring you greetings on behalf of my cousin in the hills, m'lord," he said. "I am Dranth, scion of the Raven's Guild of Yarim."

Talquist rose slowly and gestured the man forward, sizing him up as he walked nearer. The code he had uttered was an even more secret one than that of the golden measure, used only in the gravest of times.

"To what do I owe the honor of a visit from the guild scion himself?" Talquist asked, pointing to a chair before his desk. "My condolences, by the way, on the demise of your guildmistress." He watched Dranth's face carefully for a sign of surprise that he knew of her death, but the man merely nodded. "I had not met her, nor had we done business together, but her reputation was well known to me."

"Doubtless," Dranth said dryly. "M'lord." He sat down slowly in the chair.

"Since you have approached me under the auspices of the golden measure, tradesman to tradesman, one guild hierarch to another, I am obliged to help you in whatever way I can, if the request be reasonable. What do you want?"

"Actually, I believe what I bring may be of aid to *you*, m'lord," Dranth said respectfully. He drew forth a parcel wrapped in sheepskin from within the folds of his cloak and laid it on the table in front of the emperor-to-be. "Please examine this."

Talquist nodded to the package. "Open it for me," he said pleasantly.

Dranth smiled. "Gladly, though you have nothing to fear from me of traps or poisons, m'lord. Your long life and robust health are quite important to me; you will see why in a moment."

He pulled from the sheepskin parcel a sheaf of documents, each in the spidery script of assassin's code, next to carefully rendered schematics of tunnels, bunkers, and breastworks.

"The guildmistress was doing reconnaissance in the Firbolg kingdom of Ylorc at the time of her death," Dranth said softly. Talquist noted that his voice was both sweet and poisonous, like the scent of almonds in arsenic. "She had gained the Bolg king's trust, and thereby had unfettered access to his inner sanctum, his secrets, and his plans. She sent back a great deal of information, including troop numbers and schedules, hallway and infrastructure diagrams, munitions caches, and a host of other very important material." He tossed the documents on the table in front of Talquist. "Among the other things she discovered was that he is planning to move against Sorbold."

Talquist snorted. "If he is, I've seen no evidence of it. The Bolg have been busy redecorating Canrif more than building up for war. King Achmed doesn't seem the land-grabbing type to me; he wants the demi-human monsters he reigns over to be seen as men, and to that end he is pursuing manufacturing and trade agreements, not war."

Dranth nodded thoughtfully. "What is he manufacturing?"

Talquist shrugged. "The Bolg produce a strange but interesting array of goods," he said. "They make a very light, very tensile rope, that is prized in the shipping trade. They also spin some finely delicate ladies' unmentionables, which has always amused me. A unique type of wood from their inner forests past the mountains bears a faint blue tint beneath its dark natural hue, and that is highly sought after, especially overseas."

"And they also make weapons," Dranth noted. "Extremely effective and deadly weapons."

"Yes."

"But while they have trade agreements with you to buy and broker their rope, their wood, and their lacy folderol, they do not sell you their weapons." Dranth smiled icily. "Do they?"

Talquist stared at the guild scion for a long time, then looked down at his desk and smiled.

"What score are you looking to settle with the Bolg?" he said finally, tracing the pattern of the wood grain in his desk.

"The death of our mistress," Dranth answered.

"And none other?"

"No. She was seeking revenge for another matter, the theft of water, but that is no longer of consequence. The Raven's Guild has sworn to avenge her death to the exclusion of all missions, or contracts, sparing no expense, no cost of any kind, human or otherwise, until the very end of Time, if necessary."

Talquist chuckled. "My. That is certainly a very intense sentiment." He looked up into the serious face of the guild scion, his smile dimming slightly.

"If you wanted my help in achieving your revenge, you should merely have requested it under the auspices of the golden measure. It is not required that I agree with your vendetta; only that it is not against my interests." His smile broadened. "And it is not."

Dranth nodded, relief in his eyes that was not mirrored on the rest of his face.

"In fact, I believe that if we join forces, we can both exact your revenge and further my plans very nicely." He pushed his chair back, rose, and walked slowly to the tall windows that overlooked the city's central square where the Scales stood, their immense wooden arm casting a dark, rectangular shadow over the streets. "First, you do understand that our conversations are guarded by the sacred vow of the guildmason?"

"Of course."

"And that, as brothers in the guild, we are sworn to deal honestly with one another?"

Dranth's brows narrowed. "The Raven's Guild abides by the same ethics and vows as all other guilds, m'lord. Our area of business notwithstanding."

"Do not misunderstand me, guild scion," Talquist demurred, opening his hands in a benign gesture. "I fully respect your guild's reputation and your expertise. I have dealt with many of your brother guilds in my time as guild hierarch in western Sorbold. I just need to know the truth—did the guildmistress truly uncover a plot by the Bolg to invade Sorbold, or—"

"No."

"Ah. Good. Well, then, pray join me at supper to discuss how we might be able to mutually achieve our ends." Dranth nodded, and Talquist rang for the chamberlain.

When the cordials were served, and the last of the trays taken away, Talquist leaned over the table.

"Now that I understand the capabilities of your organization, I believe I have a way to fulfill your request."

Dranth interlaced his fingers. "I'm listening."

"All of the intelligence you brought to me is genuine, except for your erstwhile claim that the Bolg intend to attack Sorbold, is that correct?"

"Yes," said the guild scion, his eyes darkening. "Why?"

Talquist swirled the liqueur in his snifter gently and inhaled the bouquet.

"What do you know of the kingdom of Golgarn?"

Dranth shrugged. Golgarn was a distant realm, to the southeast of Ylorc and Sorbold. The forbidding mountain passes of the Teeth prevented overland trade and travel between Roland and Ylorc to Golgarn, so the only real method of communication was by avian messenger, the only manner of trade by sea. "There is a brother guild there. Esten was in infrequent contact with them, on rare occasions when a debtor of one kind or another attempted to make his way there, or here, to outrun a debt. She always found them very cooperative, and reciprocated quickly. They are on friendly terms with Sorbold, are they not?"

"They are," Talquist agreed. "But not friendly enough." He took a sip of the golden liquid as Dranth raised a questioning eyebrow. "You will go to Golgarn, infiltrate their networks of information that make their way back to the king. And you will tell them the same fairy tale you told me—that you have incontrovertible evidence that the Bolg king is building up his army with the intent of invading them."

"They won't believe that any more than you did," Dranth said darkly. "They have the mountains to protect them. The Bolg tunnels do not approach their realm within five hundred miles."

Talquist grinned. "Yes, you are correct. If someone were to go to Beliac, the king, and tell him such a fanciful story as you told me, he would see through it immediately. Which is why you have to let him uncover the information himself." He drained his glass, then reached for the decanter to refill it. "If documents with the authenticity of these, enhanced a little to show that the Bolg actually have tunnels with *five* miles, rather than five hundred, of Golgarn, were to be found in, say, a raid of an establishment of questionable loyalty—such as your brother guild—it might cause Beliac to worry enough to go investigate."

Dranth poured himself another drink as well. "And what would he find, should he travel five miles into the mountains?"

"An encampment of Bolg preparing for war," Talquist said.

Dranth paused in the course of raising the glass to his lips. "But there are no Bolg there."

"There can be. At least enough to convince Beliac that he has a serious problem on his border."

"A charade? A simulated encampment?"

"Exactly."

"How? How will you persuade, intimidate, or capture enough Bolg to go along with such a farce? They are singularly loyal to their king and their commander, not to mention primitive and untrustworthy. I can't imagine they would be willing to stage such a charade, even under torture or pain of death."

Talquist took a sip, then opened his lips enough to allow air to pass over the burning liquid, filling his mouth with the vapors. He swallowed.

"Dranth," he said, leaning forward, "no one in Golgarn has ever seen a Bolg. Not since before the Cymrian War a thousand years ago, anyway. I could dress an ox or a gorilla in a pink camisole and prop it in the mountains with an ugly mask and a spear beside it, and the Golgarn would believe they were about to be invaded."

The guild scion stared at the regent for a moment. A hint of a smile cracked his otherwise impassive face; he saluted Talquist with his glass, then drank.

"So are you attempting to destroy Golgarn, then?" he asked. "Mislead them into attacking the Bolg?"

"Destroy Golgarn? Don't be ridiculous, Dranth. Golgarn is an important ally, and Beliac is my friend."

The guild scion shook his head in puzzlement. "I am not following your intent, then. Because if you convince the king of Golgarn that the Bolg are massing against him, and he attacks, the Bolg will eat him and the entire kingdom alive, literally."

"Beliac will not attack the Bolg," Talquist said. "At least not alone. He will turn to me. Sorbold has a force ten times the size of the army of Golgarn which, while sizable, is certainly ill prepared to act unilaterally. Beliac is an ally who doesn't even know that he has thrown his lot in with me yet. But he will soon."

"Your willingness to manipulate your friends so mercilessly is admirable," Dranth said, finishing his drink and replacing the snifter on the table, where it caught the firelight and reflected it, in a golden pool, on the desk. "Not many men have the viscera for it."

Talquist shrugged. "I'm a merchant, Dranth. You've heard the aphorism that we would sell our own mothers for a profit? Well, I actually did. Got a respectable price for her, too."

"And when the king of Golgarn joins you in an alliance against a fictional Bolg invasion, what will that gain you?"

"An army worthy of my plans," Talquist said.

"And what are those plans?"

The regent of Sorbold smiled. "I will let you figure that out," he said amiably, rising as if to indicate that the meal, and the conversation, were over. "Rest assured, your desire to see the Bolg king pay his debt to you will more than be accomplished. But I will share one more little secret with you, guild brother to guild brother: I need a northern ally as well. The Diviner in the Hintervold—he is also my friend, a dear one. Virtually all of the prosperity I enjoyed in my career as a merchant I owe to him; he even saved my life once. And when you see how cruel the methods are that I will use to secure his allegiance to my goals, you will fully appreciate how truly worthy I am to be considered a brother to your guild."

Talquist pulled up the linen hood of his robes of regency. "And now, Dranth, go with the chamberlain and have a rest; we have specific planning to do in the morning. I have other things to attend to. A carnival of freaks has come into town, and I have arranged for a private showing. I love oddities and the like. Good night."

16

℘he sun's departure was fading the sky to colors of cobalt and indigo
at the eastern edges, turquoise where the light still touched it in the west.
Talquist inhaled the evening breeze, cooler with night's approach and with
the turn of the seasons in more northern lands. In the desert of Sorbold, autumn was mostly just a slightly fresher gust of air in the morning and evening; otherwise, the endless desert sun continued to beat down, baking the
dry land into sand.

From his balcony he could see the firebrands of the traveling circus
burning steadily, sending light and thin trails of black smoke skyward in welcome, an invitation to him and him alone. He sighed; there was a time when
he was merely a powerful merchant that he would have been able to indulge
all of his darkest fantasies in such a place, but now that he was known to the
world as the emperor presumptive of Sorbold, he would be constrained to
merely wander between the wagons, amused, but unable to partake in some
of the more sinful pleasures that traveled with such sideshows. *A pity,* he
mused as he came away from the window and made his way down the stairs
to the place where the carnival waited. *Look, but don't touch. Ah, well.*

When he arrived at the gate of the circus, the Ringmaster was waiting
for him.

"Your Excellency," the Ringmaster said, bowing low, his striped silk
pants bending comically as he did.

"Oh, come now, Garth, you and I have done business for years now,"
Talquist admonished. "We've had many high times, have protected each
other's backs in several potentially deadly circumstances. There's no need to
be so formal, now that I am, well, emperor, for all intents and purposes. You
may address me as 'm'lord.'"

"Yes, m'lord," the Ringmaster muttered, opening the gate.

He followed the emperor-to-be through the dark pathways, in and out
of the tents, as Talquist admired the strange human inventory. In one tent,
they stopped before the small woman with almond-shaped eyes who sat,
chained by an enormous collar around her neck, on a small stool. The
woman recognized Talquist, and began to tremble violently, causing both
men to laugh aloud.

"Ah, the Gwadd! I had all but forgotten about her," Talquist said. He
leaned closer; the tiny woman shrank away in fear. "No need to worry, little
lovely," he murmured, "I'm afraid I'm too important to play with you anymore." He turned to the Ringmaster as they moved along through the exhibits. "You had best be careful if you go back into Roland that the Lord
Cymrian not discover you have her. Gwadd are not technically freaks; they

are old-world people, an ancient race that came over with the Cymrian exodus. She is thereby one of his citizens, and he will take action to free her and imprison you if he discovers her presence in your carnival."

"Now, how would the high and mighty Lord Gwydion do that, unless he were to be patronizing the Monstrosity himself?" the Ringmaster asked disdainfully. "My audiences don't tend to be the type who have luncheon invitations at Haguefort where they might accidentally drop my secrets to him."

"Too true," Talquist agreed, wandering in front of a fragile glass tank with a floating morass of wrinkled human flesh in the water. "Now, this is new. What sort of freak is this supposed to be?"

"We call it the Amazing Fish-boy," said the Ringmaster, tapping on the glass to waken the creature, "but as you can see, it could just as easily be the Amazing Fish-girl. We don't know what it is, exactly. I bought it from two imbecilic fishermen from Avonderre."

"Does it have a name?" Talquist asked, peering closer into the murky green water.

The Ringmaster shrugged. "Duckfoot Sally calls it Faron," he said.

The creature in the tank, waking and recognizing the Ringmaster, began to hiss menacingly. Its rubbery lips, fused in the center above soft, yellow teeth, gapped at the edges over its jaws, causing water to spurt out in streams of unmistakable anger.

"Good heavens," Talquist exclaimed, chuckling. "What a horror."

The creature hissed again, swimming forth in the tank to claw at the Ringmaster, hatred in its cloudy eyes.

"He seems to like you," Talquist said humorously, putting up a hand to avoid the spittle as the creature pressed its body against the glass, reaching for the Ringmaster.

In the light of the tent's lantern, his eye caught a flash of iridescent color, a quick twinge of a sparkle in the creature's abdomen as it futilely tried to grasp the Ringmaster with its gelatinous arms. He blinked, thinking that perhaps he had caught a grain of sand from the wind in his eye, then stared harder at the wrinkled freak's underbelly.

He had to watch for a moment, as the layers of fatless flesh undulated beneath the water, but a few seconds later he saw it again. There were spines of a sort protruding from between the skinfolds, as if they had been tucked there, the tips of oval scales that looked very much like the violet one in his possession. Talquist felt the cold rush of excitement spread through his body, the blood rushing away from his racing brain to a heart that was racing faster, leaving him weak, perspiring.

He coughed to cover his excitement. "Where did the fishermen find this—this thing?" he inquired, trying to keep his voice light, his manner nonchalant.

The Ringmaster shrugged. "They didn't say. Probably tangled in a net somewhere. Well, come along, *m'lord*, and I will show you our new man-eater." He took hold of the flap of the tent's exit.

"Wait," Talquist said, his voice hardening at the edges. He continued to stare at the creature in the tank, but it shrank away from the glass, turning its back and glaring balefully over its skeletal shoulders at the Ringmaster.

The Ringmaster let go of the tent flap and came back to stand beside the Regent, his eyes gleaming at the sight.

"It is a truly amazing freak," he said, frank admiration on his face. "In all my years of travel, I have not come upon one quite so grotesque, quite so hideous, that was still alive. It's been a windfall—our gate has increased enormously ever since I bought him."

"I want him," Talquist said impulsively. "Name your price."

The words knocked the Ringmaster speechless; he laughed shortly, as if he had been hit in the midsection.

"Do be serious," he said a moment later, forgetting he was addressing the Emperor Presumptive.

"I am entirely serious," insisted Talquist. "I will give you ten times what you paid for him."

The Ringmaster shook his head. "I have made that back already," he said, his face beginning to harden at the unwanted negotiation. "He is not for sale, *m'lord*."

Talquist's hands were starting to sweat. "Twenty times, then."

The Ringmaster turned his back and walked to the tent flap again. "That thing guttles down a gallon of eels in a sitting; it has eaten all but a dozen of my breeding goldfish, thanks to Duckfoot Sally, who risks stripes across her back to give it treats. It is tremendously hard to maintain and sickly to boot. Besides, what possible use could you have for it? No, m'lord, I cannot sell him to you, and as your friend, I cannot imagine you really want him. Come along, and I will show you some new horrors almost as fascinating." He looked over his shoulder nervously; the regent was still staring at the fish-boy, entranced. Another thought occurred to him in his desperation. "I also have a new pleasure wagon; I could have the keepers stand guard if you would like some private entertainment, much as in the old days—"

Talquist turned and shot him a look that stung like an arrow in his forehead. "My final offer—twenty times what you paid for him, and your safe passage from my lands." The threat in his voice was unmistakable.

The Ringmaster inhaled deeply, then let his breath out slowly, seething silently. "Very well. I paid two hundred gold crowns for him—plus two," he added quickly, still rankling at the thought of the arrogant fisherman.

"You're a liar," Talquist said contemptuously, "but I don't care. I will send my soldiers to get him in two hours. They will deliver your money then, but I will be paying you in gold Sorbold suns—our coins are worth two Orlandan crowns."

"I expect you'll want his food as well," the Ringmaster said angrily. "You are unlikely to have the amount of fish he requires in the middle of this desert. That'll be costly."

"That won't matter, keep your food," the emperor presumptive replied, his eyes never leaving the tank. "Now leave. I want to observe my new purchase for a while without you. It's obvious he doesn't like you much."

He continued to stare into the green water, watching the pale, fishlike creature, its cataract-covered eyes following the Ringmaster out of the tent and into the darkness of the Monstrosity.

17

Achmed's suspicious nature was an entrenched part of the culture he had established in Ylorc, and occasionally it made for unusual protocols that would be unrecognizable in most courts on the continent. His leavetaking was generally a closely guarded secret; whenever the king vacated the mountain, it was done not with the pomp and ceremony favored by many monarchs, but under cover of darkness, with as little folderol as possible, to minimize the number of people who even knew he was gone. The only instance that caused a deviation from this custom was when it suited Achmed's purposes for his known enemies, as well as his unknown ones, to be aware that he was away.

The Sergeant-Major participated in the charade willingly, knowing that it served to quiet Achmed's raging paranoia to a small degree. He did not waste his time or breath explaining to the Bolg king that every beating heart within Achmed's kingdom was more than aware when he left, primarily because they could feel the tension break palpably. Within a few hours of Achmed's departure, virtually every one of his subjects that lived in the tunnels of the mountains before the Blasted Heath had felt his absence, and had breathed a little easier because of it.

Achmed himself was beginning to pick up the threads of this paradox—that the only thing his subjects feared more than his absence was his presence—and it served to make him even more irritable, even more anxious. Secretly he was looking forward to seeing Rhapsody for reasons other than the ones he had stated to Grunthor. Her natural music, the vibration she emitted into the air around her, was the one sensation he had found in his lifetime that soothed the angry nerves and exposed veins in his skin, that quieted the natural prickliness of his odd physiology. For all that his journey was one of self-interest and holding people to their promises, he was almost eager to get under way so that for a short time he might find a little bit of physical peace while extracting favors owed him.

So it was with more than a little annoyance that he found himself delayed in his own throne room, a satchel in one hand, the glass calipers in the other, by the arrival of Kubila, the Archon of Trade and Diplomacy, who nervously hovered at the entranceway to the Great Hall, awaiting permission to come in.

"What is it?" the king said crossly, gesturing for the young man to enter.

The Archon cleared his throat. "There is an ambassador here to see you, sire."

"An *ambassador?*" Achmed demanded incredulously. "It's the middle of the night."

"Yes, sire," Kubila replied uncomfortably. He, like the other Archons, was not in particular fear of the king; Achmed treated them with enough respect to prevent that. But he was also aware of the import hovering in the air, and it chilled him.

"Idiot," the king muttered, switching the satchel to his other hand. "Send him away."

The Bolg diplomat cleared his throat again. "Sire, this man has come from very far off. It might be wise to entertain his request; he claims he needs but a moment of your time."

"I don't care if he sailed from the Lost Island of Serendair," Achmed retorted. He inclined his head toward the door behind the throne; Grunthor nodded and started for it.

"Sire, this ambassador is from the Nain," Kubila stuttered.

The sound went out of the vast room. Achmed froze in his tracks, then turned slowly to eye the trembling Archon. He inhaled deeply, and exhaled deliberately. Then he handed the satchel to Grunthor.

"I will meet you there," he said, giving him the glass calipers. The Sergeant nodded.

Achmed waited until the giant had left the room, then turned to Kubila.

"Send him in," he said curtly.

Kubila nodded, then returned to the main doorway. He pulled open one of the two enormous doors that had been carved and gilt with pure gold in Gwylliam's time, then stepped out of the way.

A moment later a man strode into the room. He was broad of neck and shoulder, with a chest shaped like a wine barrel and strong, sturdy legs. His height was less than Achmed's own by half a head, but his bearing was straight and proud enough to give the illusion that he was as tall as the king. His beard, which hung to the center of his chest, was brown at the chin, silver in the middle, and white at the curling tips. His skin was tawny with a sallow undertone, the sign of a life lived within the mountains away from the sun, yet exposed to the intense heat of forge fire. As he entered the room Achmed saw the light of the wall torches catch his face, causing the blue-yellow tapetum at the back of the man's eyes to glow in the dim hall like those of a feral animal.

"Well met, sire." The man saluted Achmed briskly. "I am Garson ben Sardonyx, sent as an emissary of His Majesty, Faedryth, Lord of the Distant Mountains."

"I know who you are," Achmed said snidely. "I suffered your presence, and that of many of your kind, during my investiture, and later at the Cymrian Council four years ago. Your contingent consumed ten times the victuals and spirits as all the other delegations combined, and left an unholy mess that has only recently been scoured clean. What do you want?"

The veneer of politeness vanished in a twinkling from the Nain's eyes. He reached unconsciously for the end of his beard and angrily smoothed it into place.

"I can see you are in a pleasant mood, as always, Your Majesty," he said testily. "As am I. Receiving a visit at midnight in Ylorc can only be slightly less foul than having to make one. I needed to catch you before you left for the winter carnival in Navarne, to which I know you have been invited. I will be brief; I have come with a direct message from His Majesty, King Faedryth."

"And what is it?" demanded Achmed impatiently.

The Nain ambassador's gaze met the Bolg king's and did not waver.

"He knows that you are attempting to reconstruct the Lightforge," he said, his voice heavy with import. "He bids me to tell you that you must not."

For a full score of heartbeats the Bolg king and the Nain ambassador locked eyes in silence. Then the mismatched pair belonging to Achmed narrowed behind his veils.

"You traveled all the way from your lands to dare to instruct me in such a manner? You're a brave man with too much time on his hands."

Garson did not blink. "My king commanded it."

"Well, I am puzzled, then," said Achmed, sitting down on the chair of ancient marble scored with channels of blue and gold giltwork. "I know of no Lightforge. And yet Faedryth has risked my ire, which as you know is considerable, by sending you to barge into my rooms in the middle of the night to issue me an *order* regarding it? Even I, who places less stock in diplomacy and matters of etiquette than anyone I know, find that offensive."

"Perhaps you do not call it by the same name," said Garson evenly, ignoring the king's objections. "But I suspect you know to what I refer. The Lightforge is an instrumentality that the Nain built for Lord Gwylliam the Visionary eleven centuries ago, a machine formed of metal and colored glass embedded into a mountain peak, which manipulated light to various ends. It was destroyed in the Great War, as it should have been, because it tapped power that was unstable, unpredictable. It poses a great threat not only to your allies and enemies, but to your own kingdom as well. You are attempting to rebuild something you do not fully understand; your foolishness will lead to your destruction, and very possibly that of those around you. You have already seen the effects of this. The tainted glass from your first attempt still litters the countryside. This is folly of unspeakable rashness. King Faedryth commands that you cease at once, for the good of the Alliance, and for your own as well."

The Bolg king's hands went to his lips, where they folded in a contemplative gesture. He stared at the Nain diplomat, who remained rooted to his spot on the polished marble of the Great Hall floor. Then a crooked smile crossed the lower half of his hidden face, visible in his eyes.

"And how precisely do you know of all this?" he asked casually. "Your hidden kingdom is so distant that it cannot be reached even by extended mail caravans; the Nain are all but invisible in the sight of the world. If the ocean separated us we could not be more isolated from one another; how is it that you are so aware of my undertakings?"

"King Faedryth makes it his business to monitor events that could have a disastrous impact on the world, sire," Garson said haughtily. "Information finds its way to him when it is important that it do so."

Achmed's amusement dissipated, and he rose from his seat slowly, deliberately, like a snake preparing to strike.

"Liar," he said contemptuously. "The Nain turned their backs on the world four centuries ago; you have no interest in the day-to-day goings-on of the world outside your own, and no means of hearing of them, even if you did have the interest. And yet here you are, telling me the details of the most secret of my projects, at the command of a king who believes he has the domain to tell me what to do about it?"

He walked down the aisle and stood directly in front of the Nain ambassador, looking down into his smoldering eyes.

"You have one yourself," Achmed said levelly. "You have built your own instrumentality, and you make use of its scrying ability to spy on my lands. It's the only way you could have known."

Garson glared at him in stony silence.

Achmed turned his back on the ambassador and returned to his seat. "Get out of my kingdom at once," he ordered, gesturing to Kubila, who had remained in a shadow at the back of the Great Hall. "Return to your king and tell him this from me: I once had respect for him and the way he conducts his reign; he has as low an opinion of the Cymrians as I do, and is a reticent member of the Alliance, just as I am. He keeps to himself within his mountains, as do I. But if he continues to spy into my lands, or send emissaries who tell me what to do, when my own version of your so-called Lightforge is operational, I will be testing out its offensive capabilities on distant targets. I will leave it to you to guess which ones."

"I doubt very much that you wish me to convey that message to Faedryth," said the ambassador.

"Doubt it not, Garson. Now leave."

Achmed waited until the Nain diplomat had stalked out of the Great Hall, then turned to Kubila.

"Have Krinsel waiting here for me when I return."

Grunthor was putting the calipers back in their leather case when Achmed appeared at the summit of the mound of gravel and ash that served as the final barrier in the Earthchild's sepulcher.

The giant said nothing as the Bolg king approached, but Achmed could see, even at a distance, the quiet despair in his eyes. When he finally reached the catafalque on which the Child lay, he could see the shadowy outline of where she had lain the last time they had been in this dark place, her body smaller within it.

"The withering continues," he said aloud. He spoke the words just to give voice to them; before that they were hanging painfully in the air, heavy above his head.

Grunthor merely nodded and laced the caliper case shut.

Achmed brushed his gloved hand delicately over the Earthchild's hair, parched golden brown now as the dry wheat chaff on the steppes beyond the mountains. Then he followed Grunthor back up the passageway to the Cauldron again.

Krinsel was waiting in the Great Hall, as he had commanded. She appeared slightly haggard, her dusky face grim but expressionless, having passed most of the night on her feet at attention, awaiting his return. In her hands she bore the list of casualties, the victims of the Sickness that still lingered in their torment, their conditions detailed in notes carefully documented by the midwives and their aides who had been tending to them.

"Any new deaths?" Achmed asked as he came to a halt before her.

The head midwife shook her head.

The Bolg king nodded. "I believe we've come to the end of the main wave of casualties," he said, nodding his readiness to leave to Grunthor. "Those that survived the picric exposure and are still alive will probably make it. Gurgus has been scoured of all traces of it, as have the hillsides on which the dust from the explosion fell. All that is left now is to try and make those who are recovering comfortable, and to attempt to return to normal as quickly as possible. Do you agree?" The midwife nodded again. "Good. Then I will be on my way. I will be traveling a route parallel to the guarded caravan, so if you need to reach me, have Trug send out a hawk."

"Tell 'Er Ladyship Oi said hullo," Grunthor said dryly as Achmed made his way to the doorway that would lead him through the exit tunnels of the Cauldron, out through the breastworks and onto the open steppes beyond. "An' don't forget my sugared almonds. If we're gonna put the kingdom at risk, we might as well 'ave somethin' nice to eat. On second thought, bring back any Lirin ya might see at the carnival. Especially the dark-'aired variety; they 'ave the best flavor."

"I'll be back in a fortnight," the Bolg king said. "And when I return, nothing had better have exploded, imploded, or shattered—unless it's the head of that ambassador from the Nain."

$\mathcal{T}$raveling through the earth was a mixed blessing, the dragon found.

There was a power around her now that had been missing in the frozen wasteland of her lair, a warmth and vibrancy she could feel in the strata of the crust of the world. The earth welcomed her, though it was a somewhat cold welcome still. The return of her name had brought back only fragments of memories; still lost were the ones that tied her to the element from which her mother's line had sprung.

Below the ground, the song that had echoed her call was harder to hear, muffled, though still ringing somewhere in the distance. The dragon was never completely certain of its bearings, and in her singlemindedness she often found herself doubling back, confused by the echo of it. Her mind, once as brilliantly honed as a gleaming blade, was still thick, confused easily, and frequently she found, to her dismay bordering on rage, that she had circled back, or lost the path, or taken a route through the darkness that had misdirected her.

Still, the wail in the distance remained, guiding her southward, returning her to the path when she lost her way.

It may take time to get there, she thought after one particularly disappointing diversion. *But when I do, what I find will be worth it.*

The bloodlust within her heart burned brighter in the darkness of the earth.

18

THE SEXTON'S MANSE, HILLSIDE ABUTTING NIGHT MOUNTAIN, JIERNA'SID

At midnight that night Talquist pounded on Lasarys's door.

It took the sexton of Terreanfor a few minutes to answer, hurrying to the door of the manse set in a rocky grotto outside Night Mountain, half-dressed, opening it in between outbreaks of violent knocking. As soon as the latch was lifted and the door open a crack, the Emperor Presumptive pushed his way inside.

"My—m'lord," Lasarys gasped, clutching at his nightshirt, the candle in his elderly hand trembling so that wax dripped onto his forearm, "what—what's wrong?"

"Is it done?" Talquist demanded, shutting the manse door quickly. "The soldier—is it felled?"

The sexton hung his head and sighed. "Yes," he said dispiritedly. "And wrapped in linen soaked in holy water. But it has not been transported to the altar yet."

"Good—belay that and bring it instead to the square of Jierna'sid."

"Now?" The sexton looked horrified.

"Yes, now. Summon your acolytes; wake them."

"They—they are exhausted, m'lord. It was a very emotional and difficult day."

The Emperor Presumptive's face hardened in the candlelight. "It will be a difficult night as well, but then they can rest. Go get them, Lasarys."

"Yes, m'lord." The sexton disappeared into the darkness of the manse.

$\mathcal{I}$t took every acolyte in the temple's monastery to drag the dray sled containing the giant statue of Living Stone to the square in front of the palace of Jierna Tal.

Talquist had ordered his guard, the mountain regiment dedicated to protecting Jierna Tal, and thereby the emperor, to ring the pathway between Night Mountain and the square where the Scales stood, to keep the peasantry away. They had maintained the evening's peace with little difficulty; no one lived in the square around the Scales except the occupant of the palace, and so it was possible to have a large wagon pull into the square in the middle of the night without notice.

Lasarys, who had been silent and pale throughout the journey, watched in trepidation as the acolytes slowly unloaded the wagon, carefully bearing the wrapped figure between a score of them by bracing it with heavy timbers and carrying them, two men to a beam, slowly up the steps to the weighing platform on which the Scales stood. As the priests placed the huge statue onto the easternmost of the two weighing plates he finally turned to Talquist, anguish in his voice.

"What are you doing, m'lord?" he whispered desperately. "Please tell me that this desecration has some meaning, some higher reason. I feel as if I have perpetuated an atrocity for which the Earth Mother will never forgive me."

Talquist turned and watched the suffering priest with eyes that a moment before had been shining with excitement, now dimmed into the soft light of compassion.

"Lasarys, take heart. What we do here is not destruction, or desecration— it's a rebirth." He patted the sexton's arm comfortingly. "Do you remember, all those years ago when I was your acolyte, how you would tell me the tales of the formation of Terreanfor? How it was believed that the ancient peoples planted seeds of the flowers and leaves from the trees, and that the Living Stone, still alive and full of the power of creation, grew those glorious statues that still grace the basilica? That the animals and birds were carved in the same way, by the earth itself, from some piece of those selfsame animals?" Lasarys nodded distantly. "Then, Lasarys, if that be the case, where do you think those statues of soldiers came from?"

The sexton blanched. "I—I have no idea," he stammered.

"Is it possible, Lasarys, that they are, in fact, buried heroes from early days, interred in the warmth of the living earth, grown into statues to honor them as great warriors?"

"Yes, it is possible, m'lord, but whatever—whatever is given into the Earth Mother's arms should be left there," said Lasarys haltingly. "It is folly to try and take it back, to raise the dead. It is against nature."

Talquist's brows drew together in displeasure. "I am not trying to raise the dead, Lasarys," he said sharply, watching the acolytes remove the beams from beneath the statue, now lying on the weighing plate. "I am merely trying to tap life that is unused—to transfer it, so to speak." He nodded benevolently to the acolytes who were wiping their brows and who had signaled that their task was complete. "Well done, gentlemen. Thank you." He turned to the captain of his guards and spoke loudly enough for the acolytes to hear him.

"Take these holy men into the palace, where a repast has been prepared for them. After they've supped, lead them to the wagons, return them to their beds at the monastery, and withdraw, that they might rest themselves after such a difficult task—all but two." The weary acolytes bowed and followed the captain of the guard into the palace.

Talquist gestured to the soldiers as the two priests, Dominicus and Lester, came to Lasarys's side and stood, exchanging questioning glances but otherwise still.

"Bring out the creature's tank," the regent ordered.

Slowly a dray cart was wheeled out from the royal stables, wrapped in canvas. The priests continued to watch as the tank was unwrapped, then shattered. From the detritus a creature was lifted, pale and sickly in shape, its flesh hanging limply from bones that appeared to be little more than cartilage.

"Sweet All-God, what is that?" Dominicus whispered to Lasarys, but the sexton silenced him by raising a hand.

The creature in the soldiers' grasp hissed and flailed weakly, but was no match for the men in armor. They bore their struggling burden up the steps to the Scales and deposited it into the empty western weighing plate, then stretched its curved arms out and weighed them down with bags of sand. Finally, when it stopped struggling, the soldiers withdrew as well, leaving Lasarys, the two acolytes, and Talquist alone in the square, their footsteps echoing away into the emptiness. A moment later they could hear the distant clattering of cartwheels, as the wagon bearing the acolytes made its way from the cobbled streets of the city to the hillside monastery next to the sexton's manse where they lived.

Silence returned to the streets of Jierna'sid.

The regent of Sorbold slowly mounted the steps to the ancient instrumentality, the Place of Weight, where the golden pans had weighed decisions of life and death, war and peace, the survival of nations, and the overthrow of despots for millennia, in this land and the one before it, now sleeping beneath the sea on the other side of the world.

"Lasarys," he said softly, "unwrap the statue."

The sexton remained frozen for a moment, then reluctantly nodded to the two acolytes. Together the three holy men gently removed the wet linen wrappings while Talquist continued to gaze at the Scales as if in a trance.

Beneath its linen coverings the statue was still warm from the heartbeat of the Earth in the Living Stone, its smooth clay flesh pulsing with a static hum. The extreme edges of it, where the shoes were carved, the rough-hewn sword in its right hand, and the tips of the mail gauntlet on its empty left hand had begun to harden into lifeless clay, but otherwise it was still damp, still multicolored clay formed into a tall man with irisless eyes, staring blindly up into the night sky, its heavy features expressionless.

Once the statue was laid bare, Talquist moved silently in front of the priests to gaze down at the enormous piece of Living Stone. He ran his hand over the massive shoulders gently, almost lovingly, his face transfixed in an excitement that bordered on holy ecstasy.

"Imagine, Lasarys," he whispered, "imagine all that can be done here. I have been planning this since before my ascension—the first time I saw those soldiers, I knew they held the power of an entire army in each one of them! I am the keeper of the scale of the New Beginning—don't you understand, Lasarys, these things are meant to work together! This is the key to all of the plans I have been crafting since I discovered the power of the violet scale. If the Scales can take the life essence of a useless freak, a barely alive piece of flesh, and put it into this stone soldier? If it can stand watch, alive, over my palace, unmoving but animate, it would be a wonderful guard, a fearsome deterrent to any who might try to enter in malice. And if it can move—if only it can move! It might be the perfect weapon, a stone neolith functioning completely under my command, perhaps able to understand the same primitive commands as the being whose life was sacrificed to animate it? Imagine then an army of them—every statue of Terreanfor harvested and brought to life? Not just the twenty or so in the cathedral, but the hundreds, perhaps thousands down in the City of the Dead in the crypt below? Just imagine—"

"This is heresy, m'lord," Lasarys whispered in return. "I pray you, you do not know what you are doing. The properties of Living Stone are all but unknown to us. It is a gift of the Creator, a primordial element, a rare treasure—"

"Get out of the way, Lasarys," Talquist said impatiently, shoving the sexton aside and crossing to the other plate where the pale, limp form of the freak he had purchased that evening was outstretched.

"Good evening, Faron," he said pleasantly, watching the recognition come into the creature's eyes. "Can you understand me?"

The fish-boy's heavily veined eyelids closed over its milky eyeballs, as if it were squinting, but it did not otherwise respond.

As I thought, Talquist noted. *Only animal-level intelligence. Like a dog, it can respond to its name, perhaps simple commands. Good.*

He examined the heavy layers of skin that made wrinkled folds around the creature's stomach. Tucked within them were three tips of hard, multicolored material, dried with blood from the creature.

"This must be painful," he said soothingly to the freak on the plate in front of him, gently running a finger over the top of the skinfold. "Allow me to hold on to them for you."

He carefully lifted the flap of skin and slid out the first tip; as he expected, it was a scale much like his own, the same gray hue but with a flash of yellow as it slid forth from the creature's belly. Faron moaned in agony, but Talquist was not deterred; he continued to remove both of the other scales, all part of the same original set, ignoring the trembling of the creature from which they had come. He held them up to the light of the torches in the square.

The tattered ovals were of the same multihued gray that his prized scale was, scored with tiny, geometric patterns like the hide of a reptile. When they caught the firelight they gleamed prismatically, as if all the colors of the spectrum were contained within them, yet each had a dominant hue; one yellow, one red, and one a dark blue the color of indigo blossoms. Each bore a crude etching on it, runes in a language, like his own scale, that he could not read.

Years before he had translated the writing on the violet scale by finding a key to the language, the tongue of the Ancient Seren race, in the dusty museum of Haguefort, the ancestral home of Stephen Navarne, the Cymrian historian. He had also found a sketch of his own scale. It was in an old relic, the fragment of a tome entitled *The Book of All Human Knowledge* that had been rescued from the sea. Most of the book had been destroyed by the salt water, but in the few pages that remained intact, he had read of a deck of cards owned by a Seren seer named Sharra, and had come to believe that his scale was part of the deck. It was said that, in the hands of someone possessed of Firstborn blood, blood of a race that had descended from one of the primordial elements, the scales had power, power to see things the eye could not see, to heal wounds that could not otherwise be healed, to bring about change that otherwise would never happen.

Power unimaginable.

This is the deck, he thought, his hands sweating in excitement. *These scales must be part of Sharra's deck.*

The creature in the plate hissed at him angrily.

"Where did you get these, Faron?" Talquist asked, almost to himself.

He reached into the folds of his robe and drew forth the violet scale, then held it up with the others to the flickering light.

The milky eyes of the creature widened.

All the scales matched.

Talquist's hands grew warm. At first he was unaware of the sensation, believing it was merely the result of his excitement, perspiration, and the ferocious beating of his heart. A moment later he realized that the scales themselves were generating the heat, as if together they were unlocking some distant cache of heat, of fire.

They recognize each other.

"Lasarys," Talquist said softly, "give me your ceremonial dagger."

"M'lord—"

The regent's hand shot out with finality, its palm open.

Lasarys sighed, drew forth his dagger made of polished obsidian, and placed it regretfully in Talquist's hand.

"You may leave now," the emperor presumptive said, finality in his voice. "Go sup, and return to the monastery with your fellow clerics. You have served me well."

Lasarys and the acolytes exchanged a glance, then hurried away from the Place of Weight. Dominicus and Lester started for the door where the other acolytes had been led, but Lasarys raised a hand and silently stopped them. He glanced back over his shoulder and, seeing that they were unobserved, led them to a sheltered spot near the palace wall where they could continue to watch the atrocity unfold.

The regent placed the three scales atop the creature's belly, returning his own to the folds of his garment. He took the knife and held it up before his eyes, then lowered it to Faron's heart.

In the shadows, the acolytes and the sexton stood, transfixed in horror, as Talquist carefully scored the freak's skin with the sharp stone blade, then dipped it into the line of black blood. He walked back to the plate where the stone soldier lay and stood above it, knife in hand. Then he deposited black drops, one by one, onto the plate of the Scales, ignoring the whimpers of pain issuing forth from the grotesque mouth of the creature in the other plate.

Each drop fell with a ringing sound.

In the darkness, the Scale plates began to gleam, the chains that hung from the arm of the instrumentality taking on their light.

Slowly, the plate with the heavy stone statue began to rise, balancing against the plate with the helpless creature.

Through their tears, the Earth priests watched, their faces pale and gray with the sweat of revulsion, as the Living Stone soldier and the twisted body of the creature began to shine with a painful radiance. The light grew brighter, more intense with each passing second, until the radiance became too agonizing to bear. Lasarys, Lester, and Dominicus shielded their eyes, just as the misshapen form on the one plate burst into dark flames, black fire that stank with rancid fumes, and withered to ash.

The Scales balanced.

Then the eastern plate thudded to the ground. The western plate rocketed aloft at the change in weight, the cinders that had once been the body of the creature exploding into the air with the sudden blast of force, then catching the night breeze and wafting away.

The light vanished, plunging the square of Jierna'sid into lantern-lit darkness again.

At first there was no sign of life at all.

Talquist stood, rooted to the spot at the foot of the Scales, his eyes darting from the immobile statue in the eastern plate to the empty western plate, now devoid even of ash.

Then, after a moment, the giant soldier let out an enormous shudder and exhalation of breath.

The vibrant striations of color deepened as the statue took its first gulp of air, the multicolored strand of purple and vermilion, green and rust took on the gleam of life and breath.

The eyes, without irises to break the stone-colored sclera, blinked.

"Praise be the Earth Mother," whispered Talquist.

The statue's limbs flexed awkwardly. Slowly the arm without the sword moved; the soldier raised its empty hand up before its rough-hewn face. The fingers curled inward, then stretched arthritically.

"Rise," Talquist commanded.

The statue turned its head in the regent's direction.

"I said *rise*," Talquist repeated, his tone harsher. A thought occurred to him, and though he felt foolish doing so, he spoke the name of the creature whose life had been sacrificed to animate the statue. "Faron."

The soldier's head jerked in Talquist's direction.

The regent exhaled in disappointment. Not having any true understanding of the power of the Scales as regarded Living Stone, he had hoped that the blood sacrifice of the creature would form the living incarnation of whatever ancient warrior of the indigenous people of the old continent had been buried in the Living Stone of Terreanfor. Instead it appeared that the entity was actually the embodiment of the freak itself he had purchased from the Monstrosity, mindless as a fish. But his dismay fled quickly upon seeing the statue flex its arms again. *Next time I will be certain to sacrifice a human with a good and capable mind,* he thought, still pleased with the sight of the ten-foot soldier, formed of clay, breathing and moving on its own.

The statue rolled suddenly to one side and fell heavily out of the weighing plate, thudding loudly on the boards of the stand on which the Scales stood. It curled up at first like a baby in the womb, scratching the hand that held the rough sword against the wooden boards, as if trying to rub it off.

Talquist started to step forward but stopped quickly as the enormous soldier brought its right hand violently on the Scale platform, slapping the sword repeatedly against the planks. It scratched at the stone weapon with an urgency that made panic start to rise in Talquist's throat.

"No, Faron, that's a sword. It's all right—do not try to disarm yourself—"

In response, the giant figure began to peel the sword from its left hand with the other.

"Faron—"

With a brutal wrench, the statue tore the stone sword from its hand and heaved it across the platform at Talquist. The regent dodged out of the way just in time to avoid being crushed by it. Then slowly the Living Stone soldier pushed itself awkwardly to its knees.

Talquist watched with mounting concern as the giant struggled to stand, as if believing its limbs were flexible, soft. *It remembers its old form,* he thought as the statue dragged itself to its feet. It reached down to the ground around it and hurriedly and clumsily gathered its scales, dropping them several times in the process.

"Faron, I command you, stop!" Talquist shouted.

The living statue stared for a moment, its irisless eyes fixed on the scales in its hands. Then it lurched forward, awkwardly locomoting toward the steps of the platform, clutching the three scales.

Talquist raised his own hands for Faron to stop, then, seeing that the moving titan was thundering toward him without any sign of halting, dove out of the way just in time to avoid being trod beneath its feet. The titan stumbled down the stairs and out into the cobbled streets of the square of Jierna'sid, where it fell heavily to the ground. Again it curled, as if unsure of its legs, then slowly, deliberately rose, casting an enormous shadow in the faint light of the torches.

"Faron!" Talquist called again, but weakly; having seen the stone musculature flex, his voice was strangled by the rictus of fear.

The thud of boots could be heard coming up one of the feeder streets to the square.

A squad of four soldiers approached, running, shouting to each other. They stopped dead in the shadow of the towering statue.

"No!" Talquist shouted, but Faron had already begun to move, lurching down the feeder street toward the guards. "Get out of the way!" he screamed.

Two of the soldiers obeyed blindly, dashing toward the palace walls.

Another hesitated a moment, then threw himself behind a cart for cover. The fourth was frozen to the spot; he raised his halberd in defense, the polearm shaking.

The titan of Living Stone slammed him into the palace wall as if he were no more than a pile of rags. A sickening *crack* resounded through the streets as his body hit the wall, the reverberation of bones shattering.

The animated statue did not pause; it gained speed along with its footing, quick strides blending into a running gait. It hurried down the streets toward the battlements, melting into the darkness, heading for the open ledges of sandy mountain crags that ringed the city of Jierna'sid.

Numb, Talquist rose to a stand and stared into the shadows, trying to find some sign of the titan, but seeing nothing but night and torches that had burned down to the stalk-joints. He continued gazing into the distance until the leader of the squad knelt before him, the two surviving soldiers behind him, bearing the shattered corpse of the fourth.

"M'lord?"

"Yes?" Talquist answered distantly.

"What was that?"

"A bad idea," the emperor presumptive murmured, running the toe of his boot along the edge of the great earthen sword that had been ripped from the statue's hand. The clay rim cracked and tumbled like sand onto the stones of the street.

He continued to watch the empty street. "And a terrible waste. A harvest of living earth that is about to crumble to dust, unused." Finally he turned, as if shaking off sleep, and looked down at the body at his feet.

"You," he said to the two soldiers who carried their dead compatriot, "take him to the monastery at Terreanfor. Leave him on the steps." He looked directly at the leader. "Are all the holy men back in the monastery and the manse?"

"Yes, m'lord."

"Good. Once you have left the body, return to the barracks. The acolytes will attend to his burial. Speak to no one of what you saw, on pain of execution. Tell the others as well. If word returns to me on this matter, I will know from whence it came."

"Yes, m'lord." The soldier bowed and hurried to catch up to the other two.

As soon as the soldiers were out of sight, Talquist went to the gates of Jierna Tal and summoned his captain of the guard.

"Have the monastery and the manse been prepared with oil and magnesium?"

The captain nodded silently.

"Good. There are three soldiers headed there now with the body of a fourth. As soon as the soldiers have deposited the body on the steps of the monastery, light the oil."

The captain swallowed, but showed no other reaction. "If they somehow dodge the explosion?"

"Drive them back inside with arrow fire."

The captain, accustomed to such orders, merely nodded. "The holy men as well? Should they survive the flames, that is."

Talquist shook his head. "They are dead already. The poison from their meal has no doubt taken effect by now. I just want there to be no witnesses, and no trace. There will not be; magnesium burns hotter than the flames of the Underworld. A tragic fire; the benison will doubtless be greatly aggrieved. Perhaps he will take pains to make certain his followers have safer lodgings hereafter."

The captain of the guard bowed and withdrew.

Talquist continued to stand in the square of Jierna'sid throughout the night until morning came. He scanned the rising mountain peaks for any sign of the titan, but saw nothing more than the pink rays of dawn spilling light onto the vast desert below, heard nothing but the autumn breeze whistle through, no words of wisdom hidden in its whine.

*W*hen the square at the Place of Weight was at last truly empty, when the light in the regent's tower in Jierna Tal finally was extinguished, and nothing remained but the tiniest glow from the streetlamps that had burned down to the wick bases, the sexton of Terreanfor and his two surviving acolytes crept cautiously from the shadows, trembling as they had been for the last few hours.

They stood in silence and watched the flames light the distant sides of Night Mountain, knowing that it was their manse burning. Finally Lester touched the sexton's arm with a hand that shook.

"What do we do now, Father?" he whispered. His voice sounded far younger than his years.

Lasarys stared at the leaping flames, lost in thought. Finally his eyes met those of the young priests-in-training.

"We must go to Sepulvarta, to the holy city," he said softly, glancing about to be certain they were not seen. "The benison is there; we must find Nielash Mousa and tell him of the terrible sights we have witnessed. But we must go carefully; Talquist has spies everywhere."

"Sepulvarta is a week by horseback," Dominicus said in a low voice. "How will we make it there, crossing the desert without supplies, without aid? We will surely die, or worse, be discovered."

"Not if we are discreet and careful," answered Lasarys. "Talquist believes we are dead. In the eyes of the world, we must be—at least until we can speak to the Blesser of Sorbold and inform him of what happened this hideous night."

He pulled up the hood of his cassock in the bitter sand wind; a moment later the others followed his example, and his lead, out through the dark alleys of Jierna'sid, into the vast desert beyond.

19

HAGUEFORT, PROVINCE OF NAVARNE, ROLAND, FIRST SNOW

In younger days Gwydion Navarne had loved the winter carnival.

The feast was a tradition begun by his grandfather and continued by his father for the dual purposes of celebrating a secular holiday with the people of his province and gathering with the leaders of the two religious factions, the Filidic nature priests of Gwynwood and the adherents to the faith of the Patriarch of Sepulvarta, to observe their common rites at the time of the winter solstice. The fact that the event had traditionally fallen on or around Gwydion's birthday had counted among his reasons for considering it special, at least when he was a young child. When he was somewhat older, especially after his mother's murder when he was eight, he began to realize that even a party of tremendous merriment could be more of an obligation than a chance for enjoyment, at least where the host was concerned.

His father, Stephen Navarne, had loved the carnival even more than he had. There was something about the arrival of First Snow that made Stephen's already jolly nature even more cheerful. Gwydion recalled fondly the sound of the traditional trumpet volley on the morning when the first cold flakes appeared, signaling that winter had begun. The thrill in Stephen's aspect was infectious, even to habitually grumpy household servants, who preferred a few more moments of sleep to the joy of being blasted out of bed by the duke's horn at something that could not be avoided, like the coming of snow. On the morning of First Snow they could be seen bustling around with a new energy, smiling at each other, laughing even as they went about their tasks.

The winter carnival in Stephen's time was the event of greatest goodwill in the year, when religious acrimony, land disputes, and other matters of contention were put aside for the sake of harmony, friendly competition, and good fun. On the day of First Snow, the year's official contest was announced, revels of differing sorts—a treasure quest, an ice-sculpture challenge, a poetry competition, a footrace with a unique handicap—along with traditional sport and games of chance, awards for best singing, which Lord

Stephen insisted upon judging himself, comedic recitation and performance dance, as well as folk reels, man-powered sleigh races, snow sculpting, and performances by magicians, capped finally by a great bonfire. It was an enormous undertaking, an expensive endeavor, a revel without peer, and a source of renewal for the spirits of the people of the central continent.

Until the year of the bloodshed.

Gwydion, standing now on the balcony of the library overlooking his ancestral lands, breathed in the air in which the tiny drops of frozen moisture were finally falling; First Snow had come late that year, only a day before the winter carnival was scheduled to begin, known as Gathering Day. He watched in relief as the snow began to blanket the ground, the large feathery flakes wafting down on a brisk wind. The carnival games and revels were generally better after a few weeks of accumulation, the drier the better, but Gwydion was not in the mood to be particular about the kind of snow.

Mostly because until the moment it started to fall, he was wondering if its absence was a sign, a portent that tragedy would strike again.

It had been three years since the last winter carnival, the first one that had been celebrated within the boundaries of the high wall his father had built around the lands nearest the keep, to protect his populace from the horrific and random violence that had been a scourge across the continent. The wall had been a saving grace when a cohort of mounted soldiers from Sorbold, under the demonic thrall of a F'dor spirit, had attacked the carnival and the merrymakers who had just finished witnessing the penultimate event of the festival, a sledge race that took place beyond the barrier in an open field. The mayhem that ensued had been ghastly; before Stephen and his cousin, Tristan Steward, the Lord Roland, had shepherded the terrified festivalgoers back inside the walls, more than five hundred of them were dead. Gwydion would never be able to expunge from his memory the look of controlled terror on his father's face as he hoisted Gwydion and Melisande over the wall into the care of the defenders, and the relief he saw in Stephen's eyes once they were out of harm's way, as he turned and went into battle.

Why are we doing this again? Gwydion wondered; he had asked himself the question repeatedly since the day two months prior when Rhapsody and Ashe had declared their intent to resume the carnival. *The magic of it all is broken now. How can there be a winter carnival without my father? His spirit was the winter carnival.*

Ashe's hand came to rest on his shoulder; Gwydion looked up at his godfather, now taller than himself by only a hand's measure. The Lord Cymrian's cerulean blue eyes, considered a sign of Cymrian royalty, were fixed on the fields of revel, where scores of workers now scrambled to erect stages, tents, bonfire pits, and reviewing stands. The vertical pupils in those eyes contracted in the brightness of the rising sun.

"Looks as if the weather is favoring us after all," Ashe said. "I was afraid we might have to beseech Gavin the Invoker to summon the snow if the warm winter continued."

Gwydion nodded but said nothing. Ashe's father, Llauron, had been the previous Invoker, the leader of the Filidic order of nature priests that tended the holy forest of Gwynwood. In that last, terrible carnival, Llauron had broken the charge of the demonically compelled regiment by summoning winter wolves from the snow itself, spooking the horses of the Sorbold cavalry and buying the fleeing populace time to get inside the gates. Llauron had given up his human body for the elemental form of a dragon, the blood he inherited from his mother, Anwyn, daughter of the wyrm Elynsynos, and now was off communing with those elements, hovering near but never seen. Ashe rarely spoke of his father; Gwydion once told his godfather that he understood his loss, but the Lord Cymrian had looked away and merely said that the situations were very different.

"The guests began arriving yesterday," Gwydion said as the falling snow began to thicken. "No problems thus far."

Ashe turned to him and took him by the shoulders.

"There will be no problems, Gwydion. I've taken every possible measure to prevent them." He gave the young man's arm a comforting squeeze. "I know you are worried, but try not to let it overshadow the import of these days. This is a special moment for you, and for Navarne. There is good reason for revelry and merrymaking; the future is being well assured with your ascension." He smiled reassuringly, the corners of his draconic eyes crinkling with fondness. "Besides, rather than worrying, you should be saving your strength for the tug-of-war. My team intends to drag yours mercilessly through the mud, and there is a considerable amount of it this year. You best pray that the ground freezes quickly."

A smile finally came to the corners of the young man's mouth.

Ashe saw the change, and patted his ward's shoulder. "That's better. Now, I understand that Gerald Owen has taken it upon himself to convince the cooks to make an early batch of Sugar Snow, just for you, Melly, and me, as soon as there is enough accumulation to cool the boiling syrup." He shielded his eyes and glanced at the back of the buttery, where the falling snow had covered the bricks with a thick layer of pocketed white, coating the graceful limbs of the silver-trunked trees with frosting. "I think it may almost be ready."

Gwydion laughed halfheartedly and turned to leave the balcony. Just before he reached the door, he heard his godfather call his name quietly again.

"Gwydion?"

"Yes?"

Ashe did not turn, but continued to stare off over the now-white fields of Navarne as the carnival came to life below him.

"I miss him, too."

THE REALM OF SUN,
THE WESTERN SORBOLD DESERT

*F*aron did not understand what had happened to him.

Initially after he had awoken on the plate of the Scales he thought, in his limited capacity to reason and understand, that he had died. The blinding light and the intense heat had scorched his withered flesh in agonizing purity; Faron was no stranger to pain, but this suffering was so overwhelming that he imagined it could only be the death he longed for. So when the light vanished, and the sky above him cleared, he was despondent.

The father he had been waiting to reunite with was not there.

He did not remember breaking away, did not have any concept of the obstacles that had attempted futilely to rein him in, to thwart his escape. He had merely run as fast as he could, once the concept of running had come to him, away from the pain and into the warmth of the desert he could feel beyond the Place of Weight.

Now he wandered that desert alone, passing over, and sometimes through, the sand and dry scrub as naturally as if it had been air. The Living Stone body that encased his spirit was born of the earth, and it had no weight to him while he was touching the ground. If anything, every step he took, every moment he felt the sunbaked ground beneath his feet, brought him new strength.

He no longer unconsciously thought of himself as neuter; something nascent in the stone warrior's spirit had instilled in him a gender, though it was not something he realized other than innately. It had imbued him with memories as well, fragments of images that flashed through his primitive mind which were beyond his understanding. There were scenes of battle, of endless marches, that came and went with the speed of a half-formed thought, leaving him confused. There were other images that came to his mind as well, human memories and scenes that were decidedly not from the mind of a man, but from the Earth itself; instinctive thoughts that whispered to him on the most elemental of levels.

Winter comes, it said. *The fallow time. The sleeping time.*

But for now the sun was high. The earth was warm beneath his stone feet. Giving him strength.

In the distance he could feel the scales as surely as he had felt them in his glowing pool of green water. Each called to him with a vibration unique in all the world, vibrations that had been an integral part of his makeup before the awakening. He could not see them yet, but he could sense the directions from which they called. Thinking about them both soothed his tortured mind and agitated him as the missing vibrations nagged at his consciousness.

And there was something more, something even more distant. In the back recesses of his conscious mind, fragmentary and shrouded in the darkness of ambiguity, was the memory of fire.

Dark fire.

20

GATHERING DAY, HAGUEFORT, NAVARNE

"This is mortifying," Rhapsody said.

Ashe sighed. "So you've indicated three times already in the last hour," he said indulgently, watching his wife wriggle uncomfortably in her thick cape beneath an even thicker blanket. She was ensconced on a large padded chair with a high back in the center of the reviewing stand, her feet propped on a tufted ottoman, her distended belly elevated to a point that she could barely see over it. Ashe leaned over and kissed her cheek, rosy from the wind, and brushed a strand of golden hair out of her eyes.

"I can stand," she insisted.

"Well, that makes one of us," Anborn chimed in humorously. He was seated to her left, watching the parade of festivalgoers from the reviewing platform as well. "Now you know how I feel."

"She can't stand, either," Ashe retorted. "When she stands she vomits or gets light-headed."

"I vomit and get light-headed when I sit as well," Rhapsody said crankily. "At least if I'm going to be sick, it would be nice to be able to *see* who I am going to be sick *on*."

"Oh, m'lady, by all means, don't aim at the peasantry," said Anborn, nudging her playfully. "Turn your lovely head clockwise toward your husband. He is, after all, responsible for your woes—or at least he thinks he is."

Rhapsody glared at Anborn, then settled back down beneath the blanket, attempting to maintain a pleasant official expression. The crowd of merrymakers was a blur to her, a sea of jumbled faces and clothing passing beneath the flapping banners of colored silk that hung from Haguefort's towers and guardposts and the reviewing stand on which they were seated.

Melisande hovered nearby, her face shining with excitement, rimmed in a fur hat that matched the muff that encased her hands. Her black eyes were sparkling in the wind, her nose and cheeks red with the bite of it.

"Look at the puppets!" she said gleefully to Rhapsody as a line of giant articulated harlequins paraded past the reviewing stand, their limbs controlled by the large sticks of their puppetmasters, who walked behind them, dwarfed by their size.

Rhapsody smiled at her in return. "Are you going to compete in the Snow Snakes competition this year?" she asked the young girl.

"Yes, definitely," said Melisande with a knowing glance at Gwydion. "I have to defend the family honor; last time Gwydion lost in the final round."

"That's right," Gwydion murmured to himself. He had forgotten that aspect of the carnival; the thought opened a floodgate in his mind and the memories poured back in, the good-spirited competition, the comic races where Melisande and the other little children had to race with a sled tied to their waists on which a fat sheep had been placed, the excitement of the sledge races, the humorous dunking of the winning teams by the losing ones. Such good memories that had been overshadowed by what came later. Over it all he could hear the pealing of Stephen's merry laughter. *I have to hold on to these*, he thought. *That was my father's last carnival. I need to remember him that way.*

He turned to Anborn, beside whom he was sitting, and motioned into the crowd.

"Isn't that Trevalt, the swordmaster?" he asked, indicating a black-mustached man, tall and rapier-thin, accompanied by a small retinue, making his way from the line of carriages outside Haguefort's wall to the central festival grounds.

Anborn's lip curled in disdain. "I would never call him by such a lofty title, but yes, that's Trevalt."

Gwydion leaned forward in his seat and addressed his godfather.

"Third-generation Cymrian?"

"Fourth," Ashe corrected.

"But a First Generation damfool," said Anborn scornfully. "A simpleton dressed in the robes of a scholar, a thespian who wraps himself in the titles of soldiers because he lived through a war in which even children and blind beggars fought."

Gwydion blinked at the acid in his mentor's voice, and looked questioningly at Ashe. His godfather motioned to Gwydion, who rose and walked over to him. Ashe leaned closer so as not to be overheard.

"Anborn loathes Trevalt because he once claimed, for personal gain, to have been invested as a Kinsman," he said quietly. He needed to say nothing more; the look of horror on Gwydion's face indicated clearly that he understood the severity of the offense. Kinsmen like Anborn were members of a secret brotherhood of warriors, masters of the craft of fighting, sworn to the service of soldiering for life. They were accepted into the brotherhood for two things: incredible skill forged over a lifetime of soldiering, or a selfless act of service to others, protecting an innocent at the threat of one's own life. It was a sacred trust to be one, the ultimate honor coupled with the ultimate selflessness, and with the membership came the unspoken understanding of its secrecy, and its honor. Anyone who was boasting about being one was clearly lying. And that was considered an affront almost too egregious to be borne.

He looked back at Anborn, whose face was still flushed with purple rage, sitting impotently on his litter, his useless legs motionless beneath the massive barrel of his chest. Gwydion's heart went out to him, but a moment later he saw Anborn glance at Rhapsody, a Kinsman herself, and the anger drained out of his face as she smiled at him. They both sighed, then returned to watching the assemblage of the crowd and the festivities.

"Become accustomed to this torture, Gwydion," Anborn said as the line of dignitaries passed the reviewing stand. "Alas, this is the sort of useless nonsense that takes up one's days when one is saddled with a title."

Rhapsody slapped the Lord Marshal playfully. "Stop that. *Your* title never stopped *you* from distancing yourself from court obligations."

"Ah, but you forget, m'lady, my titles have only been military," said Anborn. "I was the youngest of three. No one ever had any illusions about me being to the manor born, I am relieved to say."

"Well, except for the Third Fleet, who nominated you for my title, I remind you," joked Ashe. "Had you not refused it, you might have a lot more 'useless nonsense' to attend to today."

Anborn snorted and returned to his mug of hot spiced mead. Trevalt and his retinue stopped before the reviewing stand, per custom, and bowed deeply with flourishes to the Lord and Lady Cymrian. Rhapsody's hand shot out and covered Anborn's mouth in time to prevent him from spitting his libation at the swordmaster. She smiled pleasantly at Trevalt; he blinked, confused, smiled wanly in return, and moved on.

"Now, now, Uncle, this is Gwydion's last day before his investiture tomorrow," Ashe said, trying to contain his amusement. "Let us not christen his ascension to duke with a brawl, shall we?"

"You will be lucky if that's all that comes to pass," muttered Anborn into his mug.

Rhapsody, Ashe, and Gwydion exchanged a somber glance and returned their attention to the opening of the festival.

"I believe I see Tristan Steward arriving," said Gwydion.

"Oh joy," said Rhapsody and Anborn in unison under their breath.

Gwydion sighed and returned to his seat. It appeared it was going to be a long day.

*L*ater, after the Gathering Day's festivities had come to an end, and the First Night feast had begun, he had to admit to himself that he was enjoying the carnival in spite of it all.

Ashe had wisely limited the attendance to the citizens of Navarne and a few invited dignitaries from across the Cymrian Alliance, rather than holding it open to the entire population of the western continent, as Stephen always had. Since the tents required to accommodate a very much smaller attendance were able to be spread out and more carefully managed, the settling in took only a few hours, rather than the whole of Gathering Day; Ashe had anticipated this as well, and had arranged for the afternoon to hold several highly favored events, as well as a remarkable performance by the Orlandan orchestra that Rhapsody had patronized. The result was a jolly populace, fresh with the excitement of the sporting events and music, ready to sup heartily at the First Night feast. The wine and ale were flowing freely, courtesy of Cedric Canderre, duke of the province that bore his name. Gwydion was quietly amazed that the elderly man had even been willing to attend, let alone provide such a generous donation of his highly valued potables; his beloved only son, Andrew, had died a hero's death at the battle of the last winter carnival.

As Gwydion stood talking to Ashe while the roasted oxen were being carved and the ale being passed, Tristan Steward, the Lord Roland and his cousin once removed, sidled up to them both and greeted them pleasantly, his auburn hair gleaming in the light of the open fire.

"A splendid beginning, young Navarne," Tristan said, saluting Gwydion with his glass. "I confess at first when I heard of your godfather's intention to hold the carnival again, I thought it in poor taste at best, and foolhardy at worst. But it seems to have worked out well, so far at least."

Gwydion felt the air around him go dry, no doubt the dragon in Ashe's blood bristling in ire at the insult, but the Lord Cymrian merely took another sip from his tankard and said nothing.

"And where is Rhapsody this evening?" the Lord Roland asked, oblivious of Ashe's annoyance.

"To bed," Ashe replied. "Tired from the day's revels, as we all are. I intend to join her shortly."

Tristan's cheeks glowed red in the light of the bonfires. "Glad to hear it. I do have a gift of sorts for you—though it is on loan." He signaled to his retinue, and three women came forward, clad in the attire of the house servants of Bethany, Tristan's seat of power as regent of Roland. One of the women was elderly, the second of middling youth, and the last of tender years, perhaps twenty.

Ashe's brows knit together. "I don't understand."

Tristan smiled and put out his hand to the eldest of the women, who came to his side immediately.

"Renalla was my wife's nanny, and a very much beloved member of the household of her father, Cedric Canderre. Madeleine sent for her when our son Malcolm was expected, and she has served as nanny for him as well. She is without peer as a governess, and wonderful with children. I have brought her to you so that you might make use of her skills when Rhapsody delivers your child." He pointed to the next oldest woman. "Amity is a wet nurse, and as you've seen, Malcolm has grown healthy and strong on her supply." He glanced over his shoulder at the last, the youngest woman. "And Portia is a chambermaid."

Ashe looked uncomfortably at the three women. "Ladies, please sup; the ox is carved, and you have traveled a long way today," he said, dismissing them to the feast. Once they were out of earshot, he turned back to the Lord Roland. "I thank you, Tristan, but I can't imagine that we will need any of their services. Rhapsody plans to nurse the baby herself, especially given the rareness of its bloodline—we don't know what to expect of a wyrmkin child born of a Lirin and human mother. I'm certain if she needs any help with caring for the baby, she will want to select the nanny herself as well. And we have no end to chambermaids at Haguefort."

"Undeniably," said Tristan idly, watching a magician who was mixing colorful powders into the enormous bonfire and setting off brightly hued explosions that formed pictures that hovered in the night air, to the delight of the crowd. "But you will be moving to Highmeadow soon, and I thought, perhaps foolishly, that you might appreciate experienced servants to help ease the tremendous load of Rhapsody's transition there. My mistake."

Ashe held out his tankard to the waitservant who had offered a pitcher.

"That is very kind of you," he said awkwardly. "I apologize if I seemed ungrateful. I will consult with Rhapsody in the morning and see what she thinks."

"Why don't I just leave them in the custody of your household until the baby arrives?" Tristan suggested. "It's impossible to know right now just how truly demanding and all-consuming an infant—even a royal infant— can be. Wait and see if you need any or all of them then, and if not, send them back to Bethany with the guarded caravan. Otherwise keep them as long as you like."

"Thank you," Ashe said, draining the glass and putting it back on the servant's tray. "I appreciate your kindness. Now, I bid you good night. Enjoy the feast."

"Indeed," remarked Tristan as the Lord Cymrian hurried away from the festivities toward his wife's bedchambers. "You enjoy the feast as well."

Contrary to Ashe's beliefs, Rhapsody was not asleep, but was in fact sharing her bedchamber with another man.

Young master Cedric Andrew Montmorcery Canderre, known to his family as Bobo, the three-year-old grandson of Cedric Canderre, was gleefully tearing through her rooms, playing in her closets, pulling all the pillows from the chairs, hiding amid the bedcurtains, and giving spirited chase to the panicked tabby cat, causing his widowed young mother, Lady Jecelyn Canderre, supreme embarrassment and the Lady Cymrian great amusement.

"I'm terribly sorry, m'lady," Jecelyn said, struggling to catch up with the energetic tyke. She grasped him in midstride and swung him up over her shoulder, amid howls of angry protest. "He slept in the carriage all the way from Canderre, and now has enough energy to run all the way home. He was keeping all the rest of the guests in your quarters awake."

"I am delighted to see him," Rhapsody said, reaching for the struggling toddler. "I've missed him terribly. And besides, if there are that many guests sleeping already, we surely are not putting on a very good carnival." She reached into a box on the bedside table as Jecelyn set the child on the bed beside her, pulled forth a ginger biscuit, and held it up for his mother's approval. Jecelyn nodded, and Bobo immediately came into her lap, seized the biscuit, and consumed it forthwith, scattering crumbs over the bedsheets.

Rhapsody ran a hand over his glossy black curls, the same curls his father Andrew had sported, and quietly hummed a song of calming as he sat in her lap and ate. She patted the bed next to her for Jecelyn to sit down; the weary young mother sighed and dropped onto the mattress in relief.

"There will be many fun things for you to do tomorrow," Rhapsody said to Bobo, who nodded and dove for the biscuit box. The two women laughed, and Rhapsody handed it to him, restraining him from falling head-first off the bed. "These are really quite wonderful concoctions," she said, filching two of the biscuits and handing one to Jecelyn. "They make them in Tyrian; ginger is an herb that offsets nausea. They are the only thing that I can eat first thing in the morning."

"I remember those days," said Jecelyn wistfully. Her eyes darkened, and Rhapsody took her hand. Her husband Andrew had died when she was early in her pregnancy; he had never seen his son. After a moment Jecelyn rose and went to the tower window, where the gleaming torchlight from the two carillon towers that stood before Haguefort's front gate could be seen, lighting the dark night and the silvery snow that still fell in gentle sheets on the wind. "Are those the towers where he fell?"

"Yes," Rhapsody said, running her fingers through Bobo's hair. "Rebuilt now."

Jecelyn turned to her. "Which one was it?"

"The rightmost, I believe," the Lady Cymrian said gently. "I'm not certain—I was not here during that last carnival."

"Yes, it was the rightmost," said Ashe, who had just entered the room. He crossed to the bed, bent and kissed his wife's cheek, then snatched the munching youngster from her lap and lifted him high in the air. He tilted him upside down, eliciting squeals of glee from the boy and glances of consternation from the women. He held Bobo by his feet and swung him between his own legs, brushing the silk carpet with the child's inverted curls, then pulled him back up onto his hip and came to the tower window with Jecelyn.

"I was not here at the time, either, but I have read the reports carefully. He and Dunstin Baldasarre saw the attack coming—they were past the gate—and they each ran for a tower, knowing if they could sound the bells of the carillon they could warn Stephen and the others on the fields beyond. Dunstin took the left tower, Andrew the right. Dunstin's tower was felled by fire from a catapult just as he reached it, but Andrew was faster, and managed to ring the alarm before—before he, too, fell." Ashe took Jecelyn's hand and looked into her face; he understood the need to have the questions answered, the pieces of the puzzle filled in.

Lady Jecelyn nodded, then took her son into her arms. "Thank you," she said. "It helps to see, to understand a little. Well, we have disrupted your evening enough. Thank you, Rhapsody, for the biscuits and for your patience. We'll see you in the morning."

"Good night, Jecelyn. Good night, Bobo," Rhapsody called as they disappeared into the hallway, Bobo's wails of protest echoing off the rosy stone walls of Haguefort.

As the shrieks died down in the distance, the lord and lady burst into laughter.

"See what we have to look forward to?" Rhapsody said as Ashe unlaced his shirt, still chuckling.

"It's a joyful noise," he replied, sliding out of his clothing and into the bed beside her. "It's been good to hear such noise around here today; the place is filled with the sort of music Stephen loved, the music of laughter and merriment and good-natured argument. I know he is watching from wherever he is. I hope the ceremony tomorrow makes him proud."

"He was always proud of Gwydion and Melisande, Sam," Rhapsody said, opening her arms and welcoming him into the warmth of the bedsheets, running her hands over his shoulders to loosen the muscles. "I hope tomorrow is sufficient to make Gwydion proud of himself."

"It should. The ceremony will be dignified, modest, and, above all, brief, both for his comfort and for yours. Then we will get back to the festivities." Ashe put out the candle and pulled the covers up around them, settling down in the darkness, exhaling as he took his wife into his arms. For a moment there was only the sound of rustling blankets in the darkness. Then a shudder rose in the night, audible over the snowy wind and the distant noise of revelry below.

"What?" Rhapsody asked.

From the depth of the blankets came two words.

"Biscuit crumbs."

The fire on the hearth in the royal guest chamber crackled and leapt in time with the whine of the winter wind outside the tall panes of glass in the windows overlooking the festival grounds, where the revelry had died down into sleep and calm celebration among the most hearty of merrymakers.

Tristan Steward heard the door open quietly. He smiled, and took another sip from the heavy crystal glass into which some excellent Canderian brandy had been decanted.

"About time you arrived," he said without looking behind him. "I was wondering how long you could maintain your demure demeanor."

"I'm sure I don't know what you mean." The woman's voice behind him had a throaty chuckle in it.

That chuckle never failed to inspire a rush of warmth through Tristan. He set the glass down on the table before him and stood, turning around slowly to let the fire warm his back.

Backlit by the lanternlight of the hallway, the woman's form was half obscured in the shadow that stretched forward toward him. She turned and closed the guest-chamber door behind her, then ambled over to where the Lord Roland stood and stopped before him, smiling up insolently at him.

"Are you enjoying the revels, Portia?" Tristan inquired, stroking the porcelain cheek of the chambermaid.

The young woman shrugged. "It's very different from what I expected."

"Oh? How so?"

The woman's dark brown eyes sparkled wickedly. "From what you had described, I was looking forward to wild drunkenness and public debauchery. It's all very much more tame than I had hoped."

"It's early yet," said Tristan, pulling the white chambermaid's kerchief from her head and dropping it to the floor. "This is still First Night; most years this day was more for settling in than anything else. The real revelry begins tomorrow. But you are correct; there is a rather dull pall over this festival, no doubt owing to the horror that it sustained the last time a few years back. The Lord Cymrian has clamped down on the size and scope of the festival; I imagine we will have to settle for debauching in private."

Portia's lovely face contorted in a mock pout. "Now, what fun is *that?*" she said humorously. "We could have stayed in Bethany if that is all there is to be had."

"Now, you know better," said Tristan, unlacing the stays of her sedate bodice and untying the ribbons of her apron. "You have work to do here after I leave—and it's very important to me that you accomplish your task well."

Portia brushed his hands away from her breasts. "Don't I always?" she said, her eyes flashing with amusement. *"M'lord?"*

Tristan inhaled deeply. Portia's impudence was what he liked best about her, the ability to appear as demure and proper as any peasant chambermaid in his household's employ in public, while rising to a dominance and brashness of spirit behind closed doors. Doubtless her fiery nature would not have been appreciated by a lesser man, but Tristan had a weakness for strong women.

Her rude teasing and domineering sexual proclivities reminded him of an old paramour, now dead, whom he had loved more than he had realized while she was still alive. Prudence and he had been born in the same castle on the same day, minutes apart, he the oldest son of Lord Malcolm Steward, she the daughter of his father's favorite concubine and serving wench. They had been inseparable friends; she was his first lover and tireless confidant, willing to call him on his bad behavior and failings while never ceasing to love him unquestioningly. Her death had devastated him, but he had moved on, grimacing through a loveless marriage to Madeleine, the Beast of Canderre, as well as countless trysts with female servants.

And an unrequited obsession with the wife of his childhood friend, Gwydion of Manosse, the Lord Cymrian.

Portia had been his favorite bed partner for a while. Her wild spirit and willingness to fornicate on a moment's notice, barely hidden in public places where the possibility of detection added fuel to their passion, had gone a long way to sating the emptiness he had felt in recent years. It was, at its best, stimulating and emotionless sexual satisfaction. At its worst, it was better than nothing.

And anything was better than Madeleine's cold and formal submission to wifely duties.

"Stand still," he ordered, turning her around again. Portia's eyebrow arched in surprise, but she allowed the Lord Roland to pull her back to him.

"Now, tell me, Portia, how you plan to accomplish what I've asked of you," he said, untying the laces from the back of her skirts, then pulling her free of them with an impatient tug which implied an intensity that had not been in his eyes the moment before.

Portia shrugged as his hands slid over her breasts again, unrebuffed this time, pulling her completely free of the last remnants of clothing.

"The same way I accomplished it when *you* were the prize," she said nonchalantly, though the unexpected fire in her lord's voice was beginning to excite her. "One must first be an unobtrusive and extremely useful servant, so as not to attract the notice or ire of the house's lady. After that, it's only a matter of time. When the wife is bloated with child, it makes it all the more simple."

"You have not seen his wife," said Tristan Steward, his hands moving lower. "Even on her worst day, she is a hundred times more beautiful than you ever dreamt to be on your best day. There is a magic to her that is inde-scribable; I wonder how you will compete with that."

Portia turned suddenly, her eyes blazing violently.

"Tell me about her scent," she said hoarsely, struggling to keep the ire from her voice and losing.

Tristan thought for a moment, oblivious of the gleaming naked woman standing before him.

"Like vanilla, and spiced soap," he said finally. "The faintest scent of flowers. And the sharp odor of sandalwood smoke."

Portia smiled. She leaned against the Lord Roland and pressed her lips to his, sliding her arms around his neck. Suddenly, in his nostrils was the scent of vanilla and clean, sweet spice, with an undertone of fire in it. Though not exactly the same as Rhapsody's, it was close enough to make his hands shake. He pushed away in surprise.

"How—how did you do that?" he asked haltingly.

The black eyes danced with laughter.

"There is much you do not know about me, m'lord," she said, her voice silky with an undertone of threat. "I have not even seen her yet. But mark my words; you will not be disappointed." She pushed him back, and set about undoing the laces of his trousers while he stood still in shock. "Have you ever been?"

Numbly Tristan shook his head. There was something suddenly terrify-ing in Portia's aspect, something cruel and dark and deeper than he could fathom that he had never seen before. He did not recognize it at first, aroused as he was, but later, when he was alone in his bed, he realized that what he felt in the presence of this woman, this servant he had had his way with countless times, was fear.

She pushed him to the floor, covering his mouth, and then his body, with her own, his fully clothed, hers utterly naked; sliding him inside of her, riding him ruthlessly. He began to tremble, wondering what it was he had set in motion.

And as the tall windows mirrored the writhing dance of their bodies commingling on the floor of the guest chamber, he realized that, even in the traditional role of master and servant, he was helpless to stop it now.

The dragon was growing impatient.

All around her the earth was cooling, falling into dormancy, cold be-neath a blanket of snow that she could sense above, even in the southlands through which she traveled. As the world fell asleep, the ground became thicker, harder to pass through, deadening the sound of her name that she was following.

Let me pass, she thought angrily, struggling through the clay of the Earth's crust. *Do not hinder me.*

The beating heart of the Earth was slowing; it flickered at her ire, but then settled down again. She felt its answer in her mind, or at least imagined she did.

This cycle is older than you are old, the Earth seemed to say. *Take your time; it is unending.*

No, the dragon insisted, flailing about in the clay and the layers of rock. *Help me!*

But the earth merely settled back, thickening, making the way more difficult.

In the darkness of the crust of the world, the dragon's gleaming blue eyes narrowed, shining like lanterns in the blackness.

I may be waylaid, she thought in slowly building fury, *but I will not be denied.*

And when I finally arrive, even the Earth will suffer.

21

HAGUEFORT, NAVARNE

*W*hen she entered Haguefort's garden in the gray light of foredawn the following morning to prepare for her aubades, Rhapsody thought she caught sight of a thin shadow at the edges of her vision. She turned as quickly as she could without losing her balance, but saw nothing except the gray haze that was thinning in the advent of sunrise.

Then she felt it again, a vibration she recognized, and she broke into a wide smile.

"Achmed! Where are you?"

"Here," a voice behind her said, closer than her own shadow. "As I told you I would always be."

She turned and threw her arms around the Bolg king, laughing with delight.

"I'm so happy you are here," she said, clinging to her oldest friend in excitement. "Where have you been?"

"I arrived this morning," Achmed said, extricating himself after a quick return of her embrace, gently pulling her away, mindful of her belly. "You didn't really expect that I would come for First Night and have to endure all the nonsense of the arrivals and the pomp that goes with it, did you?"

"No, I suppose not," Rhapsody chuckled, taking his arm and walking with him through the gardens. "But I have been waiting so long to see you that I just suppose I hoped you would arrive sooner. It doesn't matter; you're here now. How are you? How is Grunthor? And everyone in the Bolglands?"

"Grunthor is well, but the Bolglands have been suffering," the king said bluntly. "If you are truly concerned, you can be of great help."

"Of course," Rhapsody said haltingly, her good cheer fading away like water running down a drain as her nausea returned. "What's wrong? Why are the Bolglands suffering?"

"We can go into that at greater lengths later," Achmed replied hastily, noting the change in the color of the horizon. "You have not sung your morning devotions yet, I take it?"

"No," Rhapsody admitted. "I had just entered the garden when I felt your presence."

"Well, don't let me interrupt. I have to see Gwydion Navarne before he becomes too wrapped up in the preparations for his investiture. Which window is his?"

"That one," Rhapsody said, pointing to a balcony above the Great Hall. "But spare yourself the climb and the arrest. Ashe is taking no chances; there are guards everywhere, and soldiers at all points around the province perimeter."

"I noticed," Achmed said dryly. "Good for him; he's finally learning. Perhaps your kidnapping had some lasting value after all."

"Gwydion is probably in the burying ground," Rhapsody said coolly, ignoring the slight. "That is usually where he begins his day. I expect he is there already this morning. Give him a moment alone before you seek him out, please."

Achmed nodded. "I will be back afterward, and then we will talk. I need your focused attention, so be prepared to send away anyone who comes nattering at you about minutiae."

"Gladly," said Rhapsody as his arm slid out of hers. He had just vanished from the edge of her blurry sight when she became aware of another presence, felt another vibration in the garden, an older, more musical sound.

"Good morning, Jal'asee," she said without turning.

"Good morning, m'lady." The sonorous voice drifted toward her on the warm wind, light as ether. A moment later, the Sea Mage seemed to appear out of the morning light, although Rhapsody was certain he had been standing just beyond her vision.

Rhapsody inhaled deeply. The Sea Mage and his retinue had been away from Haguefort since the morning after Ashe's announcement of Gwydion's investiture, visiting the Lirin kingdom of Tyrian with her viceroy, Rial. She had hoped he would return earlier, so that he might spend some time instructing her in the science of magic that the Sea Mages practiced, as he had promised, but his absence meant the secrets of the Isle of Gaematria were still a mystery. She suspected that his timing was intentional. He smiled disarmingly and shielded his eyes, looking into the sky.

"Have you greeted the daystar yet?"

"Not yet," Rhapsody said. She turned toward the east, where the star was setting; a thin line of pink had cracked the gray vault of the horizon, and was pulsing with impending light.

"I am sorry I am so late in arriving; I know I had offered some instruction in lore you had not yet been made aware of. If it pleases you, m'lady, I would be happy to teach you the elegy for Seren, the aubade that the ancients composed upon leaving the old world. It is a song of praise to the Creator for the wonder of that star. We find it helps to maintain the connection we had when we sang our hymns beneath her light in Serendair."

Rhapsody considered for a moment. "I'd be honored," she said finally.

The tall golden man smiled, took her hand in his own, and closed his eyes. She followed his example, and a moment later felt the breeze whisper over her; it was in pitch with *ela,* her Naming note, the vibration on the musical scale to which she was attuned.

Behind her eyes she saw, or perhaps felt, a shimmering light appear, singing in the darkness of the universe. The star she had long welcomed with music was returning the laud that Jal'asee was chanting, but it was a different response than Rhapsody was used to. It seemed present, not on the other side of the world; inadvertently she opened her eyes and blinked in shock. Her aubade faltered to a halt as she dropped Jal'asee's hand.

An ethereal light was emanating directly from the head of the Sea Mage, shining brilliantly from his eyes.

He finished the song, then turned to her.

"When one is baptized in ethereal light, he carries it with him wherever he goes," he said. "It is really not necessary to wait for evening or morning to chant the praise, because it is always with me."

"Well, thank you for the instruction," Rhapsody said, observing the preparations with a wary eye.

"And now, has the Bolg king arrived yet?" Jal'asee inquired politely, though Rhapsody could detect a modicum of impatience in his eyes; otherwise, his ambassadorial countenance was perfectly serene.

"Yes, as a matter of fact, he has," Rhapsody said, watching with consternation as a bevy of cooks marched by in the snow, each carrying a towering array of trays of sweetmeats, winter fruits, and pastries. "He should be back in a moment. I didn't get a chance to tell him you wanted to see him."

"Good, that's just as well," Jal'asee said smoothly. "Well, I believe I will leave you to your preparations, and have a walk about in the snow. Gaematria is tropical, thus we do not see much snow unless we manufacture it ourselves."

The Lady Cymrian shook her head. "I hope someday before I die I will be invited to see your island, Jal'asee," she said, putting her hand on her belly as the baby began kicking ferociously, causing her stomach to turn. "It certainly sounds like an interesting place."

"It's the place you must come if you are interested in learning magic as a science, m'lady," said Jal'asee mildly, "which is very similar to your Naming studies now, but with additional areas of expertise and a maritime focus. As an academic, I am a firm believer that one should seek out the best teacher, or physician, or mentor that one could possibly have, and place oneself utterly in his or her care. Those people at least know all the missteps, and everything that can go wrong in their area of expertise; it's probably something they've had to solve before."

Rhapsody smiled. "Actually, I was thinking something very much along those lines, Jal'asee. Now, if only my husband will agree."

*f*ond as he had been of Lord Stephen Navarne, Achmed had never been to his grave. Such visits were not in his makeup; he had dispensed enough death in his career as an assassin and king to understand the finality of it, to recognize the separation of soul from earthly substance, and so did not make a practice of observing anniversaries or tending to cemetery plots. If he ever had need of remembrance, he combed the wind and his own memory, rather than planting flowers on burial ground.

So it took him a few moments to find Gwydion Navarne in the quiet garden behind Haguefort, gated in wrought iron and evergreen bushes.

He had thought perhaps that one of the taller monuments that gleamed in various shades of aged marble might have stood to mark the resting place of Haguefort's beloved master and caretaker; no one could have done more to renovate and tend to the rosy-brown stone keep than Stephen had. Stephen had also built the Cymrian museum that stood within its gates, a squat marble shelter for the artifacts of the enlightened age that had been born, had its heyday, and ended in war while he, Grunthor, and Rhapsody were still in the course of their travels through the Earth. If anyone deserved one of the foolishly ornate headstones pointing toward the winter sky in this place, it was Stephen.

And yet, to Achmed's gratification, Stephen was not buried in a mausoleum guarded by a towering obelisk of stone, but rather was entombed in snow-covered earth beneath two slender trees, along with his wife, Lydia. A simple bench and a small piece of inscribed marble were all that marked the place; he would never have even seen it were it not for the presence of Stephen's son, who sat quietly on the bench in reflection, attired in silver-blue court brocade and a grim expression.

"Your grandmother wore the exact same look on her face the night before the Lirin invested her as queen," Achmed said wryly.

The young man turned around and smiled slightly. "Well, I suppose I am in good company, then." He stood and offered his hand. "Welcome, Your Majesty. I didn't see you yesterday; did you just arrive?"

"Yes," the Bolg king said, shaking Gwydion's hand with his gloved one, a practice he participated in rarely. "I brought you something."

"Oh?"

From within his robes Achmed produced something wrapped in oil-cloth and handed it to Gwydion. The duke-to-be took it questioningly, but when Achmed said nothing, he slowly untied the bindings and unwound the wrapping. As he peeled the last layer back, Gwydion's hair was suddenly touseled by a stiff breeze, cold and stingingly clear, that seemed to rise up from the layers of the package.

Within the cloth lay a sword hilt of polished black metal the likes of which he had not seen. It was carved in ornate runes, its crosspiece curled in opposite directions. It had no blade.

"This is an ancient weapon, the elemental sword of air known as Tysterisk," Achmed said quietly. "Though you cannot see its tang or shaft, be well advised that the blade is there, comprised of pure and unforgiving wind. It is as sharp as any forged of metal, and far more deadly. Its strength flows through its bearer; until a short time ago it was in the hands of the creature that took Rhapsody hostage, part man, part demon, now dead, or so it seems at least. In that time it was tainted with the dark fire of the F'dor, but now it has been cleansed in the wind at the top of Grivven Peak, the tallest of the western Teeth. I claimed it after the battle that ended the life of its former bearer, but that was only because I wanted to give it to you myself. Both Ashe and I agree that you should have it—probably the only thing we have ever agreed on, come to think of it."

Gwydion stared at the hilt. He could see within the swirls of its carvings movement, but it was evanescent, fleeting; he blinked, trying to follow the motion, but lost it. A shiver of excitement mixed with dread rose up inside him; the sword handle was heavy, humming with power.

"I—I don't know that I am ready for such a weighty gift," he said haltingly, though his hands were beginning to shake from the vibration as well as his own exhilaration. "I haven't done anything to be worthy of such a weapon."

Achmed snorted. "That's a fallacy long perpetuated by self-important fools," he said scornfully. "You cannot be 'worthy' of a weapon before you begin to use it. It's in the use of it that your worthiness is assessed. It is an elemental sword—no one is worthy of it."

"Don't—don't you want it?" Gwydion asked nervously, his eyes beginning to gleam.

Achmed shook his head. "No. Despite what I just said about worthiness, in truth weapons of this kind of ancient power do choose their bearers, and make them, in a way. I prefer to choose my own weapon, and make it."

"Like your cwellan?"

The Bolg king nodded. "That is of my own design," he said, shrugging slightly to bring forth from behind his shoulder the machine shaped like an asymmetrical crossbow, with a curved firing arm. "I made it to heighten my strengths and accommodate my weaknesses, but mostly it is tailored to the sort of prey I once hunted." He indicated a spool on which whisper-thin disks were housed. "It fires three at a time, each one driving the previous ones deeper in. And it can be adapted as I have need—this one I developed to be able to pierce the hide of a dragon." He glanced over his shoulder in the direction of the reviewing stand. "Ashe is around here somewhere, no doubt. Perhaps I can test its efficiency later."

Gwydion chuckled. "How did you adapt it to dragons specifically?"

"This one has an especially heavy recoil," Achmed replied. "Dragon hide is as thick as stone. The disks are specially made as well; they are of rysin-steel, a metal that is extremely malleable when heated, which has been shrunk to a compact size by cold manufacture. Once inside the body and exposed to heat they swell in vast proportion with jagged edges, expanding the original damage many times over." He turned the cwellan over lovingly. "I got many of the ideas from a weapon Gwylliam was working on before his death; I suppose he had his own problems with the dragon he was married to. The properties of fire and earth make the disks expand—that's mostly what a dragon is inside, despite all the other elemental lore they possess."

"You know it won't work on Ashe," Gwydion said humorously, trying to break his attention away from the humming sword hilt in his hands and failing. "He's mostly water."

Achmed stared down at the weapon in his hands.

"Hmmmm," he said finally. "Back to the drawing board."

Gwydion laughed. "You don't need it against Ashe, anyway," he said. "Even though you may argue, I know you are really allies. But I have seen your weapon in successful use—it was this cwellan that took Anwyn from the sky in the battle at the Moot, was it not?"

Achmed slung the cwellan again. "I hit her, and took off a claw or two, but the credit for that kill goes to Rhapsody," he said, securing the cover beneath his robes. "She was in the dragon's clutches; she carved her way out with Daystar Clarion. Once free, she called starfire down on Anwyn, then sealed her in her grave. But I suppose you could say I assisted—as did Anborn, at the cost of his legs." He looked over his shoulder as trumpets blared, sudden and loud, in the distance. The Bolg king winced. "I assume that is your godfather's subtle way of indicating your presence is needed."

Gwydion nodded. "What should I do with this?" he asked anxiously, nodding toward Tysterisk.

Achmed shrugged. "It's yours to use, to bear, to live with," he said nonchalantly. "It should be with you upon your ascension to duke, assuming you wish to accept it. Remember, if you are going to take on the responsibility of such a sword, you will be expected to use it when needed, even at the cost of your duchy. But somehow I doubt that will be a problem for you. Get Anborn to instruct you in its use." He turned to leave, then paused and looked back at the nervous young man. "It's best to be ready. This is what I came to tell you, why I wanted to give the sword to you myself. The world in which you are about to claim a part is an uncertain place, but one thing can be predicted without fail—sooner or later, you will need to fight. You may as well have the best blade in your hand when you do. Just remember that *you* wield *it*; do not let the weapon wield you."

Gwydion nodded and looked down at the hilt once more. As he stared at it, he thought he could see the blue-black outline of the blade against the brown oilcloth, gleaming dully, with tiny currents of wind swirling randomly within it. He continued to watch it in fascination until the trumpets blared again. Then he shook off his reverie and looked up.

"Thank you—" he said, but Achmed was already gone.

As Faron moved west, the winter was catching up with him.

Day into day his body became more melded to his mind; his hands and feet, once totally foreign and unwieldy, now served him with the same unconscious direction with which anyone else moved. His mind was still cloudy, still roiling in a sea of confused thoughts and the combined memories of an ancient soldier, an even more ancient demonic father, and the asexual creature he had once been.

The uninhabitable desert eventually had given way to steppes and dry grasslands, where only nomads and caravans passed. Faron had taken to hiding when such things came into view; his sun-deprived eyes were slowly gaining strength, and now he put them to use scanning the horizon for anything that moved. As he followed the sun across the sky he found that winter had hold of the places into which he was now coming. He had a vague recollection from his time as a soldier of snow, which stung the edges of his earth-hewn legs, but otherwise did not bother him. It gave him little hindrance, except that its presence added difficulty to his ability to hide.

Across the frost-blanched plains of upper Sorbold and into the southern province of Navarne he traveled, deeper and deeper into winter's grasp.

His fragmented mind seething, bent on destruction.

22

THE WINTER CARNIVAL

When Achmed returned from visiting Gwydion Navarne, he came directly into the garden where he had left Rhapsody. As luck would have it, she was inside the buttery, preparing to return to the festival, so instead he was alone when he met up with the ambassador from the Sea Mages.

He stopped in his tracks, and stared over his veils at Jal'asee, his mismatched eyes sighting on the man as if he were leveling a cwellan at him.

"You lived," he said accusatorily.

Jal'asee sighed and tucked his hands into his outer cloak.

"Yes," he replied. "I am sorry about that."

Achmed glanced around the garden for Rhapsody. "Well, at last you and I agree on something, Jal'asee," he said shortly. He turned to leave, only to be stopped when the Sea Mage raised his hand.

"I have been waiting to see you for almost three months, Your Majesty," he said in his interesting voice. "I beg you do me the honor of favoring me with your attention for a few moments, and then I will withdraw and allow you to enjoy the festivities."

Achmed snorted. "Do be serious."

Jal'asee's face lost its natural expression of serenity. "Believe me, Your Majesty, what I have to say to you is very serious."

"Then get on with it. I have more pressing matters to attend to, such as informing Rhapsody that should she ever invite us to the same event again I shall burn down her almost-completed house."

"Did I hear my name being bantered about in disrespect?" the Lady Cymrian asked humorously upon entering the garden. "It must be that Achmed has returned."

"Had I known you planned to ambush me with this academic, I would have gone directly home from my meeting with Gwydion Navarne," Achmed said, the hostility in his voice unmistakable. "There are three types of people I despise, Rhapsody—Cymrians, priests, and academics. You should certainly know this by now."

"I see no need to be rude to an ambassador from a sovereign nation who is also my guest," said the Lady Cymrian tartly. "Perhaps you can at least hear the gentleman out, Achmed."

"No need to defend my honor, m'lady," said Jal'asee, a twinkle in his eye. "I have been fielding the Bolg king's insults for millennia now." He walked a few steps closer and tucked his hands into his sleeves, crossing his arms. "It is our understanding that you are seeking to rebuild the instrumentality in Gurgus Peak," he said seriously.

Achmed sighed. "Perhaps I should just have sent a royal notice to be posted in every port of call, every judiciary, and every brothel from here to Argaut," he said angrily. "Do yourself the favor of making a wise choice, Jal'asee; I didn't seek your counsel about this originally because I do not care what your thoughts are on the matter. Please do me the favor, therefore, of not sharing them with me."

"I have no choice in that matter, Your Majesty," Jal'asee retorted. "That is the precise reason I was sent from Gaematria. The Supreme Council of the Sea Magistrate respectfully asks that you suspend all work on this project until such a time when—"

"Tell them by all means, I will do that," sneered the Bolg king. "Their opinions are even more edifying to me than yours are."

Jal'asee's patience seemed to run suddenly thinner.

"You must heed this advice, Your Majesty."

"Why?"

The ambassador glanced around the garden.

"Shall I leave?" Rhapsody asked, pointing to the gate. "I truly don't mind."

Both men shook their heads.

"I'm really not at liberty to go into the specifics, Your Majesty, but I believe you know the reason, or at least should be able to surmise it."

Achmed stepped up to the ambassador and stared up into the tall man's golden eyes.

"Tell me why, or go away."

Jal'asee stared down at him seriously.

"Just remember the greatest gifts the earth holds, sire."

Silence fell in the garden. Then Achmed turned and walked past Rhapsody.

"When you have time to speak to me alone, seek me out," he said, heading for the garden entrance.

Jal'asee coughed politely. "You know, it's a shame you chose to leave the study of healing behind for another profession. Your mentor had great faith in your abilities. You would have been a credit to Quieth Keep, perhaps one of the best ever to school there."

Achmed spun angrily on his heel.

"Then I would be as dead as the rest of the innocents you lured to that place," he said harshly. "You and I do not have the same definition of what constitutes 'a shame.'"

He stalked out of the garden, glaring at Rhapsody as he left.

She stared after him as the gate slammed shut.

"Do you mind telling me what that was all about?" she asked Jal'asee incredulously. In all the time she had known him, she had never seen Achmed become so engaged in a conversation he had stated up front was of no interest to him. Achmed was quite talented at ignoring subjects, discussions, or people in whom he had no interest.

The Sea Mage sighed. "Many years ago, when he was a fairly young man, a terrible tragedy occurred at Quieth Keep, the place of scholarship I mentioned to you several months ago, where I taught," he said solemnly. "Someone he apparently cared a great deal for—perhaps several such someones—did not survive the mishap. I take it he has never forgiven me."

"So it would seem," said Rhapsody. "I'm sorry."

"No need to be, m'lady," Jal'asee said. "Just because someone is rude and unreasonable does not mean that he is wrong."

Gerald Owen stirred the boiling syrup in the large cauldron of black iron, ignoring the rising noise of the children and some excited adults who were anxiously awaiting the pouring of the next batch of Sugar Snow. He had been conveniently deaf to such noise for many years; Lord Stephen's father had introduced the custom of drizzling hot liquid sugar onto clean snow that had been harvested on large trays to cool the caramel syrup into crisp, hard squiggles of sweetness that had come to be hallmarks of the winter carnival. Lord Stephen had added the extra sin of dipping the hard candy in chocolate and almond cream; Gerald Owen was the festival's traditional candy cook, as well as the guardian of the secret recipes.

The elderly chamberlain of Haguefort finally signaled the readiness of the syrup to be poured; he stepped back out of the way, allowing the assistant cooks to position the pot as the snow boards were brought forward. He wiped his sugary hands on his heavy linen apron and crossed his arms, allowing himself a small smile of satisfaction.

The solstice festival, despite his misgivings, seemed to be going well. Owen had served the family for two generations, and it gave him great satisfaction to see the traditions Lord Stephen had cherished being carried on by his son, whom Owen had cared for since his birth.

He was secretly glad that Gwydion was about to take on his title in full; the presence of the Lord and Lady Cymrian, however consoling it had been in the aftermath of the loss of the duke, was an uncomfortable fit in the small keep of Haguefort. The heads of the overarching Alliance belonged in a more central, grander estate; from what he had heard of it, Highmeadow was at least central, if not particularly grand. But Haguefort had been built originally as a stronghold for the families who had settled the wilds of the province of Navarne early in the Cymrian Age, and had always been a modest keep, not a palace or even a castle. Once it went back to being the seat of a duke, not the home of imperial rulers, life would be closer to normal.

He sat down wearily on a cloth-covered barrel, suddenly winded, and watched the mad tussle of children vying for the fragile sweets. Gerald Owen, like the duke he served, was of Cymrian lineage, long diluted, and had lived many years more than the human friends with whom he had been raised and schooled, now long dead. He had watched many of the parents and grandparents of the children competing for his candy do the same thing in festivals past; there was a cyclical harmony to it all, this sense that life was passing by for others faster than it was for him, that left him occasionally melancholy.

The grip of a hand on his shoulder brought him out of his reverie. He looked up, squinting in the sunlight above him, to see the face of Haguefort's soon-to-be master smiling down at him.

"Is it almost time, Gerald?" Gwydion Navarne asked.

Owen rose quickly, the spring back in his step.

"Yes, indeed, sir, if you are ready to begin."

"I will be, once you have checked me over to make certain I haven't missed anything. Once I pass muster with you, I will feel ready."

Gerald Owen took the young duke by the arm and led him back into the Great Hall, where a table had been laid with the tools for his final preparations.

"Not to worry for a moment, young sir," he said fondly. "We will have you turned out in a manner that will make you and everyone who loves you proud this day."

$\mathcal{A}$she, true to his word, kept the ceremony by which Gwydion was invested brief and elegant. Rhapsody watched as the boy she had claimed as her first honorary grandson four years before, bowing at her feet, raised his eyes with a new wisdom in them, the wisdom of a young man now bearing the mantle of his birthright squarely on his shoulders. Her heart swelled with pride at his calm mien, the prudent and respectful words of acceptance he spoke. After Ashe handed him the ceremonial keys to Haguefort and Stephen's prized signet ring engraved with the crest of the Navarne duchy, Gwydion had turned and thanked the assemblage, then bade them to return to the festival, citing the sledge race trials that were about to begin.

As the crowd began milling back to the tents and the fields of competition, she felt a strong, bony hand clamp down on her elbow.

"If you are ready now," Achmed's sandy voice said quietly in her ear, "we have something important to discuss."

Without turning around, Rhapsody nodded, allowing Achmed to maneuver her out of the crowd of excited people shouting congratulatory salutes, to a quiet enclave inside of the keep.

"Tell me," she said tersely as soon as they were out of earshot of Haguefort's servants. "And tell me why it was necessary for you to be so ungodly unpleasant to one of our most distinguished guests."

"It was necessary to be unpleasant to him because I don't have any other temperament," Achmed replied irritably. "You of all people should know that by now. He's an arse-rag, and I have very little patience with arse-rags. Now, as for what I need from you, and how you can help the Bolglands, do you remember this?"

He handed her a thin locked box fashioned in steel and sealed around the edges with beeswax.

Rhapsody's brows drew together. "Yes; wasn't this the container for an ancient schematic of Gwylliam's?"

"Indeed. And I need it translated, completely and accurately."

"I believe I did this for you once before," Rhapsody said, her own ire rising. She opened the box, and carefully moved the top document, written in

Old Cymrian, aside from the sheaf of even more ancient parchment below it, graphed carefully in musical script. "Oh, yes, I remember this poem now:

"Seven Gifts of the Creator,
Seven colors of light
Seven seas in the wide world,
Seven days in a sennight,
Seven months of fallow
Seven continents trod, weave
Seven eras of history
In the eye of God."

Achmed nodded impatiently.

"I understand the poem," he said. "It's the schematic and all the corresponding documents I need translated, and carefully."

"When?"

The Bolg king considered. "What are you doing until supper?"

"I was actually planning to attend the sledge races," Rhapsody replied archly. "And after that I thought I might attend the rest of the winter carnival, thank you. What sort of time do you think this kind of thing takes, Achmed? I can assure you, there are many days', if not weeks', worth of translation time here. This is more than just musical script; it requires the composition to be played, and to be referenced in later parts of the piece. It's not something I can sit down and do after noonmeal."

"I am willing to wait until teatime," Achmed said wryly.

"You will have to wait until teatime next year," Rhapsody answered. "Additionally, didn't I tell you at the time you last showed me this that I worry about your rash experimentation with ancient lore?"

"You did, which is why I have decided not to experiment, but rather to get a careful and accurate translation, then assess for myself what to do with the information. Surely you can't object to *that?*"

She thought for a moment. "Well, I suppose not."

"Good. Then perhaps when this folderol is finished, you can turn your attention to this. As I've explained, if it works the way the one I knew of in the old world worked, it might be precisely what we need to keep the Bolglands, and consequently the Alliance, free from subversion or attack. Your ward, the Sleeping Child, all your Bolg grandchildren, and the 'people' of Ylorc are certainly worth *that*, aren't they?"

"Of course," said Rhapsody uncertainly.

"Well, just in case you still think this is ill advised, know this: While I was off pulling your charming arse out of a sea cave, my kingdom was being infiltrated by the mistress of the assassin's guild of Yarim, the very same folks you talked me into helping by having the Bolg drill them a new wellspring for Entudenin, for which we have not received payment in full, by the way. Consequently, said guildmistress not only destroyed Gurgus Peak, but also poisoned a good deal of the kingdom with picric acid."

"Oh, gods!" Rhapsody exclaimed in horror.

Achmed considered. "No, I don't believe she got them, but it may have only been by accident if she didn't. Suffice to say that at least a thousand of the Bolg have died or been terribly ill with symptoms like dysentery, bleeding out the eyes, bleeding internally—"

"All right, that's enough," Rhapsody said, fighting back nausea and losing. She ran to the nearest potted plant and retched.

Achmed waited smugly until she returned.

"So I trust I can count on your help in this matter?"

Rhapsody sighed, still pale and woozy.

"I will do what I can, Achmed, though I can't promise that I will be able to give you the information that you seek," she said, leaning against the enclave wall. "But if it is of any encouragement, know that I expect to have some time to work on it very shortly."

"Oh?"

"Yes. I need to consult with Ashe and see if he agrees first, but it's my hope to leave and spend some time with Elynsynos shortly."

Achmed's eyes widened. "You are going to a dragon's lair while pregnant?"

"Yes, actually. She is the only one I can think of who truly knows what it is like to be carrying a wyrmkin child. So I will make you an offer: If Ashe agrees I will take the manuscript with me and work on it when the nausea allows. I will do what I can with it, though again I make you no guarantees. You, in turn, will bring Krinsel to me at Thaw, so that I can keep her with me until my baby is delivered."

She could tell that the Bolg king was smiling behind his veils.

"So you trust yourself to a Bolg midwife before all the vaunted healers of Roland?"

"In a heartbeat. Do we have an agreement?"

"We do," Achmed said. "Just make certain you hold up your end of the bargain."

Faron stared down in silence at the merriment below him.

His awareness did not include the concept of holidays; having been kept in the dark basement of the Judiciary all of his life in Argaut, he was confused and upset by the noise and celebration taking place just beyond the hill on which he was standing.

23

"A good solstice to ya, Brookins."

The burly fisherman broke into a gap-toothed smile but did not pause from tying his lines.

"Glad to see you're feelin' better, and a good solstice to you as well, Quayle," he said, watching the snow in the distance whip about in the wind that rippled the water below the docks. The warmth of the ocean kept the air clear here, on the point of the jetty south of town. He winched the last of the ropes, then pulled his hat down over his red ears. "You up to helping me and Stark haul the traps in?"

Quayle wiped the mucus from the tip of his red nose with the back of his worsted sleeve, then dried his similarly red eyes with it as well.

"Let the lobsters wait another day," he muttered grumpily as Stark, another dockmate, approached, dragging the crates for the catch. "A storm's brewin'; you can tell by the sky it's gonna be a cracker."

Stark spat into the ocean and shook his head.

"Been two days since baitin' already," he said, his voice scratchy from the wind and disuse. Stark rarely spoke; when out in the harbor with both him and Quayle, Brookins occasionally forgot Stark was even in the boat. "An' a whole village waitin' to eat 'em tonight."

"He's right," Brookins said to Quayle. "You go home and get yourself a grog; we'll haul in."

"You're daft to go out now; it's almost sunset." Quayle jammed his hands inside his sleeves, as if they were a lady's muff. "Don't want to be spending the holidays consoling your widows."

Stark scowled and climbed into the boat.

"Go back to bed," he said. "Come on, Brookins. My supper's waiting."

Brookins looked from Quayle to Stark, then back to Quayle again.

"He's right," he said finally. "Get some rest. Stark and me will split the take from this catch with you; you baited, after all. We'll celebrate the holiday tomorrow, then have a whole lovely catch to pull in the next day. I'll drop you by a few for your pot on the way home." Quayle nodded gloomily. Brookins lit the oil lantern that lighted their prow, then set out into the harbor with Stark.

For a long time Quayle stood, watching the bobbing light on the waves as his friends emptied the traps of their catch. The breeze whipped off the waves and stung, sending sand and salt spray into his eyes. Finally, when the boat's light was too far out to see anymore he turned his attention north to the twinkling candles that shone in the windows of Jeremy's Landing, and the bonfires that were beginning to light the village square in anticipation of the solstice.

Merry music began to drift toward him on gusts of the icy wind. Quayle's bitterness at the thought of lost profit drifted away with it, and his humor began to rise in the anticipation of the celebration at hand. He was too far away to catch the aroma of the stewpots yet, but if he hurried, he could be there in time to sample each of the entries in the village's contest. And, as on every solstice night, there would be bread and ale and singing, with the promise of other pleasures of the flesh later, in warm brothels or cold stables. The season's excitement seeped into his nostrils along with the cold salty wind, chasing his malady away. He unhooded his lantern, turned away from the dock, and started across the salty marsh dunes at the edge of the bay, dark as pitch in the winter night.

The dunes seem higher tonight, he thought; the tiny beams from the distant candles vanished as he stepped into a swale in the marsh. He pulled his hat brim lower to shield his eyes from the wind, then cupped his hand around the battered lantern, trying to keep the wind from snuffing it.

Before him in the blackness the frost-bleached ground seemed to heave, then rise until it towered into the sky.

Quayle stopped, night blind. His lungs seemed suddenly full and heavy, as if the chill he had caught a few days before had returned, stealing his breath. Shakily he held up the lantern.

In front of him the dune shifted again, sand and marsh grass raining from it as if it were a waterfall. The dim light of his lamp flashed on what appeared to be a giant statue, taller than himself by more than half, a primitive-looking man clad in armor, shedding sand in great wispy waves. Its blind eyes seemed to be fixed on him.

"God's drawers," Quayle whispered. "What is this?"

The statue in the sand did not move.

Quayle swallowed hard, his throat sore and suddenly without spit. He tried to imagine, with a mind clouded by shock and illness and anticipation of frolic, how this statue could have come to wash up on the beach, and especially how it could have happened without his hearing of it. Jeremy's Landing was a tiny community, many generations of families who plied the sea for a living, selling their catch in nearby towns, all interdependent upon one another. Each event, no matter how insignificant, was reported breathlessly from hut to hut; how he could have missed this news was incomprehensible to him.

He shook his head, then turned northward, and took a step toward the village.

The statue's head moved in unison with his.

Quayle gasped, the lantern in his hand shaking violently.

He held the lantern up higher in the wind. There was something malevolent in the statue's stance, as if seething anger had been sculpted into it by the artisan who carved it. Quayle did not know how he knew this, but the tension, the fury was palpable. He leaned forward and stared at the figure's eyes.

Then reared back in horror as those eyes stared back, gleaming with hatred behind milky cataracts.

The lantern fell from his hand onto the sandy marsh and went out. Blackness swallowed Quayle.

In that blackness, he felt certain that the titanic figure before him was breathing.

Or moving.

Blind, Quayle turned and dashed to his left, running hell-bent for the lights of the village. He had gone a half-dozen steps before he was lifted from the slippery ground up into the air with a force that stripped the breath from him.

A sickening crack resonated in his ears; dully Quayle realized it was his pelvis shattering under the crushing weight that had clamped around him. He tried to scream, but no air would come into his lungs. All he would do was open and close his mouth silently in terror as he was dragged forward in the air, until he was a hairsbreadth away from the terrible eyes, black with a milky sheen, staring at him in the darkness.

Quayle's mind, never the keenest in the world, disconnected from his body. The unreality of what was happening was too much to comprehend; instead he decided that he must still be in the throes of the fever that had gripped him with the onset of his chill. *I'm still in bed, having nightmares,* he thought as the titan turned him onto his back, until the stone fingers gouged through his underbelly and began digging around in his viscera. Then the agony and the spinning lack of air hit him at once, and he began to shudder, the only bodily function he was capable of.

The statue ripped through his intestines, searching, then pulled its bloody fingers out of his abdomen and pushed aside the folds of his tunic. It seized the tattered scale that Quayle kept tucked inside his shirt, dropping the fisherman as it raised the object up to the light of the moon, the beams dancing off its ridges in rainbow ripples.

As the darkness started to close in, Quayle had only the momentary sight of the titanic being above him, an expression of almost piteous joy evident on its rough-featured face, before the statue turned and brought its foot down on his face, splitting his skull like the husk of a soft-shelled crab.

The pieces of him were found in the morning, first by the ptarmigans and gulls, then by Brookins, who stained the sand with all the liquid his body held at the sight.

$\mathcal{F}$or the first time in as long as his cloudy mind could remember, Faron felt joy.

No longer a formless creature trapped inside a statue, he felt the pieces of his divergent identity start to fall into place; he was a man now, a titan formed of living earth and fire, the son of a demon, blessed and cursed with the memories of ancient battles and conquests that he did not understand.

The green scale hummed in his hand, the light of the moon rippling off it like seawater flowing over the edge of the world. Reverently he pressed his treasure against his face, feeling once again the vibration that had resonated deep within him for so long. He had mourned its absence by becoming weaker, withering; now the strength of spirit came flowing back, sparking inside him. He slid it into place with the other three, forming a gleaming fan of color in his stone hand; the warmth they emitted coursed through him, filling him with something akin to bliss.

But he was still missing something.

Distantly he heard the roar of the sea; it was a sound that had struck great fear into Faron from the time his father had brought him forth from the quiet darkness of the cavernous tunnels in which he had lived to sail across the world to this place. His father had been chasing a woman, a woman whose hair he had saved and carried with him, tied with a moldering ribbon. Faron had scryed for her with the scales, and had found her. They had come to this new, frightening land, only to have his father die and their ship scuttled in the ocean.

He stared at that ocean now, shrinking from the might of it. Slowly he walked to the beach, where the foaming waves were chasing up on the sand. He stood, staring at the glittering green scale until those waves touched his bare stone feet; the sensation nauseated him, filling him with fear, and he shrank away, back to the dry land, where he could feel the warmth of the earth once more.

Then, his treasure returned to him, he turned slowly in the night and walked away from the pounding sea, leaving the noise of Jeremy's Landing and the solstice celebration behind him.

24

$\mathcal{T}$he closing banquet of the winter carnival started out festively, and ended even more so.

With the final races complete, the last of the competitions' prizes awarded, and the final round of choral singing ended with enthusiastic participation, such that the white fields of Navarne had rung with the sound of it, all without any noticeable mishap, the Lord and Lady Cymrian, the two

Navarne children, Anborn, and the household staff had wearily sat down to a late supper, reviewing the final arrangements and determining the festival's success.

"Two drunken fights leading to fisticuffs; otherwise, all in all, a fairly peaceful event, I would say," Ashe commented, running his thumb over his wife's hand. Rhapsody smiled in response, assenting. "And Navarne has a new duke now, with full participation in the council of Roland, which bodes well for the province. I think we can cautiously term this carnival a success." Gerald Owen, the last of the servants to leave the table, smiled tiredly and nodded, gathering the plates and withdrawing from the room, followed by Melisande, who was on her way to bed.

Anborn belched loudly, deadening all sound in the room.

"Indeed. Any party where no one of significance gets killed can certainly be seen as a good one," he said. "I'd like to offer my thanks to the Lady for her kind hospitality, and make known that I will be taking my leave shortly." Those around the table nodded in assent; such an announcement was never unexpected, as Anborn rarely remained in one place very long.

"This time, however, I would like to issue an invitation to the new duke of Navarne to accompany me in my travels."

"Where are you going?" Ashe asked, taking a sip from his glass of spiced cider.

The Lord Marshal waited until the door had closed behind Gerald Owen to answer.

"Sorbold. I am still troubled by things I have heard on the wind from there; I suspect it is worth investigating."

Ashe nodded in agreement. "I'm sure whatever information you gather will be highly useful, Uncle. I have been concerned about some of the reports from the shipping trade there; we've been watching the actions of the new regent emperor since his selection by the Scales, but thus far, at least on the surface, he seems to be conducting a measured regent year. I have had some doubt expressed about him from people I trust, so whatever you can determine will be valuable."

"Only if you choose to act on what I tell you, Gwydion," Anborn said darkly. "I've been warning you for some time that war is coming, and while you've taken some of my suggestions to heart, I would like to see you moving more aggressively to reinforce both the infantry and the navy."

"I've placed an order for a dozen new warships, built in Manosse and outfitted in Gaematria, this very week, Uncle," Ashe said mildly. "And the shipments of horses for the Alliance cavalry have been arriving regularly from Marincaer; training is well under way. I *am* taking what you have said, and what I have seen, to heart, rest assured." He squeezed Rhapsody's hand again; her capture had been sufficient to make him see Anborn's warnings as timely.

"So we would be going to spy, then?" Gwydion asked, barely able to contain his excitement.

"Gwydion, an invested duke does not spy on a sovereign nation," Rhapsody said reproachfully.

"No, indeed not," Anborn agreed. "He makes a visit of state, but without telling anyone, and watches from places where he cannot be seen."

"Forgive me," Gwydion grinned. "Is that all right, then, Ashe? May I accompany Anborn?"

"That's for you to decide," Ashe said, draining his tankard. "You are fully invested; your decisions are your own now. It probably is a good idea for you to make an official visit of state at the beginning of your reign, anyway—but I think you might wish to limit that visit to Tyrian or the Nonaligned States, which are safer havens for you, it would seem, and travel through Sorbold only as a means to get there." He ignored Anborn's withering glance. "I would also caution you about remaining away from Navarne for long; as the duke now, you need to be available to keep the province running." He saw the young man's face fall, and hurried to finish his thought. "But you have inherited an elemental sword, and need time to travel with it, to train. There is no better teacher than Anborn. I think it's a good use of your first weeks as duke—and I will mind Navarne while you are gone. Then you can return and assume your full duties." He turned to his wife. "What say you, darling?"

Rhapsody folded her hands.

"If you are going to venture forth, those are good reasons to do so—the official and unofficial ones—and you will be in good company," she said. "To that end, I'd like to note that I desire to leave Navarne for some time as well."

The three men at the table stared at her.

"I have been feeling ill and weak for some time, and it is disturbing to me," she continued, her face flushed from the weight of their stares. "Something Jal'asee said before Achmed left made a lot of sense to me—it seems to me that since my situation is unique, and somewhat chancy—it would make sense for me to go and spend some time with Elynsynos, to see if there is something I can learn from her experiences with wyrmkin pregnancy, or just to visit with her. There is something drowsy and comforting about being in her cave, and I have not seen her for quite a long time."

"How long a visit are you talking about, Aria?" Ashe asked, trying to not allow the reaction he was experiencing internally to become rampant.

Rhapsody shrugged. "I don't really know. I suppose it depends on how I'm feeling. I have no idea how long my confinement is going to be, given that your own mother carried you for close to three years. I think I might like to stay at least until Thaw. But I am not much good in Haguefort; I cannot even properly look after Melly, being ill so much. I am looking for a way to get better, and I believe that the search for the answer as to how to do that may reside in the dragon's cave."

She turned her attention away from the others and to Ashe.

"We have talked about this before; what is your decision, Sam? Is it all right with you?"

Ashe choked back his rising gorge. *No*, the dragon in his blood whispered. *My treasure. Stay.*

"If that's what you want, Aria; if you think you will be safer or more comfortable with Elynsynos, I will gladly take you there."

"Thank you," Rhapsody said, her green eyes shining. "You can always come to visit me from time to time." She looked at Anborn, whose face betrayed his disapproval, and said quickly, "Remember, Lord Marshal, should anything happen to you in Sorbold where you might need assistance, you know the Kinsman call. I'm sure I would hear it, even in the dragon's cave, and come to your aid, if the wind is willing to carry me as it does other Kinsmen."

Anborn chuckled in spite of himself. "Now, that's a pretty thought. The three known Kinsmen on the continent—one is lame, the second is pregnant and sick as a dog, and the third—well, the third is a Bolg."

"Indeed," said Gwydion Navarne. "But in my view, if I were ever in need, any of those three Kinsmen, however compromised, would be a great relief to have around."

"You're right about that," said Ashe, rising from the table and helping Rhapsody out of her chair. "And as long as the three of you remember to call for aid should the need arise, I will at least be somewhat comforted until you are home again."

*T*wo mornings after the festival ended, and the last of the stragglers had made their way out of the grounds and back to their homes, when the last of the debris and detritus had been cleared away, Anborn and Gwydion Navarne saddled their mounts and left on their mission together.

Rhapsody had been fighting back tears all morning, helping Ashe check Gwydion's provisions and sitting at breakfast with him and Melisande, who felt no need to hold any tears back and instead allowed them to roll down her porcelain cheeks into her clotted cream.

"I think I am finally understanding what you went through all those times when the people you loved left you at home and went off to do things they assured you were important, promising to come back," she said to her adopted grandson after Melisande had left the table. "You want to believe so badly what they say is true, but your dread prevents it. Additionally, you can't give voice to that worry, for fear that your doubt will somehow be taken as a lack of faith, or bring bad luck. So you put on a brave smile and tell your loved one to hurry home safely, all the while dreading the moment they leave your sight."

"That would be correct," Gwydion said sympathetically. "I'm sorry to have made you experience it."

"No need to be," the Lady Cymrian replied. "Do what you need to do, and come home safely. I know that Anborn will guard you with his life."

"And I will guard him with mine."

Rhapsody resisted the urge to smile. "I know that as well," she said.

A slamming sound startled them. The young duke stood as the doors opened and the litter bearers entered, carrying the Cymrian hero, who was snarling at Jal'asee as they came through the door.

"No, I did *not* try the infernal contraption, bugger it all," Anborn said, gesturing contemptuously at the Ancient Seren. "And as I have told you over and over again, I have no intention of doing so, unless the bloody thing can be used to hone weapons or ferment ale. I don't want my brother's damnable pity, or his largesse. You can tell him that rather than its intended use, I plan to donate it to a whorehouse and suggest that they use it on their guests who find it intriguing."

Jal'asee consulted his cards, then pulled one out of the sheaf.

"Hmmm, whorehouse, whorehouse, whorehouse. Ah! Here it is. 'Then at least I know you will be getting *some* use out of it occasionally.'"

"Are you ready yet?" Anborn demanded of Gwydion Navarne, glaring daggers at the Sea Mage.

"I will be in just a few more moments, Lord Marshal," the new duke said, bending to kiss Rhapsody on the cheek. "I need to say my goodbyes to Gerald Owen and Melly, and then I will be prepared to go."

"Get on with it, then," Anborn said gruffly. Gwydion nodded and took his leave.

The Lord Marshal gestured at his bearers. "Withdraw to the edge of the room; I wish to speak privately with the Lady Cymrian." The servants bowed and walked away. "And you, Jal'asee—tell my miscreant brother that the next time he wants to make something for me, he might want to be certain it is something that would not squash him flat should it drop on him unexpectedly next time he comes to visit."

"I will relay the message," said the Sea Mage dryly.

"Good. Now go away."

Rhapsody and the Seren ambassador exchanged a sympathetic glance; then Jal'asee bowed slightly and withdrew from the room.

"You know, it's a shame that you chose to go into soldiering," Rhapsody said, a sour edge mixing with the humor in her voice. "You really would have made a fine diplomat."

"Indeed, the finest sort of diplomat is the one that is plainspoken about his goals and intentions, and where he stands. I don't think anyone could seriously accuse me of vacillating on my positions, or obfuscating my statements."

"Certainly can't disagree with you there."

Anborn's azure eyes twinkled. "Well, to that end, I have to ask you if you are still planning your ill-considered visit to the lair of Elynsynos."

"Yes," said Rhapsody, taken a little aback. "Why would you think that I had changed my mind?"

Anborn shrugged. "I have no reason to believe that good sense would suddenly strike you; it has never made an appearance up until now. I had just hoped against hope that it would."

"What is your objection to my plans?" Rhapsody asked.

"For the life of me I cannot imagine why you would want to go sit in a cave with a vapid beast who might accidentally incinerate you should she get a head cold. Is my wretched nephew's company even more dull than I had imagined?"

"You have never met Elynsynos," Rhapsody said tartly, her ire rising. "I don't appreciate you speaking about her, or Ashe, in that manner."

The general chuckled. "Elynsynos is my grandmother."

"So perhaps you should take the time to come to know her. She's fascinating."

Anborn shrugged. "Perhaps. Maybe someday when I have nothing better on which to spend my time. It appears I value mine more than you do," he said, a playful note in his voice, but a serious look in his eyes. "Stay here, Rhapsody, where Gwydion can take care of you. This pregnancy was ill advised; do not make it even more dangerous by hiding away in a dragon's cave where no one can find you to help if you need it. At least at Haguefort you have access to the very best healers in Roland."

Rhapsody shook her head. "To my knowledge, none of those healers has ever delivered the child of a Lirin mother and a dragon father," she said lightly. "It's a somewhat exclusive experience. There are few in the world who have ever been involved in such a pregnancy, and Elynsynos is one of them. She conceived Manwyn, Rhonwyn, and your mother while in human form, and could not then change back to her wyrm form until they were born, so she has had the experience of carrying babies of different blood in her body and giving birth to them. I hope to learn a great deal from her, and perhaps fare better in the delivery than I would have otherwise."

"What can she possibly teach you? She was a serpentine beast of ancient race, an egg-layer that took a Seren form, mated with a Seren man, and carried triplets in a body that itself was foreign. That is not your situation."

"No, it's not," Rhapsody admitted. "But as far as I know, there is only one other person who had a closer situation to mine, whose natural form was human, and that was your mother." She sighed deeply. "I wish that events had worked out differently with Anwyn, that I could have come to know her and learn from her, as my grandmother-in-law. I wish she could come to know her grandchild. If only I had not gained her ire, perhaps—" Her voice broke off in midword.

Anborn's face was bloodlessly pale, his azure eyes gleaming with wild intensity.

"Do not ever speak those words again," he choked, his voice raw. "You are a Namer; may the All-God forbid that your wish ever be granted just because you were foolish enough to misuse your power."

Rhapsody stared at the Lord Marshal in amazement. He was more visibly upset than she ever remembered seeing him, even in the heat of battle.

"Anborn—"

His hand shot out and roughly covered her mouth. "Stop—do not utter another sound." He glanced around behind him, then above, as if listening for something in the wind. "You do not know what you are saying." His voice dropped in tone to just above a whisper. "If there is anything in this life that you have to be grateful for, it is that the misbegotten hellkite is *dead,* rotten into coal in her ash-covered grave, and therefore will never know your child, or that you even have one. She was the absolutely last entity on the face of this earth that you would want to seek maternal advice from; trust me on this."

His hand trembled as it cupped her lips.

Rhapsody's emerald eyes, wide with surprise, blinked above his fingers. Then her expression resolved into one of more calm, and she placed her hand over his and pressed his hand to her lips, then gently pulled it from her face.

"All right, Anborn," she said quietly. "I believe you."

Her eyes searched his face, trying to ascertain the reason for the intensity of his alarm. She knew that Anborn had led his father's armies against his mother's in the Cymrian War, and doubtless that had given him opportunity to see Anwyn's brutality at close range. But the war had been over for more than four hundred years; the general seemed to have made peace with other old adversaries and buried his enmity in all other matters. The strength of his reaction confounded her.

After a moment's staring at each other, she still had found nothing tenable, so she smiled, hoping to diffuse his mood. The wildness in the general's eyes seemed to pass, and he stared at her with a new clarity.

"It's time I got started," he said finally, reaching over the side of his chair for his crutches, pulling them into his lap. "Young Gwydion will be waiting; he's already champing at the bit." He continued to watch Rhapsody for a moment longer, then leaned forward.

"I have one final thing I want to say to you," he said, his voice firm but calm again. "Just in the event I don't return."

Rhapsody went pale. "Don't even think that, let alone say it," she said.

Anborn smiled slightly. "It's a possibility that occurs every time one leaves another's presence. Isn't that what you said?"

"Yes. But I don't like the way it comes out of your mouth. When I said it, it was a reminder to tell the people you love how much they matter to you. When you say it, it feels like goodbye."

"It's meant to be neither; I just wish to pass along to the only Lirin Namer I know something that I have never said to another person, for the sake of history. Both of my parents were selfish, misguided monarchs that allowed a petty disagreement and their own thirst for power to plunge a continent into war and destroy the civilization their people had built from nothing. There is an element so avaricious, so self-important, about this that it can only be ascribed as evil—both of them."

He leaned closer, so that his words, spoken softly, could be clearly heard.

"And while there are those who would discount what I say as biased, or self-serving, I swear to you, Rhapsody, that while Gwylliam, my father, may have been a man whose selfishness made him evil, my mother was wicked, malevolent, on a much deeper level. Llauron might disagree, were he to appear from the ether, or whatever elemental state he currently lounges about in, because he always took her part, but despite what my brother might say, I can tell you from firsthand experience that my mother was evil *incarnate*. She was soulless—she had been cursed with the ability to see only into the Past, for all intents and purposes, and she was reminded constantly of the wrongs that had been done to her, the slights and the betrayals, those injuries which good men and women put behind them and bury in what went before so that they might move on. Perhaps anyone so afflicted would also have turned wicked. But Anwyn had a ruthlessness that came from a deeper place. There is no doubt in anyone's mind that it was she that allowed the demon that you and your friends vanquished to grow in power, to escape notice for centuries as it sowed the seeds of its destructive plans. But I know more—much more. And I can tell you that there has been nothing in my experience more close to gazing directly into the Vault of the Underworld than looking into my mother's eyes. May she putrefy in that Vault forever."

He signaled to his bearers and was carried from the room, leaving Rhapsody watching him go in stunned silence.

25

Elynsynos's lair was exactly as Rhapsody remembered it.

The journey with Ashe had been much easier than the first one they had made to this place together. Then they did not trust each other; the land was rife with hidden evil, in the grip of an unseen F'dor, causing even those who were allies to be suspicious of one another. Now, as they returned to the hidden cave set in a hollow in the hillside near a small woodland lake, lost in the wonder of love and impending parenthood, the Lord and Lady Cymrian found that sweet memories were all that remained of that first journey, the mistrust and acrimony lost to history.

The lake at the base of the hill was frozen, its crystalline ice reflecting the trees that lined it like a mirror.

From the depths of that cave a voice sounded as they approached, a voice that held the timbres of soprano, alto, tenor, and bass simultaneously.

Hello, Pretty. You've brought your husband and your baby. How lovely.

Rhapsody chuckled. "Hello, Elynsynos. May we enter?"

Yes, of course. Come in.

Together Ashe and Rhapsody followed the winding path down into the dragon's lair.

The great wyrm, matriarch of all that lived on the continent, was waiting in her horde of glittering coins, chests of treasure and jewels, and artifacts recovered from a jealous sea—tridents and masts, figureheads from lost ships, rudders and wheels formed into chandeliers with a thousand candleless flames. As always, Rhapsody struggled not to become entranced by her eyes, prisms of colors and hypnotic light scored with the same vertical pupils that could be seen in Ashe's eyes. Those enchanting eyes were dancing with the light of excitement.

The great beast lifted herself from the salty water of the lake that filled the bottom of her horde, her gleaming scales and enormous, serpentine body fluid as the wind. Elynsynos had long ago given up her physical form and existed in a purely elemental state, in much the same way that her grandson Llauron, Ashe's father, had chosen to do.

Have you come to visit, as you promised, Pretty? the wyrm asked, settling down on the cave floor.

"Indeed," Rhapsody said. "I am hoping to learn about carrying a wyrmkin child from you, and to find a way to feel better while doing it."

How do you feel now? the great beast asked.

Rhapsody considered; the nausea had vanished from the moment she walked into the cave, lulled by the rhythmic sloshing of the small salt sea. While the darkness and closeness of the place reminded her of the Root, there was something about the love in it that seemed to keep the fear she was sometimes consumed by underground at bay. The sea treasures were signs of the dragon's love of her lost Seren sailor, Merithyn the Explorer, who had found this place a millennium ago and had inadvertently started the dynasty that would build and destroy the continent.

And was rebuilding it now.

"Better," she said. "Almost well."

The wyrm regarded her with an expression of mixed fondness and concern.

"Will you take care of my wife for me for a little while, Great-grandmother?" Ashe asked, helping Rhapsody into a hammock that had been fixed to the stone wall by a trident thrust into the rock of the cave.

Of course, the dragon said, manipulating the wind as its voice. *Have you chosen a name for the child?*

The expectant parents looked at each other.

"We have discussed one, but we wanted to see what the baby looked and seemed like first," Rhapsody said.

Very well, said Elynsynos. *As long as you understand that the child will need a name in order to be born.*

"Er—no, I hadn't realized that," Rhapsody said.

A dragon emerges from the egg in an elemental state, said Elynsynos. *Because wyrms contain mostly Earth lore, but each of the other elements as well, whatever name is given will largely determine what the child is like. So choose well; many mother dragons are grumpy after egg-laying, and the names they give their offspring when they hatch yield even grumpier wyrm adults.*

"Will that be the case for our baby?" Ashe asked, sitting down beside an enormous pile of rysin coins, forged of a blue metal found deep in the mountains. "He or she won't be full wyrm—I am actually hoping that since his or her blood will be so dilute, it will yield a low draconic tendency."

The great beast shrugged, a gesture that made Rhapsody giggle.

Every beast is different, Elynsynos said. *It's impossible to know what the combinations of blood will produce. When you consider, there really are only a few known examples of wyrmkin in the world, and all that I know of are related to me. My three daughters, Manwyn, Rhonwyn, and Anwyn, are first-generation wyrmkin; of them, only Anwyn reproduced. The only other living wyrmkin I know of are Anwyn's three sons, Edwyn, Llauron, and Anborn, and, of course, yourself, Pretty's Husband. All of you are different, though there are some family traits that are consistent. What this child will be like, who can say? He or she will be like himself, or herself.*

Ashe smiled at his great-grandmother. "Wise words—and we will cherish our child, whatever he or she is like. I just hope you are willing to help instruct this child in the use of dragon lore; no one did that for me, and

I think it would have been useful to help understand this second nature, this nonhuman side."

The great beast snorted.

Dragon nature is straightforward, Pretty's Husband, she said with an injured air. *It is human blood that makes wyrmkin inconsistent.*

Dragons are protective of their land, because they must be. We are the last guardians of the primordial earth; its lore is extant within us as it is within no other creature. We alone understand the stakes of death, the finality of ending, because we do not have souls as other creatures do. No dragon would ever consider killing another dragon, no matter how much he hated the beast, because we understand the need for our race to remain intact. This is a lore that is older than me, is older than all of us. But whether wyrmkin have the sense of it, I do not know. I suspect that Anwyn's sons had it—they never took the initiative to kill each other, or their mother, when they could have, particularly Llauron. But Anwyn—I do not know if she would have held to the dragon ways if they did not suit her purposes. The dragon eyed Ashe, causing prismatic flashes of light to dance over the coins scattered throughout the cave. *And the books of history are not written about you yet, either. We will have to see if you remain faithful to the draconic code, or if the mix in your blood leads you elsewhere.*

"I have blood on my hands, it's true," Ashe said, his voice melancholy. "As far as I know, I have never killed one of my own kind. But had I been given the chance to take my grandmother from the sky as she strafed the Cymrian Council in dragon form, or when she took my wife into the sky with her, I would have ripped her heart out without a second thought. Blessedly, Rhapsody did it for me, but I cannot say that I mourn her passing. She was a bitter, vicious, bloodthirsty woman, and her death was a good thing for everyone involved."

Untimely death is never a good thing, said the dragon sadly. *You say that because you have not truly come to understand it. I had not either, until Merithyn died. I had never before felt death, tasted its foul burning in my teeth. The creatures I had consumed—stags, harts, and the like—had experienced death in my maw, but with their passing had come life, sustenance, and so it did not have the same bitter taste. But Merithyn's death was an ending so complete that it took part of my life with it as well.*

Rhapsody reached out from the hammock and caressed the dragon's massive shoulder.

"Merithyn gave his life saving his ship, and much of the First Fleet. Out of his death came life as well, Elynsynos. It was a great sacrifice, for him and for you, but a nation lived because of it. Perhaps it is one of the greatest sacrifices in history."

The dragon shook her head violently.

No, Pretty. I will tell you of the greatest sacrifice. It is important that you both know it, because it is the heritage of your child, the legacy of his dragon blood. I will tell you of the Ending.

You know the stories of the Before-Time, of the great battles between the five Firstborn races, when the children of air, earth, water, and ether, the Kith, dragons, Mythlin, and Seren, banded together to force the destructive fifth race, the F'dor fire demons, into the center of the world where they could no longer wreak havoc upon the earth. And you doubtless know that the part dragons played was the contribution of the Living Stone to make the Vault in which the F'dor were imprisoned, yes?

"Yes," said Ashe.

But what you do not know, my great-grandson, Pretty's Husband, is that the Vault, as it was built, with the vast majority of our treasure of Living Stone, was still not enough to completely contain the F'dor. The Progenitor of all dragons, the first of our race, could see that the cage of Living Stone would not hold them. So he made the greatest sacrifice in history. That sacrifice is known to all dragons as the Ending.

A dragon's decision to die, to give up its life, is undertaken with the understanding that for us there is no Afterlife, at least not a conscious one. Most often that decision comes at the end of an extremely long life. The dragon is too tired to continue to live; it is in pain and exhausted, and so it merely ceases to try and stay alive. And it ends. That kind of ending leaves some of the dragon's lore behind—the blood that ran in the beast's veins turns to gold. And some of what was the dragon remains with it—the avarice, the possessiveness. Why are men so hungry for a soft yellow metal that does nothing to further their ends? They cannot sate their hunger with it, or heal themselves when they are ill or injured. They cannot even forge it into a weapon. And yet they fight wars over it, commit all sorts of atrocities, even lose their souls to it. Much like a dragon would.

"I had never considered that," Rhapsody said. She was taking notes in her journal.

The Progenitor saw that the F'dor might well escape from the Vault. And after all the death, all the destruction, and all that had been sacrificed in the fight to contain them, he understood the incalculable cost of that happening. So just as the lock of the Vault was being sundered, the Progenitor wrapped his body, more vast than can even be imagined, around the Vault, subsuming it. He had been in an ethereal state; once he had enveloped the Vault with his own being, he slowly let go of each of his elemental lores—the ether, the earth, the water, the air, and the fire. His body dried and hardened to a vast shell that surrounded the Vault inside it, preventing the escape of the F'dor. He just Ended. That is his legacy—and it's the legacy of your child. Each dragon has the power to End, but none, to my knowledge, ever have done so since, because it is the most complete and final form of death. Not even your lore remains behind in gold or gems that can one day adorn the empty heads of kings, or the breasts of vain women. Dragons have more of a stake in the Earth that shelters all beings, because we have sacrificed more to guard it.

The Lord and Lady Cymrian looked at each other in silence.

So, Elynsynos concluded, her multitoned voice lightening, *that is the tale. Now, Pretty's Husband, eat something, so that you will be sustained on your journey home, and will come back often to visit.*

A plate of rolls and jars of jam appeared on the cave floor.

Ashe laughed. "All right, I know a hint when I see one. Very well, Great-grandmother, I will eat and be on my way so that you may begin your visit with my wife. I know when I'm not wanted—and I surely don't want to get breathed on, so I will comply."

Don't be ridiculous, said the wyrm. *A dragon has to be solid in order to breathe on someone else. I do not do solid.*

Now have some jam! Then be on your way.

After Ashe had left, Rhapsody sat down to examine the documents Achmed had left her, as she promised to do.

"One important thing I forgot to tell you, Elynsynos," she said, sifting carefully through the papers and graphing the musical code in which the manuscript was written. "At Thaw I have asked my friend Achmed to come to this place."

The dragon inhaled slowly.

Did you tell him where it was?

"No," Rhapsody said quickly, "I would never do that without your permission. I told him to go to the Tar'afel, and I would sing him to the place I wanted to meet him. He can follow the sound of his namesong wherever I chant it. But I just wanted to warn you that Achmed and I can argue fairly harshly; it is just our way, not a sign that he is going to harm me. So if we do argue when he comes, please don't intervene. I would hate to see him roasting on a spit over his own campfire."

Very well, said the dragon, but she did not sound impressed.

And there they remained in pleasant company, the dragon reveling in her treasure, the Lady Cymrian translating the documents, until she began to tremble with the understanding of what was in them. With shaking hands, she put the manuscript back in the metal box and closed it quickly. The inclination to vomit came over her, but it was not one generated by her pregnancy.

"Oh, sweet One-God," she whispered.

26

As Ashe neared the far side of the crystalline lake beyond which the lair of the dragon Elynsynos lay, he felt an unwelcome static tingle run the length of his spine, radiating out over his skin to his fingertips. Then, a heartbeat later, it was gone.

He stopped in the crusty snow and turned angrily around, recognizing the vibration and looking for the source, but there was nothing visible in the ancient forest. The deep, rich hues of the evergreen boughs stood in marked contrast to the bare trunks and branches of the deciduous trees, silvery-bare or clothed in a remnant of ragged, dead leaves of brown and russet, waiting to be swept away by stronger winter winds. The breeze that blew through the glade was sharp and cold.

"Where are you, Llauron?" the Lord Cymrian demanded of the air around him.

There was no answer but that of the wind, and the ripples that disturbed the surface of the lake.

Angrily Ashe seized hold of the hilt of his sword and drew it quickly forth from its sheath. Kirsdarke, the blade of elemental water, roared to life in his hand, appearing like the foaming waves of the sea, gleaming with liquid anger matching Ashe's own. He held it up to his eyes and looked through it.

The world beyond the rippling waves appeared dull and flat, like an old grave marker whose inscription had been worn flatter by time. Like water on such a stone, the rivulets running into the crevasses and depressions, making them visible again, the vision Ashe had through the blade sharpened around the elemental form that was hovering, invisible to the human eye, beyond the treeline of the clearing.

A great draconic shape floated in the air just above the ground, gray and silver as the branches of the maple trees.

"I can see you, Father," Ashe said, annoyed. "You may as well show yourself."

A disappointed sigh whistled forth like the breeze. "You never were any fun to play hide-and-seek with," a sonorous baritone, light and melodious, said. "Your dragon sense was sharp, even as a child. If it took you more than a few seconds to find me, we both knew that you were merely humoring me."

"I am well past playing games with you," Ashe said bitterly, returning

Kirsdarke to its sheath with a savage snap. "I told you three years ago to stay away from my wife and family. And yet, of all places in the world you could be, hanging about in the ether, communing with the elements, the ability to do so what you chose over that family, here you are outside Elynsynos's lair. What a coincidence. What do you want?"

"No harm, I assure you," said the voice, a testy undertone in it. "And there's no need to be so harsh. I am your father, Gwydion, or at least I was in my human lifetime."

"Which you happily sacrificed for a hollow immortality," Ashe said, pulling at his lambskin gloves. "And at the expense of my wife's peace of mind; she still occasionally has nightmares about burning you to 'death' in your false pyre with a blast of starfire from her sword at your insistence. I told you then, and I will tell you again now, I want you to stay away from Rhapsody. She has paid dearly for your elemental wyrmdom, and I mean to make certain she is done with that."

"Your wife forgave me those wrongs long ago, Gwydion," said the voice. The air within the trees shifted, gaining shape and heft, thickening until it took the form of an enormous serpent, vaporous, with iridescent scales the color of ashes from a spent fire, flashing with intermittent glitters of silver and gold. Its vast wings were folded next to its sides, minimizing its breadth, leaving only the wyrmlike length of it visible, well over one hundred feet from nostrils to terminal tail spike. "It's a pity you haven't learned to follow her example."

"I care more about her well-being than she does," Ashe replied tersely, staring at the enormous ethereal dragon in the nearest multifaceted eye scored by a vertical pupil. It was a gaze that few men could hold without being lost to the beast's will, but Ashe, his own dragon blood strong, returned it without blinking. "And to that end I mean to see her kept free from annoyance, harassment, or manipulation, all of which you have committed against her at one time or another. So be on your way. You have no business here."

The wind raced through the snowy clearing, lifting the granular blanket of snow from the surface and spinning the crystals into fluttery bands that danced and twisted, then fell to the ground again, skittering along the crust.

Finally the dragon spoke, and its voice held unmistakable sadness, deep as the sea.

"You would keep me from my own grandchild, then?"

Ashe exhaled sharply. "So that's it, is it? You are looking for the baby. Why? What possible interest could you have in a child? You had one once, if I recall correctly, and it was little more to you than a tool to accomplish your goals. What goals do you still have, Llauron? I thought those things would fall away with the ashes of the mortal human body that you left behind in the coal bed of your pyre when you convinced my wife to transform you, without her knowledge, into your elemental self. Don't you have better things to do, now that you are wind itself, fire itself, earth itself, water itself, ether itself, and, of course, sheer *gall* itself?"

"It seems you believe I have always been the last of those," Llauron said, unfolding his filmy wings and stretching them lazily. They passed without resistance through the tree limbs and bracken of the forest, like mist. "And I suppose I can't really dispute that. But is it really so hard for you to imagine, Gwydion, that in my old age I might want the same joy that every other grandfather-to-be has—taking delight in his offspring?"

The ugly sound that issued forth from Ashe's throat was both a gargle and a cough.

"Yes, it is," he said flatly. "You? You want to be a grandfather?"

"Indeed." The beast beat the air with its wings, causing many of the last dry leaves to fall. "Grandchildren are a second chance at happiness we might have missed the first time around, Gwydion. Don't dismiss my desire to come to know the descendants of my blood. If you know anything about our race, you know that there is little, if anything, a dragon prizes above its progeny."

"Yes, I am well aware of that," Ashe said, positioning himself closer to the ethereal beast and interposing himself between it and the path back to Elynsynos's lair. "And as I prize mine above *all* else, I will do whatever is necessary to keep her or him from ever experiencing the sheer delight of being manipulated mercilessly by a family member, to the point of feeling useless, good for nothing, or damned. Those are feelings I know well, thanks to the tenderness of my upbringing. I have no desire for my son or daughter to ever feel that way. *Ever.* And I know Rhapsody agrees. So be gone from this place. I do not accept that your protestations are genuine. Like everything else you have ever wanted, I am certain there is an ulterior motive at play here, a hidden reason that benefits you first, at the expense of the others involved. But since those others are my wife and child, I will not brook it. Because, being part dragon myself, there is nothing more important to me. So go away."

The expression of sadness dissipated in the beast's prismatic eyes into something more studied; it was a look Ashe recognized, though until now he had only seen it in his father's human face. Llauron was regrouping, switching from the emotional, an area of admitted weakness, to the logical, which was his strength.

"So you are keeping me away from your child for his benefit?"

The headache behind Ashe's eyes stabbed sharply, and he rubbed his eyes with his knuckles, trying to fight it off.

"And Rhapsody's," he said, wincing.

The dragon nodded thoughtfully. "And in your mind, it is better for your child to grow up never knowing his grandfather?"

"Sadly, yes."

"How shortsighted of you." The great gray dragon stretched his wings slightly, causing the ice crystals on the snow's surface to whip into the air, the soft sting of the breeze blowing them into Ashe's eyes. "Had it occurred to you that your child, conceived when your dragon's blood is at the peak of its strength in you, will be more draconic than you were? He will have few of the race that is very much a part of his makeup to reach out to, to learn from; dragons as a race are rare enough. But those to whom the child will be related are few and far between—"

"He or she can learn from Elynsynos," Ashe said tersely, annoyed to still be carrying on the conversation. "She is his great-great-grandmother, a pure wyrm, not wyrmkin like you and I. No one knows as well as she what it is like to be a dragon. I'm sure she will be delighted to tutor my child in draconic ways and elemental lore. And, above all else, she has never betrayed Rhapsody or me. So thank you for your—kind offer, but I believe we have that aspect of the child's education covered."

"My grandmother has not walked the world as a human being," Llauron said smoothly, the silver scales in his hide winking in the dusty light of the glen. "She only took a human form—or, more accurately, a Seren one—to attract the notice of Merithyn. She may have knowledge of the ancient times that I did not have in human form, but since I have come to join the elements, I have learned those stories, too, Gwydion. And I do have much to impart—sure you cannot dismiss all that you learned of the world from me."

Ashe inhaled sharply, taking the freezing air of the forest into his lungs, where it weighed heavily inside him. His wife's words, spoken with a Namer's truth at the council where they were chosen to rule over the Cymrian people, rang in his ears.

If I have one message for you it is this: the Past is gone. Learn from it and let it go. We must forgive each other. We must forgive ourselves. Only then will there be a true peace.

He let his eyes wander over the face of the ethereal beast hanging before him in the air, and on his every word. The dragon's eyes twinkled with intelligence, but there was something more in them; Ashe could not be certain what it was, but for a moment it looked like longing, or something akin to it.

Involuntarily he thought back to his childhood, the earliest days he could remember, before a piece of Seren had been sewed into his chest, before his draconic nature had emerged, the days of innocence, when he was just a boy alone in the world with a father who loved to walk the forests with him, pointing out every sort of tree and plant, singing him sea chanteys and ancient folksongs, teaching him to sail and swim in the ocean that later in life became a part of him. To his shock, those good memories were still there, not obliterated as he had believed them to be by Llauron's later selfishness and manipulation, his willingness to use his son, and, worse, Rhapsody, to his ends, however noble his intentions.

"I believe you sincerely want to be part of your grandchild's life and up-bringing, Father," he said finally, wincing at the hope he could see taking root in the wyrm's gray-blue eyes. "But, as valuable as the history lessons might be, there are other sorts of lessons that you tend to teach that are very much more dangerous and scarring. I wish things could be different—I'm sorry."

He turned quickly and made his way through the forest, leaving Llauron's misty form behind him.

The beast watched him go; Llauron's dragon sense followed him for more than five miles, making note of the quickness of his son's step, the flush of blood to his face, the tightness of his throat. Then, when Ashe was finally beyond his reach and his senses, he faded slowly into the wind again and disappeared, leaving only on the dry leaves of the forest the traces of gold that can be seen where dragon tears fall.

The Slaughter

27

THE HOLY CITY-STATE OF SEPULVARTA

The outer ring of the city was a maze of white and gray marble buildings set into the foothills of the mountains that eventually became the guardian hills of Sorbold to the south. Those buildings—houses, meeting halls, and museums—shone in the light of morning from a great distance, making the entire city seem to glow from the radiance.

If that were not enough to lend a holy, almost magical patina to the landscape, in the center of the city stood an enormous structure known as the Spire, the pinnacle of Lianta'ar, the great basilica of the Star, the most sacred of all the elemental basilicas. A feat of almost magical engineering, the base of the structure spanned the width of a city block, tapering upward a thousand feet in the air to the pinnacle, which was crowned with a glowing silver star. The shining summit was rumored to contain a piece of ether from the star Melita, the entity known in Cymrian lore as the Sleeping Child, which had fallen to Earth in the First Age of history. Its impact swamped the Island, leaving it half its previous size. Thereafter, the burning star had lain beneath the waves for four millennia, boiling the ocean above it, until at last it had risen and claimed the rest of the Island. But a piece of it had traveled with the Cymrian exodus, or so the legends insisted, and now lighted the top of the Spire, which gleamed day and night, visible from a hundred leagues away.

Lasarys and the two acolytes who had escaped the purge in the square of Jierna Tal had followed that light like a beacon. Knowing that if they were recognized on their way out of Sorbold they would have been returned to Talquist, who believed them dead and would make certain of that belief if he knew otherwise, they had traveled slowly and circumspectly, joining a foot caravan of pilgrims on their way to the holy city. The pilgrims had embraced them, having similarly anonymous travelers in their midst, and allowed them to remain in their company until the Spire came into view. Then the former priests set out on their own, looking to find the Blesser of Sorbold, their nation's benison, Nielash Mousa, and tell him all that they had seen.

Now they stood at the city gates, the towering Spire casting a deep shadow over them. The priests, swathed in the robes of pilgrims, stood in silence, allowing the majesty of their holy city and its Spire to wash over them along with the crystals of ice that danced on the wind. The Spire was seen as the Patriarch's direct link with the Creator, and so looking upon it was a bit like looking at the threshold of the Afterlife.

Lester was the first to gain his voice.

"How do we find the Blesser, Father?" he asked Lasarys nervously, watching the river of human traffic, most of it composed of acolytes and priests of the Patrician religion, streaming into the city gates along with merchants and tradesmen and beggars seeking alms. "None of us has ever been here before; in asking the way, we will doubtless be recognized, as the others here all seem to be of Orlandan blood."

The elderly sexton shook his head. "Keep your eyes to the ground, my sons, and pray to the All-God to sustain us."

Dominicus tucked his hands nervously into the sleeves of his robe and fell into place behind Lasarys with Lester. Together the three men approached the city gate.

"What's your business here?" demanded the guard rotely.

Lasarys bowed deferentially. "Linen makers from Sorbold, sir," he said meekly. "Here to clean His Holiness's robes and scutch the flax for his new set."

The guard snorted, then stepped aside, his eyes glassy with boredom.

Quickly the three priests hurried through the crowded streets, making their way to the manse where the Patriarch lived. It was not difficult to locate; the rectory was a beautiful marble building with immense doors bound in brass, attached to the basilica itself, at the opposite end of the city from the Spire, but still directly beneath the light of the star at its summit. It was guarded by two soldiers with spears.

"What do you want?" the first guard demanded as the three men approached the doors.

"We're priests of Sorbold, here to see Nielash Mousa," said Lasarys in a low voice, again averting his eyes modestly. "We beg his immediate audience; it's very important."

The first soldier regarded him with narrowed eyes, then muttered a few words to his companion, who nodded. The guard opened one of the huge brass-bound doors and disappeared into the manse. Many long moments later he returned, looking smug.

"The benison is no longer here," he said. "He's returned to Sorbold, alas. Be on your way."

The three priests stared at each other in dismay, then quickly turned away, not wishing to further rouse the ire or the interest of the guards.

"Now what?" asked Lester desperately.

"Perhaps we could speak to the Patriarch," Dominicus suggested.

Lasarys choked back a sour laugh.

"The Patriarch doesn't receive the likes of us, nor should he," he said, stepping past an icy drain where street water had clogged, leaving a patch of ice that reached into the cobbled road like frozen fingers. "When he is not consulting with heads of state or the high priests and benisons, he is receiving our prayers to the All-God and offering them up." The two acolytes nodded; every adherent to the Patrician faith understood the tenet that prayer was offered by the people to their local priest, who in turn offered it to the area's high priest, whose entreaties were made to the benison, and ultimately to the Patriarch, who offered them, in a great convocation of praise, directly to the All-God. The Patriarch alone had a straight means of communication with the Creator; all others went through channels.

"Then what are we to do?" Lester persisted.

Lasarys sighed dispiritedly.

"Let us visit Lianta'ar, and offer our prayers there," he said. "If nothing else, the presence of the holy ether above us in the Spire may cleanse our minds a little of the horror we have witnessed. Perhaps wisdom will come to us then."

The priests circled the enormous building, seeking the entrance doors. They found them at the eastern side of the temple, facing the rising sun. The doors were fashioned of gleaming brass inset with silver in the pattern of an eight-pointed star, framing the huge basilica whose towering walls of polished marble and overarching dome were taller than any in the known world.

For the sexton and acolytes, who had spent a good deal of their respective lives serving the faithful of the Patrician faith but who had never until this day been to Sepulvarta, and never until this moment had been to Lianta'ar, entering the basilica through those doors was a little bit like stepping directly into the Afterlife. The basilica's architecture was unsurpassed in breadth, depth, and beauty, with countless colors and patterns of mosaics gracing the floors and ceiling, exquisite giltwork on the frescoed walls and the windows fashioned in colored glass. The men stopped, unable to take it all in and continue moving, just as the hundreds of other members of the faithful who had entered the doors moments before them were standing still in awe.

Finally, after more than a few moments of rapture, the sexton shook off his reverie and plucked at Lester's sleeve. Quickly they made their way through the assembled faithful staring openmouthed at the ceiling, past the lector's circle, where sacred texts were read aloud, and into one of the rows of seats and kneelers that surrounded the central altar on all sides.

The altar itself was elevated atop a cylindrical rise of stairs. It was fashioned in plain stone but edged in platinum, and could be seen from anywhere in the basilica. To this altar each week were brought special intentions, special prayers, and requests for wisdom or healing that had been compiled by the five benisons of the faith, and sent to the Patriarch for presentation to the All-God. Lasarys stared at the altar now, silently placing his petition at the feet of the Creator through the hands of the Patriarch, even though he was not in the position to do so.

O holy one, Father of the Universe, Lord of Life, hear my prayer, for I am in fear for your world.

He bowed his head, struggling to remain calm.

The silence of the basilica, broken by the occasional echoing of footsteps and whispering, settled on his shoulders, but no words came to his mind. Finally, after almost an hour in reflection, Lasarys lifted his head and looked at the two acolytes.

Dominicus was still bent in prayer, his hands folded before his eyes. Lester was staring without focus at the altar, a look of quiet panic on his face.

"Anything?" he asked them softly.

The two priests-in-training shook their heads.

Lasarys sighed. He rose stiffly, the joints of his elderly frame sore with age.

"Very well, my sons. Let us quit this place and look around the city; perhaps there are others of our order here we can find sustenance with. But be certain you do not share your name with them, lest it get back to Talquist."

The acolytes nodded again, and followed the sexton out of the basilica.

As they stepped into the blinding winter sunshine, another, brighter flash assaulted their eyes.

It was the blade of a spear that had stopped a hairsbreadth from Lasarys's face.

"Are you the sexton of Terreanfor?" the guard demanded. "And did you enter this city on false grounds?"

Lasarys, always a shy, bookish man, looked the man in the eye and nodded slightly.

"Come with me," the guard said gruffly.

As four other guards closed around them, the priests' eyes glittered, but they said nothing; they bowed their heads beneath the hoods of their cloaks and followed the lead guard away from the basilica.

$\mathcal{W}$ith the hardening of the earth at winter's approach came a similar hardening of Faron's will.

Each passing day drove him deeper into the frost-blanched fields, through the undisturbed snowpack of the inner continent. His primitive mind had comprehended the necessity to hide, to be unseen in populated areas, but now, as he scoured the lands southeast of Navarne, where there was little but open field, endless road, and forest, his fear and need to remain unseen was dissipating, leaving him emboldened, almost rash.

The coldness of the earth was displeasing to him; he felt like a child pushed from its mother's lap. He could still feel the heartbeat of it, still sense the warmth beneath the deep blanket of snow, but the sense of comfort that he had drawn from the ground beneath his stone feet in the heat of the desert sand was gone, replaced by a growing sense of anger, of agitation.

Of hate.

He had no need of sleep or of sustenance; the earth was sustaining him through the Living Stone that formed his body. All the while, the dark fire within him, his demonic father's legacy, was baking the core of his being, withering that stone, making it hard, too, like the earth.

Like his will.

$\mathcal{B}$eneath the crust of that same cold earth, the dragon heard the echo of her name change.

Aaaaaaaannnnnnnnwyyyyyyyyyyyyyyyyyyynnnnnnnnn!

The beast's eyes widened in the darkness. The sound that she had followed for so long, had tracked within the strata of the Earth, rang clear and high above her, signaling that she was directly beneath the place where it had been spoken.

It vibrated in waves, as if she were hearing it through water; the beast concentrated and decided after a moment that she was, in fact, hearing a watery echo from a spring-fed lake that she sensed, cool and dark, above her. Despite its distortion there was a clarity to it that could not be denied; her heart began to race with excitement darkened by the cruelty of revenge.

With all the force that her titanic muscles could muster, the beast bore up through the layers of rocks, crawling with every ounce of her coiled strength, gaining speed, gaining fury, toward the surface.

Toward sweet destruction.

28

EVERMERE, THE NONALIGNED STATES

$\mathcal{T}$he royal caravan slowed to a halt at the call of the lead driver.

Gwydion Navarne waited until his carriage had rolled to a stop, then carefully pulled aside the heavy shade and glanced outside. Salt spray blew into the carriage, carrying with it crystals of ice that stung as they made contact with his skin. He dropped the shade and looked questioningly at the Lord Marshal, who was sitting uncomfortably on the velvet bench across from him.

The visit of state to Tyrian, the Lirin forest realm over which Rhapsody was titular queen, had gone reasonably well. Anborn had remained, for the most part, out of sight, as the Lirin tended to still harbor an old grudge from the era of the Cymrian War only recently put aside at the Lady's insistence. As a result, Gwydion's first official state visit was experienced almost entirely on his own, under the guidance of Rial, Rhapsody's viceroy. He had been fascinated to walk the forest streets of Tyrian City, the capital hidden deep within the greenwood, with its ingenious defenses and elevated walkways suspended in the forest canopy between the trees. He felt a sense of wonder that he had long ago forgotten as he watched the passage of the foot traffic, where the people and forest animals traveled the same roads in harmony. His father had always been fond of the Lirin and had maintained friendly relations with them; it warmed Gwydion to see that affection returned in the greetings of the populace of Tyrian, the slender, dark-eyed people of the forest who opened their longhouses and battlements, their palace and winter gardens to him.

It had been difficult to leave, but once his official duties had been discharged, and his tour was complete, Gwydion had bidden Rial and the Lirin dignitaries farewell, indicating that his next stops were the harbor towns of Minsyth and Evermere in the unclaimed region known commonly as the Nonaligned States, as Anborn had instructed him to do. He had received their gifts of state with eagerness, reciprocating with the excellent Canderian brandy and the crystal from his own province that Rhapsody suggested he bring, then met up with the Lord Marshal, who was impatiently awaiting their departure for what he considered the real destinations of their journey. Twelve days of travel followed, much of it spent in silence as Anborn watched out the carriage window, contemplating whatever he was seeing through azure eyes that had beheld much of the region's bloody history. Gwydion maintained that silence respectfully.

"Are we in Evermere now, then?" he asked uncertainly now.

Anborn nodded shortly.

Gwydion pulled the curtain back again, more cautiously this time.

In the distance the sea was rolling to a windswept shore, crashing in icy breakers beneath ragged floating docks. He could make out perhaps a dozen ships of varying sizes, many of them sea-worn and old, docked at a pier that was similarly old and dark of timber. From the docks a walkway dotted with holes led to a small port town, its wooden and brick shops and houses having clearly seen better days.

After an awkward length of silence, Gwydion coughed politely.

"Er—Lord Marshal, why are we here? I thought you wished to concentrate on Sorbold."

Anborn leveled his piercing blue gaze at Gwydion.

"We are here because Evermere is well known for its whorehouses," he said. "An important part of any young man's education."

Beads of sweat emerged from Gwydion's brow.

"I—I had not realized that this was your intention," he stammered nervously. "Besides, are there not such things in Roland?"

"Indeed," Anborn said idly, glancing out the window again. "By the time I'm done with your mentoring, you will know each and every one from here to the middle continent." He caught a glimpse of the young duke's paling face and blinked in astonishment. "Not to frequent as a client, you young fool, although there is certainly nothing wrong with that when you are older. Brothels are an excellent source of information and refuge. I've hidden out in more whorehouses than bunkers in my life."

"So why are we here now, then? Are you seeking information on Sorbold in the brothels of Evermere?"

Anborn scowled and pulled the shade back, then shouted to the captain of the mounted honor guard accompanying the carriage.

"Roust! Bring two riderless horses round. The young duke and I wish to set out on our own—and once we're gone, you may visit the port in shifts as well." The captain's eyes shot up into his hairline, then a smile crept over his face.

"Yes, m'lord."

Anborn's face molded into a forced smile. "Don't dip your wicks into any suspicious lamp oil," he said heartily. "Every legend you've heard about the brothels of Evermere is true—so it's best to rosin yourself off afterward, or you'll be sharing lice with every sailor who plies the wide central sea. Understood?"

"Yes sir."

"Good. We'll be back in a sennight."

Anborn let the curtain fall back over the window. He reached under his seat and pulled out a bundle of clothes, which he tossed at Gwydion.

"Wouldn't want to be too conspicuous among the finer citizens of Evermere," he said, pointing to the crest on Gwydion's chest. "Imagine the scandal." He reached around his useless legs and pulled out another bundle, and began to change as well.

Within moments a pair of mounts were saddled and outfitted. Gwydion watched the guards assist the Lord Marshal onto one of them, then climbed uncertainly onto the other. Anborn dragged on the reins and rode off for the port town; Gwydion set off after him, having no idea what to expect once they dismounted.

Once they were over the hill toward Evermere, Anborn glanced back over his shoulder, then turned east and rode off along a cargo path, with Gwydion struggling to keep up.

"We—we're not going to—Evermere—then?" he gasped, spurring his mount in the futile attempt to catch up.

"Sorry to disappoint your loins if I misled them, but no, we are heading to Ghant now," Anborn called back. "If they think we are whoring, they will be discreet as to our disappearance."

"Ah," Gwydion said; his tone signaled disappointment, but his relief was immediate. The concept of lessons in a seaside whoring town had turned his stomach to porridge, especially given Anborn's reputation for wenching and some of his proclivities.

They rode in silence eastward along the windy coastline, through frost-bleached highgrass and over rocky roadways that had been all but over-grown in autumn from decades of disuse. Most of the sea traffic of the Nonaligned States came into port in the western port of Minsyth, which found Tyrian to be a more comfortable neighbor than Evermere found Sor-bold to be.

Anborn's handicap limited the length of each leg of their travels, though Gwydion was grateful each time the Cymrian hero called a halt to their ride; he found himself sore from the saddle as he helped the Lord Mar-shal down from his horse. A few hours of rest by a hastily built fire, another hour of instruction in the use of Tysterisk, and they would mount again, riding with the intent of crossing the border unseen.

Each time Gwydion drew the all-but-invisible blade from its sheath, he felt the wind around him die down, as if the very air awaited his command. Anborn seemed to be aware of his discomfort but ignored it. He had blind-folded the young duke from the outset of his training so that he was able to feel the heft of the weapon, rather than be deceived by the seeming absence of a blade. Day by day, Gwydion felt his anxiety diminish. Achmed's words rang in his head as Anborn's rang in his ears.

Just remember that you *wield* it; *do not let the weapon wield you.*

Sorbold was a nation of massive breadth, its borders long and sporadi-cally guarded, though Anborn commented more than once that the number of troops and outposts had greatly increased since the death of the Dowager Empress. Once they finally arrived at the border it took the better part of a day to find a point of entry where two horsemen might cross, unnoticed.

That night, when Anborn had ascertained that they were safely out of sight of any patrolling troops, they made camp in the lee of an old tavern that had once been a way station along the trans-Sorbold thoroughfare. Anborn deemed a fire unwise, so the two men blanketed the horses and then settled down with what blankets remained shared between them to maximize body warmth.

In the moonlit darkness Gwydion pulled his gloves more tightly against his fingers, watching the man he admired more than almost any other save his godfather. Anborn was generally much merrier in his presence; this eve-ning he seemed melancholy as he smoothed the rough horse blanket beneath which they were both huddled.

"This was Shrike's," the Lord Marshal muttered as he ran his callused hand over it.

Gwydion held his silence. Shrike had been one of Anborn's most trusted men-at-arms, probably his closest friend. Unlike the Lord Marshal he was a

First Generation Cymrian and ancient, a surly, gnarled old man that Gwydion had found hard to understand. He waited, knowing that if the General wanted to impart more than the words he had already shared, he would do so only if he was not encouraged to do it. His patience was rewarded a moment later.

Anborn stared out the broken ceiling of the way station, his eyes scanning the clear, cold sky for stars.

"Eternal life is nothing without some semblance of eternal youth," he said finally. "When Shrike left the Island he was already a fairly old man; whatever cursed entity granted the Cymrians an extended life span must have had a perverse sense of humor to condemn so many to lengthy old age."

Gwydion nodded, remaining silent. The General had not spoken of Shrike since his death some months back; he had died in the ambush in which Rhapsody had been kidnapped.

Anborn's eyes gleamed in the dark. "I always allowed him to make a fire, because he was so often cold. Sailors—" He snorted gruffly, with an undertone of amusement. "Scrawny, wiry sea rats that can stand in a gale that whips the skin from your bones, out in blasts that make this cold place seem like a tropical paradise, as long as they are on their bloody water. But bring them to land, and they shiver like children."

Gwydion chuckled quietly. "Your brother Llauron was a sailor for a while, wasn't he? And yet he seemed quite at home on land, even in the cold." He tried to blank the memory that rose up at his own words, the image of the Invoker at the bloody winter carnival, standing in the midst of the winter wind in the onslaught, commanding wolves to rise from the snow and tear at the invaders' mounts.

Anborn's eyes narrowed. "Llauron has always been more dragon than Edwyn or me. His multiplicity of elemental lores suits him, even as it damages those around him, chiefly my useless nephew, your godfather. It is just as well that he chose to forsake his human form and go commune with those selfsame elements in dragon form. Good riddance to him. May he remain in the ether, content."

Gwydion continued to listen, but Anborn said nothing more. Finally the young duke dropped off to sleep in the warmth of the shared blankets against the chill of the winter wind.

In the gray light of morning they rose and continued on their way.

29

$\mathcal{A}$ tall man with a thin body and a thinner fringe of white hair wearing sexton's robes was waiting for the three priests of Sorbold at the door of the Patriarch's manse, to which the guards had led them. In obvious displeasure he motioned them inside the marble building, dismissed the guards, and shut the heavy doors behind him. Lasarys recognized him as Gregory, the sexton of Lianta'ar; among Lasarys's order, the tenders of the elemental temples, he was the highest ordained priest. Lasarys had received training from him in the deep stillness of Terreanfor upon his investiture as sexton there; Gregory had made the journey willingly, pleased to share the secrets of tending so sacred a temple with another of the five men who devoted their lives to doing so, but had been visibly agitated from the moment he arrived, eager to return to the sanctuary of his own beloved basilica.

Lasarys understood exactly how the man had felt.

Gregory's small eyes were gleaming with fury.

"You misbegotten *idiot*," he hissed at Lasarys, the spittle of rage raining from his mouth. "How dare you disrupt the Chain of Prayer? And if you were going to be so bold as to defy the order of supplication, and pray directly to the Creator yourself, how did you have the temerity to do it in the Patriarch's own basilica? Did it not occur to you that he would feel it, and that your interruption might be disrupting the daily offering of intentions?"

"I—I am sorry, Father," Lasarys whispered, the gravity of his crime beginning to dawn upon him. "I—was—in despair and not thinking clearly."

"A sexton of an elemental basilica has no room for such a faltering of wisdom," Gregory retorted angrily. "The impact of your foolishness on the entire Patrician faith cannot even be imagined. And what are you doing here in the first place? A sexton of an elemental cathedral has no business leaving it." He leaned closer for the verbal equivalent of a killing blow. "I hope whatever your self-indulgence gained you was worth the sacrifice of your post. I'm sure your new regent emperor will be displeased to be training a new sexton before his investiture. I hope you have your affairs in order."

Lasarys swallowed as the two acolytes went pale.

"I am being relieved of my guardianship?" he asked shakily. His voice came out in little more than a whisper.

"Please, Father, we cannot go back," Lester blurted; his protestations were silenced by the elevation of Gregory's hand.

"His Grace has commanded that you be detained until he has finished righting whatever he can of your egregious mistake," the sexton of Lianta'ar said haughtily. "Follow me; you are to wait in the hospice, where you can do no more harm with your renegade prayers."

The three priests dispiritedly followed the sexton down the dark, windowless corridors in the marble manse, past tapestried walls and heavy brass braziers of incense, burning in thin wisps of scented smoke. They were led deep into the manse, through endless corridors and past numerous identical doorways, until finally the sexton stopped before a heavy mahogany door and opened it contemptuously.

Beyond the door lay a small chapel, with a plain altar and severe, backless benches. Above the altar hung a sculpture of the silver star of the Patriarchy; other than that, there was no other ornamentation.

"Wait in here," Gregory commanded. He waited until the priests had entered the room, then closed the door resoundingly behind them.

For what seemed an eternity, the Sorbolds waited on the hard wooden benches, silently contemplating their future. The windowless room kept them from watching the morning pass into afternoon, and yet they could feel the movement of the sun in the changing glow radiating from the silver star above the altar. Finally the door opened again, and Gregory returned, looking grim.

A heartbeat behind him, another man came through the door. He was taller than the sexton of Lianta'ar by almost a head, was dressed in silver robes emblazoned with the same star that hung over the altar, and on his hand was a simple platinum ring in which a clear oval stone had been set.

His hair was streaked gray and silver with age, though there was still enough white-blond hue to it to hint of what it must have looked like in his youth. His beard was long, curled slightly at the ends, and his eyes were clear and blue as the cloudless summer sky. Immediately the three priests threw themselves on the ground at his feet.

The Patriarch signaled for Gregory to close the door, then gestured somewhat impatiently at the prone holy men.

"Do get up," he said in a gruff, commanding voice. "It displeases me greatly to see my ordinates groveling on the floor."

The two acolytes helped Lasarys rise. The elderly sexton was shaking, his face white with fear. Long ago he had had the privilege of watching the then Patriarch, who was almost never seen by anyone, celebrate the investiture of Nielash Mousa, the man who now served as the Blesser of Sorbold. The Patriarch at the time had been a frail man with the same thin fringe of hair that now decorated Gregory's almost bald pate, whose aged frame seemed bowed by the weight of his own robes.

This new Patriarch, Constantin, who had been invested only a few years ago, was vastly different from that man. While he had obviously lived many years, he carried himself the way an old man who had been an athlete or soldier would. His shoulders were broad and unbowed, and there was a regal aspect to his bearing, almost an arrogance, though there was no trace of any such haughtiness in his face.

In his role as sexton Lasarys had assisted his benison, Nielash Mousa, on the two occasions that the Patriarch had made a state visit to Sorbold. The first was his own investiture, where he had stepped forth, anonymous, out of the crowd in the square of Jierna'sid and presented himself, when all other contenders had been rejected by the Scales, as a candidate for the office he now held. He had been confirmed; the Scales had held him high against the brilliant blue of the dome of the sky. It was a sight Lasarys knew he would never forget. And just before those same Scales had confirmed Talquist as the new emperor, the Patriarch had come to Jierna'sid again, to bury the Dowager Empress and her son, the Crown Prince Vyshla, who had died moments apart on the same night.

The Patriarch raised his hand in blessing, and the priests bowed respectfully, making the appropriate countersign. Then the Patriarch motioned to the benches, and hesitantly the priests went back to them and sat down again.

"I am somewhat surprised to see you alive, I must admit; word came from Sorbold a few days ago that all the acolytes and the sexton of Terreanfor had perished in a terrible fire at the manse outside of Night Mountain. The Blesser of Sorbold left our meetings and returned home at once, so since in fact you survived the conflagration, I wonder why you are not back in Jierna'sid, helping to arrange for the burial rites. Tell me, Lasarys, why you chose to come here, and pray as you did."

Slowly the sexton rose and walked over to the Patriarch, then knelt at his feet.

"May the Creator smite me into ash if my tongue proclaims anything but the truth," he said haltingly. "Your Grace, these two men will bear witness to what I am about to tell you. Talquist, regent emperor of Sorbold, is purposefully despoiling and defiling the holiest places of our homeland, especially the holy basilica of Terreanfor."

The Patriarch's eyes narrowed, and his brow blackened visibly.

"Despoiling how?" he demanded.

"At his command," said Lasarys, the flush of shame reddening his wrinkled cheeks. "And with my unwilling assistance."

The Patriarch inhaled deeply, his blue eyes blazing with cold fire, but said nothing, waiting for the sexton to continue.

"Many years ago, Talquist was an acolyte in my stewardship," Lasarys continued, his back straight but his voice trembling. "He was a fickle young man, serving in training to become a priest, not because he had heard a calling from the All-God, but because he needed information about a puzzle that was bedeviling him ceaselessly. He had found an item buried in the sands of the Skeleton Coast, a shell or scale of a sort, tattered around the edges and violet in color. It had the engraving of a throne on its surface, along with runes that I could never read. He was studying with me in the hope that somewhere in the depths of our holy scripture, somewhere in the practices of the faith, he would find clues about this object. When he discovered there was nothing about it to be found in his study, he left the temple and did not return until decades later, when he was looking to be confirmed as emperor."

The Patriarch's aspect grew more intense.

"It was my understanding that Talquist had become emperor reluctantly, that the Scales themselves had weighed in favor of the mercantile over the army and the nobility, and selected Talquist before a large coterie of witnesses, visiting heads of state and Sorbolds alike."

The sexton swallowed hard.

"It was made to appear that way, Your Grace," he said nervously, "because that was how Talquist wanted it. He had returned to Terreanfor just a few days before the death of the Dowager Empress and the Crown Prince, seeking a small piece of Living Stone from the basilica." He winced at the horror on the Patriarch's face. "He told me that if I did not harvest such a piece of stone, he would take the basilica and use it without regard to its needs. He had studied the basilica intensely when he was training with me, and so knew that there was a secret entrance to Terreanfor. If he were to occupy the basilica, his guards could effectively hold the army at bay until he had virtually destroyed it." Lasarys's mouth was suddenly dry, an indictment of his silence and at the guilt in his own heart for the darker reasons he was leaving out of the explanation.

"So I agreed, though it broke my heart. I found a place where there was stone that did not take on the form of a plant or animal, and, after praying for forgiveness, harvested the stone and gave it to Talquist."

"And what did he do with it?" the Patriarch asked, his voice going suddenly soft.

"He used it to rig the Weighing, I presume; I was not there when he did it," Lasarys said sadly. "But that is not the greatest heresy, Your Grace."

The Patriarch's eyes opened wider, but he remained silent.

Lasarys glanced over his shoulder at the faces of the two young acolytes; the men were pale as milk, their aspects grim.

"Once he was vested as regent emperor, he gave me the command that the acolytes were to harvest one of the titanic stone statues of the warriors from the basilica."

"From the ceremonial archway?"

"Yes. He insisted that the entire statue be taken, sliced from its base and brought to the Place of Weight at Jierna Tal. The sacrifice badly injured the spirit of the basilica; I could feel it suffering each moment that the statue was being—" Overcome, the elderly priest broke down, weeping.

"Tell me the rest," the Patriarch commanded.

"The statue, which was chosen because of the sheer volume of its elemental earth, was placed on one of the weighing plates of the scales. Some sort of pathetic creature, which looked like it was composed partly of human flesh, partly of pale jellyfish, was placed in the other. Through manipulation of the violet artifact, there was a terrible flash of light, and the creature disintegrated. Then the statue of living earth stood erect. Truly that was the most terrifying sight I have ever witnessed."

"Where is it now?" Constantin asked. His voice was calm, but the hand on which he wore his ring was trembling now.

Lasarys shook his head. "I know not, Your Grace. The statue—it was capable of a crude form of ambulation. It stumbled off into the desert, destroying anything in its path. It tore the sword from its hand that had been part of the original statue, and that sword crumbled into dry dust, as the statue may have done as well. We saw no sign of it when we ventured into the desert on our way to see you.

"Talquist had his troops murder the acolytes who had witnessed his treachery—the fire you heard tell of was deliberately set. Then he had all the soldiers who assisted in this horrific undertaking killed as well, except for his trusted captain of the guard. Had we not remained in hiding, doubtless we would be dead ourselves.

"We came to you as soon as we could, seeking our benison, and his wisdom, but your guards tell us he has returned already to Sorbold."

The Patriarch nodded. "Indeed; upon receiving the news from Talquist's messenger, he offered his prayers, then left immediately to return to Jierna'sid. He should arrive today, or on the morrow at the latest."

Despair came into Lasarys's eyes. "He is walking into a trap, then. There is no time to interdict him, and now that he is back inside the borders of Sorbold, any message that is sent to him would be intercepted by Talquist." His forehead ran with sweat. "I fear he is a dead man."

Constantin shook his head. "Not as of this morning," he said, turning away from the priests and staring at the altar, over which hung the silver star. "I could sense the offering of prayers that he submitted on behalf of his congregation; Sorbold is a vast nation with many faithful, and if he had not been able to attend to his duties in the Chain of Prayer, it would have been immediately noticeable."

"It is only a matter of time, Your Grace," said the sexton sadly. "Talquist is obsessed, but calculating. The power of the artifact he found on the Skeleton Coast gives him a sense not only of power but invulnerability. He has plans, vast and sinister plans that exceed my understanding, and for all that he assumed the façade of the reluctant merchant summoned by the Scales to leadership, I swear to you that his intent, and his ability to realize that intent, have been in place for many years."

The Patriarch did not turn to meet Lasarys's eye.

"You are right about that," he said in a voice that seemed far away. He stood in silent contemplation, his gaze fixed on the silver star above the altar. Finally he turned to the sexton of Lianta'ar.

"Gregory, take these men into your care," he said. "I grant them sanctuary here. Find places for them in the priory, but take care not to reveal their names to anyone. We will have a renaming ceremony tomorrow, so that they cannot be hunted." His searing blue eyes fixed on the priests of Sorbold.

"Whatever roads you have traveled in your lives until now, whatever footprints you have left in the sand between this place and the place from whence you have come, must now be erased. Talquist is a monster; I have known this for more than a lifetime. It is not for your safety alone that I command this. Your lives are secondary. If he discovers that you are here, the holy city itself is in jeopardy from his wrath."

Lasarys began to shake, as did Gregory.

"Surely he will not attack Sepulvarta?" the sexton of Lianta'ar said; his harsh voice had lost its knife's edge, and had taken on the tone of a frightened child. Such a violation was unimaginable.

The Patriarch's voice hardened, taking on a menacing, almost silky edge.

"I assure you, Gregory, not only will he, but he is planning to. It is not the presence of these men that will bring it about, we are on the doorstep between Sorbold and Roland. He will barely pause to wipe his feet on the mat of Sepulvarta on his way to the inner continent."

"But—" gasped Gregory, "Your Grace, that is—that is unimaginable. To attack, to destroy a holy city—"

"In order to hold anything holy, one has to have a fear for one's soul," said the Patriarch. "Talquist is utterly without one. Before he is done, the world itself will be torn asunder. And we will be among the first to be crushed under his heel. It is already far too late to stop him."

The priests stood, unable to move, as the door opened and the Patriarch left the chapel, taking whatever warmth had been in the room as he went.

Constantin waited, unseen, until the last of the doors of the basilica of Lianta'ar had been locked and bolted for the night, before he emerged from the sacristy and slowly made his way up the circular rise of stairs that led to the altar.

The light of the star shone down through the windows in the ceiling of the basilica, bathing the altar and most of the inner sanctuary in a silver light. As he ascended the stairs in that light, Constantin had the dreamy sensation of following a shaft of moonlight into the heavens.

This holy place, this citadel of a dead star that had fallen in another time, was one of the few places in the world he had ever felt peace. Something in the ethereal glow reminded him of another place, a realm between worlds, life and death, where his old life had ended and his new one began.

Born of an unknown Cymrian mother whose face he still remembered, even though they had shared life for only the space of one breath, fathered by a demon, his early existence had been one of cherished violence and artful bloodshed. Constantin had been, a few short years before in the counted time of the material world, a gladiator in the arenas of Sorbold, a merciless killing machine himself, until he had been rescued and taken to the realm that he was now recalling, a place of dreams known as the domain of the Lord and Lady Rowan, a place beyond the Veil of Hoen, the Old Cymrian word for joy. Those entities, the manifestation of healing dreams and peaceful death, had taught him much; time in their world passed in the blink of an eye as it was counted in the material world. Gone from sight only a few short months, he had aged a lifetime, had studied, been steeped in wisdom, and come to realize that the ignominy of his birth was not a stain but a badge of honor. He had set about being worthy of it when the Scales chose him and elevated him to the Patriarchy.

The sickening irony of his life's story twisted his viscera now. He thought back to the words he had spoken to the Lord Cymrian and the king of the Firbolg upon hearing of Talquist's elevation to Emperor.

You could not have brought me worse news.

Why? the king of the Bolg had demanded. *Tell us why.*

His answer echoed in the darkest recesses of his mind.

Talquist is a merchant in only the kindest usage of the word. He is a slave trader of the most brutal order, the secret scion of a fleet of pirate ships, which trade in human booty, selling the able-bodied into the mines, or worse, the arenas, using the rest as raw materials for other goods, like candles rendered from the flesh of the old, bone meal from the very young. Thousands have met their deaths in the arenas of Sorbold; I cannot even fathom how many more have found it in the mines, or the salt beds, or at the bottom of the sea. He is a monster with a gentleman's smile and a common touch, but a monster all the same.

And yet the Scales confirmed him, the Lord Cymrian insisted. *I witnessed it myself.*

As he reached the top step, Constantin thought about the incredulous expression in the eyes of the Bolg king, a man whose previous life had no doubt held much of the same sort of experiences as his own. *Why did you not say something before you left?* King Achmed had demanded. *If you knew this was a potential outcome of the selection process, why did you not intervene?*

The bands of platinum that edged the altar were gleaming brilliantly. His own reply reverberated in his head, nauseating him.

Because it is not for me to decry the Scales. They are what confirmed me to my position in the first place. How could I decree their wisdom to be faulty without invoking a paradox? Besides, to acknowledge my past in the arena would be to open the realm of the Rowans to scrutiny that would not be welcome there. And finally, he was not the only man with blood on his hands who was in the running. If I were to decry everyone I thought unfit to be Emperor, Sorbold would be a leaderless state.

And because I am a coward, he thought now. *I did not want to imagine what I knew would happen.*

He bowed before the stone table, then knelt on the floor in front of it. The simplicity of the stone, the purity of the platinum, was designed to allow the prayers that were presented to him through this altar to flow freely into his mind through the Spire and onto the feet of the Creator. That simplicity, that purity, made his thoughts resonate in his head now.

In the silence, he remembered the last words he had spoken to the Bolg king.

I pray that, as I have undergone a change of heart in my time behind the Veil of Hoen, Talquist too will experience such a transformation. Perhaps the fact that he did not immediately demand coronation as Emperor is a sign of that.

Achmed's eyes had met his, full of common understanding.

I doubt it. In my experience, men who had a thirst for blood and power only grow thirstier the more they are fed it. You may be the only exception I have ever met.

Constantin's hands trembled as they touched the altar.

He struggled to keep from cursing himself, pushing back the thoughts that crowded into his mind. They refused to be banished, swelling forward into his consciousness relentlessly.

You fool. If only you had stepped forward then, had recognized that the Scales had been tampered with, perhaps you could have averted the death of half the world that will come now. Now that blood joins the rest that is on your hands.

He thought of Terreanfor, one of the last repositories of Living Stone in the known world, and the vast power that was extant there. Of all the elements, earth alone had the attributes to sustain such a power; the others were too fleeting, too evanescent to hold on to it in great concentrations. The winds were too transitory, the seas too churning, starlight too distant, fire too unpredictable and destructive. But the earth remained steadfast, unchanging, passing through its cycles in patient, almost reverent, consistency, which was why so much of the world's power resided in earth, in land. And as he thought of the cool, dark cathedral hidden deep within Night Mountain, where the light would never touch it, he thought of the tale the priests had told him of the felling of the statue of the soldier of Living Stone.

And of all the other such statues, man and beast, trees and the Living Stone altar itself, waiting to be harvested.

And the power that was about to be unleashed on an unsuspecting world.

Concentrate, he willed himself.

Softly he began to chant the rites by which he received the daily prayers of the faithful of the Patrician religion. His body began to vibrate gently as he did, the power of the ethereal light above him reverberating through him, allowing him to be the channel of those petitions directly to the Creator. It was always a humbling sensation, knowing that the prayers and dreams, fears and joy of millions of souls were passing through him, making his body shine, for a brief moment, with the same ethereal glow as the star on the minaret a thousand feet above him.

From the corners of the continent, the southwestern realm of the Nonaligned States, from Bethe Corbair in the east, Navarne and Avonderre to the west, Canderre and Yarim in the north, and Bethany, the central province of Roland, and finally Sorbold in the south, one by one each of his benisons was transmitting the prayers of the faithful through the stone altar. The receipt of the praise rang like chimes, different tones in his head; he had no idea what was being asked or offered, or how many different people were entrusting him with their prayers, he only knew that together they made up one glorious symphony of praise and entreaty that gave glory and honor to the All-God while supplicating for his grace.

He never knew how long the transfer of prayers would take; time lost its hold in the presence of great elemental power. When at last the tones from each of the benisons' prayers began to fade, he caught hold of the last one, sustaining it with his own chant.

The remaining four songs of praise came to an end; the benisons had completed their evening requirements of offering to the Chain of Prayer, unaware that the Patriarch was still listening. When only the single chant of the benison of Sorbold was present in the echoing basilica, the Patriarch spoke.

Nielash Mousa, he whispered. *Tarry.*

It was something he had never done before, had never gone backward down the Chain of Prayer to a supplicant on a lower level, but he was desperate. The altar beneath his hands reverberated. He waited for a long moment, then heard a very surprised voice resound throughout Lianta'ar.

I hear you, Your Grace.

A sickening sensation swelled through him, the glorious vibration of praise and supplication changing into the racheting discomfort of discord. Constantin gripped the altar, struggling not to collapse.

It seemed as if the weight of the material world was now on his shoulders, dragging the breath from his lungs. All the lightness of being that he enjoyed in his daily offerings was reversed; now he struggled for air, struggled to bear up under the crushing pressure.

Time expanded all around him. As his daily prayers seemed to take no time at all, now each heartbeat, each breath was labored, extended, drawn out to the ends of the earth.

Concentrate, he thought again, sweat pouring from his brow.

He opened his mouth to speak, but doing so caused him agony. The joint of his jaw popped loudly under the strain; all the water disappeared from his lips, leaving them cracked as he tried to form words. Constantin's hands trembled; he closed his eyes and whispered two words, an undertaking of more pain than he ever remembered. Knowing the importance of the message he was delivering, he put the very last grain of his strength into it.

Safeguard—Terreanfor.

The words had just passed his lips when the world went dark. He was vaguely aware of hitting the altar, unconscious before his blood stained the floor of the basilica. Constantin lay, prone, in the silver light of the star atop the Spire of Sepulvarta, too far into the gray haze between waking and sleep to hear the benison's reply.

I understand.

30

THE INNER HARBOR OF GHANT, SORBOLD

*W*hile not as massive as Avonderre's Port Fallon, the largest harbor on the western seacoast, the inner harbor at Ghant was still one of the biggest in the world, the terminus for the daily off-loading of tons of goods. Hundreds of merchant ships sailed into the inner harbor with the rising of each tide, past the naval fleet of Sorbold moored in the outer harbor. Each vessel was inspected, each manifest checked by the naval harbormaster, and either turned away or allowed to pass into the smooth water of the immense lagoon that formed the inner harbor.

In his day Anborn had seen both harbors many times. Ghant was one of the first places he had annexed in the Cymrian War a thousand years before, a place from which his ground forces had been able to sustain and defend a land supply route, and from which his warships set sail for attacks on the Lirin port of Tallono to the northwest. Tallono was a sheltered harbor that had been built by the Gorllewinolo Lirin with the help of his grandmother, the dragon Elynsynos, but by the time Anborn had come to Ghant, there was no room in his heart for sentimentality, only murder and vengeance. With precision he had burned Tallono almost to the ground, much the same way he had sacked the smaller ports of Minsyth and Evermere, and had secured the seacoast all the way north to Port Fallon when the war finally ended. A millennium had not been long enough to blot out the memories that haunted him still, torturing his waking moments and plaguing his dreams.

Now the ghosts of those battles were no longer hovering over the land, as they had been each time Anborn had returned to Ghant since then. The port was busier than he had ever seen it; he could tell even at a great distance as he and Gwydion Navarne came over the rocky hills above it, looking down at the inner harbor from the trans-Sorbold passage, the main thoroughfare over which the goods were carted to places north and east in Sorbold. He grimaced as he reined his mount to a halt, remembering that his own soldiers had once built this road.

Gwydion Navarne, whose thoughts were not haunted by a history he knew little about, stared out at the harbor in amazement.

"They're doing a fair business, aren't they?" he mused, watching the scores of ships that lined the piers of the inner harbor being systematically offloaded by tiny shapes that more resembled ants than longshoremen.

The Lord Marshal nodded, his face grim.

"But in what?" he asked. He looked farther out to sea, past the inner harbor's sluice to the outer harbor, and took in a ragged breath.

From one end of the outer harbor to the other docks had been constructed, each housing a score of warships. Anborn counted a dozen of those docks, with more beyond the rim of the point.

"Dear All-God," he muttered.

Gwydion Navarne turned in his saddle. He had been enjoying the taste of the distant sea air, the bustle of the port below, after so many days' ride in the wastelands of the southern steppes, and therefore was taken aback at the sight of the Cymrian hero's face, which was now as hard as he had ever seen it.

"What is wrong, Lord Marshal?" he asked, feeling a new chill in the wind coming off the sea.

Anborn dragged the reins to his right, positioning himself for a better view. He stared down at the harbor, crawling with activity, for a long moment, then looked around him at the hillsides from which they had come.

"At the time of the Cymrian War, this was a major military center, the central port of my sea forces' offensive," he said finally. "We had a fleet that, in its time, was responsible for the destruction of much of western Tyrian, and the decimation of the coastal areas of Avonderre north to Gwynwood. I led my father's armies against my mother's forces with great success on land because of the sheer advantage of numbers and superior weaponry; that is not surprising. But until Llauron abandoned Anwyn and fled to sea, he was a formidable naval foe that would have been insurmountable; he would have destroyed my fleet if it had not been for our control of Ghant, and the size of our armada stationed here." The Lord Marshal shielded his eyes, stinging now from the glare of the sun.

"And in those days, there were far fewer warships than stand in port now."

Gwydion swallowed, but said nothing. The taste of the desert air had gone suddenly drier, clogging in his throat and burning like fiery sand.

Anborn shifted awkwardly in his saddle, straining to see behind him.

"There was a sheltered point up a ways, if I recall," he said, glancing over his shoulder at a convoy of horse-drawn wagons accompanied by soldiers in the articulated leather armor of the mountain columns, units of the Sorbold army that defended the mountain passes hundreds of miles away near the capital of Jierna'sid. The caravan was making its way up the incline toward them on the ancient thoroughfare. "I think we should take cover there now, lest we be seen. My guess is that our presence is unwelcome here."

The two spurred their horses into a loping trot over the rocky outcropping, climbing into the rough lands perched above the harbor, and took shelter behind the guardian rocks. When the horses were out of sight, Anborn gestured impatiently to Gwydion.

"Help me from this bloody saddle," he grunted, unstrapping the bindings.

Gwydion dismounted quickly, then hurried to the General's side, assisting him down from the horse. Once down, Anborn shoved him away, and lowered his body, with the strength of his arms and chest, onto the ground, then crawled to the edge of the outcropping. He signaled to Gwydion, who crouched down and lay on his belly beside him on the sandswept cliff.

Silently they watched, heedless of the time that passed, transfixed by the sight below them.

In a little less than an hour's time they noted more than two dozen ships approaching the outer harbor, merchant vessels bound for the inner docks, running the gauntlet of warships. Those ships were boarded, checked, and sent onward with military precision; once in the harbor, their cargo was immediately off-loaded and packed into wagons, unlike the harbor at Port Fallon, in Avonderre, where goods were separated into merchant orders, then debarked by longshoremen from the individual merchants who had come to claim the cargo.

"What does that tell you?" the Lord Marshal asked softly, in the tone of voice he used when instructing the young duke in matters of import.

Gwydion stared down at the barrels and crates being systematically moved into a line of standing wagons.

"All the cargo is either going to the same place, or owned by the same entity?" he guessed.

Anborn nodded. "Undoubtedly the Crown. And to some extent that is not terribly surprising; the new regent emperor, Talquist, was the hierarch of the guilds that controlled these western shipping lanes prior to his ascension to the Sun Throne. But it's not the destination of the cargo that concerns me."

"Then what does?"

Anborn pointed down the road beyond the rocky outcroppings.

"The cargo itself. Look."

Gwydion followed Anborn's finger away from the starboard hold of the closest ship on the jetty, where the barrels and crates were being off-loaded into wagons, to the port side of the same ship. He could see two lines of people, so distant as to be almost indistinguishable from the mass of others working the docks, disembarking from the vessel. The first line emerged from a higher gangplank; they were few in number, and ambulated at their leisure off the ship, where they dispersed into the crowds lining the docks. Gwydion presumed these were passengers.

The second line emerged from a lower gangplank, directly from the ship's hold. At first he assumed it was the crew, but on closer examination saw that the line was herded forward to a column of wagons, much like the cargo wagons, into which the human figures were then loaded. Gwydion counted more than one hundred from a single ship, stumbling and shading their eyes from the brightness of the morning sun. He shook his head as if to clear it, or escape a buzzing hornet, as a terrible realization took an insistent hold. When he could not escape it, the word fell out of his mouth.

"Slaves," he murmured. "He's trafficking in slaves."

Anborn nodded. He pointed slowly and deliberately to each of the two dozen ships that had docked within the time they had been watching, each of which was unloading human cargo from its starboard hold, packing the hostages into wagons, which were then disbursed in different directions along the trans-Sorbold passage.

"Slavery is not new to Sorbold," he said in a low voice. "Leitha was empress for three-quarters of a century, an impressive longevity for someone not of Cymrian blood. In her time it was practiced quietly, with criminals and debtors, or war prisoners, mostly in the gladiatorial arenas. It was generational; a slave family remained captive until a male member of it could purchase freedom for his progeny, usually through prowess as a gladiator. But it was considered an ugly, if not particularly well disguised, secret. The number of arenas was fewer than one per city-state; that's less than two dozen in total." He cast a quick glance behind him at the horses, then returned his gaze to the port below.

"In the past hour we've seen enough human cargo off-loaded to populate that entire gladiatorial structure. There are still a hundred merchants' ships outside the inner harbor, awaiting passage. And that's only today."

"Could arena fighting have increased that much in the months since Talquist took the throne?" Gwydion asked, nauseated.

Anborn's eyes narrowed, still focused on the sight below.

"Possibly—Talquist has a reputation for fondness of that kind of bloodsport. But I would hazard a guess that only a very small part of this cargo is bound for the arena. These slaves are probably on their way to the salt mines of Nicosi, or the olive groves of Remaldfaer. But the more important question is not to where the poor wretches are bound, but from where did they come? If half of those ships contain as many captives as we've seen off-loaded, that's the equivalent of the population of an entire city."

"Sweet All-God," Gwydion whispered.

"Indeed," Anborn assented. "Invoking Him may be the only thing that can help now; if this has been going on all the while that Talquist has been regent, your godfather is going to have a nightmare on his hands."

"Please elaborate," Gwydion said, his hands going cold and beginning to shake.

Anborn rolled slightly to his side and motioned the young duke into silence.

From below them a rumble could be heard as another caravan of wagons crested the rocky rise of the passage. The two men watched as they rolled past, guarded by a cohort of Sorbold soldiers both in front and behind them. Gwydion winced at the sight of the captives, a host of ragged men, forlorn women, and thin, silent children packed into the carts like cattle on the way to the slaughtering houses. He counted eleven wagons, estimating that each contained more than two dozen slaves. Gwydion watched, a knot of increasing tightness choking his throat, until the dust of the thoroughfare had settled and the sound had died away. He leaned over the cliff edge slightly and saw similar caravans making their ways in other directions, into the mountains and along the seacoast, bearing similar cargo.

"Tell me more of the implications of this nightmare," he said finally to Anborn.

The General exhaled, still watching the port below.

"A certain amount of increase in trade is to be expected when a guild hierarch, someone who has excelled in the mercantile all his life, assumes a throne," he said quietly, not watching Gwydion's face. "That's not what we are seeing here. Slaves such as these are not for the amusement of the arena; they are for the production of goods. We are seeing the buildup to war, also not unexpected, though Talquist has been hiding behind a cover of peace and the cultivation of prosperity in his lands.

"What is terrifying is the scale—we came here on an ordinary day, without being seen, and have witnessed, therefore, an ordinary day's activities. If this is how Talquist operates on an ordinary day—if Ghant has gone back to being a military port, with ships offloading supplies totally possessed by the Crown, then the scale of what he is planning is unimaginable. It dwarfs the buildup to the Cymrian War—and that conflict almost destroyed the entire continent."

"Is there any other possible explanation?" Gwydion asked, already knowing the answer.

"No," Anborn said flatly.

"Then the only thing to do is to return to Navarne at once and warn Ashe," Gwydion said.

"Indeed you must."

The young duke blinked. "Me? You're not coming?"

"No. I'm here, so I may as well make use of the journey. I'm going to ride east to Jierna'sid and scout as many of the harbor points, mines, workfields, and arenas as I can along the way. Once I get to the capital, I will gather as much intelligence as I can, then I will return and aid your godfather in planning the strategy for the war I've told him all along was coming."

Gwydion fought down his panic, which had risen above the knot in his gorge and was threatening to choke him.

"Alone?"

The Cymrian hero reached out had steadied the young man's shoulder.

"You can do this; do not be afraid. The honor guard is suitable to defend the coach if you are attacked, and the sword you carry will be a decided advantage against any brigands you should engage, or soldiers, if it comes to that, but it won't, because Talquist will not wish to tip his hand by assaulting a noble in the Cymrian Alliance, at least not yet. If you follow the route back that brought us here, you will be fine, Gwydion. Once you're out of Sorbold you can stop at any of the way stations of the guarded mail caravan and demand aid. You're the duke now; they will give you whatever you want, including supplies, a fresh horse, and escort back to Navarne. Just keep all the lessons I've taught you in mind."

"I—I meant you, alone," Gwydion stammered. "How are you going to make it across the Sorbold desert—"

The Lord Marshal's brow darkened like a thunderhead. He raised himself up on his elbows and slapped the ground, sending a scattering of sand into Gwydion's eyes.

"I'd been traveling this continent alone for centuries before your father was an itch in your grandfather's trousers," he scowled. Then he dragged himself over the rocks to where the horses waited, and slowly, painfully crawled up his mount's side, until he was clinging to the stirrup. Gwydion hurried over to him, but the ancient hero slapped him away, pulling himself with great effort into a vertical position, his useless legs limp beneath him. Gwydion could only stand there, suffering silently, as he watched Anborn struggle into the saddle. Finally, when he was atop the horse, he looked down at the young duke with a mixture of triumph and exhaustion in his eyes.

"Mount up," he said, his voice ringing with the tones of a general. "I will accompany you back to the honor contingent in Evermere, then as far back as Jakar; I want to see what is happening in the gladiatorial arena there. After that you're on your own, but you will be just over the border of Tyrian. I suggest you ride the forest road; your 'grandmother's' status as Lirin queen will assure your safety there. Tell my nephew that I will be back as soon as I have fully ascertained what is going on in this godforsaken sandbox, but in the meantime, he should be girding the loins of Roland and the entire Cymrian Alliance. It may already be too late."

The rest of the way home Gwydion's pulse was thrumming in his ears. The drumbeat grew louder when he parted company with Anborn on the crossroads of Nikkid'saar, the gambling borough in the western city-state of Jakar. From the coach window he watched the ancient hero, his mentor and friend, disappear into the endless lines of foot and mounted traffic that plied the roadways of the city, hoping that this sight of him would not be his last. Then he ordered the contingent to turn west to Tyrian, on his way back to his ancestral lands and the mantle of responsibility that awaited him there.

In his mind he practiced endlessly the words he would use to break the news to his godfather that the war Anborn had so long predicted was finally coming. He pushed the honor guard to ride at double pace, finally leaving the carriage at a way station just inside the border of Roland, riding on mount the rest of the way home. His mind focused on silly things as they flew over the ground, like how far outside his keep he would need to stop and make himself less unkempt before entering, how he would communicate to Gerald Owen the urgency of his need to see Ashe without giving away his terror to the servants, how he would break the news to them without appearing as childish and frightened as he felt.

By the time he reached Haguefort, Ashe was gone.

31

HAGUEFORT, NAVARNE

Outside the window of the vast library, the snowflakes drifted down lazily on the warm wind, melting before they touched the earth.

Ashe looked absently out the window, bored with the grain treaty he was rewriting. His dragon sense had been observing the flakes in their descent. Thaw was here; winter would return soon in its fury, making travel more difficult. He chuckled to himself; he was looking for reasons to leave again.

It had been more than a month since he had last visited Elynsynos's lair, had been able to hold his wife and sing to his child under the approving eye of the wyrm who was caring for them both. For all that he missed her presence with the intensity of a dragon missing its treasure, he had come to believe that her decision to visit with the beast was a wise one. She was much more hale and at ease under Elynsynos's magical care and fond ministrations.

The door of the library opened silently; had he not been aware, by the nature of his blood, of every minuscule happening within a range of five miles, he would not have heard Portia come in. He had to acknowledge, albeit grudgingly, that Tristan had been correct about her worth as well as that of the other servants he had loaned to Ashe and Rhapsody. The two other women were still awaiting their full usefulness, but Portia had quickly become an invaluable member of the household staff. She was quiet and unassuming, entering a room or delivering a message in a way that was never disruptive. Oftentimes she was gone without even leaving a trace of her vibration on the air of the room.

She gave a quiet cough now, a subtle verbal sign Ashe had learned was her way of informing him that his noon-meal repast was warm and would chill unpleasantly, then took hold of the door handle again.

Just as her hand began to turn the handle, the dragon in Ashe's blood caught the slightest hint of a scent on the wind, a fragment of cinnamon and a drop of vanilla, mixed with the strange and intoxicating aroma of woodland flowers. It reached down into his brain, into memory so deep it did not even need consciousness to be evoked.

Rhapsody's scent.

He shook his head infinitesimally, and the scent cleared. Out of the corner of his eye he caught a golden flash, like the movement of a fall of hair. He looked up quickly, turning in time to see Portia's tall, dark form start through the door.

Not a sign of golden hair anywhere.

He ran a hand through his own metallic red-gold hair, then called out to her just as she was closing the door behind her.

"Portia?"

The chambermaid turned, her dark eyes wide with surprise.

"Yes, m'lord?"

Now that she was there, staring at him in confusion, anything Ashe would have asked fled from his brain, and he found himself speechless. He gestured clumsily with his hands, trying to think of a way to phrase a question that didn't sound utterly insane, but no words would come into his mind.

He wanted her to explain how suddenly her presence, fleeting as it was, had reminded him, in a primitive sensory way, of his wife.

And realized in the same instant that she would think him unbalanced if he told her such a thing.

He smiled awkwardly, then shook his head as he rubbed the back of his neck.

"Sorry," he said. "I—I don't remember what I was going to ask you."

Portia dropped a curtsy.

"Ring for me if you remember, m'lord," she said pleasantly. "Good evening."

Over the next few days it happened several times more.

At first Ashe suspected trickery; his upbringing and nature did not allow for an easy application of trust, and so he began to watch Portia carefully, noting her movements, keeping track of her out of the corner of his eye, and when she left the room, with his innate dragonsense.

Each time he felt a twinge of shame afterward.

The human side of his nature had granted him his father's ability at cool, detached assessment and equanimity, so after a week or so of noting her movements, he began to look elsewhere for an explanation of what he had noticed. The new servant was discreet, modest, and kept to herself. She rose early, kept her quarters straight, worked hard, was prompt when summoned, eschewed after-hours gatherings with others who worked in the keep, and rebuffed the advances made by a young man who had come to deliver foodstuffs to the buttery from Avonderre. She was tall, broad-shouldered, and dark, with deep brown eyes and an olive complexion, a physical opposite of Rhapsody's slight Lirin frame, rosy skin, blond hair, and green eyes. Her behavior appeared to be above reproach; since Ashe could not read minds or look into people's hearts, he had little other choice but to assume she was not responsible for his odd inclinations.

Once Portia herself was ruled out he began to muse, almost to the point of melancholy, about why he was seeing aspects of his wife in a serving maid. Certainly he missed her, had always missed her in her absence, and had been driven to the brink of insanity when she was missing the last summer, taken by an old nemesis and hidden in a sea cave where the water, normally an element over which he had power, clashed against the rocks, hiding her from his inner sense. The kidnapping had loosed a wild ugliness in him, a desperation that felt uncomfortably close to the madness of dragon blood that he had seen in some of his other relatives.

I am distracted at best, going insane at worst, he thought glumly, blotting the ink on a new draft of the harbor code he was writing. *If she knew, she would come home.*

The thought kindled in his second nature an interest that took a while to extinguish. Almost as much as the man craved her company because of his love for her, the dragon sought it as well, but for different reasons. There were gemlike qualities to Rhapsody—her eyes a clear emerald, her hair like golden flax—that had been imbued in her both by nature and by her rather life-changing experience of walking through the fire at the Earth's core. It was as if all physical flaw had been burned away, and perfection was something that appealed to the avarice in the dragon's nature.

Blessedly, it was the existence of flaw that the man cherished, the pigheaded stubbornness, the occasional inability to see the forest for the trees, the wild anger that exhibited itself at inexplicable times, all parts of this woman that he enjoyed as well, and so the duality of his nature remained in agreement and in balance, despite taking opposite sides of the debate.

But now, if the physical cues that reminded him of his wife were beginning to manifest themselves for no reason, there could be more beneath the surface. Upon contemplating that possibility, Ashe felt cold.

Because it might be a signal that the dragon side of him was beginning to take over.

His desire to see her return grew stronger. He countered in by chanting under his breath, reminding himself that she was happier in the lair of the dragon than she was in Haguefort, and ultimately safer, but the diversion only worked for a short while. Then he would see Portia pass by, carrying linens or a tray to the kitchen; she would bow or smile slightly at him and hurry away, leaving in her wake a flicker of golden hair, a flash of rosy cheek and the scent of soap and vanilla.

He began to dream about his wife ceaselessly, fevered dreams that caused him to wake, sweating with unmet passion or the shivering chills of fear. Some nights in his dreams she came to him, pulled the covers aside, and settled down into his arms; from those dreams he awoke feeling lost and sick, his head pounding as if it were about to split.

After the worst of those nightmares Portia had come into his rooms, as she often did, delivering a clean basin and fresh, warm water for his morning shave. She bowed and disappeared, leaving such a strong image of Rhapsody in Ashe's mind that he pulled the covers over his head and groaned loudly enough to frighten the tabby cat in the corner into a frenzy.

Finally the last blow to his peace of mind was struck on an especially cold night.

Ashe was sitting before the fire again, warming himself by its flames and in thoughts of his wife, when the serving maid entered the room, carrying a tray with his supper. She placed it down on the table before him, uncovered the plate, and turned to go; Ashe caught the scent of spice and vanilla, and the faintest hint of summer flowers in the folds of her rustling skirts. But rather than leaving, she came slowly up behind him, the heat of her body far more intense than that of the fire on his back.

With the lightest of touches, she let her hands come to rest on his shoulders, then allowed them to run lightly over his collar as if she were smoothing it. Her hands closed gently on the heavy muscles of his shoulders, her thumbs dug deliciously into the tight bands that encircled his spine as her fingers gently massaged the soreness from his neck.

Just as Rhapsody had always done.

She had magic in her hands, magic that soothed his tension and brought warmth to the deepest places that were tight and sore. Against his will Ashe closed his eyes, surrendering for a moment to the blissful ministrations of her hands.

Then went cold with the horror of what was happening.

Rage began to burn in his belly, anger at the liberties this servant was taking with him, but a deeper fury was building, directed at himself for allowing her to take those liberties.

And enjoying them.

He tried to keep his smoldering anger from igniting too quickly, reminding himself that it was a common practice in other keeps, other castles, for the servants to believe that servicing the master's needs, physical and sexual, was part of their indenture. When he was an adolescent his own father, a holy man widowed by Ashe's birth, had had a coterie of whores, each of whom had the countersign to open the secret door into Llauron's office. So he kept himself as steady as he could, despite his inner desire to fling the girl across the room.

He set his teeth and spoke in as calm a voice as he could.

"Portia," he said quietly, "you have truly beautiful hands. Soft as milk, and gentle. It would be a shame if I have to cut them off, which I will, if you don't remove them from me immediately."

A gasp of shock went up from the doorway. Ashe spun in his chair.

The serving girl was standing in the doorframe, the lid of the serving tray still in her hands. She began to tremble in confusion, tears forming in her large brown eyes.

Ashe looked wildly around him; his meal was still on the table before him, untouched. The nap of the silk carpet showed two sets of her footprints, and his dragon sense could immediately tell from the lack of heat in them that she had made her way directly to the door, rather than lingering.

His stomach clenched.

"Forgive me," he stammered. "I—I thought—"

The young woman burst into tears.

Ashe pushed the tray aside and rose; Portia froze, her body going rigid with shock.

"I am sorry, again, I apologize," the Lord Cymrian said awkwardly. "You may go."

Portia dropped a quick curtsy and skittered through the door, closing it behind her. She waited until she had gotten all the way back to her bedroom, had thrown herself on her bed and pulled the cover over her head, before allowing herself the pleasure of a grin.

By that time, the Lord Cymrian was no longer thinking about her, and was actively ignoring anything his dragon sense might tell him about her. He had bounded up the stairs, two at a time, to gather the provisions he would need for his trip to the silent lake in the forest of Gwynwood.

He did not even wait until morning to leave.

32

THE DRAGON'S LAIR

The silence of the forest was broken occasionally by the twitter of winterbirds.

Achmed stopped long enough in his trek to point a deadfall out to Krinsel, the Bolg midwife, before stepping over a rotten tree. He waited until the woman had nodded her understanding and had circumvented the natural trap before turning and continuing deeper into the forest.

They had been traveling along a tributary of the Tar'afel River for some time, knowing that the brook would eventually empty into a quiet lake near the dragon's lair. Achmed was listening intently, paying little attention to the glistening white trees, their branches dripping soft drops of snow in the heat of the morning sun.

He was following a sound that resonated in his ears as well as his blood; the namesong by which Rhapsody had called him. The song vibrated in his soul and resonated in his eardrums, through the sensitive network of veins and nerves that formed his skin-web, to the very tips of his fingers.

Achmed the Snake, come to me.

It was both a welcome sensation, and horrific one, to be summoned thus by a Namer. While the melody being chanted in the distance was perfectly attuned to his brain and the natural vibrations that he emitted in the course of drawing breath, there was still something deeply disturbing to him about his name being on the wind, even if no other living soul could hear it. Achmed had been a solitary and secretive creature his entire life.

Some habits were hard to break, some natural impulses all but impossible to overcome.

Achmed, come to me.

The winter had faded, as it always did in the middle continent during Thaw, for one turn of the moon. The ground at the base of trees was visible, dead or emergent grass in tones of pale green and gold drying in the morning wind. The snowcap, hard and frozen most of the winter, had softened to a thin, watery layer, and the breeze was warm, but did not carry the scent of spring, because the melt was false. In a few short weeks the cold would return with a vengeance, choking back any early shoots that might have come up in response to the cruel invitation the earth issued during Thaw, burying them securely under a resilient blanket of hard white ice until the turning of the season.

Still, he had to admit to himself that it was pleasant to hear Rhapsody's voice in his ears again. She had been away from Ylorc for so many years now that he had almost grown accustomed to not hearing the morning messages she used to broadcast daily through the natural echo chamber of the ring of rocks that rose above her subterranean home in the grotto of Elysian, an underground lake in his lands.

Even though she liked living alone when she, Grunthor, and he had first come to Ylorc, away from the Firbolg who considered her a source of food and watched her hungrily when she passed by, Rhapsody was good at keeping in touch, and made of point of checking in with him each day. When she first married Ashe and moved to Navarne Achmed found to his shock that he missed her Lirin sunrise aubades and sunset devotions as well, the love songs of her people, sung to the heavens and the stars they had been born beneath, ceremonies she had marked daily all the time that he had known her. She had even continued to sing the prayers when they were traveling within the earth along the Axis Mundi, as far from the stars as it was possible to be, and so they were annoyingly ingrained in his mind, enough so that not hearing them had become even more bothersome than hearing them had been.

So it was, in a way, comforting to hear her voice again, singing his name, in the depths of his consciousness. Almost as comforting as it was disturbing.

He inhaled, allowing the air of the forest to circulate through his sensitive sinuses. Then he grimaced.

There was a taste of salt on the wind; Achmed rolled it around in his mouth, then spat it out on the ground sourly. They were a good way from the sea, and the breeze was blowing from the east, not the west, so that tang could only mean one thing.

Ashe was around here somewhere.

From what he could ascertain the droplets of salty water were a ways off; perhaps he had as much as half a day's lead on Rhapsody's husband. Achmed signaled to Krinsel to hurry; he wanted to have a chance to confer with the Lady Cymrian alone before Ashe showed up and distracted her completely, as he had done ever since he interposed himself in their lives four years before.

Achmed.

Achmed flinched and shook his head; the voice was different now, harsher, he thought, though when pondering a moment later he realized that it was not a good characterization of it. *Is she growing impatient?* he wondered as he quickened his steps, homing in on the aural beacon. *Tired of being holed up in a dragon's cave for an unknown number of months or even years, until her confinement is over and her brat born?*

Finally he and Krinsel came to the banks of a placid forest lake nestled against a hillside. Its crystal waters were perfectly calm and reflected the trees that lined it like a mirror; broken chunks of ice floated lazily in the current draining into a small stream. From the descriptions Rhapsody had given him of Elynsynos's lair, he thought this might be the reflecting pool that was fed from its depths. The grove in which the pool rested was serene, the silence broken only by an occasional chirp of birdsong, which grew lesser with each step closer toward the dragon's lair.

He motioned to Krinsel to follow him around the quiet lake, the only sound now the trickling of the brook. The song of his name grew louder as he approached; when he got to the far shore he could tell that it was issuing forth from the entrance of a cave that was hidden in the steepest part of the hillside, obscured all but entirely by trees and the grade of the land. From the mouth of the cave a small stream flowed, emptying silently into the glassy waters of the reflecting pool.

Achmed indicated the cave entrance wordlessly, and Krinsel nodded again.

No path was visible to the eye; in fact, it seemed to Achmed that the trees that grew around the lake up to the entrance of the cave had been planted, or perhaps subtly twisted, to obscure the way, to lend yet one more layer of guardian flora to the place. Fortunately, not long after she had given him the ridiculous moniker of Achmed the Snake, Rhapsody had also re-titled him with other names—*Firbolg, Dhracian, Firstborn, Assassin, Unerring tracker. The Pathfinder.* The words, spoken in the pure flames of the fire at the center of the earth, had imparted those traits to him, some of which he had had all his life, others of which were new. The ability to find paths was a useful addition to his skills, and he employed it now; the way through the labyrinth of trees became instantly clear to him.

He had started down the path that led to the entrance when the silence of the forest was suddenly shattered by a voice that rumbled through the forest floor, its pitch at once soprano, alto, tenor, and bass.

Stop.

Achmed froze involuntarily.

The odd voice sounded both annoyed and amused.

One does not walk, uninvited, into the lair of a dragon, unless one is a great fool. I suggest you knock, or at least announce yourself.

The words echoed up the tunnel beyond the cave entrance. They rippled unpleasantly over his sensitive skin, disrupting the agreeable vibration of his namesong that had been dancing there, irritating it and making his head throb. Beyond that, there was an inherent power to them, elemental in origin, that was unmistakably threatening.

He looked back at the Bolg midwife, whose face was set in the same stoic expression it always held, but whose eyes were glistening with fear.

"You can wait here," he said; the woman nodded slightly, relief evident, though her expression did not change.

Achmed walked to the mouth of the cave. On the outer wall, obscured by a layer of frost and lichen, he saw some scratched runes; upon closer examination, he recognized them, and exhaled deeply. The words were carved in the ancient language of Universal Ship's Cant, a compound tongue that was formed from Old Cymrian and the languages of the known world more than two millennia before:

Cyme we inne frid, fram the grip of deap to lif inne dis smylte land

The irony made his skin itch. This was the birthplace of the Cymrian people, the very spot where Merithyn the Explorer had carved the words given to him by his king with which he was to greet anyone he met in the new world.

Come we in peace, from the grip of death to life in this fair land.

The dragon that lived in the bottom of this cave had been fascinated with the explorer, then enamored of him; she had invited him to return home and bring his doomed people with him to refuge and safety in her lands. And the imbecile had done so, bringing with him all manner of selfish, spoiled people who had gained a sort of immortality, or at least an immense longevity, in the process. Though Merithyn died at sea on the way back, the Cymrians, as the refugees from Serendair were known, then proceeded to conquer the Wyrmlands and the lands beyond, ruling undisputed, subjugating the indigenous peoples who could not withstand conquerors with such unearthly powers and life spans, only to despoil it all with their great, stupid war.

And this was where it all began.

His teeth hurt thinking about it.

"Rhapsody!" he shouted impatiently into the mouth of the cave.

The namesong abruptly ceased, ripping the pleasant vibration from his skin, leaving it humming with a slight sting.

Silence reigned for a moment. Then the multitoned voice spoke again, displeasure evident in its tone now, replacing the humor that had been there a moment before.

You may enter, Bolg king, but mind your manners.

"Huzzah," Achmed muttered. He gestured to Krinsel to make camp outside the cave, then started down the tunnel into the dark.

The mouth of the cave began to widen a few feet in, stretching into a vast, dark tunnel that glowed farther below with a pulsing light. At the tunnel's exterior, a starlike lichen grew on the walls of the cave, spreading out into the light of day, but thinned as the tunnel deepened and eventually disappeared.

The walls of the cave twisted in ever-growing circles as the pathway descended. Achmed could hear the sound of trickling water farther in, could smell the unmistakable odor of the forge, of brimstone burning in the tunnel's depths. *The breath of the dragon,* he thought, the acrid scent irritating his sinuses. He squinted in the dark, following the glow.

He was wading now through a shallow stream that deepened the farther he went in. Rhapsody had described the lair to him years before, had told him that the wyrm lived along the banks of an inland sea. Steam rose from the water he walked through.

He lost track of time as he traversed the tunnel, much as he, Grunthor, and Rhapsody had when traveling within the Root. The sensation surprised him; he was amazed that Rhapsody was able to pass any amount of time within this subterranean cave, as it was very reminiscent of that time within the Earth's belly. Being Lirin, a child of the sky, she had suffered every moment she was away from the open air; the journey along the Axis Mundi had been torture for her. And she had been here for months.

The rancid air blasted around him in a wave of tainted heat again, and ahead of him he could hear the sound of taloned feet scraping against the stone floor of the cave, followed by the splash of water as the beast dragged itself out. Achmed stopped as he rounded a corner and looked up.

Ahead of him the dragon loomed, filling the cave from floor to ceiling, its enormous body ethereal but with surprising mass. The immense wyrm was at least a hundred feet in length, perhaps longer, in her nonsolid state, the copper scales that clad her skin glittering in the warm light from torch-fires that illuminated the bottom of the cave, causing her skin to reflect the light like a million twinkling red stars. Her eyes were prismatic orbs bisected vertically with narrow silver pupils, and gleamed like lanterns in the darkness. And in those eyes was the unmistakable look of irritation.

"Do not upset Pretty," the beast warned, her multitoned voice echoing through the cave. The multicolored eyes narrowed to emphasize the words that had issued forth from the very air itself.

Achmed nodded curtly. "Where is she?"

The dragon eyed him suspiciously for a moment longer, then moved to one side, allowing him to pass by her translucent body and continue deeper into the cave.

In the midst of all the treasure from the sea Rhapsody sat in a canvas hammock suspended between two walls of the cave, a trident buried into the stone up to the top of its prongs holding one end up. Achmed slowed his steps and came to a halt, watching her intently.

He barely recognized her.

She had changed physically since the festival, but at first Achmed had difficulty trying to isolate in what way she was different. Her features had seemed to sharpen, to have lost some of the softness of angle that her father's human blood had given her otherwise Lirin face. Now her appearance was colder, more severe; the warmth of the elemental fire that she had absorbed walking through the Earth's core had diminished, leaving her skin paler, more alabaster, less rosy than it normally was. She seemed detached; she must have heard him come in, but she did not favor him with a glance. There was an almost draconic edge to her, and Achmed swallowed angrily, bile rising in his throat at the sight.

"Are you forming this baby, or is it forming you?" he asked.

Rhapsody turned then and looked at him. Achmed's throat tightened; her clear green eyes, emerald in the torchlight, were scored with the same vertical pupils that her husband's eyes, and those of the dragon, had.

"Both," she said. There was an echo in her voice that was reminiscent of the multiple tones of the wyrm, though less pronounced. "And hello to you, too."

Achmed measured his breathing, trying to beat down the rising sense of distress that was welling up inside him.

Rhapsody slid out of the hammock then and came to him. She nodded to Elynsynos, who glared at Achmed once more and slipped deeper into the cave through a mountain of gleaming silver coins.

"It's only to be expected that a blend of such powerful blood would have an impact on both the mother and child," Rhapsody said calmly, but clearly disturbed by Achmed's reaction. "It's temporary."

"Has Ashe seen you like this?" Achmed demanded.

Rhapsody's brow furrowed. "Yes. Did you bring Krinsel, as I asked you to?"

"She is outside. Did you finish the translation?"

"I did," Rhapsody said.

"Where is it?" Achmed asked, his hackles beginning to rise from the static air in the cave and the disturbing change in Rhapsody.

Rhapsody crossed her arms. "That doesn't matter," she said. "I am not going to give it to you, Achmed."

The air in the damp cave suddenly seemed to go completely dry. The two friends stared at each other intently. Finally Achmed spoke, and his voice was calm, but with a deadly undertone.

"I must have misheard you."

"You didn't," Rhapsody said flatly. "You cannot have this lore, Achmed — it mustn't be used. Not now, not ever. For any reason. You must abandon your plans to rebuild the Lightcatcher, and find some other way to keep the Earthchild, and Ylorc, safe. This way will only make things more dangerous."

The pupils in Achmed's mismatched eyes contracted, as if drinking in a blinding light. His breath became more measured, shallower, but there were no other outward signs of the towering rage that was building within him. Both of them knew it was coming. Finally he spoke.

"Over the time I have known you, Rhapsody, you have given me many reasons and even more opportunities to kill you. You always do it so blithely that your sheer ignorance saves your life every time, because it would be difficult to summon up the initiative to terminate the existence of someone who is so clearly missing the point." His eyes narrowed perceptibly. "This time, however, you are so willfully unaware of the thinness of the ice on which you are treading that it is breathtaking."

Rhapsody exhaled but did not blink. "Do whatever you think you must, Achmed," she said evenly, but with a deadly undertone of her own. "If my death at your hands is what it takes to keep you from moving forward with this folly, then it will have been worth it."

Achmed flinched. She was using the Namer's skill of True Speaking; there was no sarcasm, no jest in her voice.

"Why?" he spat. "Tell me what is so worrisome to you about me having this information that you would jeopardize—no, sacrifice—our friendship, and possibly your own life, to keep it from me, knowing how much I have need of it? Have you lost your mind, or just your commitment to the Earthchild and her safety?"

"Neither." The pupils in Rhapsody's emerald eyes expanded in the same way Achmed's had, mirroring the control he was struggling to exert over his anger. "My commitment to keep her, and the rest of the people for whom I have responsibility, safe has not changed. Not even in the face of having to refuse my dearest friend something he craves beyond reason. Whatever that costs me is a price I'm willing to pay because, unlike you, I understand what is at stake here."

"I am fully aware of what is at stake," Achmed said softly, menace dripping from his words. "What is at stake here is the continued existence of life, and the Afterlife. Should the F'dor find the Earthchild, they will tear her rib of Living Stone from her body, and use it to unlock the Vault of the Underworld, in which all their remaining kind are imprisoned. Once loose, the demons will destroy all that lives on the earth, for that is what they crave, but since their existence is not limited to the material world, well fed with the power of that destruction, they will use it to undo even that life which exists beyond this one. Even I, godless man that I am, find that to be a fate that I cannot allow while there is breath in my body. So why is it that you, who see yourself as the savior of the world, not to mention every lost wastrel, child, and cat, cannot see the need to *help me* in this totally baffles me, Rhapsody."

She exhaled deeply, then glanced over to the wall of silver behind which the dragon had disappeared.

"For ages you have had Grunthor's loyalty, loyalty without limits, unto death and beyond. And yet there have been times over the course of your association that he has had to refuse you, has he not?"

"There is a considerable difference between Grunthor and you," Achmed said, the hint of a sneer in his voice. "I trust his judgment. He is wiser than me in many ways. So when he questions me, I listen, because he and I have the same basic goals in mind, and he never does it just to be cantankerous. You, on the other hand, are like a spinning top. Your ethics, while consistent, are frequently foolish, your loyalties ill placed. Ofttimes you defy me or what I mean to do for reasons that make no sense to anyone ruled by his head rather than by whatever body part rules your decisions."

He waited for the hurt reaction he knew would result from the cutting words, but saw none. The arrows of his words bounced off her unnoticed; her facial expression did not change.

"And does Grunthor support your decision to rebuild the Lightcatcher?"

The Bolg king's eyes narrowed. "Whatever doubts he has had have been assuaged both by his knowledge of the instrumentality's history, and of what is at stake."

"Liar," Rhapsody said contemptuously.

The air between them crackled with sudden dryness.

"Grunthor has done whatever he has to support you in the feverish intensity of your plan, which has consumed you," she continued. "He has expressed his worry to you, I am certain of it. And this is what frightens me more than anything, Achmed. It does not surprise or distress me that you would disregard my concerns, for we both know you do not hold them in any regard. You have defied the pleadings of the Sea Mage, because you despise him and blame him for losses in the past. The king of the Nain, the people who built the very mountain realm that you now rule, and the Lightcatcher itself, sent you an emissary to warn you against building it again, did they not? That was the reason he came to you, though you did not confess that when you told me of his visit during the carnival." Achmed did not answer. "All these people who are your friends, or at least your allies, have begged you not to do this, and their pleas fall on your deaf ears. I am not surprised.

"But then, your own chief Archon, your supreme military commander, your best friend who has followed you with the unquestioning loyalty of a born soldier throughout more than a millennium of time, not to mention through the very bowels of the Earth itself, tells you he doubts the wisdom of what you are doing, and you *still* do not heed? You should ask yourself whose judgment is really impaired here, whose soul is possessed of irrational ethics and goals." She put a hand to her belly and took a deep breath.

"Here is what you truly need to know about this translation, Achmed. I have told you from the beginning that this is ancient lore, the very code of power by which magic is manipulated. The roadmaps to the beginning of time, the musical score of the elements and how their vibrations make up the very fabric of the world itself. Is it even possible for you to understand the import? You have the keys to the world in that manuscript. Any man with even the slightest humility would tremble at the thought of touching it, let alone wielding it, without years of study in how to use it. But your arrogance knows no bounds, and so you are blind to how ferociously dangerous this information could be, even in the hands of someone well-intentioned." Her eyes gleamed bright in the darkness of the cave.

"So since you will not accept my wisdom in this matter, or that of the Sea Mage, or the Nain king, or even your best friend, perhaps I can put it in terms you might actually fathom. Power does not come from nowhere, Achmed. It is an elemental vibration drawn from something else, a transfer of life essence. Whether it be for healing or hiding, scrying or destruction, the instrumentality you have built, and want to rebuild, needs a source to power it. And since you are using the pure energy of the light spectrum, the colors which, like music, are attuned to the vibrations of the elements, know what it is that you are drawing from.

"These are primordial magics, left over from the birth of the world. Those magics that are purely fire-based pull power from the core of the earth, the very elemental inferno through which you, Grunthor, and I walked to come here. Those that are based in water draw from the Well of the Living Seas, the place where that element was born. Air-based magics come from the Castle of the Knotted Winds, ether from the star Seren and the pieces of others that have fallen to earth and yet remain alive still. But most of the magic of the Lightcatcher, or the Lightforge, as the Nain called it, is drawn from the earth, since it is in earth, being the last element born, that traces of all the elements are contained."

Rhapsody's breathing evened out, as she saw her words beginning to register with the Bolg king. Lest the moment be lost, she leaned closer, and whispered her final words like a killing blow.

"The machine you built, and want to rebuild, draws from the earth itself, Achmed, and more—it saps the oldest piece of it, that which has lain within it, dormant, since the world began, its power tainted with fire lore because it has been polluted by the F'dor. This machine, which you see as a bastion of protection for the Earthchild, pulls power from the very wyrm that lies, sleeping now, within the body of the earth—it is *part* of that body, a large part. You have seen that wyrm with your own eyes.

"And each time you use the Lightcatcher, you are risking waking it."

33

$\mathcal{F}$or a long time the only sound in the cave was the trickling of the water that streamed from the underground lagoon into the quiet lake beyond the confines of the cave. The two ancient friends stared at each other, neither speaking, their breaths measured in unison. Finally Achmed broke the silence.

"Give me the translation."

Rhapsody's eyes narrowed. "Have you heard nothing I have said?"

"Every word. Give it to me anyway."

The Lady Cymrian rested her hand angrily on her swollen belly.

"I want you to leave now, Achmed," she said.

"With pleasure, as soon as you give me the translation. I have been learning to be patient with reptiles, but don't push too far."

Rhapsody turned away angrily. "Or what? You'll kill me? If that will keep you from finishing and using that device, go ahead. I have already told you that the price would be worth it."

The Bolg king exhaled. "Who's being the fool now? First, let me tell you this again: The Lightcatcher *will* be built, it *will* be used, translation or no. You cannot stop that. I'm looking for something in the text to avoid having to learn how to use it by trial and error. In that you could have been useful, but instead you remain blind—perhaps it is the shrinkage in your eyes from carrying your husband's brat.

"Next, when was the last time you knew me to kill someone when it wasn't in self-defense, or, more likely, in *your* defense, my dear? I leave my kingdom and travel over the width of a continent to haul your arse out of the sea and the grip of a depraved maniac, and you accuse me of being willing to kill you? Ridiculous, on top of insulting. Just because I know how to kill well or easily doesn't mean I do it recklessly or without reason. There are plenty of individuals I would like to see dead who still walk the earth—many of them related to you.

"And don't treat me like a child. Primordial magic? Of course it is primordial magic. We are dealing with forces of evil left over from the First Age. No source of power that has its genesis any later than that will work against those forces."

Rhapsody turned back; she was pale now. "But you have no business using it," she said haltingly. "This is not a matter of reading a recipe or building from a design. The great Namers studied for centuries before they were given access to these lores; even I, who have studied these things, am woefully unprepared to understand what is written here fully. I am largely self-taught, Achmed—do not forget that much of my study was done in the absence of my mentor. Despite all the time I have practiced the science of Naming, even I would not dream of manipulating primordial magic."

Achmed pointed at her belly. "What do you think you have been doing in spawning dragonlings?" he said, unable to disguise his disgust. "If that's not manipulating primordial magic, I don't know what is. You don't even have a pretense of an idea what will happen as a result of this pregnancy. You, a vessel of elemental fire and ether, the wielder of a sword that has no doubt shaped your soul with its own powers, Lirin and human and *Cymrian,* gods help you, frozen forever in time, ageless—blending your blood with the tainted mishmash that is Ashe's? Whatever is born could be the end of the world all by itself. And don't pretend this was entirely your idea. I know enough about wyrms to know that your beloved husband is toying with your life, whether he pretends otherwise or not. All this pretense of concern about the risks of the Lightcatcher—you should be far more worried about the risks of bringing this child into the world, not only to your own life, but to the future." He saw Rhapsody wince, and felt a twin rush of satisfaction and guilt.

"So now," he said quickly, "stop lecturing me about the risks of playing with magics one does not understand and give me the translation. I assure you I will be far more responsible with mine than you have been with yours."

"I—I can't—"

"Of course you can. Ask yourself this: Knowing that there is an entire library, Gwylliam's library, at my disposal, in Ylorc, and any number of Bolg to work on it, is it better for you to give me specific directions, or allow me to experiment? Or, of course, you could abandon all this"—he waved contemptuously at the cave filled with sea treasures and lichen—"and come back to Ylorc with me; you can oversee the project, and then at least you will know how the lore is being used."

"No."

In fury he reached out and seized her wrist; instinctively she pulled away, but stopped, feeling the strength of his grip.

"You are sacrificing your status as a Namer, you realize this?" Achmed said softly, staring directly into the now-vertical pupils of her eyes. "You promised me in Yarim, when I did a rather major favor for you and the useless duke there, that you would help me with this. If you refuse now, that will be a lie. You will be going back on your word. You will be breaking your oath of truth—your status as a Namer will be forfeit."

Rhapsody's face hardened, and she struggled to pull free of his grip again.

"So be it," she gasped, her attempt to break his lock on her wrist futile. "If I was willing to die to keep you from disturbing the lore, what's the sacrifice of a profession?"

Achmed released her arm with a violent toss.

"I repeat, you are keeping me from *nothing*," he said harshly. "You are only missing the chance to keep the process from being haphazard. Let that be on your head." He turned and started up the passage to the air again.

Rhapsody's eyes opened wide with shock, the emerald green irises lightening to the color of spring grass. Achmed caught the change out of the corner of his eye. He recognized that look; it was the expression that came into Rhapsody's eyes when she was afraid.

He stopped in the tunnel and opened his mouth to ask her what she feared more, his actions, or her inaction.

Then shut it abruptly at the sight of the bloody water gushing forth from her and pooling ominously on the floor of the cave at her feet.

$\mathcal{W}$ithin a heart's beat, the whole world seemed to change.

Rhapsody's hand went to her belly, and her face contorted as she doubled over. She let loose a gasp of pain and shakily put out her hand to brace herself against the wall of the cave.

Achmed felt a sudden chill, an iciness as the heat in the tunnel dropped suddenly and dissipated. His anger melted away, leaving him dizzy; he seized Rhapsody's arm and discovered that her body was cold, as if the core of elemental fire burning within her had been snuffed.

The air in the tunnel crackled statically; the dragon appeared, sliding over the pile of silver like liquid lightning. Her multitoned voice resonated in the water and walls of the cave.

"Pretty?"

Rhapsody struggled to remain standing, but her legs buckled beneath her, and she slid to the floor. She opened her mouth to form words, but then her face contorted in pain and she gasped again.

"Your husband comes," the dragon said, her voice solid and resolute as the ages, but Achmed could see consternation glittering in the beast's prismatic eyes. "I sense him at the stream's edge, less than a league away."

Rhapsody's eyes met the Bolg king's. "Krinsel," she whispered. "Please."

Achmed fought back the acid in his throat. He slid his hand down the length of Rhapsody's arm into her own and squeezed it; he released it and bent to the floor, dipping the edge of his robe in her blood. Then he ran back up the tunnel.

He found the midwife at the cave's mouth. The command to run and aid Rhapsody he gave in Bolgish, as it was a terse and guttural tongue that required little effort to speak. As the woman hurried into the glowing darkness, Achmed exhaled sharply, then stepped out of the cave and held the edge of his cloak aloft in the wind.

He waited impatiently, long enough for the scent of the blood to catch the wind, then turned and hurried back into the dark belly of the dragon's lair.

℣wo miles away at the edge of the tributary of the Tar'afel, Ashe paused from drawing water and rose. He cast the droplets in his hand to the snowy ground, where they refroze into crystals of ice, and ran the back of his sleeve across his face to clear his nose and eyes.

Within him his dragon sense expanded, rising from its dormancy. The minutiae of the world around him became mammoth; suddenly he was aware of the tiniest of details, the infinitesimal threads of light and sound that made up all the individual things that existed beneath the sun, that stood separate from the wind that blanketed the earth. Every blade of frozen grass in every thawed circle below every leafless tree, every feather on every winter bird that flew above him, every ice-covered branch of every bush was suddenly clear to him, or at least to the ancient beast in his blood.

On the wind he could count the drops of blood he recognized more surely than he knew his own name.

And more—there was blood mixed with hers that echoed his own.

Ashe turned in that instant and surveyed the land between where he stood and the dragon's cave. *Two miles as the raven flies,* he thought, forcing down the fear that was rising within him the way his dragonsense had the moment before. At least ten to ford the river at a low enough place and then circumvent the thickest parts of the virgin forest, where no path had ever been blazed, and where snow still lingered.

The woodlands around him appeared for a split second in his mind to be filled with obstacles that separated him from his treasure, snow-covered deadfalls and white hillocks, hummocks and knolls that barricaded the forest with thick frost that had melted to mere frosting at the onset of Thaw.

And then suddenly the obstacles fell into place as his dragon sense took on a new dimension. No longer confined to being just an awareness, his dragon nature took over, and that side of him rose, rampant, struggling within him no more, but rather asserting itself over nature and the earth around him. A path gleamed in his mind like a beacon, an ethereal guide to Elynsynos's cave.

And as his wyrm nature took over, Ashe felt a loosening of the reins of control that he kept so tightly inside of himself, a calling to the power of the elements all around him.

His body remained human for the moment, even though his conscious mind was now draconic. He began to run, straight into the tree wall before him that kept him separated from what the dragon in his soul considered its treasure.

His wife and unborn child.

Bend to me; let me pass, the multitoned voice within his soul commanded.

And the earth obeyed.

Trees shrugged in the wind, their trunks bending at barely possible angles to clear the path. Mounds of snow-covered brush parted; the muddy ground hardened in places before him, all in response to the lore of the earth from which his ancestors had sprung. The forest, suddenly silent, seemed to hold its breath as the man who raced through it dragged power from the air around him, passing through the greenwood as if it were nothing more than wind.

Leaving it crackling, dry, a moment later, as if his presence had stripped the life right out of it.

As he ran, all of the thought went out of Ashe's conscious mind, sinking deeper into the primal nature of the dragon in his blood, until the solitary thought—the need to get to Rhapsody—consumed his entire being. That primacy gave him greater speed, and before he knew it he was standing at the mouth of Elynsynos's lair, panting from exertion and sweating in terror.

At the cave entrance his dragon sense was suddenly, rudely slapped away, forced into sharp submission by the greater lore that was extant in the place. Ashe blinked, then listened. From the depths of the cave he could hear a keening wail, the sobbing of pain and despair in a voice that he knew well. The sound of the agony made his blood turn cold; his skin prickled in sweat and nausea threatened to consume him.

Standing before him in the cave's mouth was a Bolg woman, a dark and somber-faced midwife he vaguely remembered Rhapsody introducing to him years before. In Bolgish culture the midwives held a special place of power; the Bolg believed that infants were to be given the best of their crude medical care because they represented the future, even while Ylorc's warriors of great skill and accomplishment might be left to bleed to death of their wounds. The midwives were an iron-fisted lot, a dominant political faction even in Achmed's new order, a silent, stern-demeanored group of women who were rarely known to show emotion or distress.

So it was even more disconcerting to see the expression of stoic fear in the eyes of the woman standing before him.

Ashe struggled to form the words. "My wife?" he whispered. "My child?"

The Bolg woman let her breath out slowly, then spoke three words in the common tongue of the continent.

"I am sorry," she said.

34

The days of endless snow passed, one into another.

Faron's mind, absent of other things to comprehend, honed a harder focus. He had lost all memory save one, had turned away from acclimating to his new body, his new reality, to keep his attention set on but one goal. Mile by mile, he followed winter's path through unbroken farmland, sighting along the trans-Orlandan thoroughfare, the frozen road that bisected the continent. There was very little traffic on that thoroughfare; Thaw had come, and the people of the towns, villages, and cities of Roland were busy making repairs, stocking up peat, wood, and dung for fuel, and settling in, awaiting winter's return. With the lore of the earth strong within him, Faron had learned to blend into the landscape, so whether it was because of that new ability, or the lack of anyone to see him, he passed unnoticed.

He was following a sound now, a distant call in a vibration he had known all his life, the ancient, primordial song of the scales he had lost. If it had been possible for him to forget the tune, he would have been reminded by the humming of the ones within his possession, their power reverberating through his stone body.

Ofttimes the noise of day served to mute the call, and when it did Faron became angry beyond all measure. The cry of a winter bird, of geese flying overhead in formation, caused him to stop in his snowy tracks, looking up to the firmament of the sky above, muttering silent curses in a long-dead language deep within his brain. He craved the silence of the world, for in that silence, he could hear the call clearly. Once he got a fix on it, he followed it ceaselessly.

Until at last one night he found what he was looking for.

He had come to the top of a rise above a small, low-lying valley, one of the undulating hills of the Orlandan Plateau, on the wide Krevensfield Plain, and there it was below him.

The full moon was shining, bright as day. Its light glazed the snowy fields, making them gleam silvery blue. Even in the dark, the moonlight was so intense that it was easy to see the brightly colored wagons, the crimson and purple flags dressing the carts that by day were pulled by horses. Those beasts were quartered together now, blanketed for the night; they alone noticed the chain in the earth, and nickered in a growing panic.

Within the Monstrosity's camp torches and barrel fires burned, sending sparks skyward to dance with the blazing moonlight.

Around those barrel fires some of the men who served as guards and laborers sat, drinking foul ale and telling fouler jokes. The hunchback ticket taker had imbibed more than he could handle, and was now being used as a human ball in a grotesque game of Tossabout, to which he seemed to proffer no objection and was, in fact, cackling aloud. The laughter echoed off the empty world of hummocks and rises around them, fading off into the night.

Masking the call of the scales.

Malik held his battered mug to his lips, blowing the dirty foam off, the ale spattering into his beard as he laughed. He had pulled his legs against his chest in the attempt to warm them when out of the corner of his eye he spied movement.

He looked again, peering out into the darkness, but whatever had been moving was gone. *Nothing more 'an a snow devil,* he decided, taking another draught. *Wind'll be a bitch tonight.*

The wagon closest to their barrel fire reared up off the ground, then was slammed down on it again, shattering into pieces.

For a split second, no sound was heard on the wide expanse of the great plain except for the splintering of the wood. Then the screaming began.

The freaks that had survived the initial impact inside the wagon started to scream; their harsh, alien voices rose in a discordant wail that sliced through the winter wind and the crackle of the fire, blending with the frightened whinnying of the horses. Malik and the others around the barrel fire fell back, covering their faces, then scrambled to their feet in shock. The keeper's mouth flapped, forming two words.

"What the—"

The next nearest wagon suddenly skidded sideways toward them, as if it were being swung from behind. It smashed into the wreckage of the first, doubling the screams and filling the night air with the sounds of gruesome snapping and grinding.

Then it was hoisted up into the darkness, and tossed in much the same manner as they had been tossing the hunchback the moment before, right into their midst.

Through the sheer luck of reflex and favorable positioning Malik dropped on the snow and rolled to his left, bruising himself from face to knee but spared from being crushed, as three of the other men he had been drinking with the moment before were.

As the cacophony swelled around him, and the blood pounded crazily in his ears, Malik's mind tried to determine what was happening, why a pleasant night's drinking in the cold had suddenly become a nightmare. All he could imagine was they had been caught in the middle of a terrible winter storm that had whipped up from nowhere, catching the wagons and sending them flying.

He struggled to regain his feet and his gorge, which had risen into his throat and was choking him; just as he did, Malik thought he saw a shadow pass between the destruction and a third wagon, from which freaks and others that traveled with the Monstrosity were streaming, gibbering in confusion and fear. In the tattered light of the remnants of the barrel fire that had been in their midst and now was scattered over the snow the shadow appeared to be human, but elongated into gianthood by the undulating flames.

The roof of the next wagon splintered into pieces as the chorus of confusion grew into screams of terror.

This time Malik looked up over the top of the broken wagon in time to see the silhouette of two enormous arms and upper body slamming down with fury again. The shadow seized the wagon, shaking it violently, causing whatever other creatures had still been inside, crowding their ways to the exit, to be thrown clear onto the snowy ground, where they huddled, their eyes fixed above them, as it brought the wagon down directly on top of them with a resounding slam.

In the fading light of the barrel fire Malik thought he could make out the entire silhouette now. For a brief moment he had believed that one of the freaks was rampaging; such things had happened before, and a number of their exhibits were very strong. But as the titanic shadow lurched away in the snow toward the Ringmaster's wagon, he could see that whatever was assaulting the monstrosity was no freak, nor was it any man he had ever seen.

And it was making its way to the Ringmaster's abode.

"Fire at it!" he shouted hoarsely to the men who had been on duty while he and the others were drinking with the hunchback. Those men were leveling their crossbows, shaking; they were in better sight of what they were facing, and whatever it was must have been far worse than Malik could imagine by the sight of their faces, frozen in a rictus of fear. His shout seemed to waken them; in unison they fired, one of the bolts going wide, but the other three finding their marks on a target that was hard to miss, even when moving.

The bolts glanced off or shattered, as if they had been fired into a stone wall.

"Again!" Malik screamed, but two of the crossbowmen had already dropped their weapons and run while the third stood motionless; only one of the guards had the presence of mind to fire again, which he did even as the moving earth in man's form brought its arms down in a single clenched fist onto the guard who had frozen.

Amid the spattering of blood and crunching bone that followed, a tiny metallic *clink* could be heard.

The statue reared upright, clutching at the vicinity of its ear, immobile for a moment.

Malik saw the opportunity. "Run!" he screamed to anyone still standing, stunned, in the area. He waved his arms wildly, then glanced about him. "Sally? Sally darlin'! *Sally, where are ye?!*"

"'Ere, Malik," answered a small, terrified voice behind him as Duckfoot Sally appeared on the step of one of the wagons, logjammed with the others trying to make their way out.

At the sound of her voice, the enormous man stopped, then turned sightless eyes toward her that in the gleam of the torches of the remaining wagons shone blue and milky.

Then began to stride in her direction, following the sound of her voice.

Malik was between them, and saw the intent in the statue's stride. "Run, Sally!" he screamed, interposing himself in the statue's path and grabbing hold of a broken tent pole. *"He's coming fer ye! Run!"*

The giant slapped him away like a leaf in the wind, shattering his bones and flinging them into the snow in several discrete sections.

Duckfoot Sally and the freaks crowded around her screamed in unison. The sound seemed to infuriate the approaching titan; its speed increased, along with the menace in its stance. For a second there was jostling on the porch of the wagon; then the freak known as the Human Bear seized Sally from behind and tossed her over the railing into the statue's path.

She squealed as she tumbled to the ground, then looked up to find two unearthly eyes, eyes whose scleras were stone, but whose irises were blue with filmy cataracts, staring down at her intently.

Choking on her horror and on her own tears, Duckfoot Sally skittered backward a short distance, hampered by the rustling tatters of her many layers of skirts and aprons. Under her breath she began to mutter soft prayers she remembered from childhood, even though their meaning was long lost to her.

The titan continued to observe her, unmoving. It watched her as she began to sob, then slowly knelt in front of her, oblivious of the arrow fire that was glancing off its back and sides.

One of the statue's enormous hands curled into a fist, eliciting a gasp of horror from Sally and every other freak who had been trapped on the wagon's porch or by fear.

Silence fell over the devastated ruin of the camp, save for the crackling of the remaining barrel fires and the soft moaning of the dying.

The titan reached out slowly and ran the back of its stone knuckles over the cheek of the terrified woman, brazing it slightly from the roughness of the stone, but wiping away the flood of tears that had cascaded down her face.

Exactly as she had always done for him.

No realization came into the terrified woman's eyes.

From his wagon across the campsite, the Ringmaster finally emerged, tucking his nightshirt into his striped pants, the double-pursed woman behind him.

"What is going on here?" he shouted, his voice thick with rum, unspent arousal, and annoyance.

The shocked silence broken, the freaks and carnies, Duckfoot Sally among them, began to shriek again.

The statue's head snapped upright.

For a moment Faron had been feeling a sensation that had not been present since he had been encased in the body of Living Stone. It was the sensation of sadness.

She no remember me, he was thinking.

There was something devastating to him about that; without Sally and her kindness, there would be no one now in the world who had known him as he was.

Had loved him as he was.

He put his free hand up to his ear, where the lucky shot had torn a chink in his flesh; there was no pain, just a sense that the damaged area was drying in a way that the rest of his earthen body was not, as if the stone was no longer alive.

Suddenly he could hear the sound ringing clearer, the song the scales emitted.

His head jerked up at the realization, but as it did, the garbage noise, the interference that deadened the song of the scales, rose to meet it, blocking its sound, hindering him from finding it.

He shook his head, trying to clear it of the noise, but that only made it grow louder.

Loudest of all seemed to be coming from immediately in front of him.

His balled fist opened, his fingers wrapped around Duckfoot Sally's neck, and squeezed until the noise she was making stopped.

In horror, the remains of the Monstrosity watched the titan rip Duckfoot Sally's head from her shoulders and drop it idly on the ground to its side, then straighten up and turn slowly in the direction of the Ringmaster.

The Ringmaster stumbled down the steps of his wagon, barefoot in the snow.

"Do something, you misbegotten idiots!" he squealed at the remaining guards, but the carnies were running, fleeing out into the darkness of the Krevensfield Plain along with whatever freaks could still move. The woman he had been attempting to fornicate a few moments prior gaped raggedly and ran back inside the Ringmaster's wagon, a miscalculation apparent a moment later when the titan grasped the rail of the porch and hurled it over the Ringmaster's head, blocking his exit as it smashed to the ground.

The Ringmaster froze. He glanced wildly around, looking for any exit he could find, but behind him his path was blocked by his shattered wagon, the bi-pursed woman's broken body sprawling from what had once been his window.

Before him was a giant angry shadow, formed of stone but moving now as a man.

A man with murderous rage in his eyes.

Quickly the owner of the Monstrosity dug his hands into his pockets, searching blindly for whatever valuables he might find, knowing there was little likelihood that anything so destructive might be bought off with gems or gold, but not knowing anything better to do.

His trembling hand caught hold of something sharp and rough at the edges; it was the tattered blue oval he had removed from the belly of the fish-boy a long while back. He kept it in his pocket for good luck, and because the vibration it emitted had a warm and sensuous effect on his nether region. He seized the scale and tossed it into the darkness at the approaching titan's feet.

$\int$aron stopped in his tracks on the snowy ground.

The scale gleamed before him, reflecting the fires and the crazy light of the moon. It was the scrying scale, the blue talisman etched with the picture of an eye surrounded by clouds on one side, the convex one, and obscured by them on the other, the concave one. It was the scale in which he had first found this place, had tracked the woman with the long hair over the sea at his father's insistence, had helped his father keep track of his fleet of pirate ships on the sea. It was possibly his greatest prize, and the loss of it had left him bereft.

Now it was lying, unobstructed, at his feet, singing its clear and bell-like song.

Reverently Faron bent down and scooped up the scale, then held it aloft in triumph to the light of the cloud-draped moon.

Then he turned away, lost in the joy of a treasure recovered.

Behind him, the Ringmaster let out his breath in a ragged sigh of relief.

Faron stopped in midstride.

For a moment he had almost forgotten, in the reverie of the scale's recovery, the torture that he had endured, the agony of the scale being torn from him, the teasing to force him to perform, the endless abuse and isolation in the darkness of a bumping circus wagon. He did not understand his torment then, nor did he understand it now.

But he remembered it.

He thought back to the image of Duckfoot Sally, swinging her nails like a sword in his defense; the Ringmaster had belted her into unconsciousness with the back of his hand. In his primitive mind Faron did not even remember what he himself had done to Sally, but the rage of the memory returned, along with that of all the other torment he had suffered at the hands of the man in the striped trousers.

He turned and was on the Ringmaster in a heartbeat; the man didn't even have a chance to open his mouth to scream before Faron backhanded him into the broken wagon. Then, for the first time since gaining this new body of living earth, he attacked for the sheer, sweet pleasure of revenge, pummeling the man's lifeless body into jelly, then flinging it out into the night where even the carrion did not recognize it the next morning.

The song of the scales swelled in his ears now, drowning out the whine of the wind, the whimpering of the injured, the agonized howls of the dying. It was the only thing he could hear, and it sustained him.

He listened as, in the distance, the last of the tones sounded, calling to the others. Faron turned to follow it, heading south, away from the broken remains of the Monstrosity.

Toward Jierna'sid.

35

YLORC

ᕗn the moments before the assault on the Bolglands began, Grunthor was experiencing a sense of foreboding that was unlike any other he had been granted in all his years of war. It was not the presence of some sort of fear, nor the queasiness in the stomach and dull thudding at the base of the brain that a commander of fighting men feels when something is not right. He certainly had known that sensation enough to recognize it. Rather, it was an artificial absence of any feeling of concern at all, as if some unknown entity had reached directly into his warrior's soul and ripped out every instinct, every trained alarm, that had been his from birth and developed over a lifetime of soldiering.

In short, he felt nothing.

Suddenly all the unconscious points of reference that a man whose life consists of perennial vigilance marks with each breath were gone, as if in all the world there was nothing to worry about. The sensation did not include a false sense of well-being, just a total numbness to the ever-present need to be on guard, at the ready.

Had he not been shocked by this sudden ripping of his soldier's wariness, he might have recognized it for what it was. It would have made no difference in the outcome of the events that followed, and perhaps would have only served to frighten him more.

Because what he felt in those moments, that utter sense of nothingness that numbed his senses and left him blank, was the total subversion of his earth lore as the dragon subsumed it.

The elemental heartbeat that rang in his blood, the thudding pounding of the world's pulse, disappeared. Had his own heart suddenly ceased to beat it would not have been more shocking. His connection to the earth, deep and intrinsic as it was to him, vanished, leaving him frozen, dizzy, for a split second, before he took another breath, and his heartbeat returned to its regular tempo.

By the time his awareness returned, the ground was already beginning to sunder.

$\mathcal{R}$hapsody had given the underground grotto, with its tiny cottage and gardens in the middle of a dark, subterranean lake, the name Elysian, after the castle of the king who had ruled in her homeland of Serendair. The daughter of a human farmer and his Lirin wife, she had grown up in wide green fields beneath open skies, and had never seen anything so enchanting as the quiet solitude of the dark lake, dotted by tiny shafts of sunlight that shone through holes drilled in the rocky ground above it. She had never seen Elysian Castle either, but its name conjured magical images in her mind as a child, so she thought the name appropriate.

But the place had had other names long before she came. The Firbolg called the ring of rocky crags that towered above the grotto, hiding it from sight and the wind of the upworld, Kraldurge, which in their tongue was translated as the Realm of Ghosts. Whether this was because of the mournful howling of the wind as it whistled around the bowl formed in those towering rocks, or for a deeper reason, was lost to memory. In any case the name was apt, because both the dark underground lake and the grassy meadow above it held unholy secrets, unforgiven sins that could only have been remembered by one living being, the beast who until her awakening at summer's end had been forgotten as well.

It was to this place of dark secrets that the dragon went first, boring up through the earth quietly, drawing the lore of it into herself. Her innate sense led the way as unerringly as a beacon, guiding her from far away to this place she had once made a lair of a sort, a hiding place of privacy and seclusion within the mountains she had once ruled. Her hated husband had given her this place, had made it for her, in fact, but she did not remember those things, only that it had once been hers, and that she had been betrayed there.

And more—she could hear the echoes of her name in the underground grotto, could sense it whistling in the wind of the guardian rocks above, trapped in endless circles, repeated over and over in an eternal howl of despair.

Aaaaaaaaaannnnnnnnnnnnwwwwwyyyyyyyyynnnnnnnnnnnnnnnnnnnn!

Now that she was finally here, in the place where the name had been uttered, she could feel the hatred, the betrayal, and the grim memory of pleasure long ago tasted in revenge. Whatever she had done to inspire that scream had a sweet flavor; it must have been a delicious payback, though she did not recall what it was.

As she waited beneath the grotto, savoring her return to this place, another taste came into her mouth, bitter this time. It was akin to the smell of another woman's perfume on the bedsheets, or a foreign taste on a lover's lips. At first the dragon was repulsed, spat in a vain attempt to clear the lore from her mouth, but eventually her compromised understanding recognized it for what it was.

This place above her, the lake and the gardens, the island and the cottage, belonged, in every possible way, to someone else now.

At the precise moment that her mind grasped that concept, it realized another as well: the person who supplanted her in this place, who had torn the lore away from her, knowingly or otherwise, who had taken away her dominion, was the woman whose misty face and green eyes haunted her waking dreams.

As the fury rose, a calming reassurance took hold, staying the response.

Because the dragon knew in that place she could smell the scent of the woman she despised, could drink in her essence, absorb it into her skin, into herself.

And thereby track that woman until she found her.

The wyrm did not feel the need to know the reason for her hatred, had no urge to understand her desire for revenge. She was still barely cognizant of anything, had lost the planes and angles and strata of consciousness, still was not reasoning or making the connections between thought and action. She knew only two things beyond doubt—that she had an endless well of acidic anger within her soul, and that venting it in destruction eased the pain somewhat.

I seek relief, she told herself as she slid along the underground spring that fed the lake, feeling the water recognize her and welcome her to this place again. *Surely there can be no reproach for that.*

Up from the bedrock at the lake bottom she emerged, swallowing the last of the earth's lore like a breath to be held beneath the water. Up she spiraled, from the endless darkness of the earth toward the muted light above the lake's surface, swimming with all the speed her anger could generate.

Past startled fish that dwelt in the depths, skittering away in terrified schools, by whisper-thin formations of crystal stalactites that rose up in great cathedral arches of brilliant color, unseen in the underground grotto, the dragon sped forward, finally bursting forth from the water onto the rocky shore of the tiny island in the center of the dark lake.

She lay for a moment, gathering her breath, then lifted her head and gazed at the place she had heard her name being called.

The long-ago scream actually had its genesis in the world above this place, this deep grotto; she could hear it wailing high up through the rock, dancing angrily on the wind that whipped through the circle rocks of Kraldurge. But there was enough memory latent here, below where it had happened, to warrant her notice.

The dragon crawled away from the bank, pulling the last part of herself from the water; water tended to mask vibrations, especially old ones, or distort them, and she wanted whatever she discovered here to be absolutely clear. How she knew this she was uncertain, but she didn't care.

Because her sensitive nostrils had already caught the woman's scent.

The dragon's piercing blue eyes scanned the dark island.

In the center of it stood a small cottage, surrounded by gardens deep in winter's sleep that had not been tended for a few years, with a tiny orchard behind it, beneath an opening in the firmament that otherwise covered the grotto. The wyrm's dragon sense made note of the contents of the cottage—a kitchen with no stores but dried herbs and spices, a bathroom with a tub whose pipes drew water from the lake and drained it into the gardens, a drawing room with a cherrywood cabinet lined in cork and filled with musical instruments. One bedchamber contained a tower with a windowseat, the other a large closet filled with rich court dresses and linen gowns, along with an array of jewels to match them.

Ah, so you are a musician, are you, m'lady? And a pampered collector of clothing as well, the dragon mused, until a moment's reflection yielded notice of one other item in the closet. It was an infant's garment, a gown of some sort, ancient and delicately embroidered in every color of the rainbow. *I recall this garment,* the dragon thought, but the space it occupied in her memory was otherwise blank.

The goodwill in the place was extant in the air; there was an unmistakable happiness in the place, something the dragon found both foreign and appalling, as if someone had taken what had once been her warm, dark lair, beautiful in its starkness, and whitewashed it with cheery paint and pretty, vapid flowers.

And, in doing so, had given it a sheen that had not been present before, had made it a home and a sanctuary, a place of refuge. There was a deeper entity here than that; the dragon could feel it, but did not understand it. Love was something she had never recognized, even when in human form, and even when she had it.

Done with her assessment of the cottage, the wyrm turned to examining the gardens. In the center of the long-dead flower beds, near an arbor of roses given over to growing wild, stood a stone gazebo, hexagonal in shape, with two stone benches entwined as if they were lover's seats.

In the corner of that gazebo stood a broken birdcage fashioned of pure gold, smashed beyond repair, its door gone.

The dragon's sense honed in immediately on that cage; within it she sensed not only great power, but also her own fear, old fear, mixed with pain and anger.

The side of her gigantic face tingled; unconsciously she lifted a claw to rest on it, to cool the sting of the memory.

It had been a grievous blow.

And it had happened here, in this place. In this gazebo, near this bird-cage.

Why? the beast screamed internally. *Why can't I remember?*

The rage returned, flooding through her veins like acid. As the fury built, she struggled to subsume the lore, to take back what had been stolen from her, but the land would not yield its lore to her.

Never one to be denied anything, the dragon struggled again, calling in her blood to the place that she knew had once belonged to her, but nothing answered her call, not the gardens nor the cottage, not the lake nor the crystalline formations in the purple caves beyond and beneath it. Not even the hexagonal gazebo, where her fragmented memory told her she had once been so greatly wronged that the entire world had suffered, would acknowledge her.

She did not know the reason, and would have been even more furious if she had—that the man who had taken the crown of Firbolg king, the warlord who had won rightful dominion over the lands of the Teeth, had given this place, in word and lawful deed, to the woman she considered her life's enemy.

It did not matter anyway.

Hatred, caustic and corrosive, rose up from the depths of her soulless being, and vented itself in acid fire.

First the gazebo; she blasted her fiery breath through its stone walls until the birdcage had melted into a pool of golden slag. Then she turned her anger around the rest of the place, torching the gardens and the orchard, which vanished quickly in a billowing cloud of orange and black smoke, finally turning to the house. There was a grim satisfaction in its destruction, like the ripping of old love letters from an adulterous liaison; the thatched roof ignited quickly, immolating the lovingly restored bedchamber, the rich gowns, the carefully closeted musical instruments—destroying, with blast after blast of brimstone flame, every trace of the woman who had supplanted her here.

When the entire island was engulfed, the smoke and ash forming a dizzying cloud of black over the dark lake, the dragon surveyed her handiwork.

It's a beginning, she thought, still unsatisfied. *But only a beginning. Now I need to know her name, and where she is.* But the dragon knew those things were not to be found in this place; she sensed the woman she sought was a creature of starlight and air, not of earth.

And needed to be sought in the upworld, the world above.

The wyrm reached down into the depths of herself, to the elemental earth, and once again, like a desert drawing in the water from an entire rainstorm and still not being quenched, still remaining deathly dry, she turned away from the burning island and sped across the surface of the dark lake, up into the windy meadow where the sound of her name rang ceaselessly around the mountains, and past the guardian rocks of Kraldurge.

Into the realm of the Firbolg.

36

THE DRAGON'S LAIR, GWYNWOOD

*W*hat do you mean?" Ashe demanded shakily, the multiple tones of his draconic voice gone, replaced by a very human one that echoed off the walls of the cave mouth.

Without a word, the Bolg midwife turned and descended into the cave.

Numbly Ashe followed Krinsel down into the belly of the dragon's lair.

The glow emanating from the treasure horde of the lost sea was tinged with the color of blood. He could hear his wife weeping, her voice shuddering as if she were trying to still the lament but failing. The sound caused his feet to gain speed; he shouldered past Krinsel and ran to the bottom of the cave, calling her name. The sight stopped him in his tracks.

The great ethereal beast was cradling his wife in the crook of her arm, gently brushing the sweaty locks of hair from Rhapsody's face with her claw. That face was contorted in pain, white with fear, but there was more; it was pale as milk and her lips were colorless.

She lay on her side, her eyes open and glassy, a river of blood staining her clothes and pooling on the ground before her, growing larger before his eyes.

"The waters have broken, but the baby is not coming," Elynsynos said softly. "And it is so tiny." He heard her voice in his ear, where she had caused it to originate so as not to frighten Rhapsody further.

"Sam," Rhapsody whispered. Her voice was dry and weak.

He knelt before her and cradled her face in his hands, smiling falsely to encourage her. Then he glanced at the two Bolg. Krinsel's face was pensive and stoic, as was Achmed's, but the Bolg king's normally swarthy skin was dusky with sweat in the reflected light of the cave.

"It's too soon," Rhapsody said softly. "Not even three seasons—"

"We don't know that," Ashe said soothingly.

"Your mother—carried you—three years—"

"Who can say?" The Lord Cymrian looked into the prismatic eyes of the dragon, which glistened with unspent tears. "How long was it for you, Elynsynos? How long did you carry my grandmother and her sisters?"

The wyrm shook her massive head. "More than a year's time," she said.

Desperately Ashe thought back to the words of the Seer. *Rhapsody will not die bearing your children,* Manwyn had said smugly. He had puzzled endlessly, trying to invent some way in his mind that the words could be twisted, as the Oracle had a way of doing, but had finally determined the statement to be unequivocal.

Then a terrifying thought came to him. Perhaps the Seer did have a cruel way out, a way that would defy the implication of the prophecy while still being accurate.

Perhaps it was meant to end like this, with the child dying inside her, before it was born.

In his head he could hear his father's voice.

Beware of prophecies, Llauron had said. *They are not always as they seem to be. The value of seeing the Future is often not worth the price of the misdirection.* Ashe cursed himself silently, having to acknowledge that his father might have been right.

"Help me," he said to Achmed as he stripped off his cloak and tucked it around her. "You are the Child of Blood, are you not? Can you not stop her bleeding, at least?"

Achmed shook his head. "I don't know how," he said sullenly. "I have used my blood lore as a trained killer, not a healer."

In the darklight of the cave, the beast's head inclined slightly, causing all random noise to still. "If you have an elemental lore, you should be able to make use of both aspects of it," the harmonic voice said. "Blood is an element, though not a primordial one. If you know how to let blood, you should be able to save it as well."

Achmed stood still, but his dusky face grew more ashen. "I do not," he repeated.

The iridescent eyes of the dragon narrowed in a solemnity that was unmistakable, and the artificial voice in which she spoke, fashioned from twisting the lore of wind, was soft with import.

"Hear me, Bolg king," Elynsynos said. "Close your eyes, and listen to no sound but that of my words, and I will tell you how to use your lore to bind up the blood of mortal wounds, rather than spilling it."

For a moment Achmed stood, rigid with indecision, in the quiet of the cave as Rhapsody's lifeblood pooled at his feet. Then reluctantly he knelt beside her.

"Tell me," he said tersely.

"All of the universe, Bolg king, is either Life, or it is Void. It is these two opposing forces that are forever at war, not good and evil, as man believes. Something is either creative, or it is destructive. And in each life, there is both creation and destruction." The wyrm's words grew warmer, as if the heat of the fire lore to which she was tied, along with that of all the other elements, was rising in her voice. "Those that are born with the gift of *Lisele-ut,* the color of red, are tied inexorably to blood, the river of life that runs through all creatures. If they invoke it in the name of force of Void, of murder, destruction, they are Blood-Letters, natural assassins, killers, as well as those who bring death respectfully when it is needed.

"But if that blood lore is invoked in the name of creation—with love— then it is a healing force. You and Pretty share the same connection to blood in many ways, but you have chosen to use your gift to spill it, often in the course of protecting what you believe to be right, while she struggles to contain it for the same reason. As a Namer she can heal, but she does not have the gift of *Lisele-ut,* nor do I; dragons are tied only to the five primordial elements. You alone are blessed, or cursed, with it, the natural tie to blood. It is not skill you need to save her, Bolg king—it is a reason. If you care for her, direct your tie to blood to heal instead of kill. The blood will obey you, as it has done countless times in the past. If your intent is to save, to heal, then that is what will happen."

"She and I have not exactly been on the best of terms," Achmed muttered.

"Your arguments, and the state of your friendship, do not matter now. All that matters is that you wish to aid her. If you do, then address the bleeding. If you do not, you should leave now." A puff of acrid steam issued forth from the beast's nostrils, a hint of menace in its odor.

Achmed stared at the growing red stain on Rhapsody's garments, then stiffly removed the glove from one of his hands and let it come to rest on her abdomen near Ashe's.

His mind wandered back, unbidden, to the tower rooms of the monastery in which he had trained. Achmed shook his head sharply, violently, as if to snap away the memory.

A shame you chose to leave the study of healing behind for another profession, Jal'asee had said. *Your mentor had great faith in your abilities. You would have been a credit to Quieth Keep, perhaps one of the best ever to school there.*

A hollow sting filled his ears at the recollection of his reply.

Then I would be as dead as the rest of the innocents you lured to that place. You and I do not have the same definition of what constitutes "a shame."

Warmth crept through him, followed immediately by the chill and the flinching pain of recall, as he thought of a particular one of those innocents.

Beneath the sodden fabric of Rhapsody's clothing, her belly moved, fluttering, then stretching, then subsiding immediately.

Achmed recoiled, his arm drawing back with a jerk.

The child within her was kicking, its effort listless.

Rhapsody moaned, and her eyelids flickered.

"I—this is not the first time I have attempted such a use of lore," the Bolg king said haltingly. "The outcome was not good the last time."

Elynsynos eyed him, the multicolored irises gleaming in the partial light of the cave.

"This time you have incentive, Bolg king," the dragon said. "This time you are trying to stanch the blood of one of the only people you care for."

Achmed snorted, but internally the irony was almost more than he could keep from giving voice to.

Now I see where Ashe comes by some of his most irritating traits, he thought as he rolled the sleeves of his shirt back to the elbows, revealing arms scored with surface veins. *Dragons. They speak as if they are in sole possession of the world's wisdom, when in truth they know nothing. Come to think of it, priests and academicians must be part dragon, also.*

His irritation cooled upon touching Rhapsody again. The warmth in her body was fading quickly, ebbing with each heartbeat, as if she were expelling her life force with each exhalation of breath. Guilt, a sensation he did not normally experience, clutched at the outer recesses of his mind, then wound quickly through his viscera. It seemed impossible to believe that their argument had caused this, but perhaps it had.

"All right, Rhapsody, enough of this," he muttered. "The last time you needed healing I had to *sing* to you, and believe me, nobody wants to repeat that."

Rhapsody nodded incoherently.

"Nobody," she whispered faintly in assent.

Achmed smirked in spite of himself. Somewhere inside this draconic woman was a trace of his friend still. He concentrated on the beating of her heart, one of the few rhythms he could still hear from the old world, and found it fluttering weakly within her chest. Achmed's hand trembled slightly. There was no wound as there had been the last time; the bleeding was coming from within her.

"I don't have a place to begin," he said tensely. "There is no external wound."

"Find the path," said the dragon. "Blood flows through the body as water travels the pathways through the earth."

The airy words reached back into the recesses of Achmed's mind, drawing forth memories he had hidden there. Half a lifetime before he had climbed into the root of Sagia with the only person in the world he trusted—Grunthor—and a struggling hostage who had complicated his escape plans and turned his world on its ear. As unwelcome a companion as she had been at the beginning, over the timeless centuries they had traveled together she had become only the second living person to gain his trust. The three of them had crawled through the very belly of the earth, witnessing horrors that no living man had seen, surviving challenges that seemed insurmountable by remaining together, bonded in their odd triad, while time passed them by in the world above them.

The woman he had dragged along with them as insurance in their escape from his F'dor master had irritated him, crossed him, and, when loathing finally turned to ambivalence and finally to friendship, had sung to him and to Grunthor, sharing the lore of the upworld, the green fields and plains beneath the open sky. It had kept the madness at bay for the most part. And while Grunthor trained her to use a sword, and she taught him in turn to read, perhaps the greatest gift she had given both of them was the purification of their names.

At the center of the world an inferno of elemental fire burned, impassible. While he and Grunthor believed it meant the end of their journey, trapping them forever inside the earth in a grave of wet tunnels and hairlike roots, their hostage companion had chosen to sing them through the fire, wrapping them in a song of their names, or what she presumed to be their names, and endowing them with lore they had lost, or never had before. While the song she sang had tied Grunthor beautifully and inexorably to the Earth, whose heart rhythm now beat in time with his own, she had given Achmed back his tie to blood, and more, by virtue of the name she had bestowed on him in her song.

Achmed the Snake, she had called him, eradicating the name by which he had been called for centuries, the Brother, freeing him from the bonds that had enslaved him through it. *Firbolg, Dhracian. Firstborn. Assassin.* Those appellations had been true before they had entered the earth, but then she added something more.

Unerring tracker. The Pathfinder.

With that nomenclature had come those powers.

From the moment the namesong had left her lips he had never been lost again. Concentrating on a path he had never seen, his mind's eye suddenly took on a new perspective, a dimension high above him. An inner sense he had not had before guided him now, showing him the way he wanted to go to anything he sought. That sense had led the three companions along the Axis Mundi, through the countless tunnels, roots, holes, and passageways in the flesh of the world, to this new land, this continent on the other side of the world, and of time. It had served him well since.

The woman who gave it to him now lay before him, her life spilling onto the floor with each breath.

Achmed dipped his finger into the pool of blood on the cave floor.

He closed his eyes and sought the path, hearing her words in his mind again.

Unerring tracker. The Pathfinder.

The blood on his fingertip hummed in the sensitive nerve endings of the digit.

An image of tunnels, now veins and arterial pathways rather than root passageways, filled his mind.

One of them ran with a river of dark blood turning brighter as it fled her heart.

Slowly Achmed expelled his breath, then loosed the path lore he had gained from Rhapsody's namesong in the center of the Earth. His mind cleared; the dragon, the wyrmkin, the midwife, and the lair faded into mist at the edge of his consciousness and vanished, leaving nothing but the tunnels in his mind, passageways inside the woman who had become the other side of his coin.

A sickening nausea came over him, a chill recalled from other sickbeds. He beat the sensation back and concentrated.

His mind's eye followed the trickling blood up through dark hallways, internal caverns that made him cringe. He tracked its path as he would the scent of an animal or the heartbeat of human prey; having been born with the gift to track those born in his birthplace by their heartbeats, he was used to hearing them, to feeling them in his own skin, to lock his own life's rhythm on to theirs.

But nothing he had ever done had prepared him to visually see inside another living person. Especially not one for whom he felt the damnable emotion of love, denied, confused, and forbidden as it was.

The trip along the internal path moved with a lightning speed; in a heart's beat he was seeing the inside of Rhapsody's womb, where blood welled from a tear in the wall. He concentrated, willing the wound to close, the blood to cease, and to his amazement, he saw the spongy tissue swell for a moment, then slip back into itself, stanched and red. Then the wound disappeared. The veins in his own skin pulsed, as they did when he was tracking a victim and had successfully locked on to that victim's heartbeat.

Achmed shuddered. He closed his eyes, preparing to unbind his mind from the path, but hesitated for a second, long enough to see what floated near the former wound.

Wrapped in a translucent membrane, torn down the middle, was an almost human form, a form with eyes closed as if in slumber, the shape of a head with facial features obscured by the broken caul. The membrane was gleaming in the dark, as if it had once been a sack filled with light, striated with streaks of every imaginable color.

The child within it lay motionless, the only movement a weak flickering beneath its breastbone.

With his mind's eye Achmed stared at Rhapsody's child, captivated by the sheer beauty of what he was witnessing. Rather than the despised spawn of wyrmkin, the very thought of which gave him to nausea, the infant was tiny, perfect, wrapped in light and color and darkness all at once. Even through the sticky caul golden wisps of hair were visible, and a warmth emanated from it that was compelling to behold, the same warmth that had radiated from its mother before she had come to this dank cave some months ago.

The path now found, his vision faded to darkness again. As it did, Achmed was struck with two thoughts in the same instant.

The child was not the freak he feared it would be. It favored its mother, but had a light about it of its own, and rather than emitting the ancient avarice and twisted lore of a wyrm, it seemed human, tiny, and vulnerable.

And it was dying.

Achmed pulled his hand from the pool of blood as the vision disappeared, leaving him cold and shaking.

"The bleeding is stanched," he said, his face gray with sweat. "But you have to get the child out now."

$\mathcal{J}$ar away, within the depths of his kingdom, unbeknownst to the Bolg king, another Sleeping Child's heart was beating more faintly as well.

37

YLORC

$\mathcal{A}$s chance would have it, the guard of the Blasted Heath, to the immediate west of Kraldurge, was changing just as the beast bored up through the dry riverbed that had served as a barrier against human attack for centuries. A consequence of this timing was that twice as many soldiers were on hand to witness the arrival, and twice as many bolts from crossbows were loosed at her a moment after she did, thudding through the air with a dull war tom that served to gain the notice of many who otherwise would have been caught unawares.

It also meant that twice as many died in the single moment that followed.

At first it began with a rumble of earth; the rocks of the crags of the Teeth loosened and began to rain down into the crevasses of the east and onto the steppes to the west with the force of a violent hailstorm. The Eye clans, holding their customary watch over those crags, scrambled down from the summits, trying to find purchase in the rocky terrain shifting beneath their feet, but many were caught in the beginnings of avalanches, and tumbled with those rocks a thousand feet or more into the canyon below.

The Claw clans were guarding the inner and outer passes of the Cauldron, also not far from Kraldurge. Their training had led them to be ever watchful from all directions—the four compass points and the air above—as an attack might come from anywhere. And while they had been schooled to believe that the earth itself might be a point of entry, in reality it was difficult to imagine that the very ground upon which one walked could be monitored as a hazard. So when that ground sundered suddenly, splitting open like the maw of a great stone beast and erupting fire, the Claw soldiers could do little more than roll and run, shielding their heads from the broken earth that rained back down upon them, burying them alive.

The Guts, who by heritage had claimed the lands beyond the canyon to guard, could only stand by, exposed, and watch as a great shadowy beast rose out of the ground, light glittering madly off the copper scales of its hide from the innumerable fires that ignited in bare trees and wintergrass along the Blasted Heath. It was to this group of soldiers that the dragon turned her attention first.

All of the building anger, all of the unspent rage, fostered over the months of travel, listening endlessly to her name cursed aloud in unmistakable loathing; all the betrayal, the loss of these lands that she knew were once hers, all of the confusion and terror at being unable to clearly recall the Past, and, above everything, all of the blame she held for the woman whose face haunted her every waking and dreaming moment, was given vent in the scourge of her first attack. The beast vomited the fire that had been stewing in her belly, inhaled and breathed it again, at every living being she could see or sense in her old lands, tingling with joy as her dragon sense felt them roast alive.

Another round of arrow fire and crossbow bolts were unleashed; they bounced off her ironlike hide, futile. The sensation was little more than a tickle; in fact, it delighted her to the point that the dragon began to laugh, a hideous guttural sound that formed in the very air and echoed harshly off the canyon.

Then, crouching low to the ground, she slithered along it, dragging power from it, devouring the lore of the Bolglands as she devoured the unfortunate soldiers trapped on her side of the canyon, sucking the power into herself, becoming more invulnerable each moment that passed, as she stripped power from the earth.

Able to do so because the king who claimed that power was not there to defend it.

Making her way to the summit of the nearest crag, to taste the wind, searching for any sign she might find of the woman.

Grunthor knew within seconds that the dragon had come, though where it had come from, and who it was, still was unknown to him.

He tossed back his head and roared aloud, a war scream known for its frightening effects on men and horses alike, startling the Archons and tribal leaders with whom he had been meeting.

"*Hrekin!*" he shouted, slamming his heavy oak chair back from the meeting table and lunging to his feet. "Jump to! We're under attack!"

Instantly the chairs were cleared of their occupants as the elite of the arch-Archon's fighting forces readied for the orders they knew would follow.

"Ralbux, take Harran to the tunnels into Grivven post," Grunthor commanded. "It's a dragon, by the feel o' it; nowhere's safe, so try and stay low, near somethin' stone." The education Archon and the Loremistress nodded and headed to the door of the room; both understood the need to keep alive at all costs their training and knowledge. Without the history Harran had studied, the Bolg would return to the demi-human status they had been saddled with before Achmed, or, more accurately, Rhapsody, came to Ylorc, though both had been trained to fight.

Harran stopped at the threshold.

"Reciting," she announced; Grunthor's ears perked up. "Dragons are sensitive to an extreme, a quality commonly known as dragon sense. Within a radius of approximately a league and a half, five miles above ground, or twice that within the earth, their ordinary senses are magnified to five hundred times that of Bolg. Taste, sight, odor, hearing, and tactile senses are extended thus, as well as an inner sense of awareness. The firegems within the belly of any dragon whose scales are based in a red or copper-colored metal contain a chemical commonly known as Red Fire, which burns at one and a half times the temperature of true fire. Being an acid, it is also corrosive. Most vulnerable spots include the eyes, behind the ear hole if one is present, and under the wing, also if one is present."

"Go!" the Sergeant shouted impatiently. Harran and Ralbux disappeared through the doorway. He exhaled angrily; Grunthor had had more than enough experience with dragons to understand how truly outflanked they were.

Within seconds, thudding bootsteps could be heard approaching rapidly in the inner corridor; the Eyes that survived from the parapets were rushing through the underground tunnels of the Cauldron with their report. While he awaited their intelligence, Grunthor turned to his aide de camp.

"Blast muster," he ordered. "Get me every bloody commander within earshot o' this place; all Oi got now is tribal leaders." The aide fled into the passageway. Grunthor turned to the Archons and pointed to the interior and exterior schematics of Ylorc that hung, rendered in minute detail, on the wall of every interior meeting room.

The Eye spies, their normally dark and hirsute faces stained with ash, came into the room, three in all.

"Report," Grunthor demanded. His skin, normally the color of old bruises, had flushed to an angry leather color, his amber eyes blazing almost gold.

"Dragon; out of ground above Kraldurge," said the first of the Eyes in the tongue of his tribe. Grunthor smacked the table angrily, and the shaken man quickly switched into the common dialect. "Copper hide. Keeping to the ground, not taking to the air like one at council. Same color."

The second Eye nodded. "Torn wing," he said quickly. "May not be able to fly. Perched on Trexlev crag now, not attacking; seems to be watching or listening."

"Blasted Heath is burning," reported the last of the Eyes, a woman. "Brushfires on wintergrass; frozen ground will stop the spread at frost line."

Grunthor nodded. "Back to yer posts," he said, then turned to the Archons. "Assessments?"

"Traditional weapons will be useless," said Yen the broadsmith. "Can't even use the heat of the forges against a dragon; fire will not harm it. Need special arrows, special blades to pierce dragon hide. We have none."

"Correction," Grunthor snarled. "We have *one*, but o' course it's not 'ere, as usual. Next?"

"Breastworks, redoubts, defense, irrigation, and sanitation tunnels will all be vulnerable," Dreekak, the Master of Tunnels, said solemnly. "Beast can use them as we do; can travel wherever they reach. Our own defenses will work against us in this."

"Good point," noted Grunthor with a grudging admiration. "'Oo else?"

"Many catapults working," suggested Vrith. "In peacetime have used them to fling hay and seedbags across the Blasted Heath to deeper settlements. Perhaps rocks, if not weapons, can injure it?"

The mining Archon, Greel, the Face of the Mountain, spoke up quickly.

"Much scrap rock outside of Gurgus from tower rebuilding," he noted. "Much sharp, full of glass shards. Might even make dragon sick."

Grunthor's bulbous lips pressed together appreciatively. "Hmmm," he said.

"One more thought," added Trug. "If we knew anything about this dragon, we might have a better idea how to attack it."

Omet, the only non-Bolg Archon, stood up suddenly. He said nothing; his elevation to his feet was more a sign of a sudden realization than an intention to speak. The Sergeant recognized this, and held up his hand to stem any other commentary.

"You were all here three years ago, when the council was assaulted by the dragon Anwyn?" he asked, trying to recall history in which he had not taken part.

"Yeah," said Grunthor irritably.

Omet spoke even more slowly and deliberately. "And was not the wing of that dragon injured as well? Didn't Rhapsody drag her blade through it when the beast had her in the air?"

All sound left the room; the Archons ceased to breathe at the expression on the Sergeant's face.

"Yeah," Grunthor said again, a deadly dryness in his voice. "But that bitch is *dead;* Oi saw 'er fall out o' the sky, and closed the grave on 'er myself. She's *dead*."

Dreekak coughed nervously. "Late summer, a patrol near the breast-works reported some rumblings in the Moot," he said quietly. "Thought them to be aftershocks of Gurgus explosion." His last words came out barely above a whisper. "Sent you the report, sir."

Grunthor's face flushed an even deeper shade of purple. He threw back his head and roared again; the blast echoed through the corridors of the Cauldron all the way out to the openings above the canyon, and reverberated below.

The Archons waited for the string of hideous profanities that followed, some in Bolgish, others in Bengard, Grunthor's mother tongue, to subside before exhaling.

"*Hrekin,*" the Sergeant muttered finally. "Dragons; ya can't never get rid of the bastards. Guess ya got to kill 'em more than once. Wonderful."

The door opened, and eight of his military commanders crowded into the rooms. The Sergeant went over to confer with them about troop position and casualties, while the Archons began quietly conferring among themselves.

Finally, when he turned back to them, they were standing, the light of inspiration shining from their faces.

Grunthor eyed them suspiciously.

"All right," he demanded, "what are ya thinkin'?"

*T*he dragon was too lost in the search for a name, too intent on finding the woman from the grotto, to pay much attention to the movement of the Bolg. She was aware of it, of course, in infinite detail; the minutiae of the inner realm of the Cauldron, everything else within five miles, was apparent to her. But her mind, fractured and limited as it was, obsessed as it was, considered the movements nothing more than the pathetic scramblings of the equivalent of insects. She had destroyed hundreds of them with little more than a breath; she would destroy more before she was done, but whatever meaningless attempts they were making to defend against her wrath were not worth the diversion of her attention from the search for the woman.

She could sense a rush to retrieve the dead, the movements of the old and the young to deeper bunkers, lower ground, an effort that amused her. Moreover, she did not sense the presence of many weapons. The bows and crossbows had proven useless against her, a fact that had sent her already-insane sense of invulnerability even higher.

Had she been more cognizant, more aware of her surroundings, she might have noticed the ruins of an ancient instrumentality that she had loathed in another life almost as much as she loathed the golden-haired woman in this one. When she was in human form, the ruler of a great nation and the champion of a mighty army, her first order in war had been to destroy that artifact; it had taken her soldiers almost five hundred years to accomplish that directive.

But that memory, along with most of the others she had made in her long lifetime, was buried deep in the recesses of the Past, where she could not find it.

Where is she? the dragon demanded of the evanescent winds. *Where is the woman I seek? And her name! I want her name!*

The wind howled around the mountain crag, saying nothing; very few words were spoken close enough to the summit to linger there, and those that were had blown away, off into the wide world.

Her fury returning, the beast rained fire down again from the mountain summit; no Bolg were above ground by now, so she had to content herself with the destruction of a few outposts and watchtowers, taking little satisfaction in watching them burn.

Perhaps I'm not able to hear because I am hungry, she thought, remembering with pleasure the feast in the Hintervold, not just the satisfying fullness of meat, but the joy of destruction, the orgiastic sensation of utter fear and helplessness in the faces of the hunters. *Those few on the Heath were but appetizers. Well, we can rectify that.*

Her dragon sense told her that the majority of the population on the western side of the canyon was cowering in bunkers deep within the mountain, but that a substantial cadre had remained behind, large enough to provide a decent meal.

She slithered down the crag, toward the tunnels leading into the Cauldron.

The first shaft she came to was narrow; she did not know it, but it was merely a ventilation duct, used to circulate the heat from the forges into the tunnels to warm them in winter, and the cool wind of the mountain to bring fresh air in all other seasons. She considered squeezing through, but noticed another, wider tunnel nearby, one that led to a central duct system, through which she could chase down anything that she wanted.

Quite a bit of the remaining prey was at the end of it.

She crawled across the lip of its ledge and into the tunnel, her eyes gleaming with blue fire.

Grunthor could sense the change in the earth as soon as the dragon entered the tunnel, stripping the lore from the land as she did.

"Ya bloody 'arpy," he muttered under his breath. "Thought Oi'd buried ya three years ago. Well, keep comin', darlin'. Oi'll kill ya as often as need be."

He waited until she had come to the first bend before turning to Kubila, who was waiting beside him, ready to deliver his orders.

"Now would be good," the Sergeant said casually.

The messenger nodded, and sped off like an arrow on the string.

Down the empty corridors and tunnels he ran, his route planned out to the footstep. His destination was almost a quarter mile away, but Kubila could cover that distance in a little over a minute.

He could see the light in the open doorway; the others were awaiting his signal.

"Now!" he shouted, still a few paces outside the central tunnel.

The Archons waiting past the door heard and nodded to each other.

Trug, the Voice, echoed the Sergeant's order into the central speaking tube, the instrument through which his words would be heard throughout the mountains.

"Now!"

Dreekak, Master of Tunnels and responsible for the network of vents through which the beast was traveling, seized the great valve and turned the wheel with all his might until it opened the floodgates.

All over the Cauldron, his tunnel workers were doing the same.

The dragon felt a shift in the air of the tunnel as the vacuum was released, but too intent on her prey to be distracted, she continued crawling forward until her sensitive nostrils were suddenly, viciously assaulted with the stench of raw sewage.

Which had been released in one enormous flood from the central cistern and all the collection pipes simultaneously.

And was heading, with all the force the ventilation system's pumps could muster, directly for her.

Shock flooded the dragon's awareness; she was overwhelmed with nausea, made even more acute by the sensitivity of her dragon sense. What to an ordinary being would have been revolting, vomitorious, was utterly incapacitating to the wyrm. All of her senses, her motor abilities, and her equilibrium were immediately unbalanced by the onslaught of offal and excrement that was rolling in a great, odious wave toward her.

She tried to right herself, to turn in the tunnel and escape, to burrow into the earth, even, but the tunnels built originally by her long-dead, much hated husband had been fashioned from and reinforced with steel, and so did not yield to her. She could only roil helplessly, twisted in a tangle of draconic arms and legs to which she was still not totally accustomed, when the sea of filth blasted around the turn and swelled over her, choking her, threatening to drown her.

In *hrekin*.

Gasping in horror, swallowing and vomiting simultaneously, the beast was subsumed in the mudslide of Bolgish waste, made even more foul by the vagaries of their diet. She struggled to breathe but her nostrils were filled with feces; she kicked her taloned feet, trying in vain to gain purchase on the tunnel wall, finally being flipped ignominiously onto her head as a great plug of sewage formed around her, obstructing the tunnel completely.

For a moment.

Then the pressure from the ventilation system backed up sufficiently to blast the clog of dragon and a kingdom's worth of waste out of the tunnel and into the canyon below.

Whereupon the mountain guards, under the direction of Yen the broadsmith, Greel the master of the mines, and Vrith, the lame accountant, unleashed a hail of glass-shard-imbued boulders down on her.

Sickened and bruised, the beast lay at the bottom of the canyon for a moment, trying to return to consciousness. In the distance, her dragon sense noted weakly that the catapults on the ledges above her were training upon her again.

Heedless of direction, with the last of her strength, the beast burrowed hastily into the ground of the canyon floor, following the long-dead riverbed out of the kingdom of the Bolg to the north, where she collapsed in pain and exhaustion.

She was too far away, or perhaps just too spent, to hear the shouts of victory and the songs of jubilation, chanted in harsh bass voices, ringing off the canyon walls and up into the winter night.

$\mathcal{G}$runthor lifted a glass and toasted the Archons.

"Well, Oi've always told you lads to use what ya got, and use what ya know. Oi guess this proves ya all know *hrekin*."

38

THE CAVE OF THE LOST SEA, GWYNWOOD

$\mathcal{A}$she ran his hands over his wife's forehead. The skin beneath his palm was cooler, but papery thin, dry. Her lips were pale, almost the same color as her skin, having lost a good deal of their redness with the loss of so much of her blood.

"Dry," she whispered. "My throat is so dry."

Ashe looked at Krinsel. "Is the baby any closer to coming?" he asked the midwife quietly. The Bolg woman shook her head.

The Lord Cymrian glanced from Rhapsody's face to those of the others standing in the dark cave. Each aspect, each being was utterly different, and yet they all bore the same look of bewilderment, of quiet despair, as if there was nothing to be done in the world save for watching this woman labor and die.

Quickly he took off his cloak of mist and covered his wife with it, hoping the cool vapor would ease the dryness she was feeling. With a shaking hand he drew his weapon, Kirsdarke, the elemental sword of water; the blade came forth from its scabbard, waves of billowing mist running along it like the froth of the sea. He held it in his left hand, allowing his right to rest on her belly, and concentrated, willing the water to seep into her, to sustain her, to bring hydration and healing where the water within her blood was lost.

"How can we get the baby out?" he asked the midwife again.

Krinsel shook her head. "There are roots I have—buckthorn and evening primrose, black lugwort—can open the womb, but it may kill one or the other. You will need to choose which to save."

"If you are going to resort to such extremes, allow me to help."

The multiple tones of the draconic voice filled the cave, along with a sudden glow of scattered light that danced over the walls like the evening sun on the moving water of a lake.

Achmed and Ashe turned to see a woman standing behind them, a tall woman, taller than either of them, with skin the color of golden wheat and similarly colored eyes that twinkled with the radiance of the stars. Her hair, silvery white, hung in rippling waves to her knees, and her garment was a filmy gown that seemed woven from fabric more starlight; it cast an ethereal glow around the dark cave.

Achmed looked for the dragon.

She was gone.

Ashe was staring at the woman, a smile lighting his face for the first time since he had entered the cave.

"Thank you, Great-grandmother," he said.

Rhapsody, half conscious, stirred at the change in the dragon's voice.

"I thought—you had given up your human—form," she whispered.

The glowing woman smiled broadly and bent to kiss her on the forehead.

"Shhhh," she said, resting her ethereal hands on Rhapsody's belly. "I have. Bolg woman, open the womb."

Krinsel was staring, her eyes glazed slightly over. She shook off her reverie and reached into her bag, drawing forth the evening primrose oil, into which she dipped a small piece of cheesecloth and held it to Rhapsody's lips for her to drink.

The two men watched the ministrations of the midwife in silence, uncertain of what they were seeing. From time to time Rhapsody's forehead wrinkled as if in pain, but she made no sound, nor did she open her eyes, but Ashe was certain that she was at least partially awake.

His eyes went from his wife's face to that of his great-grandmother, who in all the elegance of her regal beauty wore the plainly excited, childlike expression he had often seen her wear in dragon form. He continued to watch in a mix of fear and awe until he felt Rhapsody's hand clutch his.

"Sam," she whispered.

"Yes, Aria?"

She reached up falteringly and rested her hand on his chest.

"I need the light of the star within you. Our child is coming."

Ashe bent closer to her and rested his hand atop hers.

"Whatever you need," he said soothingly, though he had no idea what she meant. "How can I give it to you?"

She was struggling for words now, her face contorted in pain.

"Open your heart," she whispered. "Welcome your child."

All Ashe could do was nod.

Softly she began to sing the elegy to Seren that Jal'asee had taught her, the baptismal song that she had never had conferred upon her before the Island was lost. As she sang she wept; the midwife and the dragon were moving about her, touching her belly, whispering to one another, but she did not hear them. Rather, she was listening only to the music radiating from within her husband's chest, the pure, elemental song of the lost star.

Come forth, my child, she sang, her voice strong in the skills of a Namer, quavering in the emotion of a mother. *Come into the world, and live.*

From within her belly she could feel a warmth radiate, the warmth of elemental fire she had carried within her soul for longer than she could count. Blending with it was the cooling rush of seawater, the water she had been steeped in not long before, and lore that came not from within her but from the child's father. She closed her eyes and listened now to the whispered words of the midwives, the deep song of the Earth that came from Ashe as well, and the whistle of the wind from which her own race was descended, a symphony of the elements coming to life from within her, baptized in the light of the star that had been all but lost.

She continued to sing until the pains grew too strong; now she groaned in the contractions of labor, her song the story of the pain she accepted, as all mothers accept it, to bring forth life from within her body.

Elynsynos conferred one last time with Krinsel; when the Bolg midwife signaled her readiness, the dragon in Seren form raised her hands in a gesture of supplication, then reached into Rhapsody's belly from above, her hands passing through as if they were made only of mist and starlight.

Rhapsody moaned aloud, her song faltering, as Krinsel squeezed her hand, but regained it as Elynsynos drew back her hands, and lifted aloft a tiny glowing light, pulling it gently from her body.

"Name him, Pretty, so that he can form," the glowing woman said, smiling brighter than the sun in the darkness of the cave.

Rhapsody reached for Ashe with her other hand. When his fingers had entwined with hers, she whispered the Naming intonation.

Welcome, Meridion, Child of Time.

For a moment, nothing remained in her hands but the glowing light. Then slowly a shape began to form, a tiny head, smaller hands held aloft, then waved about. A soft coo erupted a moment later into a full-blown wail, and suddenly the cave was filled with the ordinary, human music of a crying infant.

Krinsel set about finishing the delivery as Rhapsody's head fell back against the cave floor, spent. Elynsysnos glided over to Ashe, who was still staring in wonder at the entire sight, and gently placed the baby in his arms.

He stared down at the screeching child, transcendent joy twinkling in the vertical pupils of his eyes, eyes that matched the tiny blue ones that were staring up at him now. Then he grinned at his great-grandmother.

"Now, as never before, I understand," he said to her.

Elynsynos cocked her head to one side, as she was wont to do even in dragon form.

"Understand what?"

Ashe looked down at his son again, unable to take his eyes away for more than a moment. He bent and brushed a kiss again on Rhapsody's brow, then reluctantly turned away again to meet the dragon's eyes.

"Why Merithyn lost his heart to you upon seeing you," he said simply. "You are truly beautiful, Great-grandmother."

The glowing woman smiled broadly, then disappeared, replaced a moment later by the ethereal form of the wyrm once more.

"Thank you," she said as Krinsel indicated that the delivery was complete.

And while they stood, drinking in the miracle, the cave of the Lost Sea resonated with the elegy to the lost star, the intonation of a new name, and the song of life beginning.

In the only dark corner of that cave, Achmed alone remained silent, watching.

39

𝒪n the red clay desert of Yarim, outside the city of Yarim Paar, Manwyn, the Seer of the Future, waited in the bitter winter wind.

While she awaited the arrival of her sister, which she knew was imminent, she passed the time crooning a soft melody to herself, and absently tangling the snaggled tresses of her flaming red hair, tinged with streaks of gray at the temples. In her other hand was a tarnished sextant, a relic from the old world given to her mother by the Cymrians of the First Fleet in memory of her explorer father, who had used it to travel the wide world, but she had no concept of its history, only that it served to help her see into the Future.

From a distance she might have been seen as a handsome, if bedraggled woman; she was tall and slim, with a well-sculpted face and long, slender hands. Additionally, she had a regal bearing, as had all the triplet daughters of Elynsynos. But closer examination would have revealed a single physical characteristic that set her decidedly apart from the ranks of average handsome women. One look into her eyes revealed only the aspect of the person beholding her, for her scleras were silver reflective mirrors, the irises shaped like the tiny hourglass mark a black widow carries on its belly.

Also like her sisters, she was mad. Cursed with the ability to see almost exclusively into the future, she had gained a reputation as a valuable oracle that she did not deserve, because her predictions, while often accurate and always truthful, contained at least a drop of her own madness.

Sometimes more than just a drop.

She had foreseen Anwyn's arrival but did not remember coming out into the night to meet her; the Past was her sister's realm, and it did not hold any sway over her. So she continued to wait, confused and disoriented, and more than a little afraid, as she had always been intimidated by her younger sister. Manwyn had been born first, followed by Rhonwyn, and finally Anwyn, but the sisters of the Present and the Future quickly learned that, while they saw into realms that foretold of what was to come or understood the moment as it was unfolding, it was the Past that held the power of history. Since neither of them could hold on to time save from moment to moment, or as a prediction of what was to come, passing from each of their memories a second later, it made the one who could keep Time the dominant one.

The earth split a stone's throw away, and the dragon appeared, a keen light burning in her searing blue eyes. She was battered, her hide tattered and reeking still, but even a mad oracle knew better than to deny a dragon her due, especially one that had come such a great distance for it.

Well met, sister. The beast's voice was smooth with an undertone of desperation.

Manwyn shrugged. "You will find her," she said absently, ignoring the forced pleasantries and jumping to the question she knew was coming. "But you may not want to."

The beast's eyes narrowed into glowing azure slits. She slithered forth from the ground, her enormous form dwarfing her sister in the empty desert. Manwyn pulled the thin silk of her tattered green gown closer around her shoulders.

What do you mean by that? The wyrm's wind-spun voice held more than a hint of menace.

Manwyn blinked; whatever she had uttered was now gone from her memory.

Curls of angry smoke began to issue forth from the dragon's nostrils.

Tell me where the woman I seek will be in the near Future, the draconic voice in the wind insisted. *At a time when I might be able to meet her, not more than one turn of the moon. I wish it to be soon, but I will need time to travel.*

The question was phrased in precisely the manner that Manwyn could understand. The clouds in her silver eyes cleared; she raised the ancient sextant and peered through it at the night sky.

"Today, until four days hence this night, she will be in the lair of our mother."

The dragon's heart burned at the words, hatred rising without the memory of where it had come from.

And where is the lair?

Manwyn lowered the sextant, pondering the words.

"Deep in the forest of Gwynwood, on the western coast, beyond the Tar'afel River."

Hot flames shot forth from the dragon's mouth, and the air roared with her fury.

The sea is more than a thousand miles to the west! I cannot travel through the earth in that time! Do not play with me, Manwyn; sister or no, I will burn you to smoldering cinders—

"You can be in Gwywood in a heart's beat if you travel along the roots of the Great White Tree," the mad Seer whispered, shaking in the wind. "The taproots run throughout the whole of the world, and tie in to the main root of the tree, which is bound to the Axis Mundi, the centerline of the earth. Those of dragon blood can travel along those roots in ethereal form, because the earth is ours. The roots lead directly to the Great White Tree in the center of the forest. From there the lair is only a few days' travel for man, less for beast."

The wyrm inhaled slowly, trying to calm her racing heart.

Where will I find a taproot? she asked casually, noting that the Oracle's skin had gone gray and her eyes were clouding over again. *Read the stars for me, sweet sister.*

Manwyn looked into the sextant again.

"You will burrow into the desert sand here, following the clay until it turns brown in the north, to the dry bed of the Blood River. It is there that you will find the taproot you seek."

The dragon's eyes gleamed with victory.

Thank you, sister, she said distantly, her mind already turning to her path. She slid back into the rip in the clay from whence she had emerged and disappeared into the earth's crust while the Oracle watched in confusion.

The earth had barely settled into peace in the dragon's absence when Manwyn spoke again.

"You will kill your own progeny in pursuit of her," she said vaguely.

Anwyn was already too far away to hear her.

The Seer stared up into the starry night, watching the southern tip of the aurora blazing in abundant color; the pulsing lights caught her fancy, and she watched until the wind became too chill.

Then she drew her filmy silk tatters around her and made her way slowly back to her decaying temple, having forgotten why and how she had come to leave it.

40

When the song of Meridion's birth had finally faded, when the warmth of the cave had begun to dim, and the afterbirth and blood had been cleared away, Krinsel took the baby from Ashe's arms, scowling at him as much as she could get away with, and carried him to his mother to be fed. Ashe motioned to Achmed, who had remained in a quiet corner of the cave, and came forth reluctantly. Both men traveled a way up the tunnel to be out of earshot of the women.

"Thank you for your help," the Lord Cymrian said, offering his hand.

The Firbolg king snorted. "I don't think observing from the corner counts as 'help,'" he said sourly. "You might wish to consider thanking my midwife, however; she's the one with the blood on her hands."

The warmth in Ashe's eyes dissipated.

"Well, in some way we all have blood on our hands, Achmed," he said evenly, trying to force the wyrm in his blood from rising in ire. "At least hers comes about for a happy purpose. And I do thank you for saving my wife."

The Bolg king nodded perfunctorily.

Ashe cleared his throat awkwardly.

"So you will be heading back to Ylorc now?"

"Shortly."

Ashe nodded. "Then I won't delay you. I don't suppose I could prevail upon you to divert your travels to the Circle, or to Navarne, and send back a coach for Rhapsody and the baby?"

"No, you could not," Achmed said testily. "The Circle and Navarne are both to the south, and quite a distance out of my way. I have already spent far too much time at parties and investitures in your lands, to the detriment of my own kingdom. I've done as she asked, and brought her the midwife she trusted to deliver her child. Now that is done, I see no need to stay, nor to delay our return further by running errands for you. Perhaps your position allows you to abandon your post for extended periods of time, but mine does not. Each time I journey west to attend to yet another of Rhapsody's whims or needs I return to an abominable mess. I can barely wait to see what I am returning to this time."

"Well, thank you, nonetheless," Ashe replied, struggling to maintain his happy mood. "I hope you will travel well."

The Bolg midwife coughed politely from behind the two men.

"Rhapz-dee needs two days of rest and watching, but after that, baby must return home," she said cautiously. "Thaw is coming to an end; soon it will be too cold for him to travel—will harm his lungs."

"They can remain with me until spring," said Elynsynos idly, dangling a shiny necklace of glittering gems from a claw over the baby's head and chuckling as his tiny vertical pupils contracted in the light that sparkled from it.

The Bolg woman shook her head.

"Rhapz-dee is weak. Has lost much blood. Needs healers, special medicines; must return soon."

Ashe felt his throat constrict. "Will you stay with her the two days at least?" he asked Achmed, noting the look of concern in Krinsel's eye. "I will leave for Navarne immediately and get the carriage myself. If you can find it in your heart to wait with Rhapsody here for the two days Krinsel says she needs watching, at least I will be able to leave her, assured she is as safe as she can be."

"By all means, I will happily divert my plans, then, Ashe, as your peace of mind is paramount to me," said Achmed unpleasantly. He glanced over his shoulder and met the eye of the midwife, who nodded her agreement wordlessly.

"Thank you," the Lord Cymrian said, seizing his hand and shaking it vigorously. "If I have to leave them, it will give me comfort to know that they are safe with you. I will leave forthwith—just let me take a moment to say goodbye."

Achmed waited until the Lord Cymrian had been gone long enough to have crossed the Tar'afel before he approached Rhapsody, who was cuddling the sleeping baby in a corner of the cave, crooning a wordless melody.

He watched her for a moment; her golden hair, normally bound back in a staid black ribbon, cascaded over her shoulders, making her appear younger and more vulnerable than he usually thought of her. She looked up at him, her smile bright, and he felt an unwelcome tug at his heart, much as he had in their earliest days together, during their travels along the Root that bisected the world. Those were lost times, long-ago times that he occasionally found himself longing for, back before the responsibilities of kingdoms and other people had come into their lives, back when the whole world was little more than Rhapsody, Grunthor, himself, and the continuous struggle to survive one more day in a place where no one even thought to search for them.

"He's asleep?" he asked awkwardly.

"Yes, deeply," Rhapsody said, her smile broadening. "Would you like to hold him?"

The Bolg king coughed. "No, thanks," he said hastily. He glanced around the glittering cave. "Where is the translation? Since I am stuck here for the next two days, I may as well make good use of my time and get started on reading it."

Rhapsody's face hardened, and her voice lost its gentle tone.

"Did we not go over this already?"

"We did. Give me the translation."

Silence fell, a silence so deafening that it disturbed the child, and he began to whimper in his sleep, then wail aloud.

Rhapsody shook her head and looked away.

"Unbelievable," she said angrily, rocking the baby as his crying increased in volume and despair. "After all we've just been through, after everything I've said, you are still insistent on carrying out this folly?"

Achmed glared at her.

"Carrying out folly is a tradition with us, Rhapsody," he said, his voice harsher. "You never listen to my concerns, and I reserve the right to disregard yours. You've made your position completely clear, as clear as the promise you made to help me in whatever I needed in this matter. Since I believe I have come through for you in your hour of need, *again,* I would think that you would be willing, if not grateful, to return the favor. Now give me the bloody translation."

The dragon's head appeared, misty and ethereal, above a mountainous pile of gold and gems at the water's edge.

Shall I eat him, Pretty? the beast inquired tartly.

Rhapsody continued to meet Achmed's stare, matching his intensity, for a moment, then finally exhaled.

"No," she said firmly. "Give it to him." She drew the baby closer to herself and watched as the dragon blinked in surprise, then disappeared into the ether. A moment later a bound journal, half the pages empty, appeared on the ground at Achmed's feet among the coins.

"Take it," Rhapsody said bitterly. "And then be gone. I do not want to see you again."

Achmed seized the book.

"Thank you," he said. He opened the journal quickly and began to peruse the pages, carefully graphed in Rhapsody's neat handwriting; much of what she had written was in musical script, but each staff had been carefully annotated.

"Go," Rhapsody demanded. "I mean it, Achmed."

The words rang through the cave, the Namer's truth ringing in them.

The Bolg king raised his mismatched eyes and met hers; they were gleaming, green as summer grass.

"I told your husband I would stay two days," he said shortly, conflicted and hating the feeling of it.

"I relieve you of your promise, even if you were unwilling to relieve me of mine," Rhapsody said shortly. "Take your bloody translation, and Krinsel, and anything else you have ever given me, including your friendship, and go. What you have demanded has put an end to our association; I cannot save you from yourself, or from your own foolhardiness, but I do not have to watch you as you blunder into lore that you do not understand. You threaten this world, the world my child has just entered, with your actions. I can't forgive you for that, Achmed. Go away."

The Bolg king considered for a moment, then nodded. He turned and silently gestured at the midwife, who was watching with concern in her eyes, but she said nothing, stooping to collect her bag and its contents, before following her king up the long, winding tunnel to the light and cold of the forest again.

Rhapsody waited until their footfalls could no longer be heard echoing in the tunnel before she gave in to the tears.

The air of the cave glimmered behind and around her; Elynsynos appeared, cradling her in the crook of her claw.

There, there, Pretty, the dragon intoned softly.

Rhapsody shook her head.

"Do not comfort me, please, Elynsynos," she said weakly, brushing her fingers over her son's downy hair as he returned to his sleep. "What he contemplates may assure that there never is a reason for any of us to feel comforted again."

41

NORTHERN YARIM

The dry bed of the Blood River was a deep length of sand above a layer of red clay, covered in a thin coating of snow. The dragon found the three strata to be the perfect place to cleanse the stench and remaining offal from herself; she bored up through the clay, spiraling, allowing herself the painful luxury of rolling in the sand until the snow finally coated her, cooling her angry flesh.

Any fury she had known before the assault on Ylorc had only been an irritation, an annoyance, beside what she felt now. Her anger had transmuted from the glowing hot rage of volcanic wrath to a far more frightening state, the cold, emotionless mechanisms of a dragon reviled. It was this same cold state in which she had planned the death of half a continent, had committed some of her most unholy acts, the unpardonable sins which she was grateful to have been born soulless, lest one day she should have to pay for them.

None of that mattered now. She did not remember her actions, her sins; her mind had placed but one goal into play, shutting down all other thoughts, all other desires.

She searched in vain for almost a day before she located the taproot of the Great White Tree her sister said she would find in this arid place. It had dried and withered to little more than an underground branch, but its power was still nascent in its fibrous radix. She did not directly remember the Tree itself, but somewhere in her memory there was a space where she believed those recollections should be, as if it had at one time been important to her.

The dragon steeled her nerve and concentrated, allowing her despised wyrm body to transcend material flesh and become ethereal.

Then she slid into the thin, dry root hairs, crawling along them as they thickened and grew moist, taking on speed, racing along the thicker root now, drawing the power of the tree her mother had tended so lovingly into herself as she passed from one side of the continent to the other in a beat of her three-chambered heart.

THE CIRCLE, GWYNWOOD

Gavin the Invoker had been summoned to Sepulvarta to meet with the Patriarch, the only religious leader on the middle continent of his stature. In his absence, his Filidic followers, nature priests who tended the Tree and the holy forest of Gwynwood, were clearing winter's deadfall, harvesting the herbs and hardy flowers that had bloomed in the time of Thaw, making ready for the return of snow when the dragon appeared, hovering in the ether at the base of the Tree.

At first the Filids stopped in shock, believing they were witnessing an apparition. Three years before, Gwydion of Manosse, the Lord Cymrian, who was wyrmkin, had passed through their forest on his way to wreaking his vengeance on the apostate Invoker, Khaddyr, the thrall of a F'dor demon who had supplanted Gwydion's father, Llauron. In his wake, much of the forest had been consumed in cleansing fire, though it was mostly the huts and settlements of the traitors that had managed to burn, while the rest had been spared.

One look into the hypnotically terrifying eyes of this beast, and any hope that such evenhandedness was forthcoming vanished.

The beast inhaled, then spewed her breath. It rushed forth in fire that burned black at the edges, glowing blue in the center as it left her maw from the sheer heat that was boiling in her belly.

Then she quickly closed her eyes and concentrated, so that she could enjoy the agony, drink in the pain and fright that was hanging in the smoky air when the fire diminished above the piles of charred bone and ash.

It was a delicious sensation.

The wyrm opened her eyes. Now that her murderous impulse was satisfied, she saw that she was looking out at a grassy meadow surrounding the Tree, whose glistening white branches rose above her for as far as the eye could see, and stretched out over the wide meadow. Beyond the sickening haze reeking of burnt human flesh she could see a settlement of huts, some longhouses, others tiny cabins, fairly newly built, each with a tiny garden or kraal, most decorated with strange hex signs above the doorways. The image was familiar; she looked to the edge of the meadow, trying to remember what was missing, but nothing resonated.

All around her was the song of the Tree; it issued forth in a deep, melodious hum, reverberating the tones of the living earth itself, achingly beautiful. The dragon felt it tug at her heart, or whatever vestige of one she possessed. On some level she knew this place had once been important to her, that if she tried hard enough, she might locate memories that would constitute pieces of her soul here, in this natural cathedral, where one of the five trees that grew at the birthplaces of Time still stood.

The holiness of it was unmistakable, impossible to deny.

The dragon steeled her will.

I choose to be unholy, she thought grimly. It annoyed her to see that the bark of the Tree had sustained no damage from her breath, that not even the leaves had withered or burned while the grass was scorched, the tenders of the Circle reduced to human rubble. It was yet one more defiance of her power which had just been laid low by a mountainful of demi-human Bolg, and served only to drive her smoldering rage into even greater fury.

She cocked her head, looking for signs of the woman, but there was nothing on the wind, nothing but the shouting of the Filidic priests and the foresters as they evacuated the area, fleeing the onslaught they believed was coming.

Deep in the forest of Gwynwood, on the western coast, beyond the Tar'afel River, Manwyn had said.

The dragon closed her eyes again, listening for the sound of the river. It was beyond her sense, but she could tell by the water table, the winding of the stream basin and the patterns of tree growth that the river must lie to the north, so she burrowed back into the ground and followed the sound of the water.

The voice of the Tar'afel was much easier to track than the ancient echoes of her own name. Like a beacon beneath the earth it sounded, rushing endlessly, unhurried, to the sea, in its low phase, carrying with it huge chunks of ice that had broken up and floated downstream with the advent of Thaw.

The winter was returning, causing the current to slow. The dragon could hear it from miles away; as she approached the riverbed, the earth through which she traveled grew ever damper, its silty strata unpleasant to ford.

Finally she could stand it no longer; she bored up through the ground again and traveled through the greenwood in the realm of air now, passing through the uninhabited wood unseen. The forest creatures had long since vacated the place, upon sensing her presence, even beneath the ground.

The river was flowing a league away; she made note of its depth, its speed, and then made her way to its muddy banks, frozen almost to the water's edge. There was a chill to the air here; she was closer than she had been to her lair since leaving it, though it was still almost a thousand miles away. At the water's edge she prepared to cross, hoping to return to the ethereal form in which she had traveled to the Circle, but without the power of the Tree, she found herself trapped in material form, her body heavy and stolid, a burdensome prospect in the attempt to cross the river.

The anger burned darker within her, driving her on.

Gingerly the dragon waded into the water. At the place she had chosen to ford it, the river itself was not as wide as she was long, so it was only a matter of bearing up under the current, finding as solid a footing as possible in the rocks along the bottom of the riverbed, avoiding the sinkholes and crosscurrents she could feel upon entering it.

Halfway across she had a sudden flash of memory, or something approximating it.

The woman she sought had forded the river at this very place, or near enough to it to have left a trace of herself in the streambed.

The dragon's ire burned hotter. Steam rose in rippling waves, hovering over the water in ominous clouds of hatred, palpable in their anger.

She pressed on, her taloned feet leaving great trenches in the cold mud, then pulled herself out of the river and onto the floodplain.

As she began heading north again, the air in front of her shifted, glimmering.

The dragon stopped, as if the breath had suddenly been dragged from her lungs.

The elemental power that hung in the air of the forest, invisible to the eye and unfelt by the vast majority of the living world, thinned out, crackling dryly.

The dragon struggled to breathe.

Directly in front of her a shape began to form; it was as large as she was, and vaguely the same shape, with a great horned head, a long, whiplike tail, and vaporous wings that were extended high in the air. There was the tiniest trace of copper in the scaled hide that was forming on the wind, but for the most part it was gray like the smoke of a brushfire, shimmering with an elemental sheen.

The dragon froze.

In front of her another wyrm finally appeared in solid form. A voice, deep and warm with a pleasing tone, resonated in the icy air around her.

Hello, Mother.

Anger shot through her hide; the beast's skin dried instantly, giving off a seething glow of steam.

I am delighted, if somewhat surprised, to see that you are alive. The gray wyrm's voice rang in a light, almost musical timbre, unmistakable in its sincerity.

Who are you? she demanded, but her multitoned voice of air quavered a bit; this being was the first to greet her with respect and fondness since she had awakened, and there was something about that fact that was both enthralling and unnerving, leaving her weak and defensive at the same time.

The blue-gray eyes of the wyrm before her widened for a moment, and it exhaled slowly.

I am your son, Llauron, your secondborn. Do you not remember me, Mother?

I do not, answered the dragon bitterly. *I have no memory of you.*

Sympathy came into the gray wyrm's eyes. *Ah. Well, perhaps you are just a bit disoriented. Your memories will return, and if they do not, I can help you find them. I made many of them with you, over the course of history.* Sadness crept into the sympathetic gaze. *Although many of those memories are probably best left unremembered.*

I seek but one memory, the dragon said quickly. *Help me find the golden-haired woman.*

The sadness turned to surprise. *Rhapsody? Why do you seek her?*

The dragon's blood warmed instantly, her heart pounding with excitement. *Rhapsody!* she shouted in her draconic voice; the word hissed upon hitting the air; it echoed across the river and over the frozen highgrass, rippling with the acid of hatred. *Where is she? Take me to her.*

Llauron saw his error immediately. *She is far from here, last I knew,* he said casually, turning subtlely to the east, away from the direction of Elynsynos's lair. *And she is insignificant. Come with me, Mother; I will take you to places where we have spent time, places where we will be undisturbed, and we can chat. If you are seeking to put your memories in order—*

NO! the beast bellowed; her voice tore through the winter wind, shattering the elemental vibration of it. The trees and highgrass that had been bending before the stiff breeze in supplication froze and snapped, the water in the river rippled in contrary ways. All of nature in the vicinity shuddered at the tone in the dragon's voice. *Tell me where she is, Llauron. As your mother, I command you.*

The gray wyrm folded its solid wings and regarded her seriously.

Let us speak reasonably, please, he said in a sensible tone that carried a barely veiled displeasure in it. *We are far from the days when you could command me by virtue of that fact, Mother, though perhaps you do not recall why. I tell you, with every ability to speak the truth that I have ever had, no one who has ever drawn breath on this earth has been more loyal to you than I. I gave up everything I treasured, everything I held dear, to do your bidding once, and it tore a world apart. My love for you should not be in question; whatever else you have forgotten, surely you must remember that.*

The dragon shook her head violently. *I remember nothing but the need to destroy this woman,* she said bitterly. *And if you love me, Llauron, you will prove it. Tell me where she is.*

I cannot, the wyrm said firmly. *I really have no idea. Come, Mother; let us quit this place—*

The dragon reared back and inhaled, sucking much of the power from the air as she did.

In a twinkling the gray wyrm vanished into the ether, just in time to avoid the eruption of caustic fire aimed at him that ignited the frozen winter grass and set it blazing.

The beast breathed again, a red-orange flame that crackled black at the curled rims. It spread futilely on the wind where Llauron had stood the moment before, billowing waves of swimming heat that dissipated impotently after a moment.

Now fully enraged, and feeling even more betrayed than she had, the dragon stormed northward, inwardly chanting the woman's name, tasting the air, hoping for any possible trace of it on the wind.

42

$\mathcal{U}$pon exiting the cave, Achmed spent a moment turning over the firepit that Krinsel had made to warm herself in his absence, and reclaim the campsite. Then he nodded wordlessly to the Bolg midwife, who laced her boots and adjusted her winter gear, then nodded her silent readiness in return.

They had not gone more than a hundred paces from the opening of the cave when the air before them glimmered with a sudden disturbing display of gray light.

In between the gusts of wind an enormous draconic figure appeared, half-ethereal, half-material. Achmed stopped in his tracks, dragging Krinsel instinctively behind him and lowering his cwellan, the one he had shown Gwydion Navarne some months before. His instinctive reactions were instantaneous; his reasoned ones took a split second longer. Just as he prepared to fire, the picture of this particular beast flashed into his mind; he had seen it before at the Cymrian Council, curled up at the feet of Ashe, much to its son's chagrin.

"Llauron?" he demanded, sighting the weapon.

Achmed, the familiar voice said urgently, *Where is my son?*

The Bolg king's eyes narrowed.

"He's returned to the Circle, or possibly to Navarne, to obtain a carriage to transport Rhapsody and your grandbrat home," he said nastily.

The gray wyrm's eyes gleaned.

The child's been born?

"Yes," said Achmed. "Now kindly stand aside, and don't interpose yourself in my path again unless you want to test out my dragon-killer disks."

No, the wyrm insisted, its anxiety causing the air around the Bolg king and the midwife to grow warm and dry. *Tarry; you must help me. Anwyn is coming; she is seeking Rhapsody with a horrific vengeance. She will be here momentarily; you must help me get your friend and my grandchild out of here at once.*

"What are you babbling about?" the Bolg king demanded. "Anwyn? Anwyn is dead, as you well know, buried in the Moot these three years."

So we thought, but we were wrong, Llauron said desperately. *There's no time for analysis and second-guessing; she is coming, and she will kill anyone and everyone in her path in her attempt to find Rhapsody. Is she with Elynsynos?*

"Yes," said Achmed shortly, casting a glance around the woods. The white trees, bare and gleaming in the cold winter air rustled as the wind blew through, seeming to shudder visibly. He looked back at Krinsel, who was trembling violently as well.

Get them out of here, Llauron commanded, his draconic voice ringing with authoritarian insistence. *I will try to divert her.* He faded into the wind again, leaving nothing behind a moment later but a sense of panic.

Achmed turned on his heel, snagged the midwife, and ran back to the lair of the ancient wyrm, muttering snarled Bolgish obscenities all the way.

ℛhapsody had barely ceased weeping when Achmed and Krinsel appeared at the mouth of the tunnel again.

Your friends return, Elynsynos said, puzzled. She cocked her enormous head to one side; her prismatic eyes widened suddenly, sending rainbows of light dancing incandescently around the cave. *Oh no,* the dragon whispered over the sound of the Bolg's footfalls. *No, it can't be.*

In the warmth of her arms, Meridion began to whimper again, his cries rising to a howl of fear a moment later.

"What's the matter?" Rhapsody asked nervously, glancing from the wyrm to the child, both of whom were now panicking without any visible reason.

Anwyn comes, the dragon said, rising from the floor of the cave, raising clouds of sandy dust in the process. *And she is rampaging; the forest is burning in a wide swath between the river and my lair.*

"Anwyn?" Rhapsody asked incredulously, struggling to her feet with the baby in her arms. "What—how can that be?"

Achmed appeared at the bend in the tunnel.

"Come with me if you want to live," he said sharply. Rhapsody recognized the words; they were the same ones he had spoken to her a lifetime ago in Serendair, words that had begun their association and led them down the long, difficult road to this moment in time.

"Is it Anwyn?" Rhapsody asked, swaddling the baby more tightly and walking with difficulty toward the Bolg king.

"Llauron says so, and I don't doubt him, even if he was a liar in life. Come on, we have to get out of here."

"Wait, wait," Rhapsody said, closing her eyes in pain and rubbing her hand across her forehead. "What good will running do? Besides, I'm safe with Elynsynos. And surely she will not harm Meridion." She turned to the dragon who was hovering now in the air, ethereal, with a look of quiet despair on her gigantic face. "Did you not say that a dragon values its progeny over all other things in the world?"

Yes, Elynsynos replied quietly. *But if she is rampaging, she is not thinking about anything but destruction, probably* your *destruction, Pretty.*

"You are endangering Elynsynos by staying here," Achmed said harshly, reaching for her arm. "Come."

Rhapsody handed Meridion to Krinsel and began pulling on her boots, her face white, her arms shaking with the weakness that follows childbirth.

"Anwyn cannot kill her mother, even in a rampage," she said, lacing quickly. "Isn't that the Primal Lore, Elynsynos? Dragons cannot kill each other, worlds colliding, and all that?"

The great beast shook her head sadly.

Anwyn is not a wyrm, but wyrmkin, she reminded Rhapsody. *She is not bound to the Primal Lore if she doesn't choose to be. I cannot say what she might do.*

Rhapsody's face took on a harsh determination.

"All right," she said seriously. "I will go—Achmed, Krinsel, leave this place now, head due west toward the sea, and hide. You need to get as far away from here, and from me, as you can."

Elynsynos shook her head.

Bolg king, take my friend and yours, she said sadly. *Save the child; he is more important than any of you know. Get her to safety; Llauron and I will do what we can to divert Anwyn, but you must go now.*

Achmed nodded and seized Rhapsody's arm. "Go west," he directed Krinsel, who nodded and hurried up the cave tunnel. "Can you walk?" he asked Rhapsody, who nodded as well, though her face was ashen. "All right, then, come with me. We've done this before."

Together they ran out up the tunnel. Elynsynos watched them leave, then disappeared into the ether.

*T*hrough the forest they bolted, Rhapsody following blindly behind Achmed, who was doubling back to the Tar'afel. In his mind he remembered something Llauron had told the Three long ago about Elynsynos and the explorer Merithyn.

If Merithyn had not loved Elynsynos as well, she would have known what befell him. He had given her Crynella's candle, his distress beacon. It was a small item, but a powerful one, because it contained the blending of two opposing elements, fire and water. Had it been with him when his ship went down, she would have seen him, and perhaps might even had been able to rescue him. But he had left it with her to comfort her, as a sign of his commitment. Alas, such it is with many good intentions.

Perhaps dragon sense is limited by water, he thought, knowing that the element obscured his own ability to track heartbeats. *If I can get Rhapsody into the river, we may be able to hide from her inner sight.*

Even as his mind planned it, his better sense told him he was fooling himself.

In the distance they could hear the crashing of trees and the ripping of the earth as the two dragons sought to divert their rampaging kinswoman, moving earth, opening chasms, diverting streams, tossing large branches into her path, exercising their elemental power over the earth, each action followed by a bellowing roar of anger and an audible eruption of flame. The ground trembled beneath their feet; Achmed glanced behind him at Rhapsody, whose hand was clutching his gloved one in a death grip, to find her face white and bloodless but set in a grim aspect as she climbed over deadfall and rotting trees, beneath bowers of thorned berries and around forest glades, panting as she ran.

On the breeze that whipped through the forest they could hear the voice of the dragon, screaming, howling, bellowing in rage.

Rhapsody! Rhapsody, you cannot hide from me!

The wind howled around them with the onset of dusk; there was snow on its gusts, icy from the water of the river, and it stung as it pelted their skin and eyes. There was not a sound from the bundle in her arms; Achmed wondered dully if the child was even alive.

Each moment the fire approached ever closer.

Finally, as the heat was beginning to lick his back, he felt Rhapsody's grip falter, then slip from his.

He turned to find her, pale as he had ever seen her, doubled over, her child clutched against her stomach. With the last of the strength in her arms, she shakily held the bundle out to him.

"Please," she whispered. "Please—take him—Achmed. Take—him and run. It's me—she's after." Her voice faltered in exhaustion and weakness. "Take him."

Achmed hesitated, then slung the cwellan at his side, snatched the bundle from her arms, tucking it under his own and grasping her hand again. The baby remained silent, unmoving.

"I'll carry him, but you must come as well," he insisted, dragging her over a moldering tree stump, pulling her along as she stumbled. "The brat will die without you anyway; I can't very well be his wet nurse. Come on."

Together they struggled, around impenetrable brambles, through half-frozen streams, until the sound of the river could be heard in the distance.

"Not too much farther, come on, Rhapsody," Achmed urged, feeling the grip of her fingers loosen again.

Under their feet the earth began to sunder in long, thin cracks. The bellowing of the dragon had gone silent; now the only sounds they could hear were the screaming of nature, protesting in reply.

"Leave me," Rhapsody panted. "The—sword I carry—protects me from—flame—"

"But not from acid, nor from claws," Achmed muttered, pulling harder on her arm. "Come on."

They crossed the last field of highgrass, ran along the floodplain, and were in plain sight of the Tar'afel when suddenly the riverbank split with a great tremor into a yawning crevasse, ripping open before their eyes as the dragon reared up, rampant and solid, hatred darker than the fires of the Underworld blazing in her glowering blue eyes. For a moment her face contorted in rage, a hideous anger so palpable that it caused the air around her to stop moving in that instant.

Achmed's reflexes reacted, bracing for the attack.

Then, without warning, his body lurched as Rhapsody shoved him from behind with all her strength, pushing him and the infant away and falling herself into the dragon's line of sight.

Shakily she drew Daystar Clarion, the elemental sword of fire and ether; the luminous blade trembled for a split second in her hand, then stopped as Rhapsody drew herself up to her full height, her own eyes blazing with fury.

"Direct your wrath at me, Anwyn, you coward," she said, her voice ringing in a Namer's commanding tone.

The beast's nostrils flared, and she rose up, her torn wings spread wide, blotting out the light of the sun. The air crackled and hissed with malevolence.

She inhaled deeply.

Achmed fired.

Three whisper-thin disks, forged of blue-black rysin-steel, sliced into the dragon's underbelly as she reared back, each driven more deeply in by the force of the one that followed.

The recoil, and the impetuous shove from Rhapsody, left him off balance and he stumbled; he dropped the cwellan, clutching the bundle under his arm.

The dragon screamed in pain and in rage; the heat of her scorching blood was causing the disks to expand rapidly, tearing open the flesh below her throat and into her abdomen. Her first attack of breath went wide, lighting the trees above them and the brambles to an inferno of yellow-orange flame. As the forest caught fire she inhaled again, bleeding profusely, and aimed her acid breath directly at the golden-haired woman whose face had haunted her dreams.

In the fragment of a second before the immolating flames washed over Rhapsody, the air in front of her turned gray and silver with just the tiniest hint of glittering copper. A great translucent figure appeared from the ether before and around her, thin as a breath of the wind, barely visible, surrounding the Bolg king and Lady Cymrian with its body, interposing itself between them and the rampaging dragon.

Just as Anwyn exhaled, loosing fire so acidic that it melted the stones of the ground beneath her, Llauron loosed a lore of his own, letting go of the elemental earth that was within his blood and soul.

Going solid.

Forming a vast, ossified shell around the man, the woman, and the child.

Saving them.

Ending.

43

The flames washed over Llauron's rocklike form, licking the perimeter, burning the grass beneath it. Rhapsody and Achmed could hear the blast, recognized it by the intensity of its hollow roar, could distantly make out the shrieks of wrath, then the silence.

Inside the shell it was dark; the palest of light remained, glowing ethereally. The Bolg king felt around in the darkness until he found Rhapsody's hand, and clutched it; she was shaking violently, watching the process of Llauron's Ending going through its terrible stages.

With the release of the earth lore came the dissipation of the starfire that was also his birthright; the cool light hardened the shell of his body, solidifying it. Her heart beat painfully against her ribs as the water within him evaporated; she felt the tears and the rain both on her face, both drying as the lore vanished into the world from what had once been the soul of a man who had loved the sea. As the water left, the shell hardened further, tempered and cooled. Only the element of wind remained; it took the form of sweet, heavy air hanging in their midst.

For a moment, no sound could be heard inside the dark cavern of Llauron's body.

Then, quietly, Rhapsody began to weep.

Achmed's eyes, the night eyes of a Bolg, watched as she walked over to the wall, striated in the pattern of ribs, and reached out her hand to rest it there. She slowly slid down to the floor of the cavern, overwhelmed with grief.

In his arms, the baby began to whimper as well.

Achmed stood for a moment, unmoving, then slowly lifted the swaddled bundle up against his shoulder and rocked it, swaying awkwardly back and forth.

"Shhhhhh," he said. "Hush now."

Outside the enormous shell of the dragon that had once been her son, Anwyn stood, frozen in shock.

At first her astonishment came from the immediacy of what had happened; a second before, she had the woman she hated in her sights, vulnerable, was anticipating the relief of her pain that would come with Rhapsody's death, was looking forward to breathing in the bitter scent of her ashes once her body was immolated.

Then the wyrm calling himself Llauron had intervened, had appeared from the very ether, had surrounded the woman and her child and the monster who was guarding them both, and Ended. Anwyn had forgotten much of the lore of her race, but even in her fragmented awareness, she comprehended the horror, the finality, the sacrifice of what had just come to pass.

And she resented it with every fiber of her tattered, bleeding being.

The rysin-steel blades were expanding in the heat of her body; she could feel them growing larger, compressed by their cold manufacture no longer. Each breath she took tore a little more at her muscle, rent her flesh by inches, as they worked their way toward her three-chambered heart. The wyrm willed her breath to slow, tried to compress her bodily functions as much as she was able, but she could not control the beating of her own heart, the circulating of her blood.

She wanted to scream, wanted to vent her rage in fire and blood, but the disks hovered within her thoracic cavity, threatening her life with every tiny movement.

Finally she decided that she had no choice but to slowly, cautiously make her way back to the frozen north, to her lair of ice and frost. She hoped that the cold would help contain the disks with her, allowing her to pry them from her flesh, but knew that even if that were not possible, she would rather die in her lair than in this alien forest, this place where she should have memories and instead found only emptiness and denied gratification.

This place where a dragon had Ended.

That alone was enough to terrify her. In her mind she heard dark chanting, voices of beings of a different elemental race, cackling as the lore of Earth was diminished by the loss of one of her kind. She no longer could stay; the sight of the massive stone statue, its wings extended forward, wrapped around the people it had died protecting, gave her chills that resonated throughout her body, made her tremble, though later, as she crawled into the Tar'afel and swam against its hardening current, she realized that her shaking was not only from fear, but from her proximity to death herself.

Achmed listened in the darkness to Rhapsody weep. It was a sound he had hated from the first moment he had heard it, a harsh, horrific vibration, unlike the natural music she emitted that he found soothing. It tore across the sensitive nerve endings in his skin, making them vibrate with agony. He set his teeth against the pain and remained silent, allowing her to vent her grief; weak as she was from giving birth and from fleeing the dragon, she had little strength to keep it up for long.

Instead he was watching her child in the darkness. He had laid the little boy down on his back; the floor of the dragon's stone body was warmer than the ground of the forest would have been. The child seemed to like the position, waving his tiny arms aimlessly, breathing in the cool, sweet air that hung heavily above his head.

Rhapsody leaned back against the cavern wall, spent. She did not have the night vision that Achmed was blessed with, so, to dispel the darkness and cold from the place, drew her sword and rested it on the ground, allowing the cavern to fill with its warmth and light.

"The irony is threatening to choke me," she said dully, watching her baby entertain the Bolg king.

"How so?"

"All Llauron wanted to do was to come to know this child, and to have the child know him. He made a sacrifice to save him, and us, that is unimaginable—like sacrificing your Afterlife along with your life. And here Meridion is trapped within the shell of his grandfather's own body, a grandfather he will never know now."

Achmed sighed dispiritedly.

"Don't you Lirin Namers have something you are supposed to do when these sorts of things happen?" he asked pointedly. "Like singing a Song of Passage or something, rather than just freeform bemoaning? I find your current lyrics a bit tiresome. Llauron was a complicated man, a draconic man even before he gave up his human body for an elemental state. He never let anything stand in the way of what he wanted or thought was right, not the well-being of his family, or the safety of his allies, or any small consideration such as that. That he was willing to do whatever this was may have been the first truly noble gesture the man ever made. Why don't you just do whatever you are supposed to do to elegize him, and leave your grief, and the grief you are borrowing for you child, out of it? Meridion may not even miss him."

Rhapsody exhaled, then pushed herself up a little straighter.

"You're right about the elegy," she said shortly. "As a Namer, it's the least I can do. But I don't want to sing the Lirin Song of Passage for him; I did that once, when he tricked me into immolating him with the sword, that he might attain his elemental dragon state. I don't think I could bring myself to do that again."

"Fine," said Achmed, shifting to find a more comfortable place in the dark. "Sing a bawdy brothel song, or one of Grunthor's lewd marching cadences; I'll bet Llauron would appreciate either of those."

Rhapsody nodded, unable to smile. "You're probably right. For all that he had a very proper exterior, he did have a raunchy sense of humor. When I first was studying with him, he used to sing me sea chanteys every night, and some of those would have curled his followers' hair." She stood and walked over to Achmed, then crouched down in front of the baby, who turned his tiny eyes in her direction. "Of course, my grandfather sang the very same songs."

She hummed wordlessly for a moment, smiling down at Meridion, then wordlessly started to croon a song of the sea. After a few moments she added the words, singing one of Llauron's favorite chanteys, a lonely tale of wandering the wide world, never able to rest, looking for peace in the sea.

Maritime lore held no interest for Achmed, but it had been a long time since he had heard her sing. He sat quietly in the flickering light of Daystar Clarion, whose cool radiance reflected Rhapsody's somber mood, remembering their journeys together along the Root and overland on this new continent, just the two of them with Grunthor. He missed those times more than he realized.

A strange tone buzzed in his ear; he listened more carefully and realized the baby was cooing along to the chantey with her in harmony. Rhapsody noticed it as well; her voice became softer, and she carried the tune past its ending until the child began to whimper.

"I suppose he does know his grandfather after all," she said as she lifted him to her shoulder, patting his back. The gesture was to no avail; Meridion continued to fuss, his whimpering turning to a cackling cry.

"Well, I believe he breathed in the last of his essence; that heavy air seemed to hang over him, almost as if Llauron wanted him to absorb it," Achmed said, his brows drawing together as Rhapsody opened her shirt and positioned the baby on her breast. He turned away hastily, to Rhapsody's surprise, keeping his back to her while she nursed the baby.

"You don't have to turn your back," she said, surprised, as she drew the swaddling blanket over the two of them. "I'm covered now, and I apologize if it bothered you." She saw him shrug, but he did not turn back to face her. "After all, we lived on the Root for a thousand years or more, and in camping conditions after that. There's not a shred of modesty left in any of us by now."

Achmed stared above him at the interior of the dragon cavern, noting the curves of the thoracic cavity and spine. "Had it occurred to you that I might not want to witness you nursing another man's child?" he asked bitterly.

The silence that answered him was heavier than the air had been.

He continued to examine the intricacies of the shell Llauron had left behind until finally he could hear her patting the child's back against her chest, humming a wordless lullabye. He turned then, finally, to see her looking above her as well.

"Gods, we're back on the Root again, in a way," she murmured. "Trapped in a cavern with no exit, away from anyone who might find us. And it's dark and close in here." Unconsciously she wiped the back of her hand across her forehead and drew the baby nearer.

"Yes, but this time we don't have Grunthor along to make it bearable."

"No, you're right, we don't." Rhapsody's eyes gleamed in the darkness. "You have changed so much in a few short years, Achmed," she said sadly, swaying the baby in her arms. "Even in the darkness, I barely recognize you."

The Bolg king's breath escaped his mouth in a hiss of sorts as he swallowed a laugh. He stretched out his legs and wrapped his arms behind his head. "Is that so?" he said. "Perhaps it does seem that way to you, Rhapsody, because you never have really understood what mattered to me. You have always assigned me altruistic motives where none exist, because you want to believe that we have the same priorities. At one time I believed we did as well. But who really has changed here?"

The child sighed in his sleep, a high, sweet sound, and she looked more sharply at Achmed.

Achmed leaned nearer, so that his words would carry the weight without the volume. "You risk your life, and the life of a child whose fate you cannot possibly be certain of, and all of the people who follow your vision, for whatever fancy moves you. I don't remember you ever being careless with those things before. And I, who never felt an obligation to preserve anything other than my own neck, now guard a Child of Earth, and a people who no longer wander the world eating their enemies—oh, and a foolish queen whose husband seems unable to do it alone.

"Who has changed? I suppose we both have."

The Lady Cymrian stared at him; Achmed noted with interest that her green eyes had now cleared of the draconic pupils. The baby drifted into soft clicking sounds, and then silence. Finally she spoke.

"When first we stepped forth into this new land, Achmed, you and Grunthor were consistently annoyed that I could not let go of the past. You had fled Serendair because there was no longer anything there that mattered to you, only death waiting to find you should you have remained. But I lost everything when you decided to drag me along with you. And then all you did was complain when I mourned. 'Serendair is gone,' you said. 'Your life is here now.' You were fairly insistent that I come to accept what had happened, put the Past aside and live in the Present."

"True," Achmed assented. "And I gave you a project that you seemed to relish—helping to end the atrocities that Roland was committing against the Bolg, and to assist in building them into a kingdom of men, albeit monstrous ones. I gave you a duchy in my kingdom, paid for all the useless trinkets you could possibly desire—there are still two dozen gowns in Elysian, rotting quietly in the grotto." He sat back heavily against the wall and exhaled. "Perhaps I should commandeer them and pass them out to Bolg women to wear while they are skinning game and rendering tallow."

"By all means, do," Rhapsody said, caressing her son's cheek. "They can wear the skirts around their necks, the way they wore the horns of the unfortunate oxen you brought into the kingdom as codpiece decorations. But don't avoid your own point—you are happy to see me living in the Present as long as by doing so I am achieving your ends. Should I choose to turn my attentions to other matters which you do not value as readily, such as the Cymrian Alliance or the kingdom of Tyrian, or raising a family, that is not sufficient to assuage you. In your twisted mind, I have 'changed' because I am no longer doing what you want of me. Perhaps it is audacious of me to expect it, but I would like to live my life as I see fit, and not by your command."

The Bolg king snorted. "Neh," he said. "You'd only bollix it up."

For the first time since the Ending Rhapsody smiled slightly. "No doubt," she acceded. "But it is mine to bollix up, Achmed. If anyone has been in support of that belief, it would be you. You have always told me that I have the strength to do things that need doing, to lead when I don't want to, keep on when I want to give up. But you never share your reasons for anything you do, so I can't understand them. You support me unfailingly, and feel betrayed when I can't do the same for you as well."

"Something like that."

"So explain it to me," she insisted. "Tell me why you are so set on building this damnable thing, so willing to risk so much for it. Maybe if you could make me understand your willingness to experiment foolishly with primordial magic, I might be able to help you."

For a long time Achmed was silent. He continued to look above him, gazing around at the interior of the cavern. Finally he spoke.

"Did I ever tell you what I was running from the day Grunthor and I were unfortunate enough to run into you in Easton on Serendair?"

Rhapsody shook her head. "I know that you were enslaved to a high priest who was the host of a F'dor demon," she said, rubbing the baby's back gently. "I thought you were running from him."

"I was," the Bolg king said dully. "But do you remember the key I used to open Sagia, to allow us to pass into it in the first place?"

"Yes—it was made of Living Stone, as if it were the rib of a Child of Earth."

"Did it ever seem strange to you that I had such a key? Did you ever wonder where it came from?"

Rhapsody thought for a moment in the darkness. "Not really. There are so many things about you that are secretive, odd, or difficult to grasp that it never occurred to me to wonder about that. I always supposed that if you wanted to tell me, you would." She looked above her in the darkness and sighed. "After fourteen hundred years, I've learned to live with knowing that you probably wouldn't."

Achmed sat quietly, listening to the echoes of sound inside the hollow shell. He saw the expression in Rhapsody's eyes as they wandered over the ossified corpse of her father-in-law, a man she had loved despite his manipulations and betrayals. The expression on her face was one he had seen before, long ago, on the day they had first emerged from the Root, only to discover how far away from home they had traveled, how lost in time they were.

How long dead everyone she had loved was.

"The demon priest you mentioned gave me that key," he said finally, in a voice that was dry and soft at once. "He sent me to the northern coast of Serendair, across the straits to the Northern Islands of Balatron, Briala, and Querel, where a failed land bridge once stood. The key was meant open a door in the base of that bridge, so that I could bring back an associate of his from the other side." He met her eyes in the darkness. "You do understand that Tsoltan was the host of a F'dor?"

"Yes."

"So do you understand where it is that he sent me, and what I was to do?"

She thought for a moment, her eyes growing wider in the darkness.

"You went to the Vault?"

Achmed nodded.

"The actual Vault? It exists in the material world?"

The Bolg king exhaled deeply. "A gateway to it does. 'The fabric of the world is worn thin there'; that's what Tsoltan said when giving my instructions."

Rhapsody's eyes were glinting now; Achmed knew she was growing nervous.

"And did you open it?"

He nodded. "I did. I looked into the Vault of the Underworld itself. And what I saw there so defies description that I have never really seen fit to attempt it. But it was enough to abandon everything I had, and everything I was, to risk running, because even a cold-blooded assassin like me, even a reprobate with no use for God or man, and no compunction about administering death as if it were a sacrament, has a limit over which he can be pushed. That experience was the limit."

"I can believe it," Rhapsody said.

"Then maybe you can believe that now, as a result, everything I do, every chance I get, is an opportunity to safeguard the world from repeating my mistake. You think I am taking unnecessary risks, Rhapsody, but in truth, I am only taking every opportunity to keep that Vault sealed for all time. It is an endless task; like trying to constantly reinforce a dike of sand against the tide of the sea. There are a limited number of F'dor, it's true, left over from the dawn of Time, but there are enough of them still out there who escaped the Vault in the first cataclysm, ceaselessly endeavoring to get a key like that one and open it, releasing their fellows. I don't mean to insult you when I say that even you, a Lirin Namer, cannot fathom what that would be like. I have been the dispenser of death myself, in truly horrific ways sometimes, and even I could not have fathomed it had I not seen it with my own eyes.

"You mentioned when you ripped my skin from me, metaphorically speaking, that the Nain had objected to my building of the instrumentality for which you translated the schematics. There *is* a reason I didn't confess all that the Nain said. Do you wish to know how they were aware of our construction? They have already built one of their own." He took some satisfaction at her intake of breath.

"And I wish you wouldn't lecture me about primordial magic. I know several things about primordial magic that you don't. It is not immutable, it is fragile; it can die. The death of Sagia left a huge hole in what was possible for primordial magic. The tools we have now are diminished, the weapons denatured. We lost so much constructive power, so much magic from the world when the Island died. I am trying with all my strength to build up our arsenal in this last, greatest battle of all, in every front."

"But if your fear is that a F'dor will find the Earthchild, and take her rib to use as a key, and release the F'dor, who will then waken the Wyrm, what good is any of your guardianship if your use of the Lightcatcher bypasses all of this and merely wakes the beast up itself?" Rhapsody asked, holding her baby tighter.

Achmed sat up straighter, shaking a cramp out of his neck. Then he met her eyes.

"On the highest peak of Serendair, guarded at its highest pass in air so thin the winged lions who patrolled it could not fly, could barely whisper, was a Lightcatcher. I saw it, Rhapsody. I saw it used, or at least I saw the results. I spoke with the guardians.

"The reason it was built atop the highest peak was so that the power it drew on was the *star,* not the earth. Every time Faedryth spies on me he tickles the Wyrm; he roots his movable Lightforge near a vein and rattles the world. The Sea Mages undoubtedly take calculated risks with tremors all the time, which is why the currents near their island run amok." The intensity in his voice made the cavern walls tremble. "But *I* know, I *know* that if you ignore the workings of the earthbound navel examiners like Faedryth and Gwylliam, who only looked to the depths for their power, that I could light a flame with the *sun*. It wouldn't draw as quickly, it doesn't draw on a whim, but it doesn't reach toward annihilation every time you turn it on, either. I need the information in those scrolls to know what I have to do to make sure my peak is not just a Lightforge, but a Lightcatcher. Taking power not from the Earth, but from beyond it. From a star, from the sun—from before the element of Fire was ever born. I can use that instrumentality to see where I cannot now see, to defend where I am vulnerable, to hold the wall of the world stronger than I can without it, and perhaps, just perhaps, we can keep that Vault sealed if we do not disrupt the earth in which it lies."

He cast one last glance above him.

"It looks a great deal like this inside, by the way."

"There's a reason for that," Rhapsody said sadly. And while the baby drowsed, she told him the story Elynsynos related of the first Ending, and the building of the Vault of the Underworld.

"I am tormented now, wondering what has become of Elynsynos," she said softly when she had finished the tale. "I don't know whether Anwyn killed her, or if she is back in her lair, injured. Otherwise she'd be outside right now, trying to free us."

Achmed sighed. Comfort was not one of his skills.

"Perhaps she's alive and is outside, but she merely cannot do anything to free us," he said awkwardly. "Whatever substance is left when formerly living dragonflesh is fired by the release of elemental powers in Ending, it is impervious to all the magic of the demons in the Vault. I can't imagine that a dragon has the power to open it. The only thing that might is a key like the one that opened Sagia. And that remains hidden back in Ylorc."

"Even if she's alive, I'm sure she is distraught to a level no one but a dragon can fully understand. And I ache for Ashe. Sooner or later he will return to collect the baby and me, and he will come upon his father. And, being wyrmkin, it will devastate him."

"Unfortunate as that may be, it's the least of our worries now," Achmed said. "For when he does come upon our stone prison that once was his father, we will have long since run out of air."

44

JIERNA'SID, SORBOLD

The middle day of the week in Jierna'sid was known as Market Day. On that day, the red stone streets were even more crowded than they usually were with every sort of merchant and waremonger, sellers of salted fish and shoes, leather and cloth, spice and rope, cutlery and salt and any other possible type of good that one might want to buy. As a result, a majority of the citizenry was in the streets as well, taking advantage of the abundance to stock up on their stores for the winter, unlike the populace of the outlying areas, that had to set their stores in before the snow began to fall, as they might not have another chance at procurement until Thaw.

Along with the merchants and the townspeople, others were out in force as well: ratty children ran through the streets, invigorated by the sense of drama in the air; pickpockets plied their trade, under the increased presence of the emperor's constabulary; beggars and cripples and all kinds of alms seekers lined the dirty alleyways, hoping to benefit from an increase in traffic, if not generosity. As in all of Sorbold's twenty-seven provinces, there were soldiers everywhere, their numbers and visibility increasing by the day.

Another sort could also be seen in greater numbers during Market Days—thugs. Sometimes wastrels, sometimes former members of the imperial army, there seemed to be an entire class of them scattered throughout Sorbold, a strata of human beings whose only living purpose seemed to be adding to the misery of other human beings. Generally harmless, but always irritating, these louts prowled the streets of Jierna'sid from the Place of Weight to the farthest reaches of the mercantile district, avoiding the constable and soldiers but harassing passersby, jostling well-dressed men, leering at or sometimes groping women, threatening children, all of which seemed to generate gales of laughter that could be heard for city blocks.

On this Market Day one such thug came by chance upon a group of sleeping beggars huddled beneath a few tattered rags in an alleyway avoiding the bright morning sun, their breath shallow and stinking of sour ale.

What ho! the ruffian thought, pleased with his find. He sauntered over to the sleeping grizzled men and prodded the first with his toe. When the man didn't stir, the brute kicked him savagely.

"Wake up, you stinkin' sot! Get off the street and out o' my sight; it pains me to see the likes of you taking up space on the emperor's thoroughfare. Move on, or it'll pain you, too."

The man, now awake and terrified, turned sightless eyes that reflected the morning light and his fear onto his tormentor.

"Please, please, sir," he muttered in the throes of dementia. "Please don't take me ta the army; I've lost my sight there once. Don't want ta do it again."

The thug laughed out loud. He looked more closely at the other two beggars, both lame, one still asleep, the other waking fitfully, and aimed a kick at the waking one's head.

"I said get up, you beg—"

His word choked off in midsyllable as the hand of the sleeping beggar shot out like a strike of lightning and grabbed him by the ankle, jerking his calf up high and sharply enough to unbalance him. His balance upended, the ruffian fell backward against the stones of the alleyway, slamming his head against them.

Dazed, the young man tried to rise, only to be gripped by a clutching hand that grasped him around the throat in a clenched fist that seemed to be made of iron.

Before he knew what was happening he found himself being dragged forward on his face over the cold, jagged stones of the alleyway, until he was eye to eye with the beggar. The vagabond's eyes were unlike any he had seen; Sorbold was a nation of swarthy skin and dark features, where almost all eyes were brown as the earth. But these eyes were an azure blue, and they were burning clearer and hotter than the fires of the streetlamps that lit Jierna'sid by night.

The beggar spat in his face, a mouthful of sour spittle rancid with bad drink and coated teeth.

"Don't you have anything better to do than to bother the downtrodden, you miscreant?" the ragged man said disdainfully. He slammed the young thug's head against the wall where the men had been leaning, then, with his other hand, seized the remains of the sour ale in the battered bowl from which they had been drinking, and tossed it down the front of the thug's trousers. Then he pulled the dazed young man's ear next to his lips.

"Now, here's the moment in your life where you will decide to either grow up and be a man worth drawing breath, or where you will sign your own death warrant as a pugnacious fool who owes his mother an apology for being born and will, no doubt, come to an embarrassing end every soon. You can leave this place, go home and change your clothing, and cease from here forward to bother old men who have done you no ill, or you can go round up your fellow reprobates to come back for more. Bear two things in mind if you choose the latter option: First, you will need to explain to them why you pissed yourself. And second, you will not find me here—though rest assured I will come to find *you*. Unless you wish to earn the wrath of the beggar with the blue eyes, I suggest you choose the former."

He slammed the thug's head into the wall again for good measure, then dropped him in the street.

"Go," he ordered in the ringing tone of an army commander.

The thug scrambled woozily to his feet and stumbled out of the alleyway; he was greeted by a chorus of shocked laughter around the corner.

Anborn waited until the noise outside the alley had died down, then reached beneath the tatters of his cloak for his crutches.

"Find another warm street, friends," he said to the blind beggar and the lame man. He watched until the two had made it to the corner, leaning on one another, then rose creakily to a stand and hobbled along the streetwall to find another place to spy.

It took him several hours to make his way, clinging to the shadows to avoid notice, closer to the palace of Jierna Tal, rising above the Place of Weight where the massive Scales stood, dark against the winter sky. Anborn had seen those Scales many times, but there was something different about them now, something ominous he could not quite put his finger on. Perhaps it was only the way the light was hitting them, casting long shadows into the streets. But it was also possible that the sights he had been witnessing during his time in Sorbold had been enough to stain his view of everything in the nation.

As he feared, there were signs everywhere that Sorbold was preparing for war. The garrisons that previously had been confined to the borderlands and along the thoroughfares had spread; now almost every few blocks within the city an outpost of some kind had been erected. It was all very discreet; perhaps someone who had never been to Jierna'sid or to any of the other Sorbold states would have even noticed. But Anborn's understanding of the signals of military buildup, and their efficiency, was legion, having been honed in the most terrible of conflicts.

And what he saw was making him tremble.

Finally he found a warm alcove beneath a small tannery across from the palace, where the fumes and stench would keep any patrol from investigating too thoroughly, and took up residence there. From that hiding place he knew he would see the quartermasters bringing in armor for repair, and believed that what he saw would help him determine even more about the army's movements. He waited until dark when the tannery had closed for the night, then crawled into the tiny alcove beneath it and settled down, as he had in each of the places between Jierna'sid and Ghant, to watch and make note of what he saw.

Nielash Mousa stood in the silence of dawn before the ruins of the monastery and the manse.

Thaw was coming to an end, he knew; even the desert clime of Sorbold had seen a few flakes of snow carried on the cleansing wind that was whipping over the scarred stones, blowing the ashes about in swirling patterns of gray.

Talquist stood behind him, his head bowed respectfully.

"A most terrible tragedy, Your Grace," he said softly. He gave the benison's shoulder a supportive squeeze.

"Indeed," Mousa replied, allowing his dark eyes, red from the ash and the tears, to rest on the irregular metal pool that had once been the manse's bell; he remembered the clear sound of it, ringing through the rocky mountainside, calling his acolytes and abbot to service in Terreanfor.

He struggled to remain still, to keep his shoulder from shrugging away the regent's hand, to keep his face set in a mien that was merely sorrowful, not revealing the fury and loathing that was bubbling inside him, eating at his viscera like Pulis, the apocryphal lake of acid in the Vault of the Underworld, where traitors were dipped eternally in endless torment. *May the legends of it be true, if only for you, Talquist,* he thought bitterly.

As if the regent emperor was reading his thoughts, Talquist squeezed his shoulder again, a little more tightly this time.

"I know this is a terrible blow to you, Your Grace, and so I have made arrangements to assist you in your grief, and in the rebuilding of your monastery and your order."

Mousa turned then and met the regent's gaze; behind the sympathetic expression in Talquist's black eyes he could see a more discerning one, a piercing stare that had sized up the benison's reaction, and already determined that he had not been misled.

"What sort of arrangements?" he demanded.

Talquist smiled slightly. "All sort, Your Grace," he replied, his voice warm and respectful but with an icy edge. "You will need a place to live until a new manse can be built, obviously, so I have taken the liberty for finding you lodging within Jierna Tal, where my servants and guards can be at your beck and call."

"How kind of you," the benison said dryly.

"And of course we will want to be interviewing new acolytes as soon as possible, I would imagine."

Nielash Mousa arched an eyebrow. "We? I hadn't realized you had any interest or expertise in matters of the faith, m'lord."

The regent emperor opened his hands in a conciliatory gesture. "How awkward; I do apologize. I suppose Lasarys, may the All-God cradle him gently in the Afterlife, did not tell you that I trained with him in Terreanfor as an acolyte myself, many years ago?"

"I see," said the benison. "Well, what a loss it is that you did not choose to follow the call into the order, my son."

Talquist threw back his head and laughed merrily, but the piercing glance did not waver.

"Yes, I suppose that would be preferable to being named *emperor*," he said humorously.

The benison smiled benignly and made the same conciliatory gesture that Talquist had performed the moment before.

"Well, some of us would think so, m'lord."

The wind whistled down from the mountain, bringing the sharp sting of fire ash with it, and carrying away the pleasantries of both men.

Talquist broke the silence first.

"So, since these new acolytes will be under my domain, and many of them will serve at my official investiture as emperor in the spring, I would see to it that we have as loyal and capable a crop as possible, and that their training begin immediately. I have taken the liberty of sending a petition to the Patriarch, under your office's seal, to begin the recruitment as soon as possible."

"Are there any other liberties you have taken in my name, my son?" asked Mousa, his voice barely steady.

Talquist's smile hardened.

"Only the ones that would assist you, and Sorbold, in dealing with this terrible loss, Your Grace," he said evenly. "There will be a good deal of paperwork in the search for your new acolytes, so I have assigned my own personal correspondent to handle all your communications, especially those going to and coming from Sepulvarta. Additionally, because your health and safety are of utmost concern to me, I have made arrangements for my personal retinue of guards to escort you in all of your travels, so that you never need fear any harm coming to you." He leaned a little closer to the benison. "I can certainly understand how this horrific occurrence might cause you to worry for your well-being, which is a perfectly understandable concern, however unwarranted. Ofttimes when tragedy strikes, men panic, become fearful." He looked up to the ruins of the old bell tower, then met the benison's eye again. "Make unwise choices."

The Blesser of Sorbold nodded silently.

"Good," said Talquist. "Well, again, let me proffer my deepest sympathies for your loss, Your Grace, and assure you that I stand by to help in all things. Together, we can see to it that Sorbold will be stronger for this loss, that we will rise above it and build a better nation in its wake."

"I will pray that your words come to pass, my son," said Nielash Mousa, picking up his walking staff and covering his head with the cowl of his robe. "Thank you for all your efforts on my behalf."

"It is my pleasure to serve you, Your Grace," said Talquist smoothly. "After all, you will be officiating at my investiture; I have to keep you safe and well until then."

The benison smiled. "Of course. And now, if you would be so kind as to have your guards escort me to Terreanfor, I must offer my prayers for the souls of the departed holy men, and for the nation of Sorbold. You may wish to arrange for several watches, as the service will be quite lengthy; I must intone the blessing for each of the lost, and, as you know, a great number of priests were lost. And this is a very large nation."

"Of course. Consider it done, Your Grace." Talquist signaled to the captain of the guard. "Escort His Grace to the Earth Basilica, and make certain that he is uninterrupted in his prayers. No one is to enter the basilica without my express permission." The guard nodded and withdrew.

"Thank you, my son," said Nielash Mousa as the soldiers took up formation around him. "May your actions be returned to you a hundredfold."

He bowed slightly and walked away, both men fully understanding the intention in each of their words.

45

The regiment of guards followed the Blesser of Sorbold on the long walk to Night Mountain within which Terreanfor was secreted, through a wide pass in the dry mountains that seemed to go on forever.

Finally at midday they reached the single entrance to the basilica, a low-lying door carved into the mountain, an overhanging ledge assuring that sunlight was not let inside. Beside the opening was a large, flat ceremonial stone; the benison signaled to two of the guards, one of whom had been grudgingly enlisted to carry a golden symbol of the sun atop a long pole, the other of whom was bearing a flask of holy oil. These tasks were traditionally performed by priests of Terreanfor, so the guards had little choice but to undertake them now.

The benison ignored their obvious consternation and ugly expressions, freezing his own aspect into a mask of serenity. He gestured to the first of the soldiers to come forward and place the golden symbol on the stone, which he quickly did, then stepped away, as if he feared proximity would yield divine retribution. The benison then reached for the oil, which he poured onto the golden symbols; he stood back to wait for the sun to kindle the oil into the only kind of fire that would be allowed into the basilica in shielded lanterns of cold light.

While the benison waited, he watched bemusedly from beneath his hood the growing boredom and irritation of the guards. *Interesting that you can stand watch in a mountain pass or a field column for days on end without losing focus, but a few moments at the feet of the All-God makes you nervous to the point of dereliction of duty,* he mused. *Well, we will try not to keep you waiting too long.*

When finally the sun overhead sparked a flame, Nielash Mousa transferred the fire reverently into a small ceremonial lantern; he was lighting it for tradition's sake only. Having been all but raised in Terreanfor, he could find his way around the basilica in the dark with his eyes closed.

Once the wick had kindled, he turned to the guards.

"Thank you for your assistance, my sons," he said graciously. "Now I will be undertaking my prayers and burial rituals; since that will take much longer than your watch here, I bid you goodbye."

The soldiers nodded and walked away, taking up their positions at the door of the basilica. The benison ducked below the overhang, uttered the words of opening, and entered the basilica, closing the doors slowly and quietly behind him.

Immediately he could hear the song of the Earth ringing in the depths of the basilica, the slow, melodic timbre of the world's beating heart. It was a sound that resonated in his soul, and had done so from the first moment he had become aware of it; its timbre was so deep, its tune so subtle, that until he had spent many years in the depths of Terreanfor, he did not even know it existed. Now it was immediately recognizable, like the voice of his mother, calling to him from her heart.

At last, alone in his beloved sanctuary, the benison broke down. He fell to his knees just beyond the doorway and wept, mourning the men who had served tirelessly with the same love of the dark earth, who had prayed beside him and stood vigil over this last enclave of one of the Creator's Paints, the primordial element from which the world itself was made.

The Earth wept along in unison.

Finally, when he could weep no more, Nielash Mousa rose slowly, with the hesitance of age, and descended the passageway leading to the basilica proper.

Down here in the interior of the Earth cathedral, the dry, stony exterior, dead from contact with the heat of the upworld, quickly gave way to the fresh, cool scent of moist, living earth. The heat of the Sorbold desert dissipated, replaced by colder air, heavy with life. The lamp in the benison's hand reflected off the smooth walls, trim and clean, gloriously colored in random swirls and stripes of deep, rich brown, gold and vermilion, green and purple, the hues of life that made their way up from the primordial world and bloomed on its surface in the form of flowers and wheat, grass and grapes, and all the outer signs that deep below the crust, the Earth was alive.

The noise of the upworld faded away, leaving nothing but silence and the resonating song of the Earth, growing louder with each step he took deeper into the basilica. He followed the song under the high archway that was the entrance to the Antechamber of the Sisters, which housed altars to three of the other primordial elements. Within that vast circular chamber were alcoves containing a vent to a flamewell from the center of the Earth honoring the element of fire, a bubbling stream to honor Water, and a captured gust of wind that eternally praised the element of Air. The fourth Sister, the element of Ether, could be found deeper within the basilica, where no light of any kind was allowed, in the glowing rocks and organisms that contained its cold light, light left over from the birth of the universe.

The benison doused his lantern, plunging the antechamber into appropriate darkness.

Through the outer sanctum, beneath the gargantuan columns of Living Stone fashioned in the shapes of tall trees filled with earthen birds, past the towering statues of elephants and tirabouri, gazelles and lions, through the archway guarded by titanic soldiers, one of which, to his horror, was missing, the benison made his way quickly to the inner sanctum, the holy altar of elemental earth. He could hear the song of it emanating in the darkness, singing a dirge so painful that it brought him to tears again.

The basilica, his basilica, had been ravaged.

Never again, he thought, shaking his head as he bowed low before the altar. *Never again.*

In his ears the words of the Patriarch were still ringing.

Nielash Mousa, tarry. Safeguard Terreanfor.

I understand, Your Grace, he whispered again.

His eyes dry, his expression resolute, the benison began to chant, opening his mind and the elemental altar to the petitions the congregation of Sorbold had directed toward it. When the rite of receiving was concluded, he began the rite of sending, directing those petitions along the Chain of Prayer toward Sepulvarta, where the Patriarch would offer them to the All-God.

Once his offering was finished, the benison began the rituals of burial, the rites for the dead. For each of the acolytes that was murdered in the manse he bowed five times over the altar of Living Stone and intoned the blessing.

*Oh our mother the Earth, who waits for us beneath the everlasting sky,
shelter us, sustain us, give us rest.*

Finally, when the last of his priestly duties was finished, he walked through the inner sanctum, up the wide, dark stone stairs to the base of the burial tomb of Sorbold's emperors. Less than a year before he had performed the funerals of the Dowager Empress and her son, Crown Prince Vyshla, who had been taken by death within an hour of one another. It had not occurred to him at the time that they might have been murdered; now the sickening realization of how it may have come to pass added to the nausea of the rest of Talquist's crimes.

No more, he intoned, hurrying up the stairs. *No more.*

As light began to filter into the holy darkness, he came into the burial chapel to the base of the Faithful's Stair, the tight, winding passageway up to the stained glass–filled sepulchers. It was a sealed tomb, but Nielash Mousa knew that the windows presented a possible entrance, a back way into Terreanfor, the only other place where Night Mountain's hidden cathedral could be broached.

Nielash Mousa knelt at the base of the Faithful's Stair.

Slowly he began to chant, intoning the words he had learned a lifetime before, words he prayed he would never have to utter. They were the Words of Closing, words of power, of destruction, in a language long dead, that had been taught in secret to each of the benisons who'd had stewardship over Terreanfor since it was built, with the understanding that they were never to be used unless there was no other way of avoiding them, and then only in a time when the basilica itself was under attack, in danger of being destroyed or, worse, its magic misused. That time had never before come to pass, not even in the wake of the war that had torn apart most of the continent, a war in which no weapon of destruction had been deemed too unholy to use.

That time had finally come.

46

GWYNWOOD

The darkness within the cavern of Llauron's body seemed to close in. "Is there no opening, no hole—"

Achmed held up his hand gently to silence her. He closed his eyes and loosed his path lore, seeking an egress, any small egress, from within the enormous stone structure. Finally he shook his head.

"None," he said. "That Progenitor Wyrm knew what he was doing when he encircled the Vault of the Underworld. If there had been any small crack, any hole, those formless spirits would have been able to escape. None ever did, not for thousands of years, until the Sleeping Child hit the Earth and shattered the Vault. It appears that in his attempt to rescue us, Llauron may have condemned the three of us to suffocation."

"Ashe will return soon with the carriage," Rhapsody said, her eyes glittering in the dark as the panic within her rose. "He will be able to get us out of here."

"How? What power does Ashe have over a fired shell of elemental earth, any more than Elynsynos does?"

The bundle within Rhapsody's arms began to move; the baby's voice rose in the beginnings of a wail. Achmed watched as Rhapsody's face changed completely, the sadness now replaced with horror. She crawled weakly to a stand and ran her hand up the ribbed wall of stone, banging on it.

"Elynsynos! Help! Elynsynos!"

She banged again, the sound dull and muted beneath the screams of the baby.

Achmed seized hold of her wrist; as he did, he felt light-headed. The world shifted for a moment, and he remembered suddenly the first time he had taken her by the wrist, dragging her away from her homeland, through the bowels of the world, a lifetime ago.

He loosed his grip slightly so as not to cause her pain, noting the thinness of the skin on her arm, the loss of blood in her face as she turned panicked eyes on him.

"Shhhh," he said gently, in the same tone he had used to gentle down her child. "Save the air. If she's alive, she already knows we're in here. Calling won't help."

Rhapsody sank back to the floor of the cavern, clutching the crying child closer, her eyes spilling over with tears of desperation. She caressed the infant for a moment, then looked up suddenly.

"Yes, it will," she said slowly. "Yes, it will help, if I can reach a Kinsman. Anborn, or Grunthor—if my call can reach them on the wind—"

"What wind, Rhapsody?" Achmed asked quietly.

He could feel the breath go out of her, along with her hope.

"Come over here," he said, leaning against the wall. "You Lirin are so wasteful of air, because you are used to endless quantities of it. Take it from a cave dweller; it's best to try and meditate. You will last longer." He met her gaze as the baby began to whimper more weakly. "Calm is perhaps the last gift you can give your child." He smiled slightly, trying to take away the sting of the words.

Rhapsody continued to stare at him for a long moment. Then realization came into her eyes. She rose shakily to her knees and crawled over to him, leaning against the stone wall that had once been Llauron's body. Achmed exhaled shallowly as the baby fell silent, his tiny chest heaving, then put his arm around Rhapsody and drew her head down to his shoulder.

"Meditate," he whispered with great effort. "Try and—remember—the best of things. There's not . . . air . . . for anything . . . else."

"You . . . are . . . one," she said softly, leaning back against his shoulder, her head heavy now. "Even if . . . we have fought, I—I do love—"

"Shhhh," he said again. "Don't . . . be a Waste . . . of Breath."

Through his very skin, he could feel her heartbeat begin to relax and slow, until he could barely detect it at all.

Nielash Mousa's head began to hum with a negative static as he chanted; a stabbing pain emerged above his left eye, making his forehead feel as if it were about to sunder. Resolutely he pressed on until the base of the Faithful's Stair began to shake, then tremble violently, at last collapsing upon itself, sealing off the upper tomb with the sepulchers and stained-glass windows above.

Dizzy, he lowered himself to the ground in the utter darkness. He sat, unmoving, on the floor until he could regain his senses, concentrating on the Earth's own song, which was beginning to resound in less of a minor key.

Weakly he walked to the enormous pile of rubble that had once been the Faithful's Stair, and examined it. As soon as he determined that the seal was complete, and the basilica would never be able to be entered through it without the dome of the sepulcher collapsing onto whoever was attempting to enter, he made his way back down the wide staircase, through the inner and outer sanctum, past the Antechamber of the Sisters, until he was standing before the only remaining place in all of Night Mountain through which the basilica could be entered.

The basilica's front door.

Surreptitiously he peeked out of the dry earthen doorway, past the bored guards, seeking one last look at the sunshine he knew he would never see again. It was there, hazy with flecks of snow; silently the benison bade it goodbye.

Then he turned his back on the light of the upworld and made his way to the altar of Living Stone once more.

Softly he began the chant the Words of Closing again; the irony choked him, because those words were the countersign to the song that had sung the cathedral into being, the holy prayer that had revealed Terreanfor for the first time to man, or at least to men who had been able to record history. He tried not to think about that moment of discovery, when the living earth first was seen in all its dark and sacred beauty, because the loss was incalculable.

Safeguard Terreanfor. The Patriarch had risked his own life and soul reversing the Chain of Prayer to utter the words in a way the Blesser of Sorbold would be certain to hear.

Fighting the nausea, the splitting pain, the blood as it began to pour forth from his nose and eyes, Nielash Mousa continued to chant until the entire opening of the basilica past the Antechamber of the Sisters collapsed upon itself, bringing down a goodly section of Night Mountain with it, burying the guards who were waiting outside in the landslide, trapping himself inside.

Sealing the basilica forever.

$\mathcal{D}$eep within a distant mountain, in a realm that bordered the lands of Sorbold, the last living Child of Earth took in a breath. The fever in which she had been tossing broke; the smoothly polished skin of her forehead glistened with the dew of its leaving.

And once again, she fell into dreaming.

$\mathcal{R}$hapsody ran trembling fingers over Meridion's downy hair. Too weak to sing, she started to hum the musical note that was his own, *ela*, the same as her own, the sixth note of the scale, the New Beginning, hoping it would give him some strength, or at least some ease.

She thought back to the times that singing her note had brought her comfort, had served to remind her of the star beneath which she had been born, and her tie to it that remained, even when she was entombed in the Earth, crawling along the Axis Mundi. As the air of the cave became thinner she felt warm and light-headed; in her mind it was easy to believe she was crawling along the Root again, fighting the vermin that fed off it, struggling to survive, teaching Grunthor to read as he taught her to fight, following Achmed as he guided them all through the endless tunnels of darkness, confident in his unerring path lore.

I gave that to him, she mused as Meridion gasped for air, tears she did not feel falling from her eyes onto his fragile skin. *What was the name I called him by, that allowed him to pass through the fire at the Earth's core, unharmed?* The darkness seemed to grow thicker. *Oh, yes. Unerring tracker. The Pathfinder. Firbolg, Dhracian, Assassin, Firstborn.*

My friend.

She felt too dizzy to turn her head, but she sensed his eyes might be on her in the dark, able to see in the dimness as cave dwellers could. She thought of Grunthor, and how easily he could travel through tunnels and caverns, and of the name she had given him, too, the lore that had allowed for his safe passage through the fire as well.

Child of sand and open sky, son of the caves and lands of darkness. Bengard, Firbolg. The Sergeant-Major. My trainer, my protector. The Lord of Deadly Weapons. The Ultimate Authority, to Be Obeyed at All Costs. Faithful friend, strong and reliable as the Earth itself. It had been the nomenclature that had tied Grunthor to the Earth, had allowed its heartbeat to echo in his own.

In the deepening fuzziness something occurred to her.

No, he was already tied to it, she thought hazily. Elynsynos once said that the race of Firbolg came from a pairing of Children of Earth, the race of the Sleeping Child, and Kith, the Firstborn race born of elemental wind. The name itself, Fir-bolga, meant *wind of the earth. So he had that tie from birth,* she mused.

With great effort she brought her son's head to her lips.

Wind of the Earth. The words were louder, as if she was hearing them from somewhere—or someone else.

Suddenly the darkness cleared.

Che perimeter of Ylorc secured, Grunthor made his way in the dark down the long earthen tunnel to the Loritorium, trembling with fear at what he might find in the wake of the dragon's attack.

As he crested the mound of rubble, the last barrier between the upworld and the Child of Earth, his face was brushed by the cool rush of air in the underground chamber, a wind of the earth that carried with it a sense of ease he had not felt in a long time.

He made his way down the moraine as quietly as he was able and approached the sepulcher, relief spreading over his broad face.

The Child slept on, undisturbed, her smooth face of polished stone cold and dry, her eyelids motionless. The sunken circles around the bones of her face had vanished, the withering of her body had ceased. The tides of her breath were gentle, rhythmic, in tune with the beating heart of the Earth he could feel in his soul. Grunthor would not have been able to form words to explain what he was witnessing, but the return of well-being to the subterranean chamber which had seen so much destruction was palpable.

He leaned over carefully and pressed his bulbous lips against her forehead, finding it cool, its tension gone.

"Sweet dreams, darlin'," he whispered.

Rhapsody struggled to sit up. She carefully lowered Meridion onto Achmed's lap and, seeing his hands clasp around the child in surprise, turned to the wall that had once been the body of her father-in-law, a kindly, scholarly man whose desire to right the wrongs of his youth and his family had severed him from the family he so dearly wanted to see prosper.

Now was nothing more than a vessel of fired elemental earth.

Her hands trembled as she clutched at the wall.

From her throat came a sound that Achmed had never heard before, a harsh, guttural noise that vibrated against his sensitive eardrums, issued forth from deep within her. At first he didn't recognize the words, discordant and coarse as the noise was. A moment later he realized what she was chanting . . . in Bolgish.

"*By the Star,*" Rhapsody chanted from deep within her throat, "*I will wait, I will watch, I will call and will be heard.*"

She's calling for a Kinsman, he noted absently, looking down at the tiny baby in his arms. *It's a waste of time, and air. But stopping her could waste even more. Let her cling to worthless hope; it's not going to matter.*

"*Grunthor,*" she intoned in the same scratchy vibration, almost a moan now, "*strong and—reliable as—the Earth—itself.*"

Nothing happened.

Achmed's head throbbed from the sound.

"Stop it, Rhapsody," he muttered.

She shook her head, still clutching the wall, and continued to intone the call, over and over, from deep within her throat. She continued to sing for what seemed like forever, until stars began to swim in Achmed's eyes.

Darkness came for him.

47

Anborn could hear the screaming even above the cacophonous noise of the tannery.

Night was falling, and the city of Jierna'sid was beginning to shut down its legitimate operations for the night. It was during such time that the Lord Marshal took the opportunity to sleep, as the later hours were some of his prime time for watchfulness, when many of the more nefarious aspects of the city's operations were revealed. Thus he was in the throes of a fitful slumber in his cubby beneath the leathermaker's shop when Faron returned to the city.

The titan had emerged at the far end of the main thoroughfare that bisected Jierna'sid, leading at its terminus to Jierna Tal itself.

The sounds of strife at first were unnoticeable to the townspeople of Jierna'sid, who continued with their nightly preparations; the merchants closed their booths, the soldiers maintained their patrols, the workmen struggled to get a little more of their tasks finished in the fading moments of light. But Anborn's ears were more sensitive, whether from his centuries of military leadership or the latent dragon blood in his veins, he was aware almost immediately of the sound of panic.

By the time he had dragged himself to the opening of the alcove, the town itself had begun to recognize that something terrible was wrong, and it was coming toward them.

From the western gate of the city a shadow was lumbering, a titanic shadow the color of the desert earth in the fading light of the sun. Anborn could feel its approach in the tremors that resounded through the cobbled streets.

God's underpants, he thought to himself. *In this place of routine horror, what could possibly be so terrifying?*

The answer followed a moment later in the twang of bowstrings and the shouted orders of a full cohort of soldiers running forth from the barracks at Jierna Tal toward the western gate.

Screams rent the air as the soldiers who had been stationed at the western gate charged the gigantic man, a soldier of primitive race by his garb and flat facial features, with eyes of a milky sheen that seemed intently fixed on the palace of Jierna Tal. In a great fountain of blood the charge was rebuffed; bodies were hurled left and right, smashed into oxcarts and torn asunder, their limbs tossed aside as easily as chaff in front of the thresher.

From beneath the step of the tannery Anborn watched the shadow pass, saw it pause long enough to seize hold of an abandoned miller's wagon and heave it, laden with heavy barrels, out of its path and through the window of a boyar's shop a hundred yards away. But unlike the rest of the populace, which was either frozen in fright by the sides of the roadway or scattering like leaves before a high wind, he recognized in the colors of the lurching man's flesh something that no one else had seen. The sight of it caused the ancient hero, general of Gwylliam's army in the Cymrian war, Lord Marshal of the Cymrian Alliance, and a vested warrior in the brotherhood of Kinsmen, first to stare in shock, then to mutter prayers beneath his breath.

Because Anborn could see that it was made of Living Stone.

Having seen more than enough, he waited until the titan had broached the doors of the palace of Jierna Tal, then, in the confusion that was roiling the streets, dragged himself forth from the tannery, stole a horse that had been left riderless, and made his way, in all due haste, back to Haguefort.

᷂alquist could hear the screams as well.

He was in the midst of a very pleasant dinner when the noise leaked in through the windows on his balcony; it started as a high-pitched chorus in the distance, but quickly rose to the level of cacophony such that he was given to sudden indigestion.

Irate, he rose angrily from his meal, tossed his linen napkin violently onto the floor, and strode to the balcony, slamming the doors open and stepping out into the chilly air.

From the balcony he could see the world below falling into madness.

The height of the upper terrace afforded him a terrifying view of the streets of Jierna'sid, their roadways a grid visible from the air. Down the central street a human shadow lumbered, gigantic given its ability to be discerned from such a distance. Around it tiny human figures the size of ants were scattering, some of them toward it, to be flung away seconds later, others away, some successful in their flight, most not. Talquist lost his water onto the floor of the balcony.

There was no mistaking what was coming.

In a heart's beat he was screaming orders to the captain of his guard, commanding cohorts and divisions to be activated from the barracks below. He watched in terror as his orders were carried out; an entire column of mounted mountain guard thundered into the streets, firing at the approaching titan, oblivious of townspeople who were fleeing in their path. Talquist could only stare as the immense statue, now more man than stone, waded through the horsemen as if they were surf, pummeling men and beasts with brutal efficiency that led to such a bloody result he could only turn and flee himself.

He knew the statue's destination.

He ran from the balcony to the tower stairs, climbing two at a time, his heavy velvet robes no longer a cherished luxury but a fatal hindrance. He had barely broached the doorway of the tallest tower when he heard the shattering of the palace's massive gates; the screams echoed throughout Jierna Tal, shaking the walls of the minaret.

There was nowhere else left to run.

Gray sweat poured from his brow and neck as the thundering steps of the titan approached. The resistance noise had disappeared; after the decimation of the soldiers sent to battle it, the household staff had fled or was hiding. Now the regent emperor could hear the heavy footfalls thudding as mercilessly, unfalterigly, the titan came closer.

The tower shook violently as Faron mounted the stairs, climbing four at once, honing in on his prey. Talquist lost what little was left of his composure and screamed, slamming and bolting the door of the highest tower shut behind him, knowing as he did what a pathetically futile action it was.

He had taken cover behind an overturned table of shiny walnut wood when the door split open and the titan emerged, dragging his massive body through the stone opening that was too small to accommodate his height.

Talquist screamed again. Knowing that Faron had come for vengeance, he dropped to the floor on his knees, hopelessly praying that the titan might recognize the gesture of surrender and be moved by it.

Faron broke through the stones of the doorway.

With all hope lost, Talquist began to weep.

"No, Faron," he gasped, struggling for breath in the grip of terror. "Please—I meant only to—"

Fear got the better of him as the living statue's eyes, blue and milky with cataracts, stared at him stonily, and he fell silent.

Slowly the titan crossed the small room until it was standing directly in front of the regent emperor.

Its stone arm reached out at the level of Talquist's neck.

Its gigantic hand opened.

In it were five colored scales, each tattered about the edges, each inscribed with runes in a language long dead in the material world. Each was of a different hue, though in the fading light of dusk they gleamed iridescently in all the colors of the rainbow.

Humming a symphony of power.

With great care, the titan crouched down and placed the five scales on the floor at the regent emperor's feet.

Dumbfounded, Talquist could only stare at Faron for the longest of moments. Finally he found his voice and thoughts again.

He reached into the folds of his robe where he always carried his treasure, the violet scale, and drew it forth, holding it up before the statue's milky eyes.

"Is this what you seek, Faron? A return to Sharra's deck? Are you looking to join forces with me, and combine them into a set again?"

The titan nodded slowly.

The regent emperor let out a sharp gasp.

Then a chuckle of relief.

And finally an unbridled laugh of manic glee that echoed off the broken tower, down the stairways, over the grounds of the palace, and out into the night, where it rang, triumphant, through the streets of Jierna'sid.

A thudding shook the foundations of the cavern that was once Llauron.

Achmed sat upright, jolting the baby awake.

Rhapsody had collapsed against the wall where she'd sung. She barely stirred as the thudding ceased.

A light appeared on the wall, forming a doorway in the side of the great stone beast. Achmed summoned the strength to rise to his feet, his eyes stinging, and pulled Rhapsody up behind him, still clutching the baby in his arms.

A dark humanoid shape, taller than a man by half over, filled the opening.

"Oh, right, ya can't manage ta stay in Ylorc yerself, so now yer draggin' *me* away from there now?"

Achmed stumbled forward, using his right arm to shove Rhapsody into Grunthor's while cradling the baby with his left.

"Air," he croaked.

The light dimmed and vanished. The giant Bolg grabbed the Lady Cymrian and lifted her out of the cavern, depositing her quickly and gently onto the snowy ground outside, then pulled Achmed through the opening as well. Then he leaned back into the cavern, letting out a low whistle as he did.

"Criton, what's this?"

"It used to . . . be . . . Llauron," Achmed said, choking on the fullness of the snow-filled air of the forest. He took a moment to catch his breath, then looked up at the giant Sergeant. "He died rescuing us from Anwyn," he said when he could speak.

"Ah, she made it 'ere, then?" Grunthor said under his breath. "That bitch. Glad Oi brought this with me." He held up the key of Living Stone that had once opened Sagia's root. "Oi was right there in the vault when the call came, and Oi jus' 'ad a feelin'."

Grunthor looked down into Achmed's arms and froze, his amber eyes widening in the morning light. "Whatcha got there, sir?"

Achmed shook his head and nodded at Rhapsody, who was rising weakly to her knees, staring at the carriage that was waiting in the glen a short distance away.

She was watching her husband approach the cavern, the end of the world on his face.

48

$\mathcal{W}$inter had returned in all its fury by the time the caravan returned to the sheltered courtyard of Haguefort.

Gwydion Navarne watched the carriages arrive from the tall windows above the library; the firelight reflected off the glass in the panes, warming a room that had felt cold for some time. How long, he did not know; he waited anxiously for the doors to open, but the carriage driver took his time, endeavoring to position the coach as close to the steps as possible.

Melisande stood beside him, wrapped in the drapes, dancing impatiently to see the baby.

"Why aren't they hurrying?" she demanded, pushing in front of her brother again.

Gwydion's hands came to rest gently on her shoulders.

"They want to keep him as warm and safe as possible," he said, thinking back to what he had seen in Ghant, and what it portended for the future. His hands gripped her shoulders a little more tightly, as if to hold on to her without worrying her. "I guess that's the natural impulse with babies—and sisters." He smiled as reassuringly as he could as Melisande looked up at him, her face contorted in humorous doubt.

They continued to stand at the window and watch as Ashe finally exited the carriage, followed by the shadowy cloaked figure Gwydion recognized immediately as the Bolg king. The coach swayed from side to side for a moment, and to his delight the young duke saw Grunthor step out as well.

"They're—" His words choked off; Melly had already run from the room. He could hear her footfalls dashing down the steps of the Grand Stair. Gwydion smiled and followed her.

By the time he reached the entranceway of the keep, Ashe had already carried the newborn inside, and had handed him, with an awkward smile, to the chambermaid who had opened the door. The servant took the baby and moved out of the draft as the Lord Cymrian reached through the doorway and assisted Rhapsody over the threshold, where a bevy of other household staff descended upon them, taking cloaks, hats, and winter wear out of the way.

Excitement overran his natural reserve; he dashed across the foyer to the doorway and threw his arms around Rhapsody, whose smile was bright, though her face seemed pale and somewhat drawn. He looked up happily at his godfather, only to see him staring absently over his shoulder at the chambermaid, who was cooing to the baby; a chill went up his spine, though he had no idea why.

Melisande hugged Ashe, oblivious of his preoccupation.

"Can I hold him? Please, please?"

"By all means," Ashe said quickly. "Portia, please bring the baby to Lady Melisande."

The chambermaid nodded respectfully, then, seeing the door close behind the Firbolg king, carried the child across the entranceway and put him into the waiting arms of Melisande.

"I'm sorry to interrupt your homecoming," Gwydion said quietly to Ashe, "but I have a matter of great urgency that I must discuss with you once Rhapsody and the baby are safely settled in. I regret having to impinge this way, but—"

A loud metallic clanking sounded down the corridor in the Great Hall.

The two Firbolg, the Lord and Lady Cymrian, the children of Navarne, and the household staff all looked up to see Anborn appear at the doorway of the hall, standing erect and without his crutches, in the center of the great silver walking machine that had been brought to him from Gaematria.

"Sweet All-God," Ashe exclaimed. "I thought I'd never live to see this day."

"May you live to see many such days that you'd never expect to see," said Anborn seriously.

"What changed your mind, Uncle?"

Anborn exhaled deeply, his eyes going to the bundle in Melisande's arms that had started to kick.

"The need to be ready for what is to come," he said seriously. "You and I have need to speak now, Gwydion; your ward may already have told you what he and I have witnessed since we left. I have even worse news to add." He blinked as Ashe took the baby from Melly, walked over, and offered the baby to him.

"Tarry a moment, Uncle," Ashe said gently, "and meet your new great-nephew."

A change came over Anborn's stern face. He stared at the infant for a moment, then reluctantly reached out and took the infant in his arms, cradling him gently as Rhapsody came over beside him, smiling.

He smiled slightly down at the child for a moment, watching in wonder as the tiny fist curled around his finger. He looked up first at Rhapsody, then at Ashe, and spoke in a voice that was uncharacteristically gentle.

"Well done, my dear, and congratulations, nephew," he said quietly. "To celebrate this occasion, Gwydion, I am going to stand here for a moment and marvel at this child, allowing you a few final moments of contentment before I tell you what I saw in Sorbold."

Ashe exhaled deeply. "And I will return the favor by giving you yet a few more moments of happiness before I tell you what has happened to Llauron."

The two Firbolg looked at each other, then turned away and started toward the door.

"I don't envy Rhapsody her homecoming," Achmed said, pulling his cloak around him and preparing to start out into the building storm.

Grunthor cleared his throat as he opened the door.

"Yeah, well, sir, Oi don't especially envy you yours, either."

The Bolg king's eyes narrowed as he glanced back over his shoulder. "What now?"

"Well, if ya thought that the 'birthday party' we had while you were gone the last time left a mess, wait until ya see the one that's waiting for you when you get back this time, sir."

Achmed sighed in annoyance. *"Hrekin."*

"Actually, sir, that's right. And lots of it."